CUBA LIBRE

A Novel

by

Robert Shemeld

This is for Katherine Shemeld, the perfect mother, professional woman, and a lady. She has always been there when I needed a helping hand, advice, or kick in the pants. Thank you for all your love and encouragement.

I love you, Mom.

'Desperate affairs require desperate measures.'

Vice Admiral Lord Horatio Nelson

Caribbean

United States
Bahamas
Nassau
Turks and Caicos Islands (U.K.)
Grand Turk
Cuba
Havana
Cayman Islands (U.K.)
George Town
Jamaica
Kingston
Haiti
Port-au-Prince
Navassa Island (U.S.)
Dominican Republic
Santo Domingo
Puerto Rico (U.S.)
San Juan
British Virgin Islands (U.K.)
Anguilla (U.K.)
Saint Martin
Saint Barthélemy (France)
Netherlands Antilles (Neth.)
Basseterre
St. John's
Saint Kitts and Nevis
Antigua and Barbuda
Plymouth
Montserrat (U.K.)
Guadeloupe (France)
Basse-Terre
Isla Aves (Venezuela)
Roseau
Dominica
Fort-de-France
Martinique (France)
Castries
Saint Lucia
Saint Vincent and the Grenadines
Kingstown
Barbados
Bridgetown
Grenada
St. George's
Isla de Providencia (Colombia)
Isla de San Andrés (Colombia)
Nicaragua
Aruba (Neth.)
Oranjestad
Netherlands Antilles (Neth.)
Willemstad
Port of Spain
Trinidad and Tobago
Costa Rica
San José
Panama
Panama
Caracas
Colombia
Venezuela

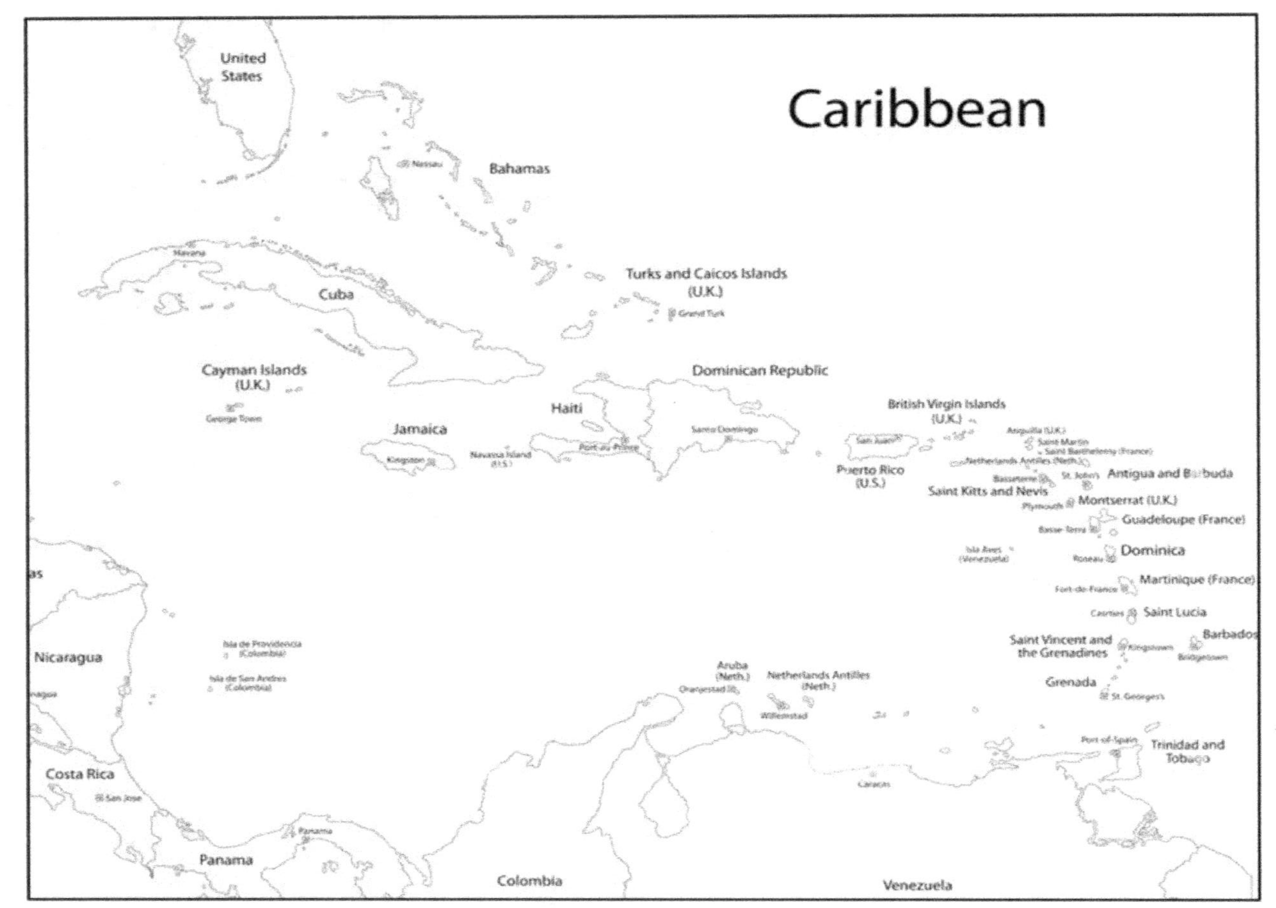

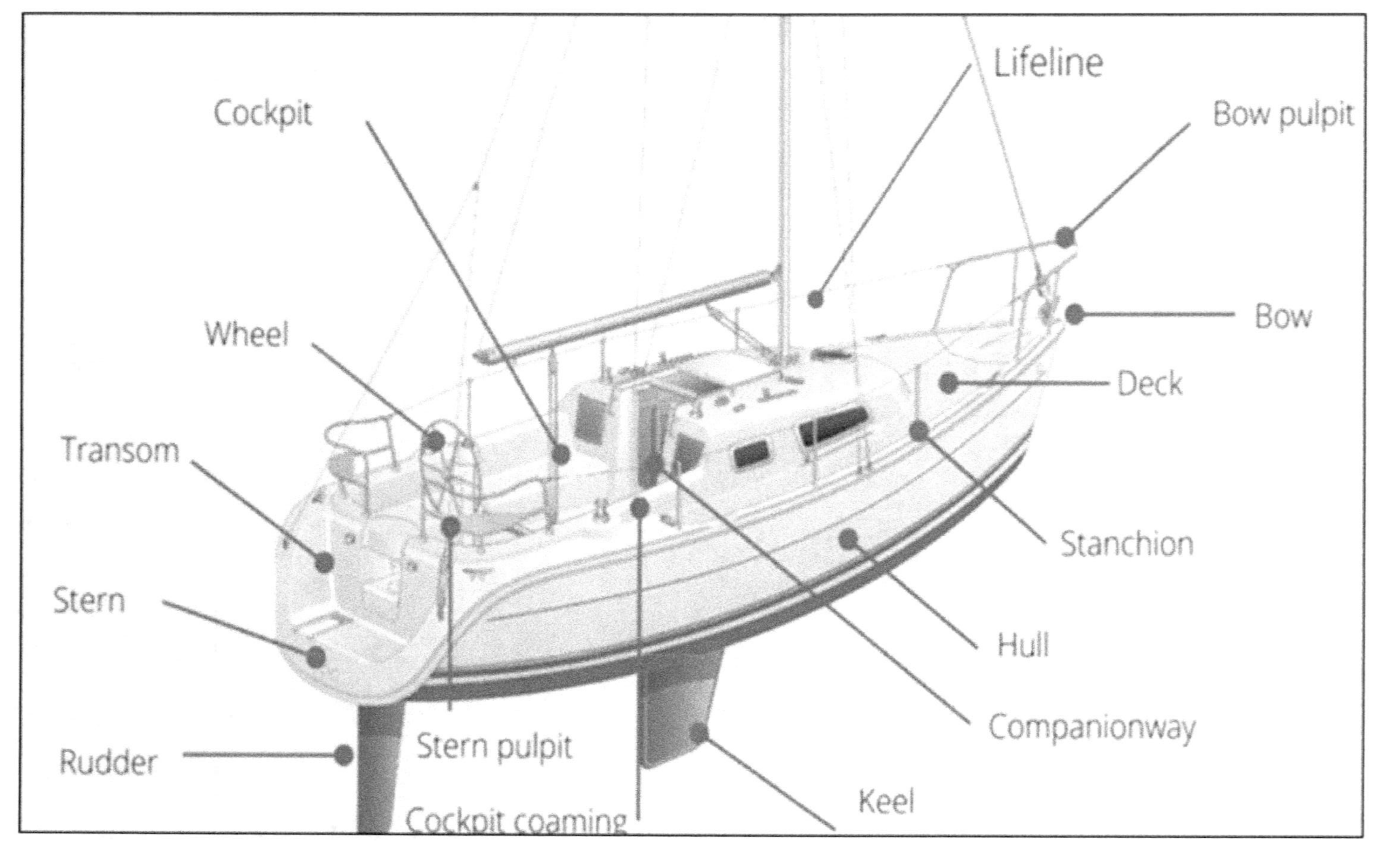

Cockpit
Lifeline
Bow pulpit
Wheel
Bow
Transom
Deck
Stern
Stanchion
Rudder
Hull
Stern pulpit
Companionway
Cockpit coaming
Keel

Prologue

A submarine glides through the abyss of a dark-blue sea. Bubbles escape from the cavitation of the two powerful propellers as they push the steel leviathan through the water toward its tiny island destination. Kapitän, Oberleutnant Otto Wermuth stands in the coning tower staring into his periscope. Wermuth is 25, he looks 35. He and the surrounding crew are sweaty and covered with grime and oil from weeks at sea.

"Allestoppen."

"Allestoppen." The XO replied.

"Radar, irgendwas?"

"Nichts Kapitän." The radar operator answered.

"Tiefe?"

"64 Meter Kapitän." The XO said.

"Sehr gut. Allevoraus, langsam."

"Allevoraus, ganzlangsam." The XO said.

Kapitän Wermuth looks into the periscope again and slowly turns it 360 degrees. "Periskopnachunten. Oberfläche!" The periscope slides into the deck.

"Allehände, Oberfläche, Oberfläche!" The XO orders.

Water is jettisoned from the ballast tanks, producing a loud swooshing noise accompanied by a shuttering of the boat. The needle on the depth gauge slowly records the U-Boat's transition to the surface.

***

Like a massive phantom floating in a liquid fog, U-530 ghosts silently through the cloudy night towards a beach of Little Tobago Island. It stops several hundred yards offshore. Hatches open disgorging men who immediately unload boxes and crates, throwing them into the water. Sparks light up the murky dark as other crewmen use acetylene torches on the foredeck.

Where the jungle meets the beach, a young boy kneels in the sand. Half hidden by the jungle foliage, his eyes are wide and expressive as he watches the incongruous scene.

CHAPTER ONE

The Yacht Pinafore, Newport, Rhode Island

Arguably one of the world's most sought criminals, he looked like your favorite uncle, if your favorite uncle looks about sixty-five, and dresses in Berluti Loafers. My wife and I had just spent our long-planned vacation in the throes of a nightmare perpetrated, in part by the man standing in front of us.

Elizabeth, though married to a sailor for eighteen years, was not particularly fond of boats. I seduced her into several weeks of sailing with assurances that our vacation would include Newport's sparkling social scene, as well as the idyllic sailing venues offered by the New England waters. Instead, we were thrust into a quagmire of improbable intrigues.

Dr. Alberto Pérez had been the previous owner of our newly acquired sailboat and because of the unfortunate coincidence, we were used, or more precisely, the boat was used as bait to capture one Pérez's rivals, a suspected drug lord. We were to learn later the scheme had little to do with drugs and everything to do with a gambit to secure the President of the United States' bid for reelection. The lexicon of a former soccer mom and her husband now included piracy, murder, and armed incursion.

Two months almost to the day of our arrival in Newport, Rhode Island we were standing in our boat, dealing with an unwanted career change— we were now what might be called 'private behind-the-scenes operatives' for the President of the United States. I couldn't wait to see our business cards.

With plans for summer of cruising behind us, we were determined to salvage the few remaining days of our vacation with a sail home. But now Dr. Alberto Pérez, former Cuban DGI, former assassin, former international drug trafficker, former orthodontist, and former owner of our 50-foot sailing yacht, *Pinafore,* was standing on the dock next to the boat.

"We had it on good authority you were dead," I said.

"It seems rumors of my death have been exaggerated," Pérez replied with a slight smile.

"Mark Twain," Elizabeth said to no one in particular.

We both looked at Elizabeth. I turned back to Pérez. "My wife has a thing for famous quotations."

"Perhaps you would be good enough to tell me how you heard of my demise," Pérez said, as more a statement than a question.

"From the guy that killed you," I replied. "He was apparently drinking heavily at the time, or maybe he was in shock. When he told me, he had just been shot himself."

Pérez laughed good naturally. "Perhaps. Might I trouble you and your lovely wife for a moment?"

"You can't have your boat back unless you're going to kill us. Then we could be persuaded to look the other way as you sailed off."

Pérez laughed again, though I thought not so genially. "Perhaps you would invite me on board so we could talk for a few minutes. There is something I should like to discuss with you both."

Not one to refuse a world-class killer, I said, "Sure, please come aboard."

Inside the salon, Dr. Pérez, Liz, and I arranged ourselves around the settee and the opposite couch.

"Dr. Pérez, please make yourself comfortable. I'm sorry we have no coffee. As you can see, we were about to get underway, but I can offer you a cold soft drink, or perhaps some orange juice," Elizabeth said.

"Please call me Berto and thank you, a glass of orange juice would be most refreshing."

Liz stood and walked to the icebox. "Berto, please call me Liz. What can we do for you?"

"I would like you to introduce me to the President of the United States."

Liz stopped, looked at Pérez for a moment, then poured the juice into a glass and set it on the table in front of Pérez. She looked at me, "Honey, would you like something to drink?" I declined and Liz placed the juice container back in the icebox. "Berto, how could we possibly introduce you to the president?"

"Please Elizabeth, I have been in the intelligence business all my life. I know you live in Washington, D.C. actually in the Commonwealth of Virginia. I know you own a consulting firm that provides analyses to your federal government, and I know your husband is a former member of your

Marine Corps, a former police detective, and a real estate developer. I also know the two of you work, if somewhat informally, for the president. I know she sent you to Venezuela to make sure President Escudero resigned and your husband's code name was Sam Spade. I know that the two of you killed a dozen of President Escudero's paid henchmen, including a former colleague of mine, Victor Fuentes. What I do not know is why you called him Beau Brummell— but that is of no importance. What matters is that you defeated a very capable agent. Personally, I would have wished you killed Victor Escudero, but perhaps I will take care of that myself.

"All that I ask is that you request an audience with President Jackson. I believe she will be most appreciative of your efforts. Perhaps she will promote you to full-time secret agents," he chuckled.

"With all that intelligence gathering, you must know, if you understand the term, we got Shanghaied into the mess with President Escudero. We are not really federal agents, we're more like private contractors and only then because the president was trying to provide us some protection from a few political types who didn't care for our interference," I said.

Pérez persisted, "I also know that should you call the White House switchboard and identify yourself as Sam Spade, the president will take your call."

"That was then, not now. I'm sure she is quite busy trying to get reelected," I said.

"Then why not give her something that will further her esteem?" Pérez replied.

"And what might that be?" I asked.

"A free Cuba."

Liz and I looked at each other, then at Pérez. "OK, you have our attention," I said. "What do you have in mind?"

"I have been languishing these many months as a guest of the Cuban government in one of their lesser prisons.

"Since 1989, when I and most of my compatriots were summarily excommunicated or killed, I have not been welcomed in my native country. I moved to Venezuela, where I met Estéban Morales, and went to work in his cartel as what the movies call an enforcer. We worked together for some years, I gained his trust and I think became quite valuable to him. When

Victor Escudero had him killed, I took the cartel records and moved to Miami, staying with my sister, whom I believe you met briefly when you bought this boat.

"After I left Venezuela, and the Morales drug cartel, I had this boat built and enjoyed several years of retirement until I learned Escudero had paid some of my old DGI friends to kill me and recover the cartel's files, the documents you called the Narragansett Files. As you know, I put them on a flash drive and hid them here on this boat in the shower sump along with seven hundred and fifty thousand dollars, which I hid in the air conditioner."

I felt my face get hot and squirmed in my seat. "Dr. Pérez, I found that money when I was trying to fix the air conditioner. We thought you were dead, and your sister had long disappeared. I donated a lot of the money, but you are welcome to the rest."

"I don't want the money. It is yours. All I ask is you do me this favor," Pérez said.

"As I said, you have our attention. And while we are on the subject, who died the night Ed thought he killed you?"

"If you knew Edward well, I assume he told you of our past association when he flew, shall we say, supplies, around the Caribbean for me."

Ed and I met in college years ago. He was, up until the moment he betrayed me, my closest friend. He said you had him flying weapons and when he found out you were DGI and not the CIA, he quit."

"Yes, quite right, though I did work with his father for a time who *was* CIA as was I. That changed when the Kennedys slaughtered many of my friends."

"The Bay of Pigs fiasco," I said.

"Yes, but to your question. One night, about ten months ago, he found me in a Fort Lauderdale restaurant. I saw him and tried to elude him, but he was very persistent and followed me for days. About the same time, I discovered I was also being followed by another man. Unfortunately, I did not make that discovery until this other man had seen me on my boat, this boat— the night I put the money in the air conditioner. At the time, I was on the dock with my hands filled with the air conditioning compressor, which you know, I had removed to make room for the money. As you might imagine, it made stealthy evasion difficult. He confronted me with a gun and told me I was to accompany him to his car. When we got to the street, I dropped the compressor on his foot and escaped."

Pérez laughed, "I would venture you would never see that on a TV melodrama, 'escape by compressor'. I assume it was this man that Edward killed. He did resemble me, and the boat disappeared as someone said on 'a dark and stormy night', or something similar."

"It was Edward Bulwer-Lytton. He also said, 'the pen was mightier than the sword'," Liz said.

I looked at Liz incredulously.

"Well, it was."

Pérez continued, "That same night, I flew to San Juan and made my way to a little village in the hills where I still have family. I was eventually arrested and held until several days ago when I was asked to arrange this meeting."

"Asked by whom," I said.

"Patriots interested in returning Cuba to a place in the world community, a world that does not include or sanction communism— in any form."

Liz got up again. "Would you like some more juice?"

"No, thank you. As you know, Cuba is a relic stuck in the 1950s. Charming for tourists and car collectors, but not for the people that live daily in poverty. Even the government lives on handouts of its so-called friends or from profits as hired guns. Cuba's army is no more than a cadre of mercenaries hired out to the highest bidder. Once the Soviet Union dissolved and Cuba lost its subsidies, things got worse."

Liz took the glass and rinsed it out and put it back in the cupboard. "I have some knowledge of the political situation in Cuba. For instance, Raul Castro is planning to retire in a few years and China and Bolivia have taken Russia's place as Cuba's piggy bank. Why not wait?"

"Because the people I represent believe Raul's son, Alejandro, will be the next First Secretary. They have no wish for another fifty years of Castro. And Alejandro is no friend of America."

"Yes, I read his book, *El Imperio del Terror*."

I stood and walked to the icebox. "What's that mean?"

"The Empire of Terror," Liz said. "It refers to the United States."

"So, he's not a fan," I said, sticking my head in the icebox.

"Then you know his ascension to power would not be a good thing," Pérez continued, "for both Cuba and the United States, he would be a continuation of the past, xenophobia and archaic ideals fed to him by his mother and father."

I climbed out of the icebox with a beer— never too early for a beer. It's one of my lesser-known observations on life, "His mother, who's his mother?"

"I thought you were a student of history. Vilma Espín was one of the leaders of the revolution. She acted as spokesperson for the cause. Smart lady, went to MIT." Liz said.

"Guess I slept through that lecture. Dr. Pérez, would you care for a beer?"

"No, thank you. Liz is correct about Vilma Espín, and she stayed very active in the party until her death."

"So, Doctor, getting back to our original question, what can we do for you?" I asked.

"I have been asked to meet with your president to convey my principal's desire to reestablish relations between our countries."

"Dr. Pérez, despite your admirable intelligence work, Liz and I cannot pick up the phone and get an appointment with the president. We would first have to go through the State Department and the president's chief of staff, Jonathan Collins. And if your research is as good as you think, you will know Collins does not care for me."

Liz added, "We would be asked some very pointed questions, chief among them will be how do we know, forgive the American parlance, you are for real?"

"I have a letter of introduction signed by Bruno Gallardo, the Minister of Foreign Affairs."

"Who is he?" I asked. "Aside from the Minister of Foreign Affairs."

"He is their guy in the United Nations, or he was," Liz said.

"That is correct, but for our purposes, he represents Miguel de Leon," Pérez said.

"Good grief, he's the President of Cuba." Liz said.

"You know all of this how?" I asked.

"You forget what I do in my actual job. Remember Gery, my South American desk, the guy that did all the analysis on the Narragansett Files?"

"Sorry, I forget you do all of this secret agent stuff for a living, not that you ever tell me about it."

"I analyze and forecast political trends sometimes for the State Department, which you know about and other customers you don't know about. It is not secret agent stuff. Dr. Pérez— Berto, please continue."

"Bruno Gallardo has been tasked by Miguel de Leon to make overtures to your government, through me, of course, in the hope we can, as I said, normalize relations."

Always the suspicious one, I asked, "So why not go through the State Department?"

"Because this overture is outside the auspices of official government. Until recently, Miguel was in line for succession to First Secretary of the Communist Party of Cuba. Now it appears Alejandro will usurp him. This is, as they say, a covert operation. And forgive me, your State Department is not known for its clandestine reputation."

"What makes Miguel better than Alejandro? How do we know he's not just mad because he was left at the altar, so to speak?"

"He is young, born after the revolution, a moderate, an educator— and he instituted countless changes unthinkable before he took office. My principals believe he is the future of Cuba."

Liz said, "I believe Miguel is everything you say. Our people have been watching him closely, so in that respect, he would most likely receive a favorable reception within the administration. But we still don't have enough to take to the president. We need some bona fides. To put a finer point on it, you need to convince us and the administration you're telling the truth."

"Suppose I presented you, or I should say the president, with a colleague long known to you and the president that would verify what I have told you?"

"Ed Columbo!" I blurted. *Pinafore* lurched from the incredulous assertion, or maybe it was the wake of a passing boat. In either case, I woke to the fact we would not be leaving for home, at least not for some days. "Liz, let's reconnect the shore power and tell the dockmaster that we will be staying another day or two. Dr. Pérez, will you join us for an early lunch?"

"Do you have room, after all, that beer?" Liz asked.

"May I assume I have diminished some of your skepticism?" said Pérez.

"Some, but I think better on a full stomach."

"And less alcohol," Liz added.

Shore power reconnected, spring lines replaced, a stop at the Dock Master's office to tell them about our plans. Then a short walk to The Black Pearl. The ebbing tourist season and the early hour helped get us a table without waiting. I explained to Elizabeth and Dr. Pérez that the Pearl had for years been a favorite place for crews to rendezvous with incoming boats and captains. With only some success, I tried conveying to both Liz and Pérez the good meals, the laughs, the adventures, and cruises in New England waters, the Caribbean, and the Chesapeake that I had enjoyed with alumni of The Black Pearl.

Of the two, Pérez understood the best. After all, he was a sailor, perhaps even as much of a veteran, old salt as I professed, but certainly kindred in spirit and deed. He told us of his youth when he sailed the Sharpie his father had given him, and about going with his father and mother around the Leeward Islands in his father's new 1940, 61' Alden Yawl. He said he spent a lot of time on the Yawl, sometimes single-handed, admitting it was often quite a handful.

"So, your penchant for sailing and Alden's was passed to the *Pinafore*."

"Yes, in fact, I designed the *Pinafore* and had her built at the King Dragon Boatyard in Taiwan."

"Ahh, that explains why she resembles a Passport! King Dragon builds Passports as well."

"Correct, an accidental good fortune."

Liz looked up. "Andrew Cavendish, Duke of Devonshire."

Pérez and I looked at Elizabeth. "What?" I said.

"Andrew Cavendish, Duke of Devonshire. He wrote the Accidents of Fortune. Kind of Downton Abbey, only true, but with less money."

Bewildered, Pérez and I stared at Liz.

"Never mind." Liz said.

Pérez continued, "I made *Pinafore* my home until Victor Escudero ordered my assassination."

The waitress brought menus.

"Elizabeth, I understand you are quite proficient with an automatic rifle."

"You should see what I can do with a violin."

"But your husband prefers your piano, or was I misinformed?"

Doing that eye arch thing she does, Liz looked at me. "He does, does he?"

"I love the way you play the violin. I just don't understand it. When you play the violin, it's intended to be in concert with others, but when you play the piano, it's you and the machine, I pretend you're playing just for me."

Liz's face softened. "Well, from now on, you will never have to pretend."

"I remember feeling the same when my mother played. I could listen to her for hours. She was a wonderful pianist." Pérez said.

"Did your mother play professionally?" Liz asked.

"No, in her time it was considered, I believe the word is 'gauche' for women of her class to work. A shame because I heard from many who would know such things that she was very talented."

The waitress returned and filled our water glasses.

Pérez seemed to settle and relax within the seaside atmosphere. "She was taught almost from birth to play the piano. As the daughter of a minor partner in Standard Oil, she was expected to marry well and have children. My father was a dashing cavalry officer when they met in Madison Square Garden."

"My, what an odd place to meet," said Liz. "Was it at a boxing match?"

Laughing, "No, father was representing Spain at the International Horse Show. My mother was also competing. They fell in love and were married soon after."

"Your father is not Cuban?" I asked.

"No, he was born in Madrid. My family-owned sugar, tobacco, and nickel companies with interests in Cuba. When the Spanish Civil War broke out, father was in Cuba looking after family business. My grandfather forbade him to return to Spain so, he and my mother lived in Cuba and New York. They returned to Spain briefly, but by then I think they considered Cuba home. When the Second World War started, they went to New York where father was attached to the consulate. The family alliance proved profitable when Standard Oil shipments to Germany had to go through Spain."

The waitress returned. We ordered three clam chowders, I had eggs benedict, Pérez a seafood crepe, and Elizabeth ordered a mesclun salad, which looked as appetizing as it sounded. Liz ordered white wine. With a nod toward caution, I had iced tea, as did Pérez.

"After the war, mother and father returned to Cuba. When the revolution broke out, he sent my mother, sister, and me back to New York. Father survived the revolution with some power, but no holdings. Since most of his cash was in the U.S., and my mother had her own money, we lived comfortably."

Looking back at that afternoon in The Black Pearl, I learned about Alberto Pérez, the person. And importantly, we perfected a bond that would serve both as time unfolded.

Between mouthfuls of eggs benedict, I asked the question hanging over the conversation, "How's Ed?"

"He is well now. As you know, he was wounded when you ambushed Reynaldo."

"We saw the blood, but he refused help."

-A man in the back gets on one knee and starts firing.

-Ed shoots, the man who slumps over.

-Other men jump up and start shooting. The scene erupts in a full-scale firefight.

-Bullets hit in front of me, spraying shards in my face. Crouching behind Reynaldo, I lifted my gun and started firing. Time turns into slow motion and the old training kicked in, each shot deliberate and aimed. Reynaldo's men wither.

-I struggle to reload my pistol.

-Several of the thugs, now on their feet, walk toward me and Ed. They're shooting. Rounds hit all around us.

-Ed, out of ammo, goes for the shotgun. He grunts, then stumbles.

-BANG! BANG! BANG! - BANG! BANG! BANG! - BANG! BANG! BANG!

-Liz opens fire from her position on the right with short bursts of automatic fire.

-Then nothing.

-Ed kneels on the ground. Blood is running down his left arm, dripping in the dirt.

-Ed, you're hit. Let us look at your wound.

"He was shot under the arm, no bone damage, but as wounds are wont to do in the Tropics, it became infected. He appears to have recovered. And he is the ideal person for our, shall we call it, intrigue?"

"I admit to being very unhappy with Ed, even thinking of him as a traitor," Liz said.

Pérez laughed. "Edward is not a traitor, far from it. Greedy perhaps, maybe not even that. After his wife died, I think he became irrational, obsessed with finding the demon he saw in me. As soon as I heard the Nicaraguans had him, I knew he was the perfect envoy. When I walked into his hospital room," Pérez laughed some more, "he nearly had a relapse. I flew him into a small airport, then arranged for him to meet all the appropriate people."

"So how or why is Ed the perfect envoy, for our, as you say, intrigue?" I asked.

"The president and you both know him well. Who better could offer validity to my request? He is the perfect person to corroborate that my appeal comes from Bruno Gallardo by order of Miguel Díaz-Canel."

"You still haven't answered the question. How can he do that?" I asked.

"Because he was there when the order was given."

CHAPTER TWO

Aboard Pinafore, Newport, Rhode Island

It was about ten in the evening. The water slapped lightly against the hull of the boat. After spending the day and a pleasant dinner with Dr. Pérez, he retreated to his hotel room, or wherever infamous thugs go at night. Liz and I were sitting at the settee drinking Blanton's on the rocks and discussing the day's events.

"How are you for time?" I asked.

"If you mean, can I stay away from work? Sure, besides, if you excuse me for being crass, there might be a payday in this. Which reminds me, did they reimburse us for all the expenses we had to put on our credit cards?"

"Mostly, there is still an outstanding issue of one destroyed Piper Cherokee."

"Well, before we get too far astray, what do you think of Pérez's request?"

I threw back the last swallow of my drink, stood and walked to the icebox, grabbed a fistful of ice, added it to my glass, picked up the Blanton's, and sat down. I poured some of the brown liquid over the fresh ice.

"I'm not sure we have many choices, particularly if we bring Ed in. The president thinks the world of him, and I'm sure trusts him implicitly," I said.

"Thanks to you for pulling his bacon out of the fire and covering for him. That little number he pulled could have put him in prison. I'm still pissed."

"I couldn't tell. Anyway, I think we have to make the call. If true, an opportunity like this may not come again. Hell, you're the spy. What do you think?"

"I'm an analyst, and I agree. Every administration since Kennedy has been trying for something like this."

"OK, let's get some sleep and make the call tomorrow. Besides, I'm—"

"I know what you are— put the booze down and follow me. You may get lucky."

The weather was dreary with fog and driving rain. Still half asleep, we jogged into town for breakfast. Our moods matched the weather. I think we were a little homesick. I know we missed Emily and Brad. Halfway up Bannisters Wharf, we ducked into Pat's Diner, a long, narrow, and friendly restaurant known for their all-day breakfast. We took off our soaked foul-weather gear and sat in a booth next to the wall. We ordered two coffees, eggs, a rasher of bacon, and an omelet.

"Why couldn't you be like everybody else and just order a side of bacon?"

"Nobody uses rasher anymore."

"Exactly. She had no clue what you were talking about."

"Well, now she does. I was just trying to keep a good word in use."

Liz glared at me for a moment, then said, "So, are you going to make the call this morning?"

"I was thinking you should make it. You two are such buddies."

"She asked me to do some work for her, that's all. That's how I make a living, remember?"

"Before we were married, you told me you were independently wealthy."

Liz made a face. "I did not. Do you think it's all right if we call from here?"

I turned and looked down the row of booths and glanced around the smallish restaurant.

"Normally I would say no, but nobody is close enough to hear and we're out of the rain."

"And the reception is crappy on the boat." Liz said.

I pulled out my cellphone and punched in some numbers that I was sure were on NSA's top ten. The phone rang twice. A woman answered, "One five, five."

"Mr. Jonathan Collins, please tell him it's Sam Spade."

"One moment, please."

I held my hand over the phone and looked at Liz. "Good sign. She didn't hang up."

"Your reputation proceeds you."

The phone clicked, and a voice came on. "What do want?"

"Good to hear from you, too. I need to see the president."

"She's busy."

"Not for this, she isn't."

"Tell me."

"No.

"Then goodbye."

"I get you we're not fond of each other, but do you really think I would call you on something that would put us within 20 feet of each other if I didn't think it was important? And I can't tell you over the phone."

"Wait, a minute." The phone went dead. In a minute, Collins came back on the phone. "Three thirty tomorrow afternoon."

"Thanks, I'll make it work. I'm in Newport, so I'll have to get a flight this afternoon or first thing in the morning."

"Don't be late." The phone went dead.

"Prick."

"So, I take it we will be in D.C. tomorrow."

"Yeah, will you call your South American Desk and see if they can wrangle a flight?"

"Actually, I have a North American Desk for such exigencies?"

"Exigencies?'

"I'm just trying to keep a good word alive. It's the coffee, it makes me cerebral. One cup and I look for the New York Times crossword puzzle."

"So, it's like a rasher of bacon."

Liz made a face. "If you say so."

"If we had to go to Rome, do you have a Mediterranean desk?"

"No, but I have a European desk," Liz said.

"All these years of marriage, who knew? You're not independently wealthy, you have a European desk, and coffee makes you crave crossword puzzles."

"New York Times crossword puzzles," Liz said.

All these years of marriage. The words rattled around conjuring up memories of our first meeting. It was over wine not coffee, in fact it was a wine tasting party. Never an aficionado, I was absent-mindedly wondering what 'fruity and buttery notes' meant when I sensed someone at my shoulder.

I turned and was caught by a matched set of intense green eyes. She was about 35, with blonde hair. About five nine, trim with a fine nose, medium mouth, and beautiful legs. I'm a leg man. She gave me a brilliant smile, said I looked bored, and asked if she could get me another glass of wine. I declined, we talked, and exchanged cards. Her card was a simple, classy cream colored, item that said *Elizabeth Carson, President* of a tech company I had never heard of— I asked her what a tech company was? She laughed, thinking I was joking. I wasn't. My card said, *Discreet Inquiries,* probably from watching one too many PBS mysteries and certainly a distaste for the moronic red tape involved in obtaining a PI license.

Weeks after the wine tasting, I was surprised to get a call from Elizabeth asking if we could meet, perhaps for lunch, your card said you were a private investigator. I think that's what it said. Am I right? She laughed. Her laugh sounded as splendid as her smile. You are correct, I said, I was trying for erudite and ended up with enigmatic. As soon as I use all five hundred cards, I'll change the wording. She laughed. How many do you have left? Four hundred and ninety-nine, I said. She laughed some more. We met for lunch, she hired me, I found the dastardly culprit, and a year later I married Elizabeth and her two small children, Emily, and Brad. I quit the detective business and eventually parlayed a real estate license into a moderately successful company.

"I'll call Pérez and tell him the preliminary meeting is on."

"Ask him how much time he needs to get himself and Ed into D.C., preferably without triggering all the alarms in Homeland Security." Liz said.

"Good point. I'll bet our buddy Silvers can help with that, but let the president make that decision."

We caught a Southwest flight— the only flight, and despite all Liz's contacts, we had to make reservations ourselves. I planned to remind her frequently.

This was not to be our first time in the White House. On one of the several occasions, we were formally inducted into the ranks of government officialdom. We became contract employees of the State Department under a program called SPEOPS, but we answered to the president.

A flight attendant brought us some coffee.

"So, do you think we are on our way to Cuba, and do you want to go?" Liz asked.

"I doubt if we are going to Cuba, we're not diplomats. As for wanting to go, for now, I'll go where our boat goes, if that makes any sense."

"OK, just wanted to know what the marching orders were."

Liz and I entered the oval office somewhat worse for wear. We were directed by a secretary to two wingback chairs sitting in front of the Resolute desk. "The president and Mr. Collins will join you in a moment." Then the secretary left the office.

A side door opened and the President of the United States, Harriet Jackson, entered the room. Liz and I stood.

President Jackson was the consummate politician. A former military pilot, and a former U.S. senator, she was fast on her feet and made decisions quickly. I found her charming and affable.

Following the president was Jonathan Collins, the President's Chief of Staff. Typical of his sort, Collins was ambitious and conniving, but without the imagination to pull it off. We disliked each other.

Richard Silvers, Under Secretary of State, followed. Silvers ran the SPEOPS program, the outfit Liz and I ostensibly worked for. He was from an old political family that had been in D.C. politics since the Second World War. He was contemplative but frequently revealed a quick mind. I thought he was a pretty good guy. High praise from me.

Liz said, "Please forgive the boat shoes and khakis, Madam President. We caught the only flight available and just came from the airport."

President Jackson said, "That you could make it is what's important." She turned to her aide. "This is my new aid, Suzan Van . . . . Suz, despite present appearances, at our last reception, Elizabeth had the officer and foreign service corps laid out at her feet."

Suzie was a leggy beauty herself, probably 25-27, tall with long blonde hair. I assumed the hyphenated, multiple syllable last name I didn't catch came with money and a degree from Vassar or similar. Suzie looked down her patrician nose at Liz and sniffed. I didn't like her.

"Please, let's all move to the sofa and chairs. Richard, Suzie turn those chairs around, so we can all be comfortable." Smiling. "First, may I say how nice it is to see you two again. Liz, you never told me where you got that gown."

I laughed, "After the last fiasco I would have thought you would be glad to see the last of us."

"To the contrary, I think you have helped me get reelected. We'll see in a few weeks."

I started to say something self-effacing when the president held up her hand.

"We know about Pérez, and I would like you to work with him."

"You do? Does he know, you know?"

"I doubt it. We have been watching him since before you completed your last assignment.

"Our intel occasionally gets it right, and we started getting some noise about some unofficial but potentially astonishing intentions coming out of Cuba. When your deceased, Dr. Pérez, and the mysteriously missing Ed Colombo slid out of the ooze, so to speak, we were intrigued. So, we waited. And here you are. Which reminds me, you and I should talk about Mr. Colombo sometime soon."

I pulled my head between my shoulders. The cat was out of the bag, or Ed was. "Yes ma'am, anytime." The last thing I wanted to do is tell her I lied about Ed being left in Nicaragua because of his wounds. I left him because he betrayed us. I omitted that nugget from my report in the hope Ed would see the light and return. Guess I was right, and now was no time to ruin his career.

"We would have asked you to come in even if you hadn't called." The president said.

I stole a look at Collins, who gave me that insincere grin thing he does. "I doubted if anyone would work with me after the last time. You will remember I got some people hurt and ended up killing several others—though that was on purpose."

"I think most saw it as protecting your country and family. I believe Jerry and Capt. Schultz would be most amenable to working with you again. Jerry, as he is known to you, said you were the least experienced, politically inept operator he ever met. But you were quick-witted and fearless. He also said something rather odd."

"What's that ma'am?"

"He said he thinks years ago you may have worked for the CIA. He overheard one of his associates discussing an operation he conducted with you."

Elizabeth looked at me in unmasked surprise.

I looked around the room. "He was referring to Bob Osborne. I was never in the CIA. Bob, and I worked with them a couple of times. I guess they thought we did a good job, so they asked us to join. Bob did, I didn't. I would prefer to forget that part of my life."

"Certainly, I'm sorry I embarrassed you. Though it explains some lingering questions."

"If you have questions about my abilities, ma'am, I'll be happy to step back."

"No. I wondered how a real estate broker could be exceedingly competent at paramilitary operations. Capt. Schultz said basically the same thing, he would be delighted to work with you again."

"Capt. Schultz?"

"Oh, you didn't know. After your last fiasco, as you call it, Schultz was promoted to Captain and the rest of the team were similarly promoted. General Barrett works with the Joint chiefs now, but the others are still in Special Ops."

I momentarily drifted away in a sea of memories. Feeling a little ill and sweaty, I tried to focus on what the president was saying but could only see *scenes from the war, the attempted piracy, the shoot-out in the hanger, the firefight in Nicaragua and the airport in Caracas.*

"Madam President, will you please ask someone to bring in a soft drink or fruit juice?"

"Suzie, see to it."

Suzie-the-nose hurried out of the room.

I snapped out of it and, as usual, plunged ahead, forgetting who I was talking with. "The first thing we should do is meet with Pérez— "

Suzie returned and handed a glass of orange juice to me, which I gratefully accepted and drank. "Thank you. Sorry, I missed breakfast." I put the glass down, "If that's OK with you. The meeting with Pérez, I mean."

"Meeting, yes, but not with me. If the press got wind that I was taking a meeting with that character. I'd never hear the end of it, and it would be immediately telegraphed to the Cubans, and I suspect heads would roll, literally.

"The meeting will be with you and Silvers. Maybe arrange another boat trip, maybe to Florida. Will your boat go that far?"

"Yes, ma'am."

"OK, take another vacation, and take Rick with you or meet him there. Your choice. Rick will take care of the expenses."

Collins interrupted, "Ma'am, perhaps I should be the one to—"

"How do you imagine you being seen with Pérez would be any different from me?"

Collins sat back in his chair. It was my turn to grin at him.

Liz spoke, "Madam President, while we're speaking of expenses, we have not been reimbursed for the airplane."

"Which airplane?"

"The one Colonel Barrett crashed on the runway in Caracas."

"Barret got the gold, and you got the shaft."

Chuckling, "Yes, ma'am, that's about it."

The president looked over at Silvers. "Rick, take care of that for me."

"Yes, Ma'am," said Silvers.

The president looked at me. "So, the plan is to set up a meeting in Florida where you and Rick will meet with Pérez."

"Madam President, I think there is a substantial political component here. If we are successful, it is good for your election. If not, I assume the opposite is true. As you say, the election is only several weeks away and it will probably take every bit of that time to get our boat to Florida, and that's assuming good weather. If this is to happen before the election, we need to fly down there right away. But we risk observation by their intelligence guys.

As you suggest, a boat full of tourists banging around Florida would be far less suspicious, but if that's the plan, it's going to happen after the election."

All eyes were on the President. The president looked at Collins. "Johnny, what do you think?"

Collins blew out a deep breath. "Assuming everything works, and we don't even know what everything is, in a perfect world, we would want this to happen before the election. It's a hard call."

The president frowned, then looked at Elizabeth. "Liz, you have your ear to the ground. What do you think?"

Liz sat forward, pursed her lips, and thought for a moment. "I will not presume to know your poll numbers, but from what I hear, the election is yours to lose. If we rush into this and it goes bad, you not only lose the election, but you will be the one that lost an opportunity to free millions of people from deprivation.

"We didn't spend a lot of time with him, but all my experience and training tell me he is very bright and committed to freeing Cuba. I suggest you have someone quietly meet with Pérez and his principals on your behalf. See what they have to say. Then develop a plan based on your envoy's observations and the commentaries from Perez's principals. But, at some point, Madam President, you will have to insert yourself into the talks."

"Alright Liz, we will proceed as you suggest. You are my 'someone' and in charge of the operation." She smiled, "You may want to keep your husband close, just in case there is a plane that needs crashing. Plus, Latin men can still be a little old fashion when comes to dealing with women."

The early night air was cool as we stood looking at the White House, lit in all its glory. Liz said, "Seems like we have been here before."

"Yes, and not so many weeks ago. How about dinner at Ebbitt's?"

"A little while ago, you were teasing me about telling you I was independently wealthy. Now I find out the man that helped raise my children, the man I sleep with, is some kind of Rambo?"

"That was a long time ago, Liz."

"What's that mean? I've seen you kill as easy as turning on a light switch. I even asked you about it. Remember? You never told me about this past of yours."

"OK! I was a gunny, a shooter. Like Ed said, I'm a *Pistolero*. Is that the guy you wanted to marry, to raise your children? Let's pull out of this. We don't need any of it."

"You know we can't do that. Does Ed know what you did?"

"He was there."

"He was there! I thought you two met in school?"

"We knew each other before."

"He was in the Marines?"

"No, he was a civilian contractor. He installed navigation aids in the boonies for our jets."

"He was a mercenary, and you two fought together."

"Yes. Can we not talk about this anymore? How about dinner at Ebbitt's?"

"You *talked* me into it."

"Cute." We walked quietly for a few minutes, holding hands. "Remember the last time we took this walk you were in five-inch heels."

"And you were in your beautiful new tux. Think they'll let us in dressed in boat shoes and khakis?"

"I'll tell them how important you are." I said.

"Yeah, that will do it."

We crossed 15th street to Old Ebbitt Grill. Once inside, we were seated at our old booth on the main aisle and greeted by a fresh-faced waiter. I ordered crab cakes with iced tea. Liz ordered the pork chop with the house white.

"A few more meetings like that. You'll be the chief of staff," I said.

"What the hell was the matter with Collins? You could tell she desperately wanted his help, but he just gave her a bunch of political speak."

"These guys are risk averse. God forbid they actually make a decision. So, do you want to take the boat down?"

"I think that's the best way to keep a low profile. What do you think of taking the kids?"

"It would add to the illusion, but it means filling them in on our true purpose," I said.

"I don't think we're kidding them anyway, but let's wait until we are in Florida, so nothing slips to a friend."

"What if they don't want to go?" I said.

"Well, we can't force them. Maybe then we will tell them the truth."

"You're the boss and the Mom."

"Yeah, how did that happen? You're still the boss of the boat. "

"I won't take you into anything dangerous." I said.

Chuckling, "You do recall the gunfights in Martha's Vineyard and Nicaragua?"

"Well, other than that." I said.

The waiter served dinner.

"How about we go somewhere in the Carolinas instead of Florida?" I asked.

"Because Florida is wall-to-wall Cubans with who knows how many intelligence guys. North or South Carolina, not so much." Liz replied.

"Right. As for the election, maybe we can move the timing up."

Liz thinks for a moment. "We should keep that to ourselves. No sense in creating false hopes." She looked up with a grin. "I trust this has nothing to do with your bizarre craving for shrimp and grits?"

"And sweet iced tea. Perish the thought."

The waiter arrived and served dinner. Looking up at the waiter I caught sight of a man at the front door just as he entered. He was tall, dressed in a business suit. As he looked around, our eyes met. He then walked to the hostess desk.

The waiter took some more drink orders and left.

"Guess what? I could swear the FBI agent that was with Tom Sawyer that night at Dulles just walked in the front door and stared at me."

Liz started to turn—

RRRRIINNG! RRRRIINNG! RRRRIINNG!

I jumped, then realized it was my phone. Several patrons frown in my direction. In a low voice, I said, "Hello— How did you get this number? Never mind, what's up? We got you your meeting, sorta— Damn. OK, thanks."

"What? It's not the kids?"
"No. That was Pérez. Ed disappeared. Guess who has him?"
"Who?"
"Victor Escudero!"

26

CHAPTER THREE

The White House – The Following Day

The Roosevelt Room contains a large conference table surrounded by leather-upholstered armchairs. A sofa sits against the far wall. On the near wall is a butler's table with a pot of coffee and a tray with a selection of pastries. Jonathan Collins enters the room, followed by Jerry McGuire. Collins said, "Please wait here. The president will arrive momentarily."

Liz and I greeted the newcomer, shaking hands. "Jerry, nice to see you again," I said.

"Hey bud, good to see you. I don't have to guess why you're here." Jerry said.

Jerry McGuire, I've never learned his real name, was brought out of retirement to command the CIA team for our recent visit to Caracas.

Jerry looked at Liz. "Nice to see you, ma'am. You all kick over another shit bucket? Or is it the same one?"

"A little of both," Liz said.

President Jackson enters the room. "Please be seated. We have a lot to go over."

Chairs are shuffled, coffee cups clink as everyone sat down. Collins sat to the right of the president, Silvers on her left. The president's aide sat behind on a chair next to the wall. I sat with Liz and Jerry McGuire on the opposite side of the table in front of the president.

"Anything new since last night?' The president asked.

"Yes, ma'am. Pérez thinks Ed is being held in one of Castro's old revolutionary-era camps in the Sierra Maestra mountains."

"Comandancia La Plata?"

"No, ma'am. A small place used primarily as an escape route to the sea from Comandancia La Plata."

Jerry said, "If it's the one I think it is, I've been there. It's a deep forest, almost impenetrable."

"Damn and shit! If Ed knows about our plans, and those plans get out, it could be devastating." President Jackson said.

"Pérez thinks it's less about politics and more about money," I said.

"It's always about money with that little shit, Escudero. So, what does he want?"

"All the money you took from him," I said.

"The money I took from him! It wasn't his. I gave it back to Venezuela."

"I guess he doesn't see it that way." My stupid remark left my mouth before I could shut it.

The president gave me a 'no kidding' look. "I assume the Cubans just let that SOB walk around."

"I don't think they care, ma'am. They think of him as a joke and ignore him," Jerry said.

"Regardless, it doesn't change the situation. We need to get Ed back and do it with the people in this room. Otherwise, we start a war with Cuba." The president looks at the three opposite her. "Well?"

"I'm afraid any plan will involve a direct assault on the camp," Jerry said.

"Since Escudero has to pay for it, Pérez doesn't think he has much security. We can't use helicopters, so we need a boat. Fortunately, the camp is close to Gitmo," I said.

"Maybe we fly into Gitmo and launch from there," Jerry said.

"The airport is on the leeward side of Gitmo, same as the camp. Maybe we can get to the end of the runway and disappear over the fence," I said.

"Is it that easy?" The president asked.

"No, but it's the start of a plan," I said.

"You'll need some help. Suzie, ask Ava to find the Chairman of the Joint Chiefs and get him on the phone."

"Yes, ma'am." Suzie leaves the room.

"OK, when I got your call, I asked Jerry to join us. I also did some checking on your pal, Bob Osborne, in case we needed to add him to our merry band of men. As I understand, you guys were real holy terrors. They took women and children off the streets when you two came to town."

"Ma'am, I—"

"Save the wounded rhino stuff. I want you and," she looked at Jerry, "and Jerry, or whatever your name is, to grab Osborne and anybody else you need and go down there and get Ed. And I don't want to hear from that son of bitch Victor Escudero again! Ever. Do you get my drift?"

"Yes, ma'am," I said.

"Remember, just like last time, you get caught. I can't help. And like last time, don't start a war." She smiled. "It would be bad for the election."

A clatter of heels brings Suzie and Ava to the room.

Ava said, "Madam President, General Wallace is on the secure phone."

"Thank you, Ava. Close the door." The president pushes a button on her phone. "Wally, you are on the speaker with Johnny Collins, Rick Silvers, and three others."

"Good afternoon, Madam President."

"Wally, I want to borrow General Barrett. Can you spare him?"

"He doesn't have to break another plane, does he?"

There is some snickering on both sides of the phone call. "I hope not."

"They say the third time is a charm."

The president laughs. "A third time?"

"Yeah, he dropped in on a big firefight the first time."

"Seems I heard about that. Tell him if he crashes again, he gets a free toaster."

Everyone laughs.

"Wally, he doesn't have to come over here, but be prepared to lose him for days at a time."

"Yes, ma'am. Truthfully, I think he's bored with staff work."

"Well, we'll try to keep him entertained. Tell him to expect a call from Sam Spade or the Queen of Spades."

"Sounds like a trip to Vegas. You know, when I was a kid, my dad took me to the casinos in Havana."

"You don't say. And I mean you don't say. Wally, pass the word that until further notice, General Barrett works for me."

"Yes, ma'am. Do you want that official?"

"No. God knows who sees those general orders. Thanks, Wally."

CLICK.

"Damn, that guy doesn't miss a thing." The president said, looking at the three across the table. "OK, now you have some muscle. Call if you need me, but otherwise, I don't want to know anything until Ed and that letter of bona fides walks into my office."

All three in unison say, "Yes, ma'am".

"And don't come back with another story about how you had to leave Ed behind. I didn't believe it the first time. Do you think I just fell off the turnip truck?"

"Yes, ma'am, I mean no ma'am," I said.

"OK, get out of here and take Rick with you. Do a good job for me. Rick, stay behind for a minute."

"Yes, ma'am."

Jerry, Liz, and I walked out of the Roosevelt Room. "If she wasn't married, I'd say there was something between the president and Ed."

"I think there was some history a long time ago when she was in flight school." Liz said.

"Ed wasn't in the Army."

"I don't know, just something she said once."

"You don't know or can't say?"

"I don't know, and I've already said too much."

"OK, now that we're done with advice to the lovelorn, what's the plan?" Jerry asked.

"I think you should forget, Gitmo. The fence is too closely guarded, from both sides. Plus, the perimeter is mined." Liz said.

"How do you know?" Jerry asked.

"I've been there and don't ask."

I looked at my wife with unabashed surprise. "Really?"

"You know I travel for my work." Liz said.

"I forgot we took our mines out, but they didn't. I guess we go in by boat. The Special Ops guys have something called a CCM Mk1, but depending on who you believe, it only has a range of 400 to 600 miles." Jerry said.

"It's got to be some 700 miles if we come out of MacDill, so we need to get closer." I said.

Silvers walked out of the door. We all look at him. "She just wanted me to grease the way as much as possible, but her words: stay out of your way." He laughed.

"So, nothing about cutting us loose and letting us go home?" I said.

"Sorry."

"Let's go somewhere and hash this out. Preferably someplace close so we can walk." Liz said.

"There is a small conference room we can use in the Executive Office Building. Let's go there." Rick said.

"Can we get something to eat?" I asked.

We were ushered into a conference room by a young man I assumed to be a politician in training. He was my hero. He brought ham sandwiches and coffee. The four of us sat around a table playing with pencils until my hero left.

"The first thing we need to do is get *Pinafore* back here, and fast." I said.

"I've been thinking about that. We sure can't take the *Pinafore* to Cuba, Liz said.

"Maybe I can help. Who will be on the boat?" Rick asked.

"Liz, me, probably Pérez."

"Why don't we use the time as a training and planning session? Jerry, are you up for a boat ride?

"I'm one of those boaters that turn gasoline into noise, but I can navigate and stand a watch."

"Rick, how about you?" I asked.

"I was raised on my dad's B-40."

"I thought a B-40 was an RPG?" Jerry said.

"It is in your world it is. Among the enlightened, it's a Hinckley Bermuda 40. One of the finest sailboats ever built."

"Rick, what do you have in mind?" asked Liz.

"We jump on a plane and bring back your boat. On the ride down, we make plans. When we get here, we will be acclimated to the boat and each other, and we'll have a plan."

"OK, we need to get some flights lined up and get to Regan." Liz said.

"No, we don't. How fast can you get to Andrews?" Rick said.

"We can go now. Jerry, how about you?" Liz asked.

"I have a go-bag in my truck."

"Rick?"

"I'll buy what I need in Newport."

"I'm going to ask you guys to stay in a hotel tonight— there may be some rooms right at the dock— so I can get some food and get the boat squared away. Otherwise, let's go." Liz said.

CHAPTER FOUR

Pinafore, Atlantic Ocean

Liz, Silvers, Jerry, Pérez and I all sit around the settee. "Some housekeeping matters first. Can any of you guys cook?" I asked.

"That's OK, I don't mind." Liz said.

"It's not fair for you to cook all the meals." I said.

"I'm a pretty good cook, nothing fancy, but you won't starve." Jerry offered.

"OK, Liz and Jerry will handle the cooking. The rest of us will take turns as dishwashers."

Everybody nodded in agreement.

"As of now, we are on autopilot, and the radar is set for a five-mile warning. During the day, everyone will want to be topside, but at night there needs to be a watch. Except for Liz and Jerry, each of us will take a four-hour watch starting at 8 pm. OK with everyone?"

Again, everyone nodded.

"OK, that's all I have. Liz."

"First, it's a beautiful day so let's adjourn to the cockpit. Help yourselves to any of the drinks in the fridge or icebox. Cookies and crackers are in the lockers. Dinner will be in about an hour."

The next day we were about 20 miles offshore in a 15-knot broad reach, sailing almost due south. Liz, Rick, Jerry, and I were sitting around the cockpit table in an impromptu meeting. We were all wearing sunglasses, shorts, and ball caps. An assortment of sweaters, jackets, and sweatshirts finished the eclectic look. Pérez was at the helm.

"What do we know about this camp where Ed is being held?" Liz asked.

"It's not very big, and it's on a sizable river close to the ocean." Jerry replied.

"It sounds like you have been to this place. Is there any way to get in there other than by boat?" Liz asked.

"No, if we're going, it has to be by boat."

"So, the river is navigable?" I asked.

"Sure, the idea was to use it as an escape to the sea." Jerry replied.

"You were talking about a boat." Liz said. "I think you called it a CCM, but it only has a range of 600 miles."

"Yeah, a CCM Mk1."

"Right. Are there other boats with a longer range?" Liz asked.

"Yeah, but they are virtually experimental. We try to use one of those things, everyone in the Navy will know about it."

"That CCT... what did you call it?" I asked.

"It's a CCM Mk1, it stands for Combatant Craft Medium." Jerry said.

"They must have some way to move it around," I said.

"C-17s and I think C-130s can handle it. But I don't think we want to fool with either. There *is* one other way. An LPD." Jerry said.

"What's that?" Liz asked.

"A ship dedicated to the Marine Corps for amphibious assault." Jerry said.

Liz looked at me. "Do you know what that is?"

"Yep. LPD is short for landing platform dock. Marines don't leave home without it."

"Some of the LPD's were assigned a CCM Mk1, more or less permanently. And they are in and out of Gitmo all the time. All we have to do is figure out how to borrow one," Jerry added.

"Why not go aboard as civilian observers? There's always a junket of congressmen, contractors, and hangers-on visiting one ship or another for a couple of days of sun and a free boat ride." Rick said.

"I've been on a few of those junkets myself. Mostly we get in the way, but the men on board seem to ignore us." Liz said. "Can we get to an LPD by helicopter?" Liz asked.

I laughed, "Sure, that's what it does. It has a flight deck devoted to helicopters and Ospreys and a well deck with a ramp that can be flooded for amphibious stuff."

"OK, let's say we are some kind of tech geeks checking on equipment for the CCM Mk1. I'll bet it has some electronics on it." Liz suggested.

"It has a ton of stuff, including night vision," Jerry said.

"Then, we tell them we are there to install new night vision capabilities and naturally, we have to take it for a test run." I said.

"So, we get on board by chopper, then on the way to Gitmo- in the middle of the night- they kick us out the back. We do our thing and hightail back to the boat." Jerry said.

I looked at Liz. "What do you think, boss?"

"Sounds like we have a plan. Now, to work out the details."

"I would think the first thing we have to do is find an LPD with a Mk1 on board." Rick said.

"Can we have lunch now?" I asked.

Deep in the Sierra Maestra Mountains of Cuba, the door to the cell scrapes open. An order is yelled. *"Tráeloaquí!"* Two brutish guards dragged Ed Colombo from the cell.

Another order, "Give me that machete. Get him up and hold his hand on the table!"

Ed struggles and kicks out. His shoe lands squarely, smashing a guard's jaw.

Another guard goes down from Ed's hammering fist, two more guards jump on and subdue Ed, holding his arm to a weathered wooden table.

With a flash, the machete swings down to the table.

In an instant, Ed turns his hand and grabs the guard's wrist, violently pulling the guard's arm under the arc of the machete. *"Aaaaaaaah! Aaaaaaaah!"*

Using the guard's severed forearm as a club, Ed swings the forearm at the man with the machete, connecting with his chin. The sound of broken jaw and teeth is drowned out by another scream. *Aaaaaaaah!*

Ed turns on the other guards,ground, swinging the severed appendage. He beats another to the ground then Ed grabs the machete and runs for the jungle, throwing the forearm to the ground.

CHAPTER FIVE

USS Williamsburg LPD-16 - Caribbean Sea

"Captain on the bridge!"

Captain Gery Briscoe walked on the bridge and looked out over the sparkling Caribbean. Briscoe is 47, 6-2 with short, grey hair. He is wearing a Ball Cap embroidered with *USS Williamsburg LPD-16* and a Navy Working Uniform (NWU) with the rank insignia of a Navy Captain and the wings of a Naval Aviator. He walked over to the Executive Officer. "Good morning, Commander Davis. How is everything with the XO this sunny morning in paradise?"

Commander Tom Davis is wearing an identical ball cap and NWU's with the rank insignia of a Navy Commander, the wings of a Naval Aviator. The ball cap is embroidered with *USS Williamsburg LPD-16.* Davis is 38, 5-10 with short, sandy blonde hair. "Hot straight and normal, Skipper. No bends or dents."

"Very well. What's on the training schedule?"

Davis steps close to the captain. In a subdued voice, "Sir, we received a low priority a couple of hours ago. I think you should take a look."

"OK, Tom, let's see what you have." He takes the radio message from Davis and starts reading. The XO turns to the watch closest to them. "Rodrigues, get the captain some coffee and get some for yourself."

"Aye, aye, sir." Rodrigues leaves the bridge.

Briscoe looks up from the message. "So, another bunch of techs are coming out to play with that new CCM. Wish I'd left the damn thing on the beach."

"Look at the originator. It's not from the Navy."

Briscoe looks at the message again. "Mmmm, Barrett. He's a Marine? From the Chief's office but not the CNO. Barrett— I think I know that name. Yeah, he's that Rambo from Special Ops." Chuckling, "They promoted him before he got himself killed."

"I did some back-channel. Barrett reports to the president."

"To the president! No stops?"

"No stops."

Looking at the message, "It says these people get here at eleven hundred tomorrow. Tom, they report to me before they take one step toward that rubber boat."

"Aye, aye skipper."

"Now, let's go play war. Officer of the Deck! Bring the boat to one, seven, five and make turns for 18 knots. Let's see if the old girl will hold together."

"Aye, aye sir, steer one, seven, five. Speed, 18 knots."

'Now hear this. Flight personnel lay to the flight deck for air operations helo.' A Navy SH-60 *Seahawk* helicopter lands on the flight deck of the *Williamsburg.* The rotor blades slow. The Crew Chief jumps out, turns, and helps a woman dressed in a green aviator flight suit exit, then he helps four men dressed in Marine Corps utilities off the helicopter. Men carrying duffel bags exit, none wear insignia. A man dressed in a white helmet and white safety vest meets them. Ducking under the spinning rotor, they hurry from the helicopter to a door in the hangar bay.

The five of us were ushered through a narrow door into the ship's wardroom. A Marine Lance Corporal stood at parade rest inside the door. The captain and XO are sitting at a large table holding coffee cups. The two naval officers stand. I walked to the captain and stood at informal attention. "Support team 3 reporting as ordered, captain." We made up the name 'Support team 3' on the flight down. Sounded official to me.

The captain moved well within my comfort zone and looked me over. "Don't I know you? Yeah, older, but you're that sergeant—"

"Yes sir, we flew a couple of missions together, and no sir; you don't know me. My name is Sam Spade."

"It was more than a couple, and you damn near got my ass shot off."

"May I say, sir, you're one hell of a pilot. I never got a chance to thank you."

"You may— and consider me thanked."

"I didn't know you were Navy."

"Yeah, it was on one of those exchange deals. We called them 'live and learns'. If you lived, you learned something. I learned not to associate with Marines."

There is laughter from the group. The captain walked over to Liz and held out his hand. "How do you do? I'm Captain Gery Briscoe." Briscoe turns to Davis, "This is my XO, Commander Tom Davis. Tom's the one that runs things. I take the credit." Davis nods at Liz. Briscoe turns his attention back to Elizabeth. "Are you with this band of cutthroats?"

"It's a pleasure, Captain Briscoe. Please call me Liz. Yes, in fact, I'm married to the aforementioned sergeant cutthroat."

"Well, some of us are slower to learn than others. I take it this is not a honeymoon cruise."

"No, we had hoped to arrive more or less under the radar."

"Hard to do nowadays, with all the new gadgets we have now. Speaking of which, I take it you are here to install some new gear on our CCM?"

Elizabeth looks at the XO and the Marine sentry. Davis turns to Lance Corporal Miller.

"Lance Corporal Miller, secure the hatch."

"Aye, Aye, Sir." Miller steps through the door. Miller closes the door, turns, and stands at parade rest in front of the Wardroom entrance just as a Marine Captain walks up. Miller comes to attention.

"Lance Corporal, is there a meeting in the Wardroom?"

"Yes, Sir. There is no admittance."

"Be good enough to announce me. I've been ordered to attend the meeting. My name is Captain Schultz."

"Please wait here, sir." Miller knocks then steps through the door, "Excuse me, sir. Marine Captain Schultz requests entry. He says he's supposed to be in your meeting."

Elizabeth looked up from her coffee. "He's one of us."

"OK, Miller let him in."

"Aye, aye, sir."

The Marine officer enters the room, takes a brief look around, then walks to Captain Briscoe and comes to attention. "Captain Schultz reporting aboard as ordered, sir."

"And you're a real Captain not one of these ruffians?"

"No, Sir. That is, I'm a real captain. I'm with special Ops, sir. I'm a communication specialist."

"So, you *are* a ruffian?"

"Ahh, yes, sir."

Briscoe looks at Shultz's ribbons. "Yea, I know about you. You're the guy who won the Silver Star for sitting out in the open, directing an airstrike on your own position."

"Yes, sir."

"You and the sergeant make an impressive duo."

"Sir?"

"Sam Spade over there won the Silver Star, too. I put him up for it."

Liz looked at me thunderstruck. *Shit, I thought to myself.*

Shultz turns to me and smiled in recognition, then turns back to face Briscoe. "I didn't know, sir."

The captain turns to the XO. "What was the name of the general we got that message from yesterday?"

"Barrett, sir."

"Right, Barrett. He was there too. Right?"

"Yes, Sir. He was the one that ordered the air strike."

"This is all coming together. You guys all work for Barrett, and that means you work for the president."

Elizabeth said, "As I mentioned, Captain, in all deference to you, we would like to keep that quiet. Very quiet."

"I think there is coffee over on the sideboard. Everyone sit down and let's see what this is all about. My bet, the good people of Cuba are in for some shenanigans. This will probably be *Williamsburg*'s last mission, so let's get it right."

There is much shuffling of chairs. Several of the group walk to the coffee urn.

"Why is that?" Liz asked.

"Why is what? Oh, the last mission. Well, she is the last of the *Trenton* Class LPDs. She's being decommissioned to make way for the new *San Antonio* class ships."

After dinner, we were shown to our 'Officers Berthing Quarters.' The room was cozy if you liked bunk beds, wall lockers, and steel desks with matching chairs.

Liz was in a mood, through dinner, and after, so I knew a storm was coming. She was dressed in a robe stenciled 'US Navy'. I was less stylish in shorts and a T-shirt.

Liz sat in one chair with her foot propped on the bunk, rubbing some lotion on her leg. "The silver star, for god's sake! That's the third-highest medal this country awards!"

"That was—"

Moving to her other leg, rubbing vigorously. "—Don't give me that 'it was a long time ago' bullshit! Don't you think your children would like to know? How about your wife? I know she would have wanted to know. So, what else haven't you told me? Any climbs to Mt. Everest, dives on the Titanic. Were you a rodeo cowboy, race car driver?"

"I told you I was a shooter. It's not something you advertise. Over the years, it became unimportant."

"Well, I'm very proud of you. You're a wonderful father and husband. And a real pain in the ass."

I chuckled a little. Out of the doghouse— again. "Thank you. I think."

Liz looking around the small compartment. "These bunk beds sure offer little in the way of romance."

"Let's improvise. I'm told I'm good at improvising."

She stands, takes off her robe, and throws it over the chair. She walked to the light switch, turned, and posed seductively.

"Ma'am, you seem to be naked."

"My, observant and improvising." Liz turned out the light.

CHAPTER SIX

USS Williamsburg - Well Deck, Night

Liz, Jerry, Osborne, Shultz, Pérez, and I stood in the cavernous and damp well deck next to the CCM. Everyone except Liz was dressed in a Marine Corps Combat Utility Uniform with dark MARPAT camouflage and matching soft hats. We all carried Heckler & Koch 416s or M4s. Most of us carried knives. There were no insignia on our uniforms.

The Navy CPO in charge explained the finer points of the boat and the launch. "When the ramp goes down, I want you all in your assigned stations. When the well deck is flooded, we will motor out and head toward the beach. From that point, we will be on our own. Questions?" He looked at each member of the team. "OK, once we get near the coast, no talking, no lights, no moving around. When we get upriver to the drop point, I'll try to find a beach. Otherwise, you go over the side and walk or swim. Questions?" The team members look at each other, then shake their heads.

"So, what you're saying, we will be getting our feet wet." Rick said.

"I would count on it."

Bob Osborne said, "I hope these new utilities dry quickly. I hate cutting throats with a chafed bottom."

Everyone laughed.

"OK, gather around guys." Liz said. All the men turned and gathered around Liz. "The ramp will come down in about 12 minutes. I know you have heard this before, but Shultz and I will be in continuous contact. It's his job to monitor the operation and give me updates so I can adjust our plan accordingly. Dr. Pérez, you're our pathfinder. Once you get to the drop point, in deference to your age, I want you to remain with the boat with the Chief Petty Officer and his crew. I suggest you man the mini-gun and keep your eyes peeled."

"But I know the area."

"Please doctor, no arguments. Stay with the gun. You said you used to sell them, so you should know how to use them. If not, stay with the Browning. It's as old as you are."

"I am very adept with both, thank you."

Everyone laughs.

"Hopefully, you won't have to use either." Liz looked at Silvers. "Rick, no one will hold it against you if you want to stay here."

"I will. Besides, as a captain in the National Guard, I have to uphold the Minuteman tradition."

"OK, you guys should be in there in about 45-50 minutes. Thirty minutes to find Ed and another 50 minutes to the pickup point, then we can all have breakfast. And write this down. Don't forget Ed!"

The men laugh again.

"And remember our credo."

All the men in unison say, "Don't start a war!"

CLANG! CLANG! CLANG! CLANG!

Yellow warning lights flash all over the well deck.

The CPO said, "OK, here we go. Grab your gear. Everyone on board? Buckle-up!"

The ramp begins to lower. Elizabeth ran over to me. We kissed passionately. She brushed my cheek with her hand, then turned and walked forward to the higher part on the well deck. She turned and watched as the rear end of the ship sinks below the ocean surface, flooding the deck until the CCM stared to float. Once fully afloat, its engines were started, and the boat slowly moved out of the ship.

Water ran out of the well deck, and the ramp closed. Elizabeth turned and walked to the closest hatch for the climb to the bridge.

The four CCM crewmen sit in tandem on the port and starboard sides of the cockpit, the five-man insertion team sit at the rear. The high-speed ride was a gentle lope with the occasional bone-jarring thump. White phosphorescent spray spewed from the bow. The noise from the engines and wind were significant.

Jerry yells to be heard, "Guess this is a little faster than you rag baggers are used to."

I yelled back, "You couldn't get a sailboat to go this fast if you strapped a jet engine to it."

"Hope we're going this fast on the way back."

I nodded at him and gave him a thumbs up.

Elizabeth stood on the bridge, looking out at the night, seeing nothing but the dark sea.

"Captain on the bridge!"

Liz turned as the captain walked onto the bridge. He spotted her and walked over.

"Did you get your ruffians out the door?"

"Sure did. That's quite the movable beach you have down there."

"Don't laugh. We use it as a beach on occasions. Hamburgers, hotdogs, sodas, the whole shebang."

"No beer?"

The captain smiled. "No comment." He nodded at the radio in Liz's hands. "Is that radio going to do the trick?"

"I was assured by Captain Schultz it would work fine. He said it's a SATCOM. I assume that means it goes through a satellite."

"Well, he should know, in the meantime, go down to Communications and talk to the Warrant Officer on duty. Ask him to fix you up with a backup plan."

The CCM slowed down to about 15 knots. The CPO motioned for me to come forward. I unbuckled my harness and carefully made my way to where he was sitting, and leaned over so I could hear him.

"We have to slow down from now on. Our bow wave can be seen from a good way off." The CPO said.

"Fine with me. What's our ETA?"

"About 30 minutes. When we enter the river, we will be dead slow to reduce our noise signature."

"OK, thanks." I patted him on the shoulder and made my way back to my seat remembering one hand for the boat, one hand for me.

When the boat entered the river, Pérez stood up in the cockpit next to the CPO, giving instructions and hand signals. About 10 minutes later, the boat suddenly turned toward the shore and glided under some overhanging tree limbs. With a scraping sound, it slid up on the sandy shore, coming to an easy stop. The CPO shut off the engines and silently walked back to the insertion team. He was followed by Pérez. The three other sailors manned the crew-served weapons and fidgeted with equipment. No one made a sound.

The CPO whispered, "OK, your pathfinder says this is the spot. Like I showed you, slide off the ramp. The water will be shallow enough to walk in under the trees."

Pérez whispered, "Once you get ashore, go to the right. There is a small rise or hill. The camp is on the other side of that rise. Or it used to be."

"It's still there. And don't ask how I know." Jerry whispered.

Schultz quietly moved around the cockpit with a Navy PO making last-minute checks of the communications. Jerry, Bob, Silvers, and I checked our equipment, then filed off the back of the boat into the shallow water. I lead the team through the dark undergrowth to the top of the rise. With hand signals, I told the others to hold in place, then crawled through an opening in the brush. Sure enough, two hundred yards to the front, the camp was down in a shallow bowl like swale. It comprised three huts with an open fire burning in the center. A truck sat next to one hut. There was some faint light coming from inside two of the huts. I looked slowly from left to right, then back again. Staying on my stomach, I slid back to the other men. Whispering, I said, "No sentries. Three huts, two lit, one dark. Cooking fire in the center. One truck. Ten, maybe more soldiers." There was some slight groaning among the guys.

"Ed's probably in the dark hut. Jerry go left. I'll go right and try to come in next to the dark one."

Jerry nods.

"Bob, you set up where you can see the camp. You must keep the area between here and the water clear. Otherwise, we don't get out."

Bob nods.

"Rick. You stay with Bob. If one of us falls, fill in. Rick, you hesitate to shoot. You or one of us gets killed."

Silvers looks scared, but nods.

I grinned at him. "Don't shoot me or Jerry."

Avoiding the guards, Ed carefully skirted the camp to a place where he could approach the hut that had been his prison cell. There was a truck parked next to the hut. He sneaked up to the truck and peered inside the cab. In the middle of the seat was a canteen. He looked around and found a stick. Reaching through the open window with the stick, he gradually pulled the canteen to him. A guard came close to the truck and began relieving himself. Ed grabbed the canteen and slinked away.

The guard cries out, "Hey, who is that?" Two of his comrades ran to where he was standing. "I thought I saw something."

A second guard looked but sees nothing. He looked at a third guard. "Ha, probably the ghost of Che." They laugh.

"Maybe it was the prisoner." The first guard said.

"Why would he stay around here? He probably caught a ride with some farmer, or maybe a tourist. Ha, he's in Miami now."

"I wish I was in Miami."

"Don't let the ghost of Che hear you." They both laugh and walked to the fire. The first guard followed.

Ed sits in a cubby of brush, eagerly drinking from the pilfered canteen.

SNAP!

He freezes. Barely moving, he looks to his left. Carefully, he moved his hand toward the handle of the machete in his belt. Slowly, very slowly, inch by inch, he removed the machete from his belt. He begins to ease away from the sound. He hears another noise— Instantly a hand reaches out and pulls Ed's chin back, exposing his jugular to the razor-sharp edge of a knife. Ed felt his assailant's whiskers scrape his ear as the vice like grip on his jaw tightened for the kill. Helpless, all he could do was wait for the searing pain of the knife.

"Pardon me, when is the next bus to Havana?"

Ed said in a horse whisper, "Jesus Christ, you scared the shit out of me."

I couldn't help but chuckle. Trying to whisper, "You do need a bath. How you doing Bud?"

"I could do with a beer."

"OK, let's get out of here. How many men they got?"

"Ten and an officer. Do you know who's in that hut over there?" Pointing.

"Victor Escudero. You don't think we came for you?"

"Who's we?"

"The president must think highly of you. She sent every decrepit has-been she could find to get you out of here."

"Well, she was definitely scraping the barrel if she sent you."

"You can thank me later. In the meantime, crawl over to the hill—carefully so they don't shoot you and introduce yourself."

"Where are you going?"

"To have a chat with Victor."

"It will be a one-sided conversation. I broke his jaw."

"That's OK, I don't speak Spanish." I watched Ed crawl toward the other men, then I went to make a call on Victor.

I made my way to the side window of the hut and looked in. A bandaged Victor Escudero was sleeping on a cot. A Cuban military officer was sleeping in a chair. He was snoring. I looked around, then raised my silenced H&K and fired twice at Escudero.

PHISST, PHISST

Escudero's body jumped as the rounds impacted. Contrary to the movie's, silenced weapons aren't really silent. The military officer woke, groaned, and said something in Spanish.

PHISST, PHISST

I killed him, then dropped to my knees and slinked back into the jungle, arriving at the crest of the hill where Ed, Bob, and Rick waited— "Any sign of Jerry?"

Bob and Rick shake their heads.

"Who's Jerry?" Ed whispered.

"CIA."

Ed nods.

BANG! BANG! BANG!

BANG! BANG! BANG! BANG! BANG! BANG! BANG! BANG! BANG!

"Shit! Ed, make your way down to the river. There is a Navy boat waiting. Looking at Bob and Rick, "You two spread out and try to give cover to Jerry."

"I'm staying." Ed said.

"God damn it, Ed! A lot of people put their asses on the line to get you out of here. Now go! Tell those Navy guys if we're not there in 10 minutes, we're not coming. Now move!"

Ed hesitates, then scampers down the hill toward the river.

BANG! BANG! BANG! BANG! BANG!

I saw some movement down in the camp. It was two Cuban soldiers. I fired.

PHISST, PHISST

Two men fell.

On my left, I saw Jerry. A Cuban soldier sees him too and aims. I fired again, and the Cuban went down. Two more Cubans standup in front of Jerry and fire.

BANG! BANG! BANG! BANG!

Jerry killed both.

"Where the hell are these guys coming from?" I yelled.

The truck is now on the move towards our position. An old Browning .30 cal. machine gun is affixed to the top of the cab. It fired in my direction, the rounds cutting leaves and bark above my head. It fired again and there was a yell. I looked over to see Rick holding his leg. "Shit, we are never getting out of here." Three more Cubans make for my position firing AKs. Jerry on their flank fires killing one, the other turns and opens up on Jerry. He goes down. "Bob! You, OK?" I yelled.

"Yeah!"

"Jerry is down. Try to get to him. He's about ten o'clock from your position."

"I'll get him."

I crawled over to Rick. "How you doing Army?"

He winces. "Hurts like hell. I don't think anything is broken."

BANG! BANG! BANG! BANG!

Leaves and twigs shatter around the two of them. "Good. When I get you over to the primary, I'm going to prop you up. You're going to cover us until we get Jerry."

"Just get me over there."

I half carried and half dragged Rick to our departure point. I looked over to see how Bob and Jerry were doing. It looked like Bob had found Jerry in the brush. Jerry was tying his belt around a wound in his thigh.

"Come on Jerry, I can't carry you, so you have to crawl." Bob said.

"Yes, mother." Bob, supporting Jerry, starts toward the hill. A Cuban soldier runs out of the brush. Bob lifts his H&K,

BANG! BANG! BANG! BANG!

The soldier falls.

Elizabeth put her satphone on the console in front of her. She looked worried. Captain Briscoe looked over at her. "What's up?"

"Schultz says they can hear heavy firing coming from the camp."

"OD, put that com on the IC." The OOD throws some switches. "On, sir."

There is a hiss and static. Then a voice comes over the radio, ". . . this is Gunsmoke. Actual this is Gunsmoke. Over."

Elizabeth grabs the satphone, "Gunsmoke, Gunsmoke, this is Actual over."

"Actual, Gunsmoke. We still hear interment firing. Blue-chip is aboard, repeat blue chip is aboard. He has orders from Tiger 1 to depart without Tiger team."

Liz yells into the satphone, "Gunsmoke. I'm running this mission! You will not, repeat not, leave your location unless Tiger team is on board. You got that! I want to hear you say it."

"This is Gunsmoke. Copy Tiger team is to be on board before departing. Out."

RATATAT, RATATAT, RATATAT, RATATAT, RATATAT, RATATAT.

"We have to get that truck. I don't suppose anyone has a grenade?" I asked. "No."

"No grenades. I hate working for a cheap outfit." Jerry quipped.

"Then I guess I go down and get it."

RATATAT, RATATAT, RATATAT, RATATAT, RATATAT, RATATAT, RATATAT

The men ducked behind a log. More leaves and twigs shred.

"If you wait a minute, you can shake hands with the SOB." Bob said.

RATATAT, RATATAT, RATATAT, RATATAT, BANG, BANG, BANG, BANG, BANG, BANG, BANG, BANG, BANG, BANG, BANG, BANG, BANG, BANG, BANG, BANG. RATATAT, RATATAT!

"I think the cavalry has arrived." I said.

BANG, BANG, BANG, BANG, BANG, BANG, BANG, BANG, BANG. RATATAT, RATATAT!

I stuck my head up and looked to both sides of our position. Ed, Pérez, Schultz, and three sailors are firing into the camp and truck.

BANG, BANG! BANG! BANG! BANG! BANG! RATATAT BANG! BANG, BANG.

Then there was silence. More silence. I stood slowly and looked down into the camp and the smoldering truck. Only silence. Nothing moved.

I yelled, "Everyone, back to the boat."

CHAPTER SEVEN

Jungle River, Sierra Maestra Mountains, Cuba

The boat drifted down the middle of the river. One of the Navy men was looking after the wounded. The others warily stare into the dark for signs of danger. I walked to the cockpit and asked the CPO, "How long are we going to be in this river?

"Depends on how quiet you want to be."

"If it's all the same to you, we've made as much noise as we can make. Let's get out of here."

"You got it. There are some uncharted rocks at the mouth of the river. We will have to slow down for those."

The CCM picks up speed. A few minutes later, at the mouth of the river, Pérez yelled, "Patrol boat! Starboard bow coming around the point!"

In an 'S' turn, the CCM swerves to the left and heads for the shore, then abruptly turns right for the mouth of the river. A flame of light comes out of the dark.

BOOM!

There is a searing light like a huge flash bulb. The stern of the CCM jumps out of the water, then falls back. Water sloshes over the sides. The rear of the boat is on fire.

The CPO yells, "RPG! Get that fire out! I'm going to make for those rocks on the port side!" He pilots the injured boat slowly making the distance toward the rocks. Trading fire with the gunboat, the CCM fires its mini-gun and .50 cal. while the men fire their automatic weapons.

RATATAT RATATATRATATATRATATAT.

BANG, BANG, BANG, BANG, BANG, BANG, BANG, BANG, BANG, BANG

BZZZZZZZZZZZZZZZZZZZZZZZZZZZZZZZZZZZZZZZZZZZZZZZZZZZZZZZZZ

BOOM!

The mini-gun found the fuel tanks of the riverboat, stopping it mid-river with an explosion, but the riverboat keeps firing.

BANG, BANG, BANG RATATAT RATATATRATATATRATATAT

"*Actual, actual this is Gunsmoke. We are taking heavy fire from a Cuban gunboat. We have been hit! We have damage to our engine from an RPG!*"

Elizabeth looks at Captain Briscoe.

Briscoe turns to the officer of the deck. "OD, get the XO on the bridge and pass the word for CPO Rutkowski."

"Aye, aye, sir." He snatches the mic for the 1MC. '*Now hear this. CPO Rutkowski call the Bridge, CPO Rutkowski call the Bridge.*'

In the CPO berthing quarters, CPO Rutkowski is playing poker with three of his shipmates. He looks up, his eyes gape. One of the poker players says, "Jesus Ski, what the hell did you do?"

"I don't know." He stands and hurries to the nearest phone.

From across the compartment there is laughing, "Ahh, the captain's pet got his tits in a ringer."

Back on the 01 level. "XO on the Bridge!" A phone buzzes. Another sailor answers. "Bridge aye, aye." He turns to the captain. "Sir, it's CPO Rutkowski."

The captain grabs the phone. "Ski, is the Hangar Queen ready to fly?"

"Yes, sir, she's fueled and ready to go."

"She still have gun mounts?"

" Yes, sir, port and starboard."

"Get her out of the hangar. Get two of our best gunners and have them go to the armory and check out a grenade launcher, two MK25s, and all the ammo you can cram on the bird. We launch in 10 minutes. Wear flak jackets and sidearms."

"Aye, aye, sir!"

CLICK.

Rutkowski turns and looks at his shipmates, who stare at him. "Jesus Christ!"

"What?" One of the other men said.

"I don't know, but it's big. Jerry, get Lewis and Ward. Tell them to suit up with flak jackets and sidearms and meet me in the armory. On the double!"

"Will do." Jerry runs for the hatch.

Rutkowski runs to his bunk and grabs his flight suit.

On the bridge, Captain Briscoe calls out to Commander Davis. "XO call PRIFLY and tell them we'll launch a training mission in ten minutes. Where's Rosenberg?"

"I suspect he's in his bunk, sir." Davis said.

"OD, get Rosy on the horn. Tom, one more thing. Call down to the armory and tell them I have some men coming down for weapons and ammo. I'll sign the chits."

"Aye, Sir."

Briscoe walks over to Elizabeth. "Anything?"

"No sir, last I heard they were sinking and ran up on a rock just at the mouth of the river."

"Tell them I'll be there soon. Break out their strobe lights and turn them on when I say. Got that?"

"Yes, sir, strobe lights. Only when you say."

The XO calls to the captain, "Sir, it's the Air Boss. He says your guys are loading live ammo on the Hangar Queen."

"Tell him to log it as a training mission."

The OD hands the captain the phone, "Sir, Rosenberg on the horn."

The captain grabs the phone. "Rosy, suit up. We're going flying. Bring your flak jacket and sidearm."

'All hands standby for flight operations helo. Nonessential personnel clear the flight deck! Standby for flight operations, helo.'

A CH-46 *Sea Knight* helicopter sits on the flight deck, its rotors turning. A Mk25 Gatling gun is mounted in the window on each side of the aircraft. Lt. Commander Gerald Rosenberg, the copilot, is in the left seat of the helicopter. Crew chief and door gunner, CPO Rutkowski, stands by the door. Captain Briscoe runs to the door and climbs in. Rutkowski follows, secures the door, and swings the gun out the window. The helicopter powers up and flies into the night. Captain Briscoe and Lt. Commander Rosenberg face an instrument panel of dials, lights, and switches. Briscoe toggles the intercom.

"Good evening, men, the five of us are flying in harm's way. This is not a training mission. Some special Ops people are in a jam, and we are the only ones that can help. All I know is the CCM we kicked out last night was hit by an RPG and has been disabled. The good guys are engaged with a Cuban gunboat that may or may not be damaged. You men have trained for this. You are combat vets, act accordingly. You have permission to test-fire your weapons. Easy does it on the ammo. That's all."

"That's enough." Lt. Commander Rosenberg said.

Briscoe laughs. "Hope this old bird will hold together."

Loud noise and vibration come from the back as the men test-fire the Gatling guns. CPO Rutkowski stands by the door behind his gun. He turns on the power and fires.

BZZZZZZZZZZZZZZZZZZZZZZZZZZZZZZZZZZZZZZZZZZZZ BZZZZZZZZZZZZZZZZZZZZZZZZ

The six barreled Gatling gun has a selective rate of fire from two to six thousand rounds of 7.62 mm per minute. At night, it makes a continuous stream of red fire. Spent cartridge shells pour out of the gun onto the deck of the helicopter. CPO Rutkowski secures the gun and turns off the power.

PO Lewis' gun points out the port window. He goes through the same procedure.

BZZZZZZZZZZZZZZZZZZZZZZZZ BZZZZZZZZZZZZZZZZZZZZZZZZZZZZZZZZZZZZZZZ

PO Ward loads and checks the Mk19 grenade launcher, which is secured and fired from the ramp of the Hangar Queen. He does not take a practice shot.

"She'll be fine skipper. A little excitement might do her good." Rosenberg said.

"Maybe you're right. I'm worried about the guys in back."

"You said it yourself, Skipper, this is what they do."

Heavy fire was still coming from the disabled riverboat. All of us were trying to stay low, thankful for the rocks that provided some cover.

BANG BANG BANG BANG BANG BANG BANG BANG BANG BANG

I yelled at the CPO, "We have to suppress that fire, or they will shoot the hell out of our chopper! How are we doing on ammo?"

"Not good, only a few more bursts with the mini-gun and probably less than 100 rounds each for the rest."

"Shit, maybe the riverboat will turn a little more and give us a better shot. Let's save that possibility for the mini-gun." I thought for a minute. I turned to the men. "OK, guys, listen up!"

The men on the CCM stopped firing and turned toward me.

"If that gunboat shoots down our chopper, we're not getting out of here. If we can't take out the boat, we need to kill the people on it."

"No shit!" Jerry said.

"We don't have the ammo to keep banging away. We have to go back to basics. Start taking well-aimed shots. Jerry, you're a sniper. Bob, I've seen you hit a target at 700 yards. You all went to boot camp. Remember what you learned, sight alignment and squeeze. Wounded or not, I need you to focus on slow, accurate fire."

The men turn to the task.

"Bob, get on top of the rock and see if you can shoot down into them."

"On it."

BANG BANG BANG BANG BANG BANG BANG BANG BANG BANG

"Men, arm your weapons. We're about five minutes out. Ward, if I can, I'm going to fly over that Cuban boat. I want you to drop as may rounds as you can on her."

"Got it, Skipper." PO Ward said.

"Ski, Lewis, I'm relying on you two to keep their heads down when we go in for the pickup. Rosy and I are going to be busy. We can't direct fire."

"Got you starboard Skipper." CPO Rutkowski said.

"Roger, Skipper." Lewis said.

Through the windscreen, tracers can be seen on the horizon, crossing from right to left, then left to right. Small flashes emanate from both sides.

"Here we go. Rosy, tell the CCM to hold fire. Turn on their strobes. I'm coming in over the gunboat."

Rosenberg calls the CCM.

"Ward, on my mark, I'll be over the gunboat. A case of beer if you put one in their lap."

"Say when Skipper."

"Five, four, three, two, now!"

The CH-46 Sea Knight helicopter flies over the smoking gunboat. Light and sparks belch from the tube of the grenade launcher. The grenades land around the boat, detonating in bright flashes. One grenade lands in the boat, there is an explosion that blooms into a fireball. "I got him, Skipper! Must have hit a fuel tank!"

"Great job Ward! Work now, beer later."

"Skipper! One o'clock low. Another boat is coming into the river." Rutkowski yells.

"Shit! See what you can do, Ski?"

"On it!" He aims the Mini-gun and fires.

BZZZZZZZZZZZZZZZZZZZZZZZ
BZZZZZZZZZZZZZZZZZZZZZZZZZZZZZZZZZZZZ
BZZZZZZZZZZZZZZZZZZZZZZZZZZZZZZZZZZZZZZZ
BZZZZZZZZZZZZZZZZZZZZZZZZ
BZZZZZZZZZZZZZZZZZZZZZZZZZ
BZZZZZZZZZZZZZZZZZZZZZZZZZZZZZZZZZZZZZZZ

The new gunboat takes heavy damage. Secondary explosions light up the sky and reflect off the water. From his perch on top of the rock. Osborne yells, "The chopper just took out the riverboat!"

The men cheer.

The CPO ran up to me. "The chopper says he's going to hover and put the ramp on the rock and take us aboard. Says Sam Spade knows what to do. Who in the hell is Sam Spade?"

"That would be me!" I turned to the men on the boat. "Listen up! The chopper is going to hover directly over us. He will lower the bird until the ramp is close or on the rock. The pilot can't see and has no reference. You must get on as fast as you can. Two men for every wounded guy."

Osborne yells, "There is another boat! There is another damn gunboat!"

"Shit!" I scrambled up to Bob's position and looked. The new riverboat was taking heavy fire from the helicopter, but it was still moving forward. "Damn and hell!" I clambered down the rock, jumped in the boat, and ran to the petty officer manning the mini-gun. "Can you reach the boat that's just come around the point?"

"Probably, but I have almost no ammo."

"When you get a shot, do what you can until the ammo runs out."

The CPO turns to me, "The chopper says get ready and try to keep the gunboat off him."

"OK, men! Up on the rock!"

Through the windscreen of the CH-46 Hangar Queen, Briscoe can see the CCM and the rock coming up. Briscoe slows and starts his hover and descent.

"How's the wind Skipper?" Rosenberg asked.

"Negligible. OK Ward, how we are doing back there, you should see the rock."

"Got it. Forward twenty– down, ten– down, five– orbit right, hold! Orbit right, hold! Down five. Contact! Hold, hold, hold."

THUNK! THUNK!

"Taking hits, no damage!" CPO Rutkowski yells.

"Hold what you have, Skipper. Boarding now." Ward said.

The helicopter hovers over the rock. It moves forward, then down, forward, then down. It pivots, then settles some more. The ramp momentarily touches the rock, raises, then settles. It wavers but holds position.

I kept yelling, "Get on! Everybody on! Move! Move! Move!"

THUNK!

The men from the CCM pile on, dragging and pushing the wounded. The CPO is the last one. I yelled, "Go, go, go!"

THUNK! THUNK! THUNK! THUNK!

"Skipper, we're loaded, get us out of here! The CCM is rigged to blow." Rutkowski yells. We're taking hits! I can only bring one gun to bear!

"We are gone!" Briscoe yells. "Lewis, when I bank to go around the point, you might get one last crack at him."

"Roger, Skipper!

THUNK! THUNK! THUNK!

"Skipper! Lewis is down! Lewis is down! We took a hit in the hydraulic system!" Rutkowski yelled.

"Can you fix it?"

"Wait one!"

"See if some of those men can look at Lewis. Rosey, watch the hydraulic pressure."

"It's dropping fast. No way we make it to the *Williamsburg*."

"Gitmo, here we come!"

"If we're lucky."

"You're always the pessimist!"

"I'm Jewish! These things are supposed to float."

"Just as soon not try. Besides, who are we going to call? Once we're down, we don't exist."

"Skipper! I can't get to the hydraulic line." Rutkowski said.

"OK, I'm trying for Gitmo, but prepare everyone for a water landing."

Elizabeth keys the mic on her satphone again. "Gunsmoke this Actual, Gunsmoke this Actual, Gunsmoke this Actual. Over." *Static*. "Gunsmoke, Gunsmoke this Actual. Over." She throws the satphone on the console in front of her. "Damn!"

The Executive Officer walks over to her. "Still can't reach them?"

"No. Nothing, since they said they were boarding the chopper."

The XO reached over his head and pulled down a phone. "CIC, this is the Exec. What do you have on our guys?" He listens. "OK, keep trying." He hangs up the phone. "Combat can't reach them either and there is no radar track."

"What's that mean?" The look on her face betrayed that she already knew what it meant.

"They could be in the water. When it gets light, I'll send out a search. In the meantime, it's a calm sea. The Sea Knights are designed to float. They'll be fine."

Her eyes water. "I hope you're right. Thank you."

"XO, we have an incoming radio. I think you better take it."

CHAPTER EIGHT

Guantanamo Bay, Cuba

A Marine Corps officer is standing at a counter inside a tin building surrounded by several other Marines, all dressed in utilities. The officer wears a sidearm. He is talking on the phone.

"Colonel Holcroft, this is Second lieutenant Rollins. Sorry to bother you at this hour.

"What is it, Rollins, the Cubans coming over the fence?"

"Ah, no Sir. A chopper, I think it's full of mercs."

"Lieutenant, there are no flights due tonight."

"That's just it, sir, it's here. It already landed."

"Well, who is it? What do you mean mercs?"

"Mercenaries sir—"

"I know what a damn merc is!"

"Yes, sir. I don't know who they are. There are 15 of them. They have no identification, and they won't identify themselves. It's mostly a bunch of old guys—"

"Old guys?"

"Yes sir, they're all in their 40s or 50s."

"Christ! How old do you think I am?"

"Sir, they're armed to the teeth. But some of them are shot up and the chopper, it's an old H46—"

"Will you stop saying old!"

"Yes, sir. The chopper— it has mini-guns mounted in both windows and a grenade launcher on the ramp— it's all shot to hell. The pilot says it won't fly. He said he was lucky to get here."

"Damn it! Get here from where?"

"He won't say sir. He just said he was on a training mission and wanted us to contact the *Williamsburg*."

"Training mission, my ass! Sounds like they invaded Cuba– The *Williamsburg*. She's due in here tomorrow, right?"

"Yes, sir, at thirteen hundred hours. I called and spoke to the XO. He said he would send a chopper to pick these guys up. What do you want me to do?"

"Find out who the hell they are and call me back."

"Aye, aye sir."

Holcroft slams the phone down. "God damn it!"

"Who is that dear?" A woman asked. "And calm down, you're going to have a stroke."

"Yes dear, it's nothing. Go back to sleep."

A CH-46 *Sea Knight* helicopter sits on the ramp of Leeward Point Field, NAS Guantanamo Bay. Bullet holes and rips in the sheet metal span the length of the fuselage. Mini-guns hang out the two windows. Thousands of spent cartridge cases cover the deck of the cargo area. Fifteen men stand or sit propped against the helicopter. They look tired and dirty. Some are bandaged. A dozen well-armed Marines stand around them. Weapons ready.

Lieutenant Rollins walks up to the man he assumes to be in charge. "Sir, Colonel Holcroft, CO of Marine Security Detachment GITMO, sends his respects and asks that you identify yourself and state your business."

The man smiles. "I'll bet he does. Lieutenant Rollins, is it? Did you contact the *Williamsburg*?"

"Yes, sir. The captain was unavailable, so I spoke with the XO. He's sending a chopper."

"That's fine. Now get a corpsman to look after the wounded, then get some food and water for my men. Offer my respects to Colonel Holcroft and tell him we are on a training mission, and he should refer any questions about said mission to General Barrett. And put a double-time on the corpsman."

"Aye, aye, sir. Corpsman, food, and General Barrett." Rollins turns to his men. "Lance Corporal Givens! Have the Doc report to me on the double. Then get these people some rations, water, and hot coffee."

"Aye, aye, sir." Lance Corporal Givens and another Marine run to a hangar. Three other Marines pull out their canteens and pass among the 'mercenaries', offering them water.

The phone rings, "Colonel Holcroft."

"Lt. Rollins, sir. I'm afraid I don't have much more for you, sir. Only the pilot sends his respects. He said he is on a training mission and if you had questions, you were to contact a General Barrett."

"Barrett!"

"Yes, sir. Do you know him?"

"Yeah, I know him. When that chopper gets here from the Williamsburg, get those men on it and get it the hell out of here."

"What about their bird, sir?"

"Drag it into a hangar and keep it out of sight until I get back to you. And Rollins."

"Sir."

"This never happened. No logbook, no nothing. It never happened. Make sure your men know it never happened."

"Aye, aye, sir. It never happened."

CHAPTER NINE

The White House - Roosevelt Room

Liz, Ed, and I sat on the far side of the large conference table. The president, Collins and Silvers sit on the near side. Suzie sits on a chair behind the president. China coffee cups and plates with pastry sit on the table. Ed hands a paper to the president. "As you will see, the document is signed by Bruno Gallardo by order of Miguel Díaz-Canel. He signed it in front of me with the expectation I would corroborate the signature. I was told that Dr. Pérez would elaborate on the plan."

"Is there any question in your mind that this was done under the auspices of Miguel Díaz-Canel?"

"No ma'am, but I only witnessed Bruno Gallardo's signature."

"Well, I guess I have no choice but to meet with the scoundrel. Liz, would you agree?" Asked the president.

"I'm not so sure now is the time. As I told you before, I believe Pérez and, by extension, Mr. Gallardo are sincere, but we still have very few details," said Elizabeth.

"So, you think I should hold off?"

"Yes, Ma'am. Let us make the boat trip we had discussed, meet with as many of their emissaries as we can and, with Rick's help, prepare a preliminary document. That way, we have their hand in the cookie jar before you commit."

"In other words, if someone gets cold feet, I'm not the wicked witch of the north and their names are all over the proposal."

"Literally."

"OK, the four of you put together the details, then let me know if you need anything."

"Ma'am, we thought it better to sail into the Carolinas instead of Florida. Less chance of being noticed." I said.

"That's fine with me. Speaking of being noticed, we told the press Rick hurt his leg playing touch football with his kids."

Collins makes an unkind noise.

"As for the rest of you and your various cuts and bruises, it's probably best to stay out of the public view. OK, get out of here. Suzie, what's next?"

The participants of the meeting push their chairs back. Coffee cups clink.

"Wait. (pause) Thank you again. I'm not unaware of the risk you faced and the adversity you overcame. I'm immensely proud of all of you, including the ones not here today.

The president smiled. "*Now*, get out of here."

CHAPTER TEN

The Hunter's Residence - Den

Liz, Emily, Brad, and I sat around a low coffee table between the couch and the fireplace playing Scrabble. Sable, our gray fluffy cat, sat on the raised hearth in front of the first fire of the season.

"Children, your father and I want to ask you something."

"What?" Brad asked.

"We are taking the boat down the Intracoastal Waterway to Norfolk and wondering if you would like to go with us?

"In the *Pinafore*?" Emily asked.

"Yes. Your Dad and I will be going on south for a few weeks, and we thought it would be a nice way to finish up the summer."

Emily looked at Brad, then at her mom. "How do we get back?"

"On the train."

"Cool, a train ride. I've never been on a train," said Brad.

"No, I guess you haven't."

"I get the spare cabin," Brad informed everyone.

"You will sleep in the salon. Ed will use one of the guest cabins and your sister will have the other."

Emily stuck her tongue out at her brother.

Ignoring her Brad said, "Mr. Colombo is coming? Cool."

"Is Stacie coming? Emily asked.

"No, not this time."

"Shucks. So, what's this sailing trip about?"

"It's something your mom and I have always wanted to do. Now we have the time."

"Why do we have to get off in Norfolk?" Emily asked.

"Mom and I have some business to take care of in Hilton Head."

"Why can't we go with you to Hilton Head?"

"As you know, sometimes your mom does sensitive work for the government. This is one of those times."

"We know you guys are spies."

"Emily save that imagination for getting a job. Now are we playing scrabble or not." I stole a look at Liz.

CHAPTER ELEVEN

The White House - President's Residence

President Jackson sits at an antique desk, working.

BUZZZZZ.

The president picked up the phone "Yes. — OK, put him through. — Good morning General Barrett. No problems I hope?"

"Good morning, ma'am. It's Captain Briscoe. The Navy is pretty upset with him. There has been talk of a court-martial. I don't think it will go that far, but he will probably lose his pension."

"What on earth for? Rescuing Americans in trouble."

"The problem is those Americans don't exist, at least officially. And he destroyed a helicopter and engaged in an armed conflict with a sovereign nation."

"Sounds like some people don't have enough to do. I thought the helicopter was surplus to the needs and as for the Cubans, I haven't heard a peep from them."

"Everything you say is correct, ma'am."

"OK, I know you. What do you have in mind?"

"Ma'am the Williamsburg is being decommissioned. The Navy needs a testbed for a new forward base concept. Why not temporally reassign the Williamsburg as a prototype. In addition, the program rates a Rear Admiral— "

"And Briscoe is on the Admirals list, or he was."

"Yes, ma'am."

"General, you are a devious man."

The president, Collins, and Silvers converse in a small office used for non-ceremonial business. "Ma'am, you can't just pilot a helicopter down there," said Collins.

"Why not? I'm a pilot in the National Guard. I have over 3,000 hours in a *Black Hawk*."

"I think it's a great idea," said Silvers.

Collins leers at Silvers.

"Rick set it up for me."

"Yes, ma'am."

I was sitting in my chair reading the editorial section of the newspaper. Sable was on my lap. She preferred the comics, so she was sleeping. Liz was at her desk on the phone. After a few moments, she hung up.

"That was the White House." She said.

"Not another reception." I groaned.

"It was Rick Silvers. Seems Captain Briscoe is having a rough time because he rescued you and the boys. There is even talk of a court-martial."

"If it was up to me, he'd get a medal. He pulled us out of a dangerous situation. How's Rick doing?"

"He said he was doing OK. Most of his mobility is back. He would like us to go down to Norfolk and attend a ceremony on the Williamsburg. The president is using some new Navy program to save Briscoe's career and promote him."

"Count me in. Let's drive. It's only a couple of hours. Speaking of Williamsburg, we can spend the night at Colonial Williamsburg."

"The Williamsburg Inn?"

"Sure, we have an extra couple thousand lying around." I said sarcastically.

"Great! I'll make reservations."

Liz and I drove the one hundred plus miles south to Colonial Williamsburg and spent two days soaking up history. In October 1699, after a fire, the Virginia legislature moved from Jamestown to Middle Plantation, later renamed Williamsburg. For the next eighty years, Williamsburg was the capital of Colonial Virginia and host to the likes of George Washington, James Madison, and Patrick Henry. In 1780 Governor Thomas Jefferson moved the capital to Richmond. In November 1927, Reverend Dr. Goodwin, rector of Williamsburg's Bruton Parish Church, convinced John D. and Abby Aldrich Rockefeller to fund the restoration of Williamsburg.

Of the 500 buildings reconstructed or restored, 89 are original. Today it is both beautiful, illustrative of 18th century living, and a living monument to Virginia and U.S. history. My parents first took me to Williamsburg as a young boy, and I never tired of the experience.

A crowd watched as Marine One landed at Joint Base Andrews. Stepping off Marine One, Jackson is greeted and escorted to one of two Sikorsky SH-60 *Seahawk* Helicopters on the ramp. President Jackson is dressed in an Army flight suit with a Master Aviator Badge. There is no rank insignia, but the Presidential Seal is attached to her breast pocket.

"Good morning, Commander Jackson, thank you for flying with me."

"It's an honor, ma'am."

"The president smiled, I assume we are no relation."

Commander Jackson laughed, "no, ma'am, I don't think so. My family is from upstate New York. I understand you are from Louisiana."

"Born and raised."

"Ma'am, this is the Navy version of the Black Hawk, so I'm sure you're checked out."

"Three thousand hours' worth. Two combat tours. Shot down once."

"Let's not go down today. I'd just as soon not serve the rest of my career in Leavenworth."

President Jackson laughed.

"Ma'am, would you like to fly right seat?" Commander Jackson asked.

"No, it's your bird. I *would* like some stick time. Shall we go?"

Onlookers and a throng of reporters watched the two SH-60 *Seahawks* taxi and take off into the beautiful morning.

CHAPTER TWELVE

USS Williamsburg, LPD-16

The 1MC blares, "*Standby for flight operations. Nonessential personnel clear the flight deck! Standby for flight operations, helo!*" Minutes later two SH-60 *Seahawks* settle on the flight deck. The engines shut down and the rotors slowly come to a stop. Men dressed in Navy Dress White uniforms form a reception line to greet the president. Captain Briscoe is the first to greet Jackson.

"Good morning, ma'am. Welcome aboard."

"Good morning, Captain Briscoe, it is such a pleasure to meet you after all the wonderful things I've heard."

"That's kind of you to say ma'am. After we shake hands, we have set aside a room should you want to change."

"Thank you. The flight suit is comfortable, but you all look so splendid I feel a little out of place. Well, shall we do the meet and greet?"

Briscoe laughs and introduces President Jackson to the guests.

After a quick ride from Colonial Williamsburg, we were standing next to the namesake, USS *Williamsburg*, LPD-16. We were dressed in our Sunday best, Liz in a blue suit with heels and pearls. I was in a blue suit with a red tie. Much to my wife's displeasure, I wore boat shoes with no socks. My appeals to her reasoning that we were to spend the day aboard a boat had been ignored. Looking up at the ship's gangway, which was several stories high Liz groaned, "How am I going to get up all those stairs?"

"I told you not to wear heels."

"It's not the heels, it's the skirt. It'll be around my neck by the time I get up there."

"At least you have the legs for it."

Eventually, the interminable climb brought us to the quarterdeck, where the officer of the deck and the petty officer of the deck, both in dress whites met us. I faced aft, saluted the flag, then faced the officer of the deck and saluted. "Permission to come aboard. My wife and I are attending the ceremony."

The officer of the deck returned my salute. "Permission granted. The ceremony is in the Wardroom on the O2 level," He pointed. "Follow that companionway around to your left."

Elizabeth was bending over to straighten her skirt, she looked up. "Do I have to salute too?"

The OOD unsuccessfully suppressed a grin, "No, ma'am, civilians don't salute. Your husband was respecting tradition."

"You already saluted with everything you have." I said.

"Hilarious." She stood up and looked at the OOD. "Speaking of tradition, you might consider bringing back the bosun's chair."

The OOD laughed. "Yes ma'am, I'll speak to the captain about that."

Liz took another stab at rearranging her skirt, then we walked toward the Wardroom.

"Bosun's chair?"

"Yeah, that's how Captain Blood, Hornblower, and those swashbucklers got laid. They hauled women aboard with a bosun's chair." She stepped carefully through a hatch.

"I didn't know you were a fan of the genre."

"Swashbucklers? Sure, why do you think I married you? Why don't we have a bosun's chair?"

"We do. I use it for maintenance." We stepped through another hatch, a sailor whistled.

Liz pulled her skirt down. "How many of these damn things are there? What do you mean, maintenance?"

"Fixing stuff on the mast. Lights, antennas, rigging."

"Can I try it? Maybe you can get laid."

I was taking advantage of the liquid refreshments when Rick Silvers limped up to me.

"Enjoying the beverages, I see."

"Can you believe they still have this stuff? We used to call it bug juice." I said.

"In the Army, the more enlightened of us called it Kool-Aid. Did you know the beverage we call Kool-Aid today was once called Fruit Smack? It was invented by Edwin Perkins in 1927."

"Fascinating. I'm not going to ask how you know that tidbit. How's the leg?"

"Much better. The worst part is my wife, she is smoking hot.

"I've seen your wife. She *is* smoking hot."

"Thanks, but I mean she is really pissed off about the whole thing, particularly the part about getting shot. She threatened to divorce me if I went on another 'field trip.'"

"Hard not to blame her. She probably thought she was signing up for a future president, not a practitioner of jungle warfare."

On the opposite side of the room, President Jackson and Liz were talking. Jackson looked down at Liz's skirt. "That must have been an interesting climb up the gangway."

"The sailor boys thought so. It's not like I don't own an A-line skirt. I never gave it a thought."

The president laughed, "Do what I do, bring your own helicopter."

Richard Silvers limped up to the president. "Ma'am, we are ready. Please come this way." Following Silvers, the president walked to a small stage at one end of the wardroom.

Silvers announced in loud voice, "Ladies and gentlemen, The President of the United States." The room erupted in applause as President Jackson stepped on the stage and stood behind a lectern affixed with the Presidential Seal.

"Thank you. Good morning, ladies, and gentlemen, it's nice to see so many familiar faces. Forgive me, but I will not acknowledge all the luminaries present this morning, but I know who you are." There is some laughter. "I ask that you join me in recognizing Captain Briscoe for his bold, decisive action, which saved the lives of fourteen United States military and civilian patriots."

Liz stood next to me and squeezed my arm. She leaned over to me and whispered in my ear. "I am very proud of you." I kissed her cheek.

Waiting for the applause to subside, the president continued, "His actions were in keeping with the finest traditions of the United States Naval service. Today I am nominating Captain Briscoe to the rank of rear admiral.

I am also awarding him the Distinguished Flying Cross. Captain Briscoe, please step forward." President Jackson stepped off the stage, takes the DFC from a naval officer, and pins the medal on Briscoe's uniform.

Everyone applauded.

CHAPTER THIRTEEN

Pinafore - Norfolk, Va - Weeks Later

Elizabeth and I are sitting in the cockpit. Ed is behind the wheel. Liz yelled down to Emily and Brad. "Hey kids, come up here and look at the ships." Brad and Emily scramble up the companionway. On the far side of the river is an assemblage of huge warships in various states of repair.

"Honey, isn't that the *Williamsburg*?"

I stood and looked across the water, "It sure is. Try calling her on the bridge to bridge and see if anyone answers.

"That's the ship you used to get me?"

"Yep. It was going to be decommissioned, but thanks to you, they're turning it into a forward supply base prototype."

"Me!"

"Yeah, the CO of the *Williamsburg* got his shorts in a ringer for his trouble and the president stepped in and saved his career. Ed let's stop for a moment." Ed stops the boat.

Elizabeth picks up the microphone and flips a switch on the radio.

"USS *Williamsburg*, USS *Williamsburg*, this is sailing vessel *Pinafore* on Channel 16, over."

We waited.

"USS *Williamsburg*, USS *Williamsburg*, this is sailing vessel *Pinafore*, Channel 16, over."

"Sailing vessel *Pinafore*, this is USS *Williamsburg*, over."

"Good morning, sir. We wish to speak with the captain."

"Sailing vessel *Pinafore*, USS *Williamsburg*, switch to Channel 68."

"Switching to Channel 68." Liz leaned over and turned the knob on the radio.

"Sailing vessel *Pinafore*, USS *Williamsburg*, go ahead with your message."

”*Williamsburg, Pinafore*, please tell the captain that Sam Spade sends his compliments. Over.”

“Wait one.”

“Sailing vessel *Pinafore,* USS *Williamsburg*. The captain is unavailable. He requests Sam Spade and guests' presence for dinner at 1800 hours. Dress informal.”

Elizabeth looked at me. I nodded. “*Williamsburg, Pinafore*. Sam Spade gratefully accepts the captain's kind invitation for 1800 hours.”

“USS *Williamsburg* returning to Channel 16. Out.”

“Now, all we have to do is find a place to park this thing.” I said.

Liz and Emily look up at the gangway, which is several stories high. Elizabeth speaks to Emily. “See why I told you to wear slacks.” Emily continues to look up at the ship. Men in hard hats work in floodlights. Grinders and cutting torches throw sparks. There is constant hammering.

“OK, *gang*, follow me up the *gang*way– Get it?”

“Just go, you're embarrassing your children,” Liz said.

The petty officer of the deck maned the quarter deck. I faced aft, saluted the flag, then faced the petty officer of the deck and saluted. “Permission to come aboard. My wife and party have been invited to dinner.”

The petty officer of the deck returned my salute. “Permission granted. Good evening, sir, you are expected.”

Everyone filed aboard. The petty officer of the deck speaks to Liz. “Ma'am, before you leave, the crew would like to present you with a gift.” He reaches down from under the lectern-like stand and pulls out a white canvas bundle and hands it to Elizabeth.

“Petty Officer, you shouldn't have— What is it?”

He grinned, “It's a bosun's chair, ma'am. We all pitched in. It's embroidered with the ship's name.”

Liz laughs, “Thank you, Petty Officer. I didn't realize my legs were that notable.”

The petty officer of the deck gave her a sheepish grin, “Well, ma'am, I can't deny your legs captured some attention. But it's more than that. We all admire you for the way you handled that secret mission. More importantly, we heard you had a hand in saving our captain and ship. We appreciate it."

Elizabeth looked as if she might cry, she leaned over and kissed him on the cheek. "Thank you again Petty Officer and please, please thank the members of the crew for their thoughtfulness."

Ed and family enter the wardroom. Briscoe, Davis, and other officers stand randomly around the room. Most hold drinks or coffee cups. Briscoe walks over to them, "Welcome aboard."

Liz shakes his hand, "Admiral, I would like you to meet our children, Emily, and Brad. Of course, you know Ed. Emily, Brad, this is Admiral Briscoe." Both Emily and Brad shook hands.

"It's a pleasure to meet you both. You should be very proud of your Mom and Dad. Ed, how are you doing? All healed up."

"Yes, thank you admiral."

"Please excuse me, I should get on with the dinner ceremony." Briscoe turned to the assembled. "Ladies, gentlemen, may I present Captain Davis."

Applause, applause.

"As you know, this is his nonalcoholic wetting-down party. I'll understand if you men go ashore later for a more traditional affair."

General laughing.

Elizabeth kisses Davis on the cheek. "I didn't know. Congratulations Tom, how wonderful."

I walked to Davis, and shook his hand, "Congrats Tom. This is my dearest friend, Ed Colombo. You may have heard his name mentioned."

Ed shakes Davis's hand. "It's a pleasure to meet you, and Congratulations Captain."

"Thank you. So, you're the guy, all the fuss was over. It's nice to meet you in person."

Davis stepped back and spoke to the room. "Thank you one and all."

The Admiral stepped forward again, "OK, we have the Navy's famous bug juice– that's punch to you young people— iced tea and coffee. Dinner will be served shortly. Choice of steak or lobster or both.

CHAPTER FOURTEEN

Coinjock Marina, North Carolina

After getting the kids to the train station we left the great naval port of Norfolk and motored south on the Intracoastal Waterway, stopping at Coinjock for the night. The Coinjock Marina and Restaurant is a collection of red shingled buildings that overlook the Intracoastal. Their dock is filled with tables covered with red umbrellas. *Pinafore* was tied up along the dock. We opted to eat inside and sat around a table in the wood-paneled restaurant studying the menus. Ed looked up at me. "I assume you've eaten here before. What's good?"

"The prime rib."

Elizabeth said, "Damn, I miss the kids already."

"Me too, but you were right. It was best to send them home."

"At least Brad gets his train ride." Liz turned a page in the menu. "Prime rib? I thought this was a seafood place."

"The seafood is great, but the Prime Rib is their specialty." I said.

"This is the heart of Blue Crab country so I'm having the crab cakes." Ed announced.

The waitress arrives with water, then takes orders.

After the waitress walks away Ed asks, "Isn't the Dismal Swamp around here somewhere?"

I pointed to my right. "Yep, about 15 miles that way. Why?"

Ed looked at the back of the menu. "Says the Coinjock population is 380. Maybe we should have the meeting here. If anything goes wrong, we can dump our mistakes in the swamp."

Liz was still looking at the menu. "Cheerful thought. If you're that bloodthirsty, you should have the prime rib. Oh, look, they're having live music tonight."

After dinner we lingered over some wine and watched as the live band at the far end of the room tuned up their instruments.

Ed watched as a man threw money on the bar and walked out of the restaurant. "You know, I think I'm going to skip the festivities and hit the sack."

"I snickered, "You're not a fan of country music?"

"It's my favorite, but I'm tired."

"I was hoping to get a dance out of you." Liz said.

"Yeah, me too," I said.

Ed stands and kisses Liz on the cheek. "Next time." He turned and walked out of the restaurant.

Liz and I stayed a couple of hours, we danced and pretended we were teenagers again. On the walk back to *Pinafore*, we held hands. Liz's rested her head on my shoulder.

"That was fun, when was the last time we danced like that?"

"Probably before we were married," I said.

I climbed aboard *Pinafore* then turned to help Liz. As she stepped on the boat she yelled, Ed!"

I turned to see what she was looking at. Liz rushed to a crumpled body in the cockpit. Both of us bent over the body, I carefully turned Ed over. Blood dripped from his scalp.

"Liz go below and get some wet towels."

Liz jumped to the companionway and took a step down. "There's a body at the bottom of the stairs!"

I dived below and turned the man over and felt for a pulse. None. I looked up at Liz.

"He's gone. How's Ed?"

"I don't know. Help me get him below."

I slid the body out of the way then climbed up to the cockpit. We positioned Ed so we could slide him down the stairs. Liz took his feet, and I took him by his shoulders. We gently coaxed him down the companionway then slid him over to the settee. With some difficulty we got him on the couch. Liz sat next to him, holding a cloth to his head.

"How is he?" I said.

"I think he needs a doctor." Liz stands to turn on the light.

"No. Keep the light off. Take a peek outside and see if anyone heard the shots."

She climbed halfway up the companionway and looked. "No, nobody around. The dance is still going strong." Climbing down, "What about the doctor?"

"I doubt if there is one in this berg. Besides, if we call a doctor, everyone within

miles will know about it, and we're still stuck with this guy, whoever he is."

There are groans from the settee. Ed turned to his side and gradually sat up.

I walked over to him. "How you feel bud?"

Ed reaches up to the wound on his head. "Like somebody shot me in the head."

Elizabeth sat next to Ed and looked at the wound. "Honey, get me a flashlight. I can't see a thing."

I handed her a light. She looked at the wound, dabbing at the blood. "Cut the scalp but not to the bone. What the hell happened?" Still holding his head. "Who is this guy?"

"I saw him at the bar. He kept looking in our direction. First, I thought he was looking at you, but when you went to the head, he didn't watch you," Ed said.

"That's it I'm going on a diet." Liz said.

"Remember the population of 380? He didn't fit. On a hunch, I looked around the parking lot and found a Chevy with a Florida tag. When I got to the boat, he was down here. He heard me, he turned and fired. No warning, no nothing, he just fired. I shot back."

"What are we going to do with him?" Liz asked.

I bent over the dead man and rummaged through the clothes. "I have a wallet." I stood and looked at his driver's license in the dim light. "Hernandez Romero, Miami." I bent over and looked at looked at the man's face. "Liz, shine the light on him."

Liz holds the light on the man's face.

"Looks like him. In the morning, let's call Gallagher and see if he'll run him for us."

Liz looked at him, "Police Lt. Gallagher— in Newport?"

"Yeah. If we use anybody else, it gets too involved." I said.

"OK, in the meantime, what are we going to do with him?" Liz asked.

"We'll stuff him somewhere and cover him with a sail bag. At first light, we get out of here and dump him over the side in one of the swamps south of here." I said.

Ed asked, "What about his car?"

"Get a screwdriver and take the tags. By the time they run the VIN, we'll be long gone."

"Are you kidding? A black guy steeling tags from what's probably a stolen car in the middle of the night. Besides, I'm grievously wounded."

"You don't look grievously wounded, and all these years you said you were Italian."

"I said my grandfather was Italian."

"Will you two stop. I'll do it," Liz said.

"Wait! Dinner- you paid. The police will have your credit card." Ed said.

"I used cash."

"So, it's four for breakfast?" Ed said.

Pinafore motored down the ICW, in a tributary called North River Ed and I shifted the dead man over the side with a splash.

"This must be like old times for you."

"Hysterical." Ed said.

"Maybe we get lucky, and the gators eat him."

"Or the Natural Resource Police find him in the next hour."

"I guess we'll find out. Ok. Honey head south."

Liz put the boat in gear, eased the throttle forward. In a couple of hours, we were in the Albemarle Sound. Liz was reading, I was steering the boat. "Liz, it's pretty deep here. Why don't you grab that license plate and throw it over."

"You want me to pollute our natural resources?"

"No, I want you to ditch the evidence, so we don't get arrested for murder."

"Since you put it that way." Liz stood and started down the companionway.

"While you're down there, look in on Ed and see how he's doing."

Liz came back from checking on Ed. She tossed the license plate overboard. "He is awake said he's thirsty. As far as I could tell, he has no fever, and he wasn't clammy. He said he feels OK, it's just that his head hurts."

"OK, we'll make him eat something in a while." I said.

"That headache worries me. Maybe we should have a Doc look at him?"

"Liz, we are literally in the middle of nowhere. Our next stop is Alligator River. I think there is a hospital about 30 miles from there if we can get a ride."

"Just great."

"It's that or Morehead City, which is three days away. If we think he's going into shock or getting a fever, we call the Coast Guard for a medevac."

"OK, I'll keep a close watch on him. Gallagher called when I was below. He said Hernandez Romero is his real name. He is wanted for murder in Florida and Mississippi. The tag is stolen."

"Anything else?"

"Yep, Mr. Romero used to be DGI."

When the sun sets over the Albemarle Sound a photograph or poet can capture it, but neither can do the tapestry of colors justice. In the late afternoon of the third day of sailing, or more correctly motoring, we arrived at Wrightsville Beach and tied up at a marina of the same name.

"Ed, how are you feeling?"

"Guys, quit asking me that. I'm fine— really."

"So, anybody for dinner?" Liz asked.

"Yes, I'm starved, just don't ask me about my head anymore."

We walked over to the Bluewater Waterfront grill and sat inside. I ordered shrimp and grits, Ed the Mahi-Mahi and Elizabeth ordered crab cakes. We abandoned our usual beer and ordered a bottle of Sauvignon Blanc. I ordered iced tea as a chaser.

"You know the name Mahi-Mahi is a misnomer. What your really eating is a fish called dolphin, but restaurants name it incorrectly, so the patrons don't think their eating Flipper."

"Fascinating. I think you mention that every time we order *dolphin*. Liz said.

"It's also called dorado." Ed said.

"Just trying to be informative." I said. "What time does Pérez get here?"

"He said he and Gallardo will be here about noon." Ed said.

"Short of any satellite or electronic surveillance, I think we're safe to hold the meeting right on the boat. From the end of that transient dock, we can see 360 degrees."

"Maybe this austere setting thing has backfired. We can see them coming, but they can find us with little or no trouble," Liz said.

"I disagree. The guy in Coinjock stuck out like a sore thumb. If we had been in Miami, we would have never seen him coming."

"I suppose you're right. But if my ass was smaller, maybe you wouldn't have noticed him."

Ed and I laughed. The waiter brought the food and drinks.

We were sitting in the cockpit eating breakfast and enjoying the early morning.

"It sure is a beautiful day for a coup d'état," I said.

"Please, we are engaging in diplomacy," Liz said.

"Maybe we are, but not Dr. Pérez. Ed, what time will they be here?" I asked.

"I just spoke to him. He flew into Raleigh this morning and should be here in about three hours."

I looked at my phone. "So, about one o'clock. Liz, instead of you making lunch, why don't we have the Grill make a lunch and send it over?"

"I'll run out and resupply our beer and wine stores," Ed said.

It was about 2 p.m. when Dr. Pérez and Bruno Gallardo arrived. Gallardo was about 60 years old, 5-11, with dark hair. He was wearing reading glasses. The three of us greeted Pérez and Gallardo warmly. "Gentlemen, please have a seat anywhere you like. What can I get you to drink?" I asked.

"*Cerveza, por favor.*" Bruno said.

"Just coffee, thank you," Pérez said.

Elizabeth thought Ed and I should remain sober while we were remapping the world, so she put out a pitcher of iced tea for us. Bruno started things off swimmingly. A good metaphor since we were on a boat. "I do not deal with supernumeraries on matters of this importance; however, Dr. Pérez asserts I have little choice in the matter."

This was not good, he just pissed off the entire female population, worse he pissed off my wife, which was possibly ruinous to his health.

"Minister Gallardo, President Jackson has asked me to evaluate your proposal. I am not here to initiate negotiations. I can only report my findings." Liz said curtly.

Bruno removed a letter from his inside jacket pocket. "This is a declaration of our intention, signed by me and Miguel de Leon. It is an assurance of our commitment not only to the United States but to the people of Cuba." Bruno handed the letter to Elizabeth. "I do not wish to do this in a manner that will embarrass my government. This is not a coup, but a foray into a new ideology, a new philosophy of governing. However, you may already suspect that should that letter fall into the wrong hands, it would probably mean prison or death for me and Miguel de Leon."

"Minister, this letter will be treated with respect and the care it deserves," Liz said.

"I appreciate your assurances, but, as I said, I am unaccustomed to dealing with supernumeraries, and I do not share your enthusiasm for its care. Dr. Pérez tells me your little group is quite formidable. However, defeating a few thugs does not rise to my idea of formable. Nonetheless, I will respect Dr. Pérez's confidence."

"You will find that the President of the United States also shares Dr. Pérez's opinion. Our little group just defeated a company of Cuban soldiers and two heavily armed Cuban gunboats— Two days ago, we defeated one of your rival agents. If you are unhappy with any aspect of our mandate, we will be happy to depart for a much-needed vacation."

"That won't be necessary. We shall say no more about the subject."

"Yes, we will say more. After you gave Ed your letter of intent, I do not believe for a moment he was ever out of your sight. We think you had Ed kidnapped to test our resolve, our investment in your cause. I'm sitting here, so you now know President Jackson is amenable to the wonderful opportunity you profess to offer." Liz puts down her drink and leans forward. "If you kidnap another American Citizen, I have been instructed to tell you that 'Hell hath no fury like a woman scorned'. And that's not Shakespeare, sir, that's President Harriet Jackson."

Pérez and Ed looked at me but said nothing. Bruno looked uncomfortable but proceeded.

"I will be in New York in two weeks. I would like to use the opportunity to sit in front of President Jackson and tell her personally of our intentions."

"I don't have sway over the president's schedule, but I will convey your wishes. Perhaps you would allow Dr. Pérez to be your man in Washington to improve communication between us."

Bruno opened his briefcase, removed some paper, and scribbled on it, signing with a flourish. He handed it to Elizabeth. "As you see, it says That I, Bruno Gallardo here and now do name Dr. Pérez as my chargé d'affaires, pro tem."

Liz takes the document and looks at it. "Thank you, Minister. Congratulations Berto"

"The virtues which have been bestowed on men given merely to make them more obedient," Pérez said.

"Samuel Adams." Elizabeth said.

Pérez laughs.

I stood and moved to the companionway. "Time for lunch. It's one of my favorite quotes."

We all sat around the settee drinking Blanton's over ice from crystal tumblers, a luxury on a boat, the tumblers I mean. The bottle of Blanton's is sitting on the polished teak table. "Jesus, Liz, I thought you were going to declare war." I said.

"You guys could have been killed. Those sailors could have been killed for what? A stupid chauvinist test, '*Is the broad going to buckle under pressure*'."

"Unfortunately, ol' Victor got carried away. He was really going to take my arm off." Ed said.

"I don't think he was following the script. He hated Jackson." I said.

"What happened to him, anyway?" Liz asked.

"I killed him." I said.

"Oh." Liz finished her glass and poured some more. "Are you guys ever going to tell me your war stories?"

"No."

"No."

"So, what's the plan?" I asked.

"The president wants Ed and me to fly to Washington tomorrow, deliver the documents and I guess help her make a plan."

"Oh great. A supernumerary is planning the new world order." I said.

Liz punched me on the shoulder.

Ed and I doubled over laughing.

The next day Liz and Ed are greeted by Suzie-the-nose and shown into the Oval Office. "Please go in. The president will be right with you. May I get you something to drink?"

"Coffee, please," Liz said.

"Something cold." Ed replied.

President Jackson, Collins, and Silvers enter the room, seemingly all at once. Ed and Liz stand.

"Good afternoon. Liz. Where's your main squeeze?"

"Good afternoon, ma'am. We left him with the boat until you decide where you want us." Liz handed a document to the president.

"Please— everyone, be seated." The president reads the document carefully, then hands it to Collins. "Any trouble?"

"We ran into a little on the way down. Ed handled it."

Jackson looked at Ed. She arches her brows. "You handled it?"

"Yes, Ma'am."

"That's all you're going to say?"

"Yes, Ma'am."

Silvers finished reading the documents from Bruno Gallardo. "So, Pérez is official."

"If the president accepts that appointment," Liz replied.

The president looks at her two aides. "What do you guys think?"

"I don't have any issues. It may be best if he stayed in the background as much as possible, at least until we do a press release," Collins said.

"I agree with Johnny. How are you going to time the release?" Silvers said.

The president looked at Elizabeth. "Liz, any thoughts?"

"Wait until he is in New York. Let's get him to bring Miguel de Leon with him. That way, when you make the announcement, the two of them will be more or less out of harm's way."

"OK, pending any objection later, that's what we'll do. Can you leave the boat in North Carolina for a few weeks?"

"Yes, ma'am."

The president stands. "I suspect there will be more cloak-and-dagger stuff, maybe as far down as Cuba. In the meantime, bring your husband home."

CHAPTER FIFTEEN

Hunter Residence - Mount Vernon, Va

Two men were sitting in the front seat of a black SUV. One man dropped a set of binoculars to his lap. "So, why are we watching this guy?"

"Why do you keep asking me that? The director said to watch him. So, we watch him."

"I'm telling you, this guy has a short fuse. If he thinks we're fucking with his family, he's going to come out here and shoot the crap out of us and ask questions later."

"Give me the binoculars."

I was sitting in the den reading *The Admiral's Daughter* by Julian Stockwin. It was too hot for it but there was a fire burning in the fireplace. A novel is meant to be read in front of a fire or on the beach. I didn't have a beach. Besides, Sable liked the fire. She was sleeping on the couch. Liz walked into the room. "Honey, that car is out front again. Do you want me to call the police?"

"No. I know who it is. I'll talk with them."

"If you want to invite them in? I can make some coffee."

"Thanks. I'll be right back." Liz left the room. I went to my safe and pulled out a Colt, walked out the back door and went around the house, coming up behind the parked black SUV. I opened the back door and slid into the SUV. I pressed the Colt into drivers' temple. "Hi guys. You move a muscle and I'll kill you both." Both men freeze. "Very slowly, throw your guns out the windows."

"But— "

"One more time. Throw the guns out the windows." The two men threw their guns out of the car. "Now, who do you work for?"

"The FBI."

"Bull shit. No Agent would leave the door unlocked or the windows down. I'll ask you one more time. Who do you work for?"

"Can I get my ID?" The driver said.

"What's your name?"

"Agent Carter."

"OK, Carter, get it. You pull a gun out, I'll kill you. You youngsters may not recognize a Colt 1911. If a round from this gun hits you, you will not survive."

Carter pulls out his credentials and hands them back to me. I looked at the wallet in the dim light. I nudged the guy in the passenger seat with the gun. "Who are you?

"Agent Fellows."

"OK, Fellows, let me see your ID."

Fellows passed his ID back to me. "Why are you following me?"

"We don't know."

"You guys have been dogging me for two months and you don't know why?"

"No."

"Do you know who is in that house? My family. My wife and children. They depend on me to keep them safe. It's a father's job, it's a husband's job. It's my job."

"May I say something?" Fellows asked.

"No. My family is not safe when there are two hot dogs with loaded guns parked at their front door for reasons they can't explain."

"We're following orders."

"Who's orders?"

"The directors." Carter said.

"You know Tom Sawyer?"

"We work for him."

"OK, this is what's going to happen. You are going to sit quietly while I get out of the car. Then you are going to drive away and never come back. If I see you on my property again, it will not be a cordial meeting."

"What about our ID and guns?"

I got out of the SUV. "I'll mail them to you. Now get."

The SUV drove off in a hurry. I picked up the guns and cred wallets and walked back into the house. I put all three guns along with the wallets in my safe and returned to my book. Liz walked into the room with a magazine. "So, did you know them?"

"Yeah, it was a couple of Sawyers' guys. They were just making sure we were OK."

"That's nice. You should have invited them in."

"They had to leave."

The next morning, I was sitting in the dining room reading the *Washington Times* and eating my way through a dozen or so warm Beignets Liz had just made. Through a huge plate-glass window, the dining room overlooked the rear patio, lawn, and woods beyond. Once in a while, a deer would wander through the yard, so I was always on the lookout. The deer didn't like Beignets, but they liked corn.

DING! DONG!

"I'll get it!" Liz called out. She opened the front door.

A man dressed in a dark suit is standing in front of the door. "Good morning."

"Tommy. How are you? Come in. How's Kay?"

"She's fine. We've been trying to get you guys over for dinner, but you're never home."

"I know. We both have been traveling a lot. Come on in, I just made Beignets. How about some coffee?"

They both walked to the dining room.

"Please." Tom said.

Liz walked to the kitchen. Sawyer sat at the dining table.

"Good morning. I was expecting you." I picked up a large, brown packing envelope and placed it on the table next to Sawyer. "I found these in my front yard."

Sawyer looked at the envelope but didn't touch it.

Elizabeth walked in from the kitchen carrying a plate and a mug. "Here you go, freshly made. There is extra powdered sugar in the silver shaker in front of you."

"Thanks, Liz. Reminds me of Café du Monde."

"That's where I got the mix. Honey, I'm going to the bank and the grocery store. Do you need anything?"

"Chocolate chip cookies."

"Already on the list. Don't worry about the kitchen. I'll clean it up when I get home. See you guys later. Give my best to Kay."

"Will do."

Liz left the dining room and house through the garage. I could hear the garage door grinding up and down. It was a fast getaway. I put the *Times* down.

"Don't worry about the kitchen is code for have it standing tall when she gets home."

"Kay is not that subtle. You scared the crap out of my guy's last night. Do you know how much trouble you could get into for that stunt?"

"My gun wasn't loaded."

"You go after two FBI agents with an unloaded gun?"

"It was my parts gun. It doesn't even have a firing pin. As for your agents, they're accountants with a couple of weeks at Quantico."

"Were they really sitting there with the doors unlocked?" Sawyer put a Beignet in his mouth, dropping powdered sugar down the front of his suit.

"With the windows down. Why do you have a tail on me?"

He used a napkin to brush off the sugar. "Orders. Rumor has it that some mercenaries killed a bunch of Cuban soldiers and blew up a gunboat."

"Really? Hadn't heard— It was two gunboats. Orders from who?"

"The whom is the Director. He's not a fan."

"What did I do to him?"

"He thinks you're encroaching on his turf. So do I."

"I'm just a real estate broker, and he can have my turf anytime he wants it."

"You have the president's ear. He doesn't like that either. I don't give a shit. There is another rumor that Cuba is making nice with the president in hopes of official recognition."

I sprinkled powdered sugar on my last Beignet. "I'm just a real estate broker."

"Word is your brokering more than real estate. And a lot of people in this town don't like that either, including my boss."

"Is that what happened to that Navy Captain Briscoe?"

"Yep, and if Jackson doesn't win this election, you and Liz could be in real trouble."

"How's that? We work for the administration."

"Did you ever hear the term plausible deniability? Did Jackson ever tell you 'Don't get caught because I can't help you'? These people will bury you with investigations. You'll be bankrupt in a year."

"And if she wins?"

"Then you survive. At least for another four years."

The light was low, the table is set with candles and the good china. Liz and I were enjoying one our infrequent dinners at home.

"Thanks for cleaning the kitchen. With the oil, flour, and powdered sugar, I know it was a disaster."

"You are a wonderful if exuberant cook."

"Thanks. So, the guys in the car last night worked for Tommy. You didn't shoot them, did you?

I laughed, "No, I just rapped their knuckles. But I had an interesting conversation with Tom."

"Oh?'

"I think we should reevaluate our employment status with State. I'm not sure our priorities align anymore."

"In English, please."

"Our necks are hanging way out and if Jackson doesn't win reelection, Tommy thinks we could be in real trouble with her political enemies."

"Like what almost happened to Briscoe?"

"Exactly."

"What do you have in mind?"

"Three things. We cease all work for the administration until after the election. We go back to the boat and hunker down, disappear."

"And the second thing?"

"If Jackson wins the election, and she still wants us to work for her, we insist Tommy Sawyer is part of the team. The third thing is no plausible deniability. We work in the open with a contract."

"Hard to come after an FBI sanctioned project."

"Not impossible, but much harder than coming after a real estate broker."

"What about Ed?"

"He legitimately works for the State Department. I assume he is safe."

"Why don't I have a conversation with the president? I have a meeting with her, anyway. I'll broach the subject and see what she says."

"That's fine, but regardless of what she says, I have no wish to spend any time in jail or spend every dime we have answering subpoenas or both." I had a forkful of dinner. "This is great. What is it?"

"Beef Bourgogne."

"Do I have to clean the kitchen?"

CHAPTER SIXTEEN

The White House – Presidents Working Office

The president and Elizabeth are sitting across a desk from each other. "OK, you have another matter to discuss?"

"Yes, ma'am. The FBI has been following us since we landed at Dulles with Reynaldo Vicente. In addition, we have been told by people we trust that should you lose the election, your enemies plan to investigate us with a look towards prosecution. Ma'am, we cannot afford that financially or otherwise."

"What would you like to do?"

"First, we get out of town until after the election. Second, when you win and if you still want us to work for you, we work with a contract. We can't go out on a limb anymore, not without knowing you have our back. Last, we want you to assign Agent Tom Sawyer to our team."

"The FBI agent?"

"Yes, ma'am. He does two things for us. He gets Director Douglas off our backs and gives us a shade of respectability among your detractors."

"Are you sure this is all necessary? I can handle Douglas."

"Ma'am, they went after Captain Briscoe, and you're still in office."

"I want you with me in New York when we meet Minister Gallardo. What if I appoint you as an aide?"

"Ma'am, that is extremely flattering, but we already have a strained relationship with Mr. Collins, and I don't wish to exacerbate those difficulties further. But I'll be happy to attend the meeting with you. My company has worked with the two previous administrations, so I doubt anyone can find fault with working with yours."

"The author Robert Heinlein said, *Never underestimate the power of human stupidity.*"

"He also said, *The price of freedom is the willingness to do sudden battle anywhere, anytime.*"

"Are you saying that's what you do for me?"

"I'm saying, at your direction, that's what we do for our country. And we have no wish to be persecuted or prosecuted for it."

A few weeks later, while Elizabeth was with the president, Ed, and I were hiding out at the Wrightsville Beach Marina. Truth be told, were getting a little bored. Nonetheless, we persevered. Currently, we were sitting on the boat drinking our lunch.

"What do you hear from Liz?" Ed asked.

"Gallardo gives his speech tomorrow. The president has her and Silvers jumping through hoops getting ready. I think the press release goes out today."

"Guess we'll see it on the news."

"I suspect." I said.

"Did you notice the black SUV on the street?" Ed asked.

"You would think they would get another color other than black."

"Do you want to roust them?"

"No, I already dealt with them. They're going to be our new partners."

Ed sits up, "Come again?"

"We told the president any future jobs will be on the books and Tommy Sawyer will be part of the team."

"We swing pretty wide for a stuffed shirt like Sawyer."

"It was his idea, though he doesn't know it. After the beltway boobs went after Briscoe, and the constant attention we get from our friends in the SUV, I decided to use Tom to help cover our collective asses."

"In case Harriet doesn't win her reelection."

"Exactly. Hey, what is it with you two?"

"What do you mean?"

"Seems like you two may have some history."

"She's married."

"She wasn't always married."

Ed took a long drink from his beer can. "Flight school. That was then. This is now, and she's President of the United States."

"Didn't know you flew choppers."

"Yep, I was an instructor. And that's all I'm going to say."

"Another beer?"

President Jackson, Elizabeth, Collins, and Silvers are sitting in a huddle in the forward cabin of one of the three VH-3D Sea Kings flying in formation over New Jersey.

"After he gives his speech, it will take him about fifteen minutes to get to the hotel. So that should put him in your suite about 1:45," Collins said.

Silvers followed, "Lunch will be served at 2:00 sharp. We'll move as many of his entourage as we can to the other suite."

"How hard should I hit him on the kidnapping?" the president asked.

"I'd say it depends on how much of the macho BS he spreads." Silvers said.

"Ma'am, I spanked him pretty hard, but macho BS or not, I'd let him know you were not pleased with his disregard for U.S. lives and leave it at that," Liz said.

"As my aunt Jeanie used to say, don't throw out the baby with the bathwater."

"Yes, ma'am."

President Jackson and Bruno Gallardo sit at a table in the Presidential Suit of The Peninsula New York. The table is adorned with a white tablecloth, flowers, and a lunch setting. Dr. Pérez, who arrived with Gallardo, Elizabeth, and Collins, are sitting in the far background. Security people are in close attendance.

The President picks up her napkin and placed it on her lap. "Minister Gallardo, before we get started. I want to be sure you are cognizant of my displeasure in regard to the kidnapping of my State Department official."

"Madam President, as soon as we were aware of the incident, we sent troops to rescue your official."

"And those efforts are appreciated no matter how ineffectual, however any similar incident will be deemed as crossing the line."

Bruno Gallardo smirked. "Ah, the infamous American red line."

The president threw her napkin on the table, partially came out of her chair, and leaned forward. "You chauvinistic bastard, do not compare me to my predecessors, you screw with me, and I'll cut your fucking balls off. That clear enough for you."

Gallardo gulped. "*Si*, quite clear."

Jackson sat down and recovered her napkin. "I noticed Miguel de Leon is not with your party."

Gallardo took a breath and arranged the napkin on his lap. "There were those that thought his presence in Havana would be more useful."

"And less suspicious."

"*Si,* less suspicious."

"And less hazardous to his health."

"*Si.*"

"My people said your speech at the UN was well received. We sent out the press release. I won't make any formal announcement until you are ready. What else can we do for the cause?"

"Well, we will, of course, exchange emissaries. Begin the process of travel agreements, setting up airline schedules. Begin trade negotiations, agricultural agreements. These things are most important."

"I get it. You need dollars. Have Dr. Pérez and Dick Silvers get together, and they can start lining up people at Commerce. First, you fix the human rights fiasco your predecessors left for you."

"We also have a delicate matter."

President Jackson sighed. "What's that?"

"There is a group of extremists that do not follow our new philosophy of democratic rule."

"Aren't there always? I don't see how we can help. You are going to make this work or not. Why not just have them arrested? You guys are good at that."

"We don't know where they are. They use the out islands as refuge and move constantly."

"Bruno, what are we talking about? Sounds like a handful of people. Just ignore them, you poke them with a stick, you're just bringing attention to their cause. That's one of the first tenants of democracy is free speech. If they don't like what you're doing, let them run for office, or talk with them, compromise, deal with it."

"But we can't find them. Perhaps you could send your operatives down to the islands to see what they can find."

"Jesus, Bruno, you want me to send a Seal Team down there to find your disgruntled citizens?"

"I was thinking something less conspicuous, perhaps Dr. Pérez's friends with the beautiful sailboat."

"First, the people of which you speak are private citizens and I cannot order them to do anything. Second, as my aunt Jeanie used to say, I think you're making a mountain out of a molehill."

Jackson, Liz, Collins, and Silvers are sitting in Marine One as it flies back to Washington.

"Last item. What in the hell was that nonsense about the extremists?"

"He wants the *Pinafore* down in the islands for some reason." Collins said.

"I know that, but why? Liz, any ideas?"

"I'm sorry, ma'am, I have no clue."

"Liz, do me a favor, reach out to Pérez and see if he knows anything, or I should say, see if he'll tell you anything. Maybe you can get something from your special Ops friends."

"Yes, ma'am."

"Rick, talk to your guys and see if they have picked up anything. I'll call Barrett. In the meantime, Liz, go back to your boat and vacation, but stay handy."

CHAPTER SEVENTEEN

Pinafore - Wrightsville Beach Marina, N.C.

Liz, Ed and I were sitting around the settee drinking gin and tonics. There is a basket of chips and a bowl of dip on the teak table. Liz had been regaling us with her adventures in New York. ". . . so, that's about it, not much else to tell."

"Given any more thought to Bruno's request for our boat?" I asked.

"A lot, but I still don't get it." Liz said. "It's not like he can't find about a million sailboats in the Caribbean."

"Schultz- why don't we call him?" I laughed. "I'll bet his net covers the entire Caribbean."

"And that's his unofficial net. The president suggested that too."

Snapping my fingers, "Cover!"

"Cover what?" Liz asked.

"That's why they need *Pinafore.* They need the cover it brings with it." I said.

"Maybe your right. They know nobody will touch *Pinafore* because it's effectively a U.S. warship." Liz said.

"Especially after the tongue lashing you gave Bruno." Ed said.

"You should have heard the president."

"The next question is why do they need a protected boat?" I wondered.

"Are you gentlemen ready to escort a lady to dinner?"

"Can't discuss world affairs on an empty stomach." I said.

We left the boat with a good buzz and walked down the dock to the Bluewater Waterfront Grill. We were quickly seated on the patio. "Oh look, they have shrimp and grits, how wonderful!" Liz said sarcastically.

"I think I'll have that." I said.

"I'm shocked."

Ed opened a package of crackers he found on the table. "So, why do our new friends need a protected boat?"

"Let's try some deductive reasoning," Liz said.

"Lead on Sherlock." I said.

"What are the properties of a sailboat?" Liz said.

"I don't know, I'm an airplane guy." Ed replied.

"Well," I said, "aside from the obvious, a shallow draft. They are inconspicuous and can handle heavy weather. They are no speed demons, but a good one is reasonably fast."

"If they need the other features, they are probably willing to give up speed," Liz said.

"Besides, there are so many islands down there, they can disappear in an hour or so, regardless of speed." I said.

A waitress brought us some menus and water. "What can I get you all? Grouper is the special."

"Liz, what are you having? I asked.

"I'll try the grouper with your house white. Ed how about you?"

"I'll have the crab cakes with a beer."

"And I'll have the shrimp and grits with iced tea."

"OK, daarlin', I'll put the order right in. You want lemon with your tea?"

"Please." The waitress winked, smiled, and sashayed away.

"You have a fan" Liz drolled.

"My magnetic personality. It's the bane of my life. You know, one other feature, relative to its size, you can load a ton of stuff on a sailboat."

"So, we have cargo space, shallow draft, and stealth." Ed said.

"Stealth?" Liz said.

"Sure, like you said, there are about a million sailboats in the Caribbean. Who's going to notice another one?

But why?" I asked.

Ed shifts his weight and drinks from his glass. Then smiles, "Sounds like smuggling to me."

"You would know." I said.

"I would."

"Maybe. I suspect these guys are not above making an extra buck, but why bring in partners they don't need?" I said.

"If they were in the trade, they couldn't make any money using your sailboat. They would need a trawler, or an offshore fisherman. Even if it was drugs." Ed said.

"You are both right. It's something else. Ah, dinner has arrived." Liz said.

The waitress set the meals in front of us.

The shrimp and grits were terrific, and I got another wink.

We were sitting in the cockpit eating the great breakfast cooked by both Ed and Liz. "The two of you do a great breakfast. You two should open a restaurant. Call it the Coffee 'n Cream Diner." I laughed at my joke. Ed and Liz glared at me.

"You're doing the dishes, funny man. Did anyone give any more thought to our conundrum?" Liz asked.

"Our what?" I asked.

"Conundrum. A confusing and difficult problem or question."

"Liz, you have to lay off the Scrabble."

"The only answer is stealth and impunity." Ed said.

"There is one other thing. *Pinafore* has a nasty set of teeth." Liz said.

"Well done, Mr. & Mrs. Sherlock. Now tell me why." I asked.

"You can bet it has nothing to do with the dissidents he was whining about," Liz said.

"Regardless, we are not taking this boat anywhere on behalf of the State Department until the president wins reelection and gives us written instructions." I said.

"Nothing says we can't take some vacation in the islands." Liz said.

"Yeah, we do that, and like always; we get sucked into some intrigue that puts us on a limb looking for a parachute." I said.

"You're right." Liz agreed.

"Tell you what. Let's jump back on the ICW and cruise down to the Keys. The election will be over by then. If we are needed, we're in place. If not, we had a nice boat ride. Ed you in?"

"I was told to stick with you guys."

"So, do we have a plan?"

"We have a plan." Liz said.

We spent the next twenty days, sailing south, mostly motoring and mostly in the Intracoastal Waterway. We fouled the prop once. Thankfully, it was with nylon rope, not steel cable, so Ed and I could take turns going over the side to cut the prop free. As it turned out, it *was* a 'pleasant boat ride.' We stopped where we wanted, ate good food and even stayed in a hotel once to take advantage of their pool. We pulled into Marathon Marina twenty-two days later. This being the busy season, Liz called ahead to make reservations. We got a good slip at the end of the dock, a little far from the showers and restaurant, but away from the weekend recreation crowd. Because of the configuration of the marina, we also had a good view of the entrance and the adjoining street.

We were tired and red from our three weeks of sun and wind. By the time we had washed the boat down, it was late afternoon, so we collapsed in the cockpit. I was drinking Blanton's over ice and Ed and Liz were drinking gin and tonics with lime. We celebrated the stable decks by drinking from crystal tumblers.

Liz pushed her hair back and adjusted her sunglasses. "I think twenty days at sea is quite enough for a while."

I laughed, "We were hardly at sea. We were never out of sight of land."

"I'm with Liz. I'm ready for a proper shower and a restaurant."

"If I get any more sun, my face is going to fall off." Liz followed.

"That *would* be a tragedy." I said.

"Thank you, dear. Now, if you will excuse me, I'm going to get off this damn boat and take a shower."

"I'm right behind you," Ed said.

We all showered, then went to the Lazy Days Restaurant, which was under a large, covered patio. The three of us sat around a square table and studied the menus.

"I've had enough seafood to last me. Looks like they have some nice steaks." Liz said.

"Again, I second the lady."

"Steaks all around it is." I said.

The steaks were just OK, but a change of pace from seafood. We stayed for some after-dinner drinks.

Ed was eating ice cream. "Did you know this place has an airport?"

"You're kidding." Liz said.

"No. It has a couple FBO's, customs, and a 5,000-foot runway."

I finished my drink. "So, that means they can get jets in here." I said.

"Small ones, but yeah you could get a jet in here."

"How about a G550?" I asked.

"No, but a G400 could. A Citation could. The Marines have a few of those. The Navy has some Lear's that could get in here." Ed said.

"Humm, good to know." I said.

"Why?" Ed asked.

"Nothing specific. But you both know how long it took to get down here. If we need to get back to D.C. or someone needs to get here in a hurry, now we have a way to do it."

Ed finished the last of his ice cream. "Liz, have you heard from Harriet since the election?"

"I got a text from her. She invited us to the inauguration."

"Can we phone or text it in?" I asked.

"No, we can't phone it in, or text it in either. We're going."

CHAPTER EIGHTEEN

Pinafore – Marathon Marina, Florida

We all flew home and attended the Inaugural Ball. I was resplendent in my tux. I even wore socks— she checked. It wasn't my first inauguration ball but the first with Liz, and I admit to having a good time. Liz was the talk of the town in her new gown. I have pictures, a newspaper article and the bill to prove it.

Liz and I came back to the boat, ready to vacation some more if one could call sitting at a dock vacationing. In truth, I was waiting for the shoe to drop, or whatever object drops, at the first sign of bad news. The phone rang.

Moments later, Liz stepped out of the companionway and sat on the cockpit bench. "That was the president. She said Rick Silvers has disappeared."

The shoe just dropped. "Disappeared from where?"

"Rick, Bruno, and Pérez took a plane from Havana to Turks and Caicos, supposedly to meet with one of Bruno's dissidents. The plane never arrived. She's hot as a pistol and told Miguel de Leon as much."

"Well, what are they doing about it?"

"She's getting the runaround. She thinks they're dragging their feet because there are still holdovers from the Castro regime that don't want this new government to happen."

"OK, give me the bad news."

"You already know what it is."

"What did you tell her?"

"I said it was up to you, I would ask, and if you said no, that would be the end of it."

I stood and walked around. The only thing I could think of was losing my temper, so I slammed my fist on the table. Liz jumped from the noise. It hurt, which made me angrier.

"Damn those people!" I thought for a moment. "OK, here's the deal. She gives us written orders that will include indemnification for any damage to the boat and a life insurance policy on us for the benefit of the kids. The documents will be held by our attorney. She pays the expenses. I want Ed and Tom Sawyer on the boat with us and General Barrett on the other end of our phone."

"I already mostly told her that."

"Well, tell her whatever you left out. If she agrees, we'll leave as soon as Ed and Tom get here. And tell her to send two women down here. No Russian tank commanders. I want them to be lookers."

"You've grown tired of me already."

"We're going to have to work close to those islands. This needs to look like a party boat, not a barge full of thugs."

"It's my ass, right? It is too big."

"Your ass is world-class perfect. Get any last known details about Rick and Pérez's location. I don't give a shit about Bruno. I wouldn't be surprised if he's behind the whole thing."

"OK."

"One other thing. Ask her to put Bob Osborne and Jerry McGuire on standby. Let them stay in D.C. but be ready to go if we need them. While you're calling the president, I'll call Schultz and see what he knows."

Liz walked forward to make the call. I sat at the cockpit table and dialed my phone. "Hello— Is this the infamous Captain Schultz?"

The president must have been worried because Ed and Tom were here in five days. Ed brought copies of the agreements I 'requested', which is a nicer word than demanded. They were executed and notarized. The originals were with our attorney. I checked. Tom was less than enthusiastic but had few arguments, particularly when I reminded him these arrangements, including his presence, were his idea. He didn't exactly see it that way, but I think he was secretly happy to get out of D.C. We sat in *Pinafore*'s cockpit drinking beer and eating from a plate of sandwiches whipped up by the Coffee 'n Cream duo.

Tom took a swig of beer. "When you and I had our chat, I wasn't expecting to be part of your merry little band."

"Sorry Tom, it couldn't be helped. I took your advice to heart, and I need your political cover and the savvy you bring to the party."

"What's the plan?" Ed asked.

"Rick, Pérez, and dear Bruno took a plane to the Turks and Caicos. I suppose we will start there. Unless you all have a better idea."

"Long trip for a guess and a maybe." Ed said.

"Six hundred miles. When do the girls get here?" I asked.

"This afternoon." Ed said.

"Who are they?"

"Rookies from Camp Perry. Jerry McGuire hand-picked them."

"Great! They'll be 200 pounds and bald." I said.

Elizabeth reached for a sandwich. "Good! And Tom, you better remember Kay and I are good friends. What's Camp Perry?"

The men laugh. "Hey, I got drafted." Tom exclaimed.

"Camp Perry is a CIA training facility in Virginia. I think they call it the farm. We passed near it when we went to Williamsburg." I said.

"I remember seeing the sign."

It was coming on to evening. The crew and I were sitting in the cockpit swapping lies when two women walked up to the gangway. One was about 25, 5-10, dark hair, attractive. The other was a little younger, maybe 22 – 23, 5-7, blond hair and bordered on beautiful. She said, "Good evening. I'm Kelly. This is Denise. Is one of you Captain Spain?"

"I'm captain Spain. Are you the agents Jerry McGuire sent us?"

"That's not his real name, but he said to use it with you all."

Liz stood. "Girls come aboard. Leave your gear on the dock for now."

The girls dropped two bags but kept one small bag each with them, then came aboard.

Liz said, "Please sit down. Can we get you something to drink?"

Kelly looked at Denise, then said no thank you.

"Did Jerry explain what's going on?" I asked.

"He said to bring some bathing suits, sit on the boat, look good, and keep our mouths shut." Denise said.

"That's good enough for now. OK, you girls find a place to bunk. I suggest the aft cabins, but you work it out with the guys. They were here first. I'll bring your bags down. Either of you know anything about boats?" I asked.

"My dad owns a marina in Michigan. I've been around boats all my life," Denise said.

"OK, you'll be standing a watch. Explain the finer points of a marine head and hot water to Kelly. Ed, you show Tom the same thing. Liz, work up a galley schedule."

Liz gave me the arched eyebrow thing she does. "Aye, aye captain."

"We'll be leaving first thing in the morning. There is a restaurant at the end of the dock, so if you're hungry, grab something to eat." I reached into a winch pocket, rummaged around, and pulled out a tube and a small bottle. I handed one to Kelly and the other to Tom. "Here, from now on, don't come on deck without rubbing this stuff all over. This is the tropics. I don't need any third-degree burns. And always wear a hat."

"What about me?" Ed asked.

"Too late, you're already well done."

The girls snickered some, then went below, the small bags never out of their hands.

I leaned over to Ed. "What do you think is in those bags?'

"Too big for a pistol. My bet is an automatic weapon of some kind."

"That was my bet too."

Elizabeth and I were playing grab ass in the master stateroom, or at least I was. In a stage whisper, "Will you stop. Someone will hear us."

"I'm sorry you have, as usual, aroused my carnal instincts. It must be this bunk."

"This bunk and any other. While we're on the subject, those girls aren't much older than Emily!

"Liz, they're CIA agents. Jerry wouldn't have sent them down here if they weren't any good."

"He sent them down here because they have big tits and tight asses."

"Keep your voice down."

"I don't want to keep my voice down."

We were in the Straits of Florida, sailing southeast and would be for the next three days if wind and weather prevailed. The more I thought about it, the more I thought this was a wild goose chase. Any number of the presidents' aides or minions could be in the Turks in two hours, look around, and be home the same day. But I wasn't the president. She must have had some reason. Who was I to complain? I was getting paid to sail my boat in the Caribbean. Of course, that didn't work out too well the last time.

Liz and I were sitting on the foredeck. "So, are you getting along with the crew?"

"If you men the girls, they're fine. In all honesty, I think they are a little bewildered. Jerry literally pulled them out of a classroom and shoved them on a plane. They think they were chosen because of their GPA and firearm proficiency." Liz said.

"Firearm proficiency?"

"They both have H&Ks in their bags." Liz said.

"I suspected as much. God, forbid they have to use them."

Denise chose that moment to call out, "Captain Spade! I think we're being followed."

"Why?" I asked.

"There is a blip on the radar about six and half miles, at two, three, zero. It was just hanging back. Now it's coming up fast."

I ran aft and grabbed the binoculars. I steadied and focused. "Gunboat! I turned dropped, the binoculars. "Denise, turn on the autopilot. Everybody get below and into uniform. Tom, you keep a shirt on. You look like you spent a year in the arctic." Everyone scrambled below except me. I looked through the binoculars again. Then leaned down the companionway. "Girls, give your guns to Liz, you too, Tom. I want all the firearms in the repel borders locker."

"I don't feel comfortable giving up my weapon." Tom said.

"You'll be less comfortable if those guys board us and find that gun."

One by one, the crew came topside in bathing suits. "Denise, take the helm." I dived below and ran into the forward cabin where Liz was storing the weapons. "Need any help?"

"No, I got it."

"OK, put on your skimpiest suit and go on deck and luxuriate."

"Luxuriate?" Liz asked.

"Yeah, it means—"

"—I know what it means. Someone else has been playing too much scrabble."

I tore off my shirt and jammed my legs into my bathing suit then ran back topside. "Ed, take the helm. Girls, spread yourselves around the boat and look— look girlish."

Liz scowled at me. "Forget what I said about scrabble."

"What?"

"Ladies, what my husband is trying to say, in his inimitable and tactful way, is that we are to artfully drape ourselves over the boat while displaying as much skin as possible. This will hopefully distract the men on that gunboat while we all pray the crew is not female. Nudity is not required but recommended."

The girls chuckle. Liz removed her top, picked up her towel, walked to the bow and laid down on the deck. Denise removed her top and followed Liz. Kelly removed her top and laid down on the cabin roof.

"Is that what you said?" Ed asked.

"We'll probably be arrested for running a sea-going brothel." I said.

"What's inimitable mean?" Ed asked.

"I don't know. It can't be good." I replied.

"You guys are going to get me divorced." Tom said.

"We're trying to keep you from getting shot. So, lighten up, and pretend you're having a good time." I said.

About twenty minutes later, a Cuban gunboat was alongside. A man walked out of the bridge and looked down at *Pinafore*. "Good morning, I am Captain Gonzalez. What is your business here in our beautiful waters?"

"Good morning, Captain. We are U.S. citizens on vacation three days out of Miami on our way to St. Thomas."

He laughed, "I think your friend is three days out of North Pole. I think you are up to no good. Perhaps you are smugglers."

"You are very wise, Captain, but you don't think we are smugglers. And we are in international waters."

"I will say if you are in international waters! You think beautiful woman fool me that you on pleasure cruise?"

"I think the Captain will remember that the U.S. and Cuba are now friends and there are many people looking for our lost *Embajadores*."

"*Si*, perhaps you also are looking for the *Embajadores*."

"Perhaps."

"I do not think so. Only a fool would take women on such a search to Mayaguez, where there are many pirates."

"Captain, we are on vacation."

"So, you have said. If you meet with pirates, I suggest you use guns, not tits. Now go." He turns from the rail, stomps into his bridge. The gunboat roars off leaving a wake of frothy water.

"What was that all about?" Tom asked.

"Girls, don't move until the gunboat is out of sight." I turned back to Tom. "He just gave us Rick Silvers' location."

Liz, now wearing her top, walked into the cockpit. "So, Rick is in Mayaguez. What was that about pirates?"

"I think he means this was a kidnapping for profit, not politics." I said.

"I remember Mayaguez. It's uninhabited, but it used to have a dirt strip. They call it Mona Island." Ed said.

"Why? I asked.

"Mayaguez is the county or territory. Plus, there is Mayaguez on the mainland. Guess they don't want to confuse people." Ed said,

"Too late." I said.

"That's why the president couldn't get the Cubans to move." Liz said.

"I'll bet Captain Gonzales was sent out here by Miguel de Leon himself." Ed said.

"OK, girls, you've given the boy's enough eye candy for now. Let's make some lunch."

CHAPTER NINETEEN

Pinafore – Mayaguez (Mona) Island

Pinafore slowly motored through a small cut in the shoreline. Beyond the long white beach covering the shore, were trees and scrub. Dressed in their bikinis, the girls stood on the cabin one to each side of the mast. At their feet, just visible in the folds of the collapsed sail, are two H&Ks. Ed is behind the wheel. At his feet is a shotgun. Tom and I stand in the cockpit, a Colt .45 and Glock at our feet. I called to below to Liz. "Honey, do you remember how to use that M14?"

"Close my eyes and pull the trigger?"

Tom groans, "God help us."

Laughing, I scanned the beach with binoculars. "Ed let's hold up here. Kelly coil one of those sheets. Denise, go forward and make like we're getting ready to anchor."

Kelly picked up a sheet and coiled it as she watched the beach. Denise walked forward, keeping an eye on the shoreline and the jungle beyond. She kneeled and bent over the anchor. The boat swings gently in the light wind. The low rumble of the engine bounced off the trees and water in a hushed echo.

I stuck my head down the companionway. "Anything on the radar?"

"No. The trees are blocking a lot— "

Kelly called out, "Captain Spade. A boat is coming from the beach. Two people in it."

Tom and Ed are looking at the boat. I stood, looked through the binoculars. Two men in a boat. No signs of a weapon. I put the glasses down. "Denise, stroll back to where your H&K is. Kelly, stay put but watch everything but that boat."

"You mean watch for a sleight of hand?" Kelly said.

"Right. Denise don't take your eyes off the boat. Tom, watch seaward. Guys, look uninterested. Smoke if you got 'em."

Tom grumbled, "Just my luck. I gave up smoking."

"Good, you'll live longer."

"Yea, that was my plan until I hooked up with you screwballs."

The boat came alongside but stood off about 20 feet. One of the passengers called out, "Ahoy, may we come aboard?"

"State your business."

"I wish to speak with Sam Spade."

"Speak."

"My name is Heraldo Hernandez. I have some information that will interest you. As you can see, I am unarmed."

"You come aboard. Your friend stays in the boat and moves away."

"*Si, si*. Of course. *Te quedas en el barco y tealejasunos metros*." Hernandez climbs aboard *Pinafore* and looks around. "This is a very fine boat. With exquisite women."

"What can we do for you?"

"A simple business transaction. You want Richard Silvers. For a small favor, I will tell you where he is."

"I don't know any Richard Silvers. If I did know him, the first place I would look is in that jungle over there."

"Ahh, my friend, you would find that very difficult. But to show you I am a man of my word, you may look anywhere you like. He is not on this island."

"Like I said, I don't know him."

"Mr. Spade, I know this is not your real name, but Hernandez is not my name either. I think these beautiful women are armed to the teeth, though the gentleman in me would not venture to guess where they keep their weapons. There is a third woman, I believe your wife. She is probably at this moment aiming a gun at my head. Your large friend there is Edward Colombo. I do not know this other gentleman."

"You are well informed."

"Yes, we have a mutual friend. You may remember Victor Escudero."

"*Senior* Hernandez, you went to a lot of trouble to get us here. What do you want?"

"I want you to take me to Trinidad."

"Trinidad! That's five days from here."

"Six days."

"Why? You could hire any number of boats to take you. You could fly there in an hour."

"Because our destination is, as you say, off the beaten path. And there are those that do not wish me to make this trip. So, I require a more covert method of travel."

"Where are Silvers and Pérez?"

"They are both in Trinidad. They are safe for now."

"What does that mean?"

"It means the longer we stay here, the greater risk to them."

"*Senior* Hernandez, if I take you to Trinidad and Silvers is not alive, I will kill you. Are we clear?"

"When do we leave?"

"First thing in the morning. You may bring one man with you. I don't have room for the army you have hidden in those trees."

"I have no need for another. You will kill me or not. *Buenas noches amigo mío, nos vemos por la mañana.*" Heraldo goes over the side into his boat.

Tom walked to Ed. "He wouldn't really kill that guy?"

"No. Because I'd beat him to it. You're not in Kansas anymore."

Hernandez, or whatever his name was, appeared first thing. He said goodbye to his companion and climbed aboard. As *Pinafore* slowly motored into the Caribbean Sea, we drank coffee in the cockpit.

"I assume you cooked this up. Very smart. *Pinafore* is the perfect ploy for this trip. We sail right down the Leeward and Windward islands like a thousand other boats." I said.

"Perhaps we should stop occasionally to enhance the appearance." Heraldo said.

"You mean somebody is following us?" Ed said.

"Possibly, I'm not sure."

I looked at Liz. "OK, I'm sure the girls will love a shopping trip here and there. Ladies, please go easy on the water. We have to buy it and it's almost expensive as gasoline."

Kelly and Denise look at each other and smile.

"One other thing, I have many interests, kidnapping is not one of them. Admittedly, I'm taking advantage, but I knew of it only after the fact."

"Who was it?" I asked.

"The Morales drug cartel. They have been most interested in finding Dr. Pérez and want the money President Jackson took from them."

"So, you're a member of the cartel?" Ed asked.

"Certainly not! I am brokering a deal for a ride on your boat. And I'm not Cuban, I don't care who runs the government. I make my money from controlling those in power. And as a power broker who sees the writing on the wall, I feel it is time to retire.

We skirted the south coast of Puerto Rico and sailed into Charlotte Amalie two days later. Elizabeth and the girls walked around Charlotte Amalie shopping while the men followed at a distance. "Not a bad way to spend a day." I said, "I'm glad we stopped."

"The girls are sure enjoying themselves." Ed observed.

"Kay has been trying for years to get me to come here. She is not going to like I was here without her."

"For Christ's sake, Tom, buy her a stuffed parrot or don't tell her. This is supposed to be classified, anyway."

How long are we staying? Ed asked.

I nodded at Heraldo. "Guess that's up to our tour guide here."

"I think we leave tomorrow, then stop at Basseterre. I have friends there who may have useful information."

The next morning, we made sail for Basseterre, which is the capital of Saint Kitts. Denise interrupted my reverie in the cockpit. "Captain Spade. I think we have someone following us."

"What do you have?"

"For the past several days, a blip has been three miles back. Always three miles and always windward."

"Ed, will you check the big screen below and see what you can make out."

Ed went below and I moved to the helm and picked up the binoculars. "Looks like a large sport fisherman."

The crew, including Heraldo, walked St. Kitts, more like friends than associates. Once I caught a glimpse of a man on the opposite side of the street. He was big and strange looking. He wore a white fedora. After lighting a cigarette, he disappeared. I forgot about him.

The next day, we were off to Rodney Bay, St. Lucia. The weather was pleasant, winds were at 20 knots, giving us a broad reach all the way. It was early evening when we arrived. Everyone helped tie up.

After the boat was washed down, I called to everyone. "Gather around, please. You guys and girls have become a real crew. To thank you, Mr. Hernandez is springing for dinner."

"I am surprised to hear this, but I would be delighted."

There is a cheer and general laughing.

"OK, there is a good restaurant just down the street. So, spiffy up— Girls, you will note we are tied up with shore water, so now is the time to go crazy with the water. Heraldo is paying for that too."

Cheers from the women and more laughing. I laughed and slapped Tom on the back and leaned close, "See if you can get his credit card receipt."

We chose the Big Chef Steakhouse because it was close, and the idea of a steak appealed. The seven-member crew sat around a table sipping wine. The women were dressed in colorful sundresses. Their hair was done up, and they were wearing make-up. The men shaved and dressed in polo shirts, shorts, or khakis. "OK, Heraldo spill."

"I assume that is American slang for revealing the reason for our surreptitious trip."

This elicited some laughter.

"Very well— In March 1944, the Japanese submarine I-52 departed Singapore for Lorient loaded with 2.2 tons of gold and 3 tons of opium."

He stopped when the waitress brought our menus to the table.

"In May 1944, the German sub, U-530, left Lorient for Trinidad but was first ordered to rendezvous with I-52 to provide them with a radar and a pilot."

"So, they could get into Germany?" I asked.

"More precisely, so they could get to Norway. By that time, the Allies had landed in Normandy, threatening I-52's original destination of Lorient on the coast of France.

"The two submarines rendezvoused on the night of June 22d, about 900 miles west of Cape Verde. On the evening of June 23d, allied aircraft attacked, sinking I-52. U-530 escaped undetected."

The waitress returned and took our orders and left.

"Please continue." I said.

"When the war with Germany ended in May 1945, U-530 did not surrender as ordered. It finally appeared on July 10th in Mar del Plata."

"That's over two months later. Where did he go?' Kelly asked.

"You are correct; her captain never explained what happened during those two months. In addition, the submarine arrived with no deck gun, no torpedoes. The crew carried no identification and the ship's log had disappeared."

"You're saying you know where U-530 was during those two months?" Ed asked.

"It was in Trinidad. I believe the German sub received word that the May '44 rendezvous with the Jap I-52 had been compromised by the Allies, which was true. So, they transferred the gold and opium to U-530 before the attack. After they escaped, they sailed to Trinidad as ordered. When they finally returned to Lorient, they did not have the cargo."

"Why risk transferring the gold? Especially with the Allies breathing down their neck. It must have taken forever." Liz said.

"A gamble I suppose. As it happened, they had an uninterrupted 24 hours. Most of these U-boat captains were fierce loyalists. And very smart. When the allies invaded Normandy, they knew the war was all but over. I think the gold was taken to help preserve the Third Reich in Argentina. Also, there was a German liaison officer, maybe an SS officer on board. Perhaps he was ordered to take the gold off I-52."

"So, you think they went back for it in 1945? Liz asked.

"I know he did." Heraldo said.

"Why didn't he have it when he surrendered to the Argentines?" Liz asked.

"Because he retrieved it, then moved it to another place in 1945."

"Why?" Denise asked.

"Things were pretty fluid then. Backwater areas before the War were forever changed. Washington, D.C., is the perfect example. It was a sleepy southern town before the war, after the war it was a metropolis. As Heraldo said, those sub guys were very smart. He was afraid it would be found." Tom said.

"I suspect you are correct. In any event, an excellent thesis. But I know where it is now."

"That would make you unique among hundreds. Versions of this story have been floating around since the end of the war." I said.

The waitress brought another bottle of wine.

"I have an eyewitness." Heraldo said.

"How in the world did you find an eyewitness?" Liz asked.

"Victor. He was my partner. The witnesses' son was imprisoned. The father was 10 years old when he saw the Germans hide the gold. He told this to Victor in return for having his son released."

"Who's Victor?" Kelly asked.

"Victor Escudero, the former president of Venezuela. He disappeared some time back." I said.

Kelly starts to say something else, but Ed catches her eye and shakes his head.

I looked at Heraldo. "Is Bruno involved in this?"

"Bruno is who he says he is. He wants a new Cuba. I control the votes he needs in the Council of Ministers. So, he tried to help me. He is with Mr. Silvers."

I looked around the room. Then leaned toward Heraldo, "Our interest is Rick Silvers. How do we get him?"

"Once we get to our destination, he will be brought to you. They are delighted you have come back into their sphere, so to speak."

"What makes you think they will let you keep the Nazi gold?" Ed asked.

"They know nothing about it."

"So, you get a boat ride. We get Silvers. What do the Morales guys get out of the deal?

"You."

The waitress brought the food.

A strange-looking man was sitting at the bar watching *Pinafore*'s crew. In reaching for his drink, he exposed a swastika tattoo on his wrist.

Chapter TWENTY

It was early morning. We had, as Liz liked to say, been at sea for four days, most of the time out of sight of land. I had spent some time in these waters when I was in the Marine Corps and forgot how big the Caribbean can be. Without being specific, Heraldo told me to 'head for Trinidad'.

Liz and I were in our stateroom. She was sitting at her desk/vanity/bureau, applying some makeup. "Do you think Victor's old pals are waiting for us?"

"You heard Heraldo, apparently, we are sailing into a trap, so we'll probably need help. Will you call General Barrett and see if he can get a dozen Special Ops into Curaçao again?"

"When do you want them?"

"I don't think we are going to Trinidad. I've been looking at the charts and, given the water depths and the isolation factor, I suspect our destination is Tobago. We should be there the day after tomorrow. So, from noon on—day after tomorrow."

A day closer to our destination, wherever that was, the guys were sitting in the cockpit drinking beer and sodas. Liz and the girls are on the forward deck sunbathing. Tom was behind the wheel.

"Heraldo, time to tell us where we are going. I am assuming Tobago." I said.

"Excellent! You are almost correct. We are going to the eastern side of Little Tobago. There is 280 feet of water almost to the shore."

"Good for a submarine."

"Precisely."

"The sport fisherman is still with us," Tom said.

"OK, nothing we can do about it." I said.

We arrived at Little Tobago early the next day. We were in a little bay on the east side of the island. There were no signs of anyone or anything. In 1944 it must have been the end of the earth. Because of the depth, we carefully set the anchor, but our hold was still precarious, and we would have to move if there were any significant swells. I was sitting at the nav desk when Liz walked up next to me and gave me a kiss on the cheek. "Good morning," she said.

"Morning sweetie. Do me a favor. I would like you and the girls to put on your suits and go over to the beach. Take a radio and the H&Ks and watch our backs. Keep your head on a swivel. Trouble could come from the land. You see something you don't like. Get me on the radio, then get back to the boat. Otherwise, just enjoy a day at the beach."

She kissed me again. "Got it."

The three women sat on beach chairs. They were wearing skimpy suits, large hats, and sunglasses. Liz faced the jungle, the other two faced the water.

"How long have you and your husband been with the company?" Kelly asked.

"Company?— Oh, you mean the CIA. My husband is a real estate developer and I like to think of myself as a soccer mom slash businesswoman. The kids are almost grown, so now I'm just a businesswoman. I own a small company that does business for the government."

"OK."

"No, that's the truth. My name is really Elizabeth. Obviously, my husband is not Sam Spade. I think he did this kind of work before we were married. He's a dammed sphinx, so I don't know what he did."

"He sure is good at it," Kelly said.

"Yes, but I don't think he likes it. When we are on one of these jobs he always seems, I don't know, depressed. He loves being on the boat, so that helps."

"You say jobs, you've done others? Denise asked.

"Some. Mr. Spade is good at sorting things out, so they asked us to be private contractors. Honestly, it gives us a lot of time together. I don't think our marriage has been happier. Mostly, we've learned to listen to each other and respect each other's opinions."

"Is that really the president you talk to?" Denise asked.

"Yes, my company does work for her and the State Department. I think we have become friends. She's a gracious lady."

"I know we're not supposed to ask questions. It's just that we were thrown into this and don't understand how all the parts fit." Kelly said.

"It's like we were sent down here to be window dressing." Denise added.

"You were, we are. It's important in this work to project an image that keeps the other guy off balance. The slightest hesitation on his part could save a life. Like now, we are three tourists enjoying the beach. But actually, we're an early warning system. We make sure the guys are safe while they do their job."

"When you put it that way, it sounds important." Denise said.

"It is important." Liz said.

"Do you enjoy doing this kind of thing? Kelly asked.

"I'm not too fond of taking my clothes off in front of a bunch of men. Other than that, it has some rewarding moments."

The two girls laugh.

"You didn't seem too embarrassed." Kelly said.

"Good, I hope not. I could feel my face burning."

"Well, you have nothing to be embarrassed about. You have a beautiful figure," Kelly said.

"Thank you. Being around you two beauties is a little daunting— I'll give you two some advice. Listen to your gut, do the job, and don't be afraid to use what God gave you to get the upper hand. And don't put up with shit from anyone, especially your boss, whoever he or she is."

"Right now, that's your husband," Denise said.

"Him too." Liz said.

They all laugh.

Liz gave me a playful salute. "Reporting back from guard duty."

I laughed. "Thanks. Great uniform, by the way."

"Thank you. I spoke to General Barrett, and he said he would have 24 men in Curaçao waiting for your call."

"Thanks. Nothing to report here. Schultz will be with the men and says the cell phones are OK."

"Then I guess we wait."

That evening Kelly was on the bow keeping a watch on the beach, Denise was below with Liz. Ed, Tom, and I were sitting in the cockpit with Heraldo. Most of us were drinking coffee. I asked Heraldo, "When do you expect your people to arrive?"

"To be honest, I was expecting them today. I don't wish to sit here any longer than necessary, tourist ruse or not."

"I think we're good for one more day before anyone gets suspicious. There's no sign that anyone is even on this island."

Heraldo looks around, then out to sea. "Perhaps."

"Hey honey, you girls need any help down there?"

"Maybe in a minute, the spaghetti is almost done."

The next day, Liz and I were still in our stateroom. I climbed out of the shower, as Liz was smearing sunblock on her face. I finished toweling off, "Honey, I would like you to do the beach routine again. Be ready with the cell phone. Have the girls take theirs too. Be sure they have the number."

"Do you think today is the day?"

"I think so. Go over well-armed. Have *Gilbert & Sullivan* ready to go. I don't know what to look for. If you see something you don't like, shoot it."

Elizabeth laughs. "How about Heraldo?"

"That's a good start."

The three women sit on beach chairs. They are wearing one-piece suits, enormous hats and sunglasses. Kelly faces the jungle, the other two face the water.

"I assume by our attire we are expecting trouble today." Denise said.

"You are correct. Shooting an automatic weapon is much more dignified in a one-piece." Liz replied.

They all laugh.

"Use your eagle eyes and pay attention. I don't care if you see a bird; I want to know about it."

"How about two boats, three miles at eleven o'clock?" Denise asked.

Elizabeth picks up her binoculars and stares to seaward. "Damn, you have good eyes." She picks up her radio. "Honey! Two boats at three miles, eleven o'clock."

"Wait one— OK, I'm told these are the good guys. Stay in your location and report further."

"Roger." Liz hands the binoculars to Denise. "You are now our chief scout." She turned to Kelly. "Kelly, focus on the tree line. Don't be tempted to turn around."

"Yes, ma'am. I have your back."

Heraldo and I were standing in the cockpit watching the approaching boats. Ed and Tom are watching from the bow. There was no sign of Silvers and Pérez. "Friends of yours?"

"They are." Heraldo said.

"So, what's the plan?" I asked.

"First, we will retrieve your friends."

"What about Morales' men?" I asked.

"As they say in American movies, I believe you called the cavalry, and they will be here in the nick of time. Correct?" Heraldo asked.

"Are you saying this was the plan all the time. Me calling in help from Special Ops?"

"I hope you did not think I just wanted your boat. I was counting on your resourcefulness, you are well known in some circles for being quite clever."

"I hope we don't have to find out if your sources were right." I said.

The two powerboats pull alongside *Pinafore* and tie off. One man climbs aboard and shakes hands with Heraldo. "*Es bueno verte amigo mío.*"

"You too Miguel. This is my host *Señor* Sam Spade."

"*Mucho gusto.*"

"Very nice to meet you, too. Are my friends safe?" I asked.

"*Sí, si están a bordo. Aurto trae a nuestros huéspedes y los ayuda a bordo de este excelente barco.*"

One man on the larger boat disappears and comes back with three men in tow, Pérez, Silvers, and Bruno. They look worse for wear but climb on the *Pinafore* without help.

Liz is standing looking through the binoculars. "Looks like three men are getting on the *Pinafore*— Yep— Oh good, it's Rick and Pérez and I thin— "

—There is another boat coming around the north point!"

"Where?"

Denise points, "There! No, two boats!"

Kelly yells, "The tree line! There are men in the tree line!"

BANG! BANG! BANG! BANG! BANG! BANG! BANG! BANG! BANG! BANG!

RATAT RATAT RATAT! RATAT RATAT RATAT!

Four men are flung to the sand by automatic weapon fire. One is doubled over moaning. Kelly runs forward, holding her H&K. "Stay down, don't move! Don't move!" She repeats the order in Spanish, *¡Quédate abajo! ¡No te muevas!* then bends over each man and tosses his weapon away.

LOUD ROAR! A CYCLONE OF WIND BLOWS SAND AND DEBRIS IN THE AIR.

An SH-60 *Seahawk* helicopter settles softly on the sand. Eleven men jump out and form a perimeter around the helicopter. One runs over to Kelly and the downed men. Liz walks up to the Marine from the helicopter. Yelling over the noise, "Hi, I'm Mrs. Sam Spade!"

The Marine turns to the helicopter and waves. The eleven men file back on the helicopter, and it takes off in another whirl of sand and heads toward the boats.

BOOM!

Everyone on the beach turns toward the water. One of boats speeding from the north explodes in a ball of flame. Everyone is mesmerized by the scene for a moment, then the Marine turns to Liz. "Morning, ma'am. I'm Staff Sergeant Williams. General Barrett said we should come out here and see if we could talk you out of lunch and a cup of coffee. Wasn't expectin' a beach party" He looked out at the burning boat. "Or a barbecue."

"You Marines will go a long way for a free lunch."

"Hope that wasn't one of your boats."

"Ours is the sailboat. I don't know who the powerboat belonged to. There are two more that came out of the south. You can't see them from here. They're hidden by our boat."

"Yes, ma'am, I have guys checking them out."

Liz looked out over the water. Three helicopters orbit *Pinafore*. "Sergeant, would you mind helping us with these men? They all appear to be wounded. They came out of nowhere brandishing M16s and didn't expect us to have weapons, so, as they say in the movies, we got the drop on them."

Staff Sergeant Williams laughs and points. "That fellow won't be brandishing anything ever again. You hit him in the groin. You lady's mind unloading those weapons. My wife and I don't have children yet."

The women giggle, remove the magazines and clear the chambers of the H&Ks.

"You girls Marines?"

"No sir, we're window dressing," Kelly said.

The Sergeant looked at them strangely.

Liz laughs. "I'll tell you later. Come on, let's get you that coffee and see who or what blew up."

As they walk to the dingy, SSgt Williams chuckles. "The name of your dingy is *Gilbert & Sullivan*?"

"Sure, the name of our boat is *Pinafore*."

I was trying to focus on the two boats coming in from the north at high speed. Suddenly, two other boats sped around the southern point. I turned just in time to see a white flame streak across the water and impact on the lead boat coming from the north. The boat disappeared. Its companion turned and ran out to sea. Three SH-60 *Seahawk* helicopters thumped overhead, machine-gun fire crossed the bow of the lead southern boat. Using loudspeakers, one helicopter issued orders, "*Come to a complete stop. If you do not comply, we will fire into you.*" The boats stopped. "*All occupants will move to the rear of your boat and place their hands behind their heads. If you do not comply, we will sink you.*" The helicopters lower two Marines into each boat. Once the Marines are aboard, the boats were driven to *Pinafore*, where they tied up on the unoccupied side. The crews were cuffed, then told to sit in their boats.

Two *Seahawk*'s land on the beach. One remained in orbit. The wounded gunmen were loaded onto a helicopter, which flew off. The remaining

Seahawk shut off its engines. Fifteen Marines file off and form a perimeter around the aircraft.

Sergeant Williams accompanied Liz and the two girls to the *Pinafore.*

Thirty minutes later, Williams walked up to me and Liz. "Mr. Spade, my men have interrogated all the men from the two boats. They won't say a thing. You said these guys are from the Morales drug cartel. Right?"

"According to my buddy Heraldo. Why?"

"These guys are all German. Argentine, but German."

I turned, looking for Heraldo. "Heraldo, will you step over here, please?" Heraldo walked over to where Liz, SSGT. Williams and I were standing. "Heraldo, the sergeant here says the men they pulled off those two boats are German. You know anything about that?"

"*Si.* I told you there might be people following us. There is a sect of militants that still hold to the beliefs of pre-war Germany. They want to promote hatred, white supremacy, and create a fascist state. You call them neo-Nazis. I call them filth. They believe the gold from U-530 belongs to them."

"So, who was on the other boats?"

"The drug cartel."

I sat down. "Anybody have a scorecard?"

Ed picks up a pair of binoculars. "Hey, Bud. There's that sport fisherman about a mile off."

Ed, Rick, Denise, Kelly, Tom, Bruno, Heraldo, SSGT Williams, Pérez sit around the cockpit table. I was sitting behind the wheel. Liz was below, handing breakfast plates to Pérez. Liz brought up the last plate and sat in the companionway, her legs dangling into the cockpit. "I don't think we have ever had eleven people around this table. Honey, you OK back there?"

"Just fine. Any more orange juice?"

"No, sorry." Liz's phone rings. "Hello— Yes, ma'am. One moment. Honey, it's the president."

I stood and worked my way around the cockpit and took Liz's phone, then went below.

SSGT. Williams looked at Ed. "*The* president?"

Ed nods. "We have her on speed dial. She comes to all our parties."

I sat down in the master stateroom. "Good morning, ma'am."

"Where are you?

"On the east side of Little Tobago."

"Give me the short version, but first, were the Cubans involved?"

"No. They actually helped. The whole thing was put together by our friend, the late Victor Escudero. He was trying to recoup his money with a ransom, plus he wanted to kill Pérez. After Victor died, the Cartel went ahead with the plan and kidnaped Rick and the others. When they found out Ed and I were down here looking around, they tried to trap us here in Tobago. I guess they thought we would sweeten the pot.

"Anyone hurt?"

"Bad guys. Three dead, one wounded. Maybe more. A cartel boat blew up. As far as we can tell, there were no survivors. There was another boat, but it took off."

"Were the Special Ops involved?"

"Indirectly. The Cartel tried a pincer movement- that's a—

"I know what a pincer movement is. You will recall I was in the Army."

"Yes, ma'am. The plan was to come up behind us from the island— we found a rubber boat— while the two boats attacked by sea. The girls from Camp Peary took care of the land contingent."

"Who blew up the boat?"

"We're not sure. About the time the cartel boats arrived, two more boats came out of the south. Best that we can tell, one of the newcomers fired an RPG at the cartel boats, destroying one. The other cartel boat turned and ran. About that time, the Special Ops guys arrived and took over. They captured the two remaining boats and evacuated the dead and wounded from the beach."

"If the guys on the beach worked for the Cartel, who were the others?"

"I'm not sure. All we know is that they appear to be German, or German speaking, maybe from Argentina. Heraldo Hernandez says they are neo-Nazis."

"So, Special Ops landed on Tobago?"

"Yes, ma'am. They put a *Seahawk*, that's a— "

"You're not going to tell me what a *Seahawk* is, are you? I have 3,000 hours in the Army version, the *Blackhawk*."

"I'm sorry ma'am. The *Seahawk* was on the ground for about five minutes to take the wounded out. There is another one sitting on the beach now. It's been there about an hour.

"Any complaints? We buy a lot of LNG from them so it wouldn't do to upset them."

"No, ma'am. The island looks uninhabited, but you never know."

"OK, I'll call the Trinidad/Tobago President, Paula-Mae Medina, and tell her we invaded her territory for about an hour because of a drug interdiction program. Does that jive with the facts?"

"Yes, ma'am, that's the truth."

"I want Rick, Agent Sawyer, Dr. Pérez, and Minister Gallard to come back with the Special Ops people. I need you and Liz to stay down there and help Heraldo."

"Heraldo— Ma'am, why are we going to help him? He's a mercenary at best."

"No, he's not. He's with INTERPOL and the French and Argentine ambassadors asked me— which means you— to give him a hand. I think his mission is important."

"Hunting for Nazi gold?"

"He'll tell you all about it."

"Yes, ma'am. Our deal included Agent Sawyer."

"I need Agent Sawyer as protection, window dressing if you will, until they get back to D.C. God forbid something else happens to those men. I'll give him a few days with his wife and send him back. You can keep Ed, and if you want them, you can keep the two CIA agents."

"How about General Barrett?"

"You can have him on speed dial."

"Thank you. I'll keep the girls. They're sharp as tacks and holy terrors with a machine gun."

"I'm always heartened to hear when young women have found fulfillment in their careers."

"To be honest, Liz is usually knee-deep in testosterone. I think she enjoys their company."

After the call, I walked back to the companionway and climbed into the cockpit. Everyone looked at me. I took my place behind the wheel, drank some of my now cold coffee.

"Bruno, Doc, Rick, Tom you go with SSgt. Williams. Ed, you're stuck here. Tom, you'll be back in a few days. Girls, you're with us. OK, Heraldo, the cat is out of the bag. Spill.

Heraldo looked at me, then at Liz.

"That's American slang for you forgot to tell us something worthy of further discussion." Liz said.

"Why don't we begin by you telling us who you are." I said. "Start with the INTERPOL part."

He smiled, "Very well. I am with the Buenos Aires INTERPOL office. My name is unimportant so, please continue to call me Heraldo and I will continue to call you Sam Spade, though you may have wished for a more convincing *nom de guerre*."

"It wasn't my idea. It was sort of spur-of-the-moment thing, and it stuck."

"How unfortunate. INTERPOL is hunting a group that identifies as *Die Auserwählten* or The Chosen. In reality, they are thugs and killers that dress their crimes in German Nationalism."

"You mean Nazis." Tom said.

"*Si*. So far, they have had free rein over the Caribbean. Their specialty is extortion and kidnapping."

"The Caribbean is a long way from Argentina. Why are you involved?" I asked.

"*Die Auserwählten* gets its origins from *Partido Nuevo Triunfo*, a small right Argentinian fringe political party which we banned in 2009. The leaders believe Adolf Hitler identified Argentina as the future of Nazism and seek to use Argentina as the new Nazi base."

"I remember reading that in his last days Hitler pointed to Argentina on a map and said from there the new leader will come." Liz said.

"*Si*, if he actually said that is of no importance, *Die Auserwählten* believes it."

"If we find them, then what?" I asked.

"INTERPOL, through its members, has outstanding warrants for most of the leaders. They will be arrested."

"Is the witness to the gold story true, or is it part of a ploy to flush out your Nazis?" Tom asked.

"The *Die Auserwählten* believe the gold is real and they believe they have an absolute right to it because it belonged to Hitler. As for the witness story, I heard it from Victor Escudero. He believed it was true."

"So, you were friends?" I asked.

"Of sorts. We were both in the Army. He was a Venezuelan cavalry officer, and I was a Tank Corps officer with the Argentine Army. We met at your Fort Benning when we were there for school."

"And you stayed in touch." I said.

"When he was deposed and fled to Cuba, he called me and said he had a very lucrative proposition for me. I met him and here we are."

"Where is the gold? Denise asked.

"About two hundred feet beneath your feet." Heraldo said.

Liz's phone rings. "Hello. One minute." Liz hands the phone to me. "It's the president."

"I spoke to President Paula-Mae Medina. She allowed we could assuage her feelings if we bought four tickets to Carnival. I think she was joking but buy the tickets anyway. Rick will see you get reimbursed.

"Yes, ma'am, I'll take care of it."

"Have you ever been to Carnival?" the president asked.

"Sure, Ferris wheel, cotton candy and hot dogs."

"Not exactly. Send me pictures. You have reservations at the CrewsInn Marina in Chaguaramas."

I handed the phone back to Liz. "We have been ordered to Chaguaramas, which is on the far side of Trinidad. We can get food and water and a night in a hotel."

"What about the gold?" Kelly asked.

"It's been here 70 years. It will be here for a few more days. Besides, the depth here is 280 feet. We can't get down that deep without a professional diver." I said.

Kelly looks disappointed but doesn't say anything else.

"Now, to appease the local government, we also have to attend some kind of carnival."

"Really! That's wonderful!" Liz exclaimed.

Elizabeth and the girls give each other high fives.

"I don't get it?" I said.

"If you have never been, I would whole heartily recommend the experience, plus it adds to our subterfuge," Heraldo said.

Ed laughs. "That's for sure."

"OK, we're going to the Carnival." I said.

CHAPTER TWENTY-ONE

Staff Sergeant Williams shepherded his flock aboard the two choppers and flew off to parts unknown, probably Tampa. During the sail to Port of Spain, I was regaled by the remaining crew with the particulars of Carnival. It seems the celebration is an annual event dating from the 18th century. The key elements are steelpan and calypso music and outlandish costumes usually made from skimpy bikinis, feathers, and beads. We were able to get rooms and a slip at the CrewsInn.

The next day we all assembled in the lobby of the CrewsInn. Elizabeth, Denise, Kelly and Ed spent all morning getting ready and were dressed in traditional Carnival costumes.

"You girls can't go out in public dressed like that!" I said.

"May I remind you we were dressed in less a week ago." Liz said.

"That was different. That was a ruse. This is well it's just different. It's in public."

"This *is* a ruse. We're tourists having a good time."

"And I'm their bodyguard." Ed said.

"I'm so relieved. Do you have to show so much of your *body*?"

"If you got it, flaunt it."

"Great. Get on the bus. Heraldo and I will meet you at Queens Park. We'll be the ones wearing clothes."

I stormed off. Liz was laughing. Kelly turned to Elizabeth. "I get why he might be upset at you, but why us?"

"Because you are about the same age as our daughter, and he feels responsible for you. He compartmentalizes things. One day your agents, today your vulnerable young women."

"He'll get over it. Come on, let's party." Ed said.

They all exit the lobby for the waiting bus.

Among the many hundreds of people celebrating Carnival in queens park, was a man in a white fedora hat. He lit a cigarette exposing a swastika tattooed on his wrist.

That evening in the Lighthouse Restaurant, everyone was seated around a table finishing dinner. "Now I know why the president of Trinidad wanted us to attend this Carnival. The thing must be half of her GNP. It was all of mine."

"Oh, relax, you'll get reimbursed." Liz said.

Ed laughed.

I looked around to see if anyone was near. "Heraldo, the administration will not pay for us to hunt Nazi gold. We are here to support your role with INTERPOL. What's the plan?"

"I think we continue with our cover story. These *Die Auserwählten* people believe the gold is here in Trinidad, so we convince them the story is true."

"The story you told us in Rodney Bay, wasn't true?" Liz asked.

"Many people believe it to be true. I am of the opinion U-530 was on a far more sinister mission.

"What?"

"One investigation concluded U-530 had been dispatched to launch a nerve gas attack on New York City in retaliation for the Dresden bombing."

"My god, they were going shell New York city with nerve gas?" Liz exclaimed.

"That much can be confirmed. Hitler was eventually talked out of this, so U-530's gun and armaments were jettisoned, perhaps to destroy y evidence of a possible war crime."

"How hideous." Liz said.

"*Si*. I believe this is closer to the truth than the gold narrative, but it is also true many strange things happened at the end of the war."

"If the gold story is true, and it was left here in 1944, he could have picked it up in '45 and taken it to Argentina." I said.

"This is also true. But the men I am trying to capture believe the gold is here in the Caribbean. So, for our purposes, this is the story we pursue. As is said, flies are better attracted with honey."

I chuckled, "So, we go for the gold."

"I think this is the best plan."

"I assume you have a diver. Because we are sure not getting to 200 feet with a snorkel."

"Victor said he had a diver. They were to meet us on the island. I presume he was on one of the Cartel boats."

"Then we need a diver and a dive boat." I said.

"How long do you think we can hang around that island before someone gets curious?" Ed asked.

"I don't know. These guys have a sizeable Navy. Pretty soon, one of their ships is going to wonder what we are doing. And a couple of pretty girls are not going to deter them."

"What do you mean, a couple?" Liz asked.

"Sorry. *Three* pretty girls— Skimpy bathing suits aside. Eventually, they are going to ask questions."

"We don't even know if we have the right spot. Victor could have told you anything," Ed said.

"What you all say is true. We need to establish the correct location before we risk another trip to the island. But the last I heard, the witness was still in prison, and I have no idea how to find his son." Heraldo said.

"Do you know his name?" I asked.

"I know the name Victor gave me." Herald answered.

"We have friends in Venezuela. Liz, will you call Teddy and see what you can find out? Then you and the girls hang out at the pool for a couple of days."

"With or without bathing suits?"

She and the girls laugh.

"Funny. Ed, I guess you and I will find a diver."

Ed and I walked into the Lobby and spoke to the man behind the counter. "Good morning," I said. "My friends and I are eager to do some diving and we were hoping you could recommend a suitable guide and certified diver."

"There are several reputable dive companies within walking distance. They take diving tours out twice a day."

"We were looking for something off the beaten path, so to speak. Perhaps a native to the area that could give us personal attention."

"There is a man named Charlie Whitt who claims he's an ex-Navy diver. He hangs out at the Hilton. He'll be in the bar where he tries to pick up some tourist trade. Can't miss him, he always wears an old dirty white captain's hat."

"Thanks, he sounds perfect."

Ed and I walked into the Hilton Trinidad Cascadoo Bar & Grille. At the far end of the marble-topped bar facing the entrance is a man in his 60s, tanned, craggy face. He is unshaven, wearing old work clothes, and a billed dirty-white captain's hat. Ed and I walked over to him. "Are you Charlie Whitt?" I asked.

"Who's asking?"

"My name is Sam. This is Ed. We want to hire a diver."

Ignoring me in favor of the bartender, "Hey Pete." The bartender walked over. "Another beer, put it on their tab. "I'm Whitt. My office is over here." He stands and walked to a table with four chairs."

Ed threw some bills on the bar and followed Charlie and me to the table where we all sat in some faux wicker chairs . "How do you know I'm a diver?"

"The guy at CrewsInn, he said you were ex-Navy." I said.

"Retired Senior Chief. Came down here on my first hitch— this was all a Navy base then— I liked it so, when I retired, I came back."

"So, are you interested?" I asked.

"How deep?"

"About 200, maybe 280 feet."

"What are you looking for?"

"What makes you think we are looking for anything?"

"Because that's too deep for a recreational dive."

"My wife and friends want to explore an old shipwreck."

"You guys aren't tourists. Your ex-military or mercs or both and you may be diving on a wreck, but it's not for fun and games."

"You want the job or not?"

"Two hundred dollars a day plus expenses plus gas for my boat. And I don't do any rough stuff."

"Who said anything about rough stuff? Ed asked.

"That bald freak that followed you two in here."

Without turning. Ed asked, "Who is he?"

"They call him Dieter. He brings a big sport fisherman in here all the time. He's a freak"

"You said that. What's he look like?" I asked.

"Why don't you turn around and look at him?

"Because we do not wish to appear inquisitive or confrontational." Ed replied.

"That's a good idea with that guy. He's bigger than you are, but white, too white, like there's something wrong with him."

"Albino?" Ed asked.

"Maybe. Looks like he was dipped in bleach. He's got no eyebrows, and a long scar down the left side of his face. He always wears a white hat. But he ain't one of the good guys, if you get my meaning.

"Why do you say that?" Ed asked.

"I have friends in low places."

"So, do we have a deal?" I asked.

"Where and when?"

"We'll let you know. One other thing. What you see and what you hear remains confidential."

"I don't do confidential."

"I can pick up the phone. You get yanked out of retirement. Then you work for us for $130 a day. Or you can keep your mouth shut and work for us at your rate, plus bonus."

"You can do that?"

"We can do that."

Charlie Witt rubbed the stubble on his chin for a moment. "I believe you. OK, we have a deal."

Ed and I had a couple of beers with our new best friend. By the time we had a chance to look at Dieter, he was gone. As we walked out of the Hilton, Ed asked, "Do you think we could have really called him out of retirement?"

"Depends on how badly the president wants to help Heraldo."

"Wonder who this Dieter is? Did you see him?"

"No, I didn't. Let's ask Heraldo if he knows him."

We were all at the pool the next day. Ed is showing off his physique to some girls in the pool. Denise and Kelly were sunbathing on lounge chairs some feet distant from us where they could watch the surrounding area. Liz, Heraldo and I sat in chairs overlooking the pool. "What in the world is Ed doing? Liz asked.

"He and the girls are watching our flanks. Seems we have attracted the attention of a local thug called Dieter."

"Dieter! He is one of the leaders of *Die Auserwählten*."

"Big albino, bald, scar down his face? "I asked.

"Yes, no one knows his last name."

"Well, we have their attention. He followed Ed and me into the Hilton bar yesterday."

"That is wonderful news." Heraldo said.

"Happy to hear it. Liz, what did Teddy have to say?"

"He said the witness Victor was talking about died recently, but Teddy tracked down his son."

"Did the son know anything?"

"He said his father used to fish for tarpon off Little Tobago and had a small fishing camp on the beach. He remembered his father telling him a story about seeing sparks dancing on the water."

"Sparks dancing on the water?" I asked.

"His father said late one night he heard boat engines. He said it was cloudy, with no moon and very dark. When he went to investigate, he saw sparks dancing on the water. After a while, the moon came out, and he saw men on a submarine throwing things in the water."

"What things?" I asked.

"He didn't know, but he confirmed the location. Right where we were anchored."

"Throwing things in the water? Not taking them out?" Heraldo asked.

"That's what Teddy said."

"This was in May 1945, yes?" Heraldo asked.

"All he said was that it was at the end of the war."

"I guess we go look." I said.

"I know this is all more subterfuge, but it is exciting. Maybe there is really gold down there." Liz said.

"That submarine didn't come here for Carnival." I said.

Liz laughs. Ed walked over to the table. "We have company."

A man dressed in a white suit and hat walked up to the table. Kelly sat up and pulled her beach bag close. Denise stood. Holding her beach bag, she walked to the opposite side of our table, where she watched the entrance to the pool. The man addressed the table with a German accent." Good afternoon. What a lovely day. I envy you, I unfortunately seldom have the time for such leisure."

"What can we do for you?" Ed asked.

The man takes a chair from a nearby table, pulls it over and sits down. "It is *I* that can do something for you. I represent a group of investors that wish to charter your boat."

"Your investors are German?" Ed asked.

"Some are. But I am Swiss by birth. My investors are of several nationalities.

"As you can see, we are on vacation. However, should we be interested, where do you want to go?" I asked.

"My colleges are historians and collectors."

"I thought you said they were investors." Liz said.

The man smiles. "They are both. They trade artifacts in the secondary markets."

"You mean the black market." I said.

"Well, that is a crude way of putting it, but yes."

"I take it you have an artifact in mind?" I asked.

"We do."

"So, what is it?" I asked.

"For now, let us say it is an item of intrinsic and historic value."

"Who owns this historic item?" I asked.

"Why the person who finds it, of course."

"Where is this item?" I asked.

"Not far. A day's sail, no more."

I paused for a few seconds. "Mr.—sorry, I didn't catch your name."

"I did not drop it."

"Cute name." I said. "Well, Mr. I did not drop it. I suspect your charter application is really a fishing expedition. You are who you say you are, or you are with the local government. In either case, my friends and I are on vacation. If there is nothing else, we wish you a good day."

"Very well. Perhaps we will meet again." The man stands. Bows curtly, tips his hat to Liz, and walks off. Once he was off the premises, Kelly and Denise resumed their sunbathing. "Ed, are the girls carrying what I think they're carrying in those bags?" I asked.

"Yep, 9mm sunscreen with an automatic dispenser."

"Heraldo, any idea who that guy was?" Liz asked.

"I've never seen him before, but I think his name is Smerkoff."

"Sounds like a Russian vodka." I said.

"He works for your friend Dieter. And you were correct, he was on a fishing expedition."

"Heraldo, is this all worth the trouble? I asked.

"My country, France, and Israel have been tracking these people for years. We consider them terrorists and a great danger to South America and the Caribbean."

"What's Israel's interest?" Liz asked.

"Foremost, *Die Auserwählten* are neo-Nazis. Second, they have roots in the 1992 bombing of the Israeli embassy in Buenos Aires. No one has ever been tried for that massacre."

"OK, I guess you have us for the duration. Everyone relax, shop, eat and be ready to sail tomorrow morning." I said.

CHAPTER TWENTY-TWO

Pinafore - Little Tobago Island

We left Port of Spain after telling Charlie Whitt where to meet us. Everyone took a turn at the helm. We read, sunbathed, ate, and drank. Once we anchored, there was more eating. Ed and Heraldo had been preparing the meal for several hours and now passed plates of food up to the cockpit.

"Heraldo what is this? It looks delicious." Liz said.

"My mother's recipe. I hope you enjoy."

"I helped," Ed said.

"I'm sure you were indispensable," Liz said.

There was some laughing as the crew sat around the cockpit table to eat.

"When is the diver arriving?" Liz asked.

"He said he would be here first thing in the morning, so probably about six," Ed said.

"Yuck, I was getting used to sleeping late." Liz said.

The next day, true to his word, Charlie arrived about eight in the morning. He anchored about 100 yards off *Pinafore* and, without ceremony, went over the side. We sent the girls to the beach to watch our backs. Leaving Heraldo in charge of *Pinafore*. Ed, Liz and I went over to *Spanky*, Charlie's 40-foot non-descript 'dive boat'.

Some thirty minutes later, his head broke water. He swam over to the ladder. Ed, and I helped him clammer aboard. Sitting on the boat combing, he began pulling off his equipment. "Sorry, no gold. I found the deck gun, though. Couldn't find any serial numbers but it's a fair bet it belongs to U-530. The deck bolts were cut with a torch."

"Sparks dancing on the water. A cutting torch." I said.

"Be my guess." Ed said.

"Why would they get rid of the gun?" Liz asked.

"Fuel. Just like an airplane, reduce drag, reduce fuel consumption." Ed said.

Throwing the last of his gear on the deck, "There are four torpedoes down there, too." Charlie said.

"Reducing weight, which equals drag." Ed said.

"There are also remnants of crates and what looks like navigation equipment. Ammo for the gun and some small arms." Charlie said.

"But no gold." Liz said.

Charlie shakes his head and wipes his face. "Sorry."

"The range of those subs was about 12,000 miles. They had already come some 4,000 miles, so they used close to a third of their fuel. With no gas stations around and a U.S. Naval base about 100 miles away, they needed all the reserve they could get," I speculated. "

Or they were getting rid of evidence of the gas attack on New York." Ed said.

"So, what did they do with the gold?" Liz asked.

"That's the question, isn't it?" I said. "Let's get over to *Pinafore* and see what Heraldo wants to do."

A short dingy ride later, we were in the cockpit of *Pinafore* drinking coffee. "Heraldo, this is your operation. What's next?"

"We know we have enticed our prey. So, we have to draw them into a trap where they can be arrested. To do that, we need to make them believe we have either found the gold or discovered another clue as to its location."

"How do we do that?" I asked.

"We have Charlie brag about it."

Charlie looked up, "I don't know. Those guys get pretty rough. I'm not anxious to have some of my fingers broken or worse."

"Charlie. Do you have some good friends you talk to regularly, particularly over the radio?" Ed asked.

"Sure, I talk to Mikey almost every day. He's a charter captain and always bragging about the huge tarpon he hooks. Mostly it's BS."

"So, when we're ready, but only when we're ready, you tell him about this great dive you had. Act excited and tell him your clients insist you take them to X."

"How do we know Dieter and his buddies are listening?" Charlie asked.

Heraldo answered, "Be most assured, they will be listening."

"So, now we have to decide where X is going to be." I said.

"It has to be believable." Heraldo said.

"I'm all ears." I said.

"Heraldo, you sounded pretty convinced that the Japanese gold shipment was transferred to U-530. Was that for show or do you believe it?" Liz asked.

"I believe it, or I want to believe it. I must tell you, I truly thought it was here in this bay under our feet."

"Then it must be somewhere. Charlie, you know these waters, Heraldo, you know the history. The other three of us are pretty smart. So, let's go over what we know about that voyage and come up with X." Liz said.

"Lunch first. Ed, shall we bring the girls in from the beach or send them some chow?" I asked.

"Send them some food. We need them on our back door. Our radar won't pick up someone coming through the jungle."

"Yeah, we found that out. OK, let's make some lunch. Then we identify X. I said.

Lizz and Heraldo fixed lunch while Ed and I spruced up the boat, stowing lines and errant equipment that had been left about. As we sat around the cockpit table eating, we started throwing around ideas.

"We know U-530 was ordered to raid in this area several times, so I suggest we confine our search to the Trinidad area, where the allies suffered their highest losses." Heraldo said.

"Why was the Caribbean so important to the Germans?" Liz asked.

"Because England needed four or more oil tankers a day just to survive, and most of the oil came from Venezuela, which came through the refineries in Curaçao and Trinidad, which at the time were the largest in the world." Heraldo said.

"And the U.S. needed aluminum for aircraft." Ed said.

"Correct, bauxite was one of the few strategic raw materials not available within the continental United States." Heraldo said.

"So, did the Germans destroy a lot of ships?" Liz asked.

"They sank over 300 ships and damaged 46 more at a loss of 12 U-boats."

"Wow. We weren't taught that in school." Ed said.

Looking at Charlie, I said, "Charlie, I would like you to use your knowledge of the area," then looking at her, "Liz, use your research skills with the computer. Put your heads together and try to determine the best locale for our search. I suspect we are looking for an uninhabited island then and probably now, so that should help."

"OK, we'll get right on it." Liz said.

"First, I think we should move the boats somewhere less noticeable. Why don't we go around to Pirates Bay? We can drop a hook there." Charlie said.

"In the meantime, I'll call my office and see if they can dig up any further information from the interrogations that took place after U-530's surrender." Heraldo said.

"Let's call Tom and see if there is anyone he can contact about the POWs. A bunch of them were taken to Fort Hunt just outside D.C. Maybe he can find some old records." I said.

"I'll make the call." Ed said.

"OK, call the girls back to the boat. Charlie, do you need any help?"

"No thanks, I'll meet you at Pirates Bay."

"Then let's get underway."

Pirates Bay was a full day sail, and we were all tired, so most of us went to sleep without eating. The next morning, ravenous we consumed all the eggs, bacon and grits and coffee Liz and Ed were kind enough to prepare. Liz put her coffee cup down. "The whole damn Caribbean is riddled with sunk tankers and freighters. It's a wonder the Brits got *any* oil out of here."

"There are those that say the Allies came very close to losing the war right here in the Caribbean." Heraldo said.

"I believe it. Most of the shipping was sunk in this area here." She made a circle with her finger on a chart in the middle of the table. "Charlie thinks Blanquillo Island, which is here (pointing) may be a place to start."

"It's uninhabited. I've been there a couple of times. There is deep water and a beach." Charlie said.

I started to say something— Liz raised her hand. "I know, It's slim evidence, but I received a text from Tommy this morning. He may have something to add. He asked us to call him when we were ready."

"OK, let's call him." I said.

Liz dialed the phone. "Tommy, it's Liz, you ready?" She pushed a button. "OK, you're on speaker."

"Good morning. I think I'll be back down tomorrow. But that's not why I called. One of our guys said he found a deposition from one of the U-530 crew. He mentioned stopping at a place he called donkey island."

Charlie leans forward. "Blanquillo is covered with wild donkeys and goats."

"I haven't found anything that makes better sense," Liz said.

"Let's say in '44 they left the gold at Tobago, planning to retrieve it later, probably after the war."

"But they lost the war and had no idea when they could come back."

"And in '45, the entire area was lousy with Allied Navies, and Tobago itself was getting more populated. They decided to move it."

"So, they dumped the deck gun, torpedoes and packed the gold in the forward torpedo compartment and headed for donkey island." Ed said.

"Where they figured, no one would go." I said. "And they were right. Charlie, where is this donkey island?"

"From here, about 240 miles due west."

"Heraldo, do you have anything better?"

"No, what I have heard is logical."

"Tom, when can you get down here?"

"I can be in Robinson International at 11 am. Can you pick me up?"

"See you then" Liz disconnected the phone. "OK. Let's try to weigh anchor tomorrow about noon. That will put us at donkey island about 5pm the day after tomorrow. Charlie, now that we know X is Blanquillo slash donkey Island, I would like you to make the radio call to your buddy Mikey. But only when we get to donkey island."

CHAPTER TWENTY-THREE

Pinafore – Under Full Sail

Ed picked up Tom at the airport with one of the few rental cars on the island. As us nautical types say, we weighed anchor, and left Pirates Bay about 12:30 the same afternoon. We sailed through the night without mishap. Daylight caught everyone trying to catch up on the sleep you never get on a night sail. Sleeping, lounging, reading, and sunbathing, each chose their own method of rest between turns at the helm.

Elizabeth's phone rang. "Hello. One minute." Liz handed the phone to me. "It's the president."

"Good morning, ma'am."

"Good morning. Any civilians around?"

"No. Ma'am."

"Put me on speaker."

I pressed a button on the phone. "Go ahead, madam president.'

"How are things proceeding?"

"I believe we may have found the location of the gold shipment. We are sailing there now. It's called Blanquillo Island. We should be there about five this evening."

"That's fine, but we're not looking for gold. The Argentines, the French and now the Israelis want that mob of thugs arrested."

"Yes, ma'am. We are using the gold, or at least the premise of gold, as bait."

"OK. I won't tell you how to do your job. But finish it up as soon as you can. I need you elsewhere."

"Yes, ma'am."

"To those of you that are listening. Thank you. I know this is time away from your families. I appreciate your service."

There is a chorus of thank-you's from the crew.

"And don't annoy the Venezuelans."

CLICK.

We were all left looking at each other. "How in the hell did she know Blanquillo Island was Venezuelan? I never heard of the place." I said.

"That's why she's president and you're not." Ed said.

Kelly gasped "Wait! You mean that was the President of the United States?"

"It was. How do you think we dragged you out of Camp Peary? And keep it under your hat," Ed said.

I looked at Ed. "I need you elsewhere?"

Ed shrugged, then picked up his coffee cup. "Sounds like your vacation is turning into a career."

Heraldo and the girls were below. Tom was sleeping on the port cockpit bench. I was pretending to sleep on the starboard bench while trying to get my head around what the president had said about needing us elsewhere and what Ed said about our vacation turning into a career. Ed was driving the boat. He yelled, "Hey skipper, you awake!"

"Yea, I'm awake." I sat up, rubbed my face, and looked forward over the bow. "What's up?"

"I have what looks like an island on the radar. I guess it's the right one. The GPS says so."

"Where's Charlie?"

"About three miles off the starboard quarter."

"Damn, I knew we should have sent someone with him. He probably fell asleep. OK, let me look at the big screen." I climbed below where the others were napping, slid behind the navdesk, and adjusted the radar. Heraldo walked up next to me. "Are we there?"

"I think so. It has that peculiar hatchet look to it. GPS says we're on the money." I made a further change to the radar set. "Hey, look at this," I pointed to the screen. "See that blip next to the island? I think that's a boat." I stood and scrambled up to the cockpit, grabbed some binoculars, then climbed up on the cabin roof. I took a long look through the binoculars. "Still too far to see anything from here. Are any of the girls awake?"

Denise appeared from behind me. "I'm awake."

"Good, I want you to take the binoculars to the masthead and tell me what you see. We get another 12 miles from up there."

"I'll need a bosun's chair."

"Yes, you will. Give me a minute." I looked at Tom, who was now awake. "Tom take Ed's place. Ed, give me a hand, please." When Tom stood up, I pulled the cushion from where he was napping, opened the top to the bench and went head down into the sail locker. I pulled out what looked like a canvas bag and some shackles. I walked over to the mast and hooked the shackles to a halyard. "Denise, have you used one of these before?"

"No, but I've seen my dad and brothers use one. They would never let me go up a mast."

"Smart Dad. OK, this is a bosun's chair. Sit in it and Ed and I will pull you to the top of the mast. When you get up there, tell me what you see. My wife says you have the best eyes on the boat. Are you afraid of heights?"

Denise's eyes followed the mast to the top, craning her neck. "Not up to now."

I couldn't help but chuckle. I handed her the canvas contraption. She wiggled her way into the bosun's chair. Ed removed the bitter end of the halyard from a stop and wound it several times around the primary winch.

"OK, when you're ready, Ed will winch you to the top. Hold on to the mast, or you will swing with the motion of the boat."

"I'm ready."

Ed pushed the button for the electric winch. As it turned, Denise was pulled up the mast. I craned my neck back to watch her ascent. "Stop!"

Ed took his finger off the winch button.

The motion of the boat was amplified at the top of the mast, and Denise was having trouble holding on and managing the binoculars at the same time. She finally got control and took a long look through the binoculars. She looked below to the deck. "I see the island! There is a boat probably anchored. It looks like the sport fisherman we saw in Tobago!"

"Anything else!" I yelled back.

"There is a helicopter on the beach!"

"Can you see Charlie?"

Denise looked around. She put the binoculars to her eyes. "Yes! He is far over to starboard about four o'clock!"

"OK. Come on down!"

I nodded to Ed, and we reversed the procedure until Denise was on the deck.

"That was fun, a little scary at first." She said.

"What kind of helicopter?" I asked.

"A black one."

I laughed and looked at Ed. "Are you thinking what I'm thinking?"

"Charlie's radio conversation with Mikey was premature, but it worked."

"Yep."

"How much time do we have?" Ed asked.

"About 30 minutes." I said.

"You want the sails down?" Ed asked'

"Time for what?" Tom asked.

"Leave them up, we'll keep up the pretense of tourists as long as we can." I looked at Tom. "We are the stealth version of the boating world. The guys on the island can't see us yet. But they will in about 30-40 minutes, so we have that much time to get ready."

"Unless they send that chopper up." Ed said.

"Get ready for what?" Tom asked.

I leaned down the companionway. "All hands on deck!" I stood and looked at Ed. Grinning, "I always wanted to say that."

Ed rolled his eyes.

Tom is behind the wheel. Everyone else is sitting in the cockpit. "Sorry to interrupt your naps. Just over the horizon is Donkey Island. Our friends with the sport fisherman have preceded us. As an added attraction, they have a helicopter sitting on the beach."

"So, we can assume Mr. Dieter, accompanied by several of his close personal friends, is looking for the gold, thanks to Charlie's radio conversations." Liz said.

"Ed and I suspect the chopper is not a good thing and we are going to prepare for all eventualities. Liz, I would like you to break out the M14 and ammo. Girls, please do the same with your H&Ks."

"Do you mean you think they will attack us?" Tom asked.

"Depends if they found the gold yet. If not, they don't want us near the island, so they will attempt to scare us away." Ed said.

"We should call the police." Tom said.

"Heraldo will do that, but they won't get here in time, so we have to help ourselves. Heraldo, why don't you take care of that now?" I said.

Heraldo stands and goes below. I continued, "The only weapons we have that will deter the chopper is the M14 and maybe the H&Ks. I'll drive the boat the girls will sunbathe here in the cockpit. The rest of you will go below and get under anything you can find, preferably below the waterline."

"Why?" Tom asked.

"Because bullets don't penetrate water very well, but they can sure punch through fiberglass. Let's get started." I said.

The crew scurried below.

We could clearly see the island in the distance. I was driving the boat, and like the others, I was in a bathing suit, except I was topless. The M14 was at my feet— just in case. Denise and Kelly sat on opposite sides of the cockpit. Their H&Ks laying under towels next to them. Ed, Liz, Tom and Heraldo were below. "Girls, I don't think they are going to go for the bathing beauty thing, but you never know, so look like a tourist. Wave if they fly over." We were close enough now that I could see what appeared to be a black Bell JetRanger lifting off from the island and swinging toward the ocean and the oncoming *Pinafore*. "OK, everyone, here they come! Girls, if they intend to make a fight of it, shoot for the pilot, he will be on the right side of the cockpit. Next, go for the transmission. It's the big box just above the cabin."

The helicopter closed with *Pinafore* very fast. As it flew overhead, it banked hard to the right. The girls and I waved as it passed. "Maybe we got lucky." I looked toward the island, then to the left for Charlie.

Denise in a surprised yell, "It's coming back!"

I snapped my head back to see the helicopter turning for us again. It crossed in front of *Pinafore*. A man was hanging out the door.

RATATAT, RATATAT, RATATAT, RATATAT, RATATAT. Geysers of water erupt some 50 feet from the bow of the boat.

"Steady! When I yell now. Fire into them."

The helicopter pulls up, then banks hard right for another run at *Pinafore*. The helicopter is very low and almost overhead.

"Now! Now!" I picked up the M14 and fired short bursts.

BAM, BAM, BAM, BAM. BAM, BAM, BAM, BAM. BAM, BAM, BAM, BAM.

As it flies over, Denise and Kelly stand and fire into the belly of the helicopter.

RATATAT, *RATATAT, RATATAT, RATATAT, RATATAT, RATATAT.* RATATAT, *RATATAT, RATATAT, RATATAT, RATATAT, RATATAT.*

Smoke streams from the starboard engine. The helicopter turns and comes back, again very low, it banks so the man hanging out of the door can have a clear shot.

"Now! Now!" I fired M14 again emptying the magazine.

BAM, BAM, BAM, BAM, BAM, BAM, BAM, BAM. BAM, BAM, BAM, BAM.

Denise and Kelly fire into the belly of the helicopter again.

RATATAT, RATATAT, RATATAT, RATATAT, RATATAT, RATATAT. RATATAT, RATATAT, RATATAT, RATATAT, RATATAT, RATATAT.

Still streaming smoke from the starboard engine. The helicopter loses altitude, hovers for a moment then spins out of control, and drops into the sea.

I yelled, "Everyone on deck!"

"It looked like we got the engine." Denise said.

"Maybe, but it has two engines. More likely we got the pilot."

Ed arrived on deck first, followed by Elizabeth.

"Ed, you, and Liz get the sails down. We're going over there and see if anyone is in the water."

"You should just let them drown." Ed scowled.

"I want to see who they work for. Heraldo keep an eye on the sport fisherman."

"Jesus Christ! You shot down a helicopter!" Tom gasped.

"Ed said it, you're not in Kansas anymore, Tom. They were shooting at us."

Pinafore motored over to where the helicopter was half submerged. There is a man in the water flailing his arms.

"Girls, we're going to fish that guy out. Denise, you watch him, Kelly, you watch everything else. You see something hinky shoot first, then ask permission. Got it?" Ed said.

"Got it."

"Got it."

Denise steps to the rail of the boat and holds her H&K unwaveringly on the man in the water. Kelly walks forward to the bow and looks seaward.

"Liz, take the helm, please. Tom give us a hand. Let's see if we can get that guy out of the water."

Liz moves behind the wheel.

"OK." Tom walks to the side of the boat next to Kelly.

"Heraldo, you have an ETA on the authorities?" I asked.

"They said soon. That could mean tomorrow or next week."

The helicopter is upside down and only a few feet of it are now above the water. *Pinafore* pulled alongside of the man in the water. Liz stopped the engine, puts it in reverse for a second, then goes back to neutral. The boat stops and rocks gently in the water. I placed a ladder over the side. The survivor, obviously losing his strength, flails to the ladder. Ed, Tom, and I reached down and pulled him to the deck. He lay on his back, gasping for breath.

"Are you hurt? *Estás herido*?"

The man shakes his head, (gasping), no.

"*Hablas inglés*?" I asked.

"*Si.*"

"Where is the other guy?"

Still gasping. "Shot. Strapped to seat."

"Was he the pilot?"

"*Si.*"

"OK, let's get him on the forward deck." Ed and Tom drag the man forward.

"The sport fisherman is leaving. He's not coming this way." Heraldo said.

"Kelly. Anything?" I asked.

"No."

"Liz. Anything on the radar?"

"Just Charlie and the sport fisherman."

"Liz, head for the island. We'll stay there tonight."

Liz moved the throttle forward and steered toward the island. The helicopter sinks below the water. We arrived at the island without further incident, though I'm not sure how one could top an air assault. Donkey Island, as far as I could tell, was devoid of donkeys— or goats, for that matter. According to the chart, it was a couple of miles across. Atypically, the elevation ascended fairly abruptly from the sandy beach to about 200 feet. There were a few trees, but mostly it was covered with seagrass and scrub. The crew and Charlie Whitt were sitting around the *Pinafore's* cockpit table eating dinner.

"Guess I missed all the excitement," Charlie said.

"Next time, maybe they'll come at you first." Ed said.

"I don't do rough stuff."

"I don't blame you, Charlie." I said.

"Are you just going to leave that guy on the beach?" Tom asked.

"Yep. He tried to kill us once. I'm not going to give him another chance. We left some water." I said.

"And he has lots of goats. He can eat one of those." Ed said.

"Heraldo, does it make sense that they would bring that chopper out here just as a gunship?" I asked.

"I doubt it. They sent the copter after us because they thought we would be easy. When it went down, I suspect the passengers departed on the sport fisherman."

"Meaning Dieter. Yeah. That's what I think, too. We'll ask him tomorrow." I said.

"If the goats don't, eat him." Ed said.

Everyone but Tom laughs.

The next morning, the guys piled in the dingy and headed for the beach. I untied the survivor's hands and handed him an egg and bacon sandwich and a couple of bottles of water. He wolfed down the sandwich and drank from one of the bottles. Ed, Tom, and Heraldo watched as I kneeled in front of him, so we were face to face. I pointed at Tom and Heraldo. "Those two men have some questions for you. They are both from international police agencies and are very nice men. They believe in rules and due process. I suggest you answer their questions. If you don't, my friend and I— " pointing at Ed— "will ask the questions. We don't care about rules and due process." I reached behind my back and pulled out a seven-inch sheath knife and held it inches from the man's nose. "This is a Ka-Bar. You will notice the razor-sharp blade— I took exception to you trying to kill my wife and I will delight in showing you the extent of my displeasure. Either way, you will answer our questions. It's up to you. Play nice with these kind gentlemen or I will remove your fingers and feed them to the goats. *Entiendes?*"

The man's eyes were wide. He nodded his head vigorously. "*Si, Si.*"

"My friend and I are going to the boat. When we come back, you will have satisfied these pleasant gentlemen. If not, you will still tell me everything, but you will never leave this island. *Entiendes?*"

"*Si!*"

I stood, nodded at Ed, walked to, *Gilbert & Sullivan*, pushed it into the surf and climbed aboard, then motored back to *Pinafore*. Ed sat quietly while I steered.

"Damn, bud, you even scared me."

I chuckled. "I doubt it. He pissed me off. Can you imagine that SOB shooting at those little girls?"

Ed laughs. "Those little girls, as you call them, shot that helicopter down with him in it."

"Well, he better talk, or I'll cut his fucking nuts off."

"And feed them to the goats."

"That too."

CHAPTER TWENTY-FOUR

The crew and Charlie Whitt are sitting around the cockpit table eating lunch. Tom and Heraldo had been back from the island for about thirty minutes. Heraldo was telling us about the interrogation of the shooter who was still on the inland. "Well, he talked."

Tom added, "We couldn't shut him up. He literally pissed in his pants."

"That's called due process. Spelled D, E, W." Ed said.

There was some giggling.

"So, what did he say?" I asked.

"He is a gun for hire. He was told he was a bodyguard. When they saw us, he and the pilot were told to go out and scare us away. He said he has done work for them before. He always reported to a guy named Dieter. Described him as big, very scary. Bald, he thinks, albino with a scar on his left cheek." Tom said.

"Charlie, is that the guy you saw in the Hilton?" I asked.

"Yep, that's Dieter."

"They arrived ahead of us because they picked up radio chatter from Charlie and his buddy." Heraldo said.

I looked over at Charlie, but he avoided my gaze. I decided to leave it alone for a while.

"Did they find the gold?" Liz asked.

"I don't think they looked. Without mentioning the gold, we asked him what they were doing on the island." Heraldo said.

"He didn't know. They had only been there a few hours. He just said he was there as a bodyguard for Dieter." Tom said.

"I doubt that. You would never hire a bodyguard from the yellow pages. You want somebody you trust. More likely, he was a gunny that was hired to take care of us." I said.

"He said on the flight out, there were two other men in the copter. He didn't know them, but they seemed important." Heraldo said.

"*Die Auserwählten* executives?" Liz asked.

"He was never on the boat, but he thinks there were four or five on the sport fisherman." Tom said.

"We have a few names and descriptions of all of them. I know one by name and believe I know two by description. Our pool side visitor at CrewsInn is one." Heraldo said.

"Can we look for the gold tomorrow?" Liz asked.

"That's why we came here, right?" I said.

She grins and clasps her hands together, "Oh, good."

The next morning, we took turns ferrying everyone over to donkey island in *Gilbert & Sullivan*. Charlie was already on the beach.

"Does anyone know what we are looking for?" Tom asked.

I laughed, "I don't know about the rest of you, but this is my first treasure hunt on a deserted island. This seems to be the perfect time to say I don't have a clue." I laughed at my own joke. "Heraldo, any ideas?"

"Look for something that doesn't belong, would be my guess."

"Too bad we don't have a metal detector." Ed said.

Elizabeth looked at Charlie. "Maybe Charlie has one on his boat."

"Sorry, wish I did."

"Ed, before we get started, let's take a look at our buddy." We both walked to where the shooter was sitting in the sand. His hands were still bound. Charlie followed us over. "I gave him some water, says he's hungry."

"Tough." Ed said.

OK, let's get started. I said.

"May I suggest we divide up into teams of two?" suggested Heraldo.

"OK, with me." I said.

"Then I suggest Liz and Ed follow the beach around to the left. Tom, you and Charlie take the right side of the beach. You, Kelly, Denise, and I will walk toward the center of the island." Heraldo said.

"When we get up that hill, it would be a good idea to keep an eye seaward. It would be bad form to allow someone to sneak through our back door." I said.

"Exceedingly good idea. Let's also make sure we all have water and hand-held radios." Heraldo said.

The group checks their packs or belts.

"OK, good luck." I said.

For an hour or more, we thrashed around the low scrub. I was always looking over my shoulder. The good news, once we got up the dune or hill, it was sort of a plateau and offered a good few of the sea beyond. We occasionally caught sight of the others, but frequently checked in with the radios.

"Over here! I found something!" Denises yelled.

Heraldo, Kelly and I ran to where Denise was standing. Trying to catch my breath, I stammered, "What did you find?"

Denise pointed down to the sand. "I think it's a grave." The three of us looked closer. Heraldo bent down and moved some weeds and debris from a wooden marker. "I think you're right." He pulled the marker out of the ground.

"Should you do that?" Demise asked.

"He won't mind." He brushed off the sand, opened a water bottle, and rubbed some water over the face of the marker. There is an inscription, *Viel Glück mein lieber Freund.*

"What's it mean?" Denise asked.

"My German is rusty, but I think it says, 'Good luck soon my friend.'"

"It says 'Good luck my dear friend,'" Kelly said. Everyone looks at her. "I spent a year in Germany with a boyfriend."

"Well, at least we know the Germans were on the island." I said.

Heraldo moved the marker into the sun. "Better than that, Germans from U-530. Look at the corner here." He pointed at some scratches on the wood.

"You don't have to read German to see that says U530." I said.

"Well, it is late. Shall we go? Perhaps the others have been more fortunate." Heraldo said. Heraldo respectfully replaces the marker in the sand.

Our rendezvous took another forty-five minutes and then we ferried everyone back to *Pinafore*. Tired and dirty, I suggested everyone take a shower— a 'short one please.' Ed and Heraldo fixed a simple but tasty meal.

Then we sat around the cockpit drinking coffee, beer, and bourbon. "What are we going to do with our friend on the beach?" Liz asked. "When I took him dinner, he looked like one big mosquito bite."

"We turn him over to the Federals if they ever get here. Otherwise, we take him with us, then dump him overboard." I said.

"You wouldn't?" Tom asked incredulously.

I laughed. "Just kidding."

Ed chimed in, "Sounds good to me. A watery grave is perfect for him. He can join his pilot buddy."

"That's too good for him, buried at sea. It's an honorable thing." Charlie said.

I bolted straight up. "What did you say?"

Charlie jumped back. "What?— I said some of my friends were buried at sea. It's what the Navy does. It's a very honorable way to be buried. Several of my shipmates were buried at sea."

I put my drink down. "Tom, did any of that Army Intel stuff show missing sailors or deaths on U-530?"

"No, not that I remember."

"Heraldo, how about you? Did your guys dig up anything like that?"

"No, nothing."

"Then who's in that grave?"

"What?" Heraldo said.

"Good luck, my dear friend. That's not an epitaph, it's a message." I said.

The next morning, we were up at dawn. Nobody wanted breakfast, so we overloaded *Gilbert & Sullivan* and headed for the beach. We looked like a Marine assault team as we all ran ashore and clambered up the hill. The shooter looked terrified until he realized we weren't coming for him. We all stood around the grave marker, not sure what to do next. I broke the ice. "Ed, hand me the shovel."

"Are you sure we should do this?" Liz asked.

"I agree. This could cause an international incident. Disturbing a war grave is a big deal." Tom said.

"Exactly. That's why it's a war grave. Only if I'm right, it isn't." I removed the soft earth from the grave with my hands, then continued to dig until the hole was about four feet deep.

"I think we should stop." Tom said.

"I don't." I kept digging while the others watched. "Girls, use those young eyes and keep your head on a swivel. We don't want to be caught in a mid-international incident."

The girls chuckled, stepped back, and looked out to the ocean.

"Hey bud, let me dig for a while."

"No argument from me." I handed Ed the shovel. "Thanks."

Ed dug deeper—

CLINK!

Everyone's eyes were riveted on the hole in the sand. Ed moved some more dirt. I got to my knees using my hands, I brushed the dirt and sand away. There it was! A metal box. I tried without success to move it. "Ed, if you can get the shovel under here, I think we can lever this thing out." Ed jammed the shovel blade under the box and pushed down on the handle. The box moved. "Guys, help me drag this thing out of here." Ed and Tom kneeled, then reached down into the hole and helped me. We coaxed and cursed until the metal box was sitting beside the hole.

"Look at those markings!" Liz said. "I think they're Japanese."

"I think so too. Ed, knock that lock off, please."

I straightened, stretched my back, and looked around. The girls were standing some yards from the excavation. "Girls! Anything?"

"No." Denise said. "What did you find?"

"I'll let you know in a minute."

Ed bangs at the ancient lock until it breaks. I turned back to the box, leaned over, and opened it. "OK, girls, come on over and watch." I removed some rice paper, and there lay three shiny gold bars, each stamped with a small Chrysanthemum.

"Those stamps are the Imperial Seal of Japan!" Liz said.

I stood and looked down into the box, "That, ladies, and gentlemen, is U-530's answer to a 401(k)."

***

AUTHORS NOTE:

On March 10, 1944, the Japanese submarine, *I-52* departed Kure[1] for Singapore then sailed for Lorient. Her cargo included 9.8 tons of molybdenum, 11 tons of tungsten[2], 2.2 tons of gold in 146 bars packed in 49 metal boxes,[1] 3 tons of opium[3] and 54 kg of caffeine[4]. The gold was payment for German optical technology. She also carried fourteen passengers, primarily Japanese technicians, who were to study German technology in anti-aircraft guns and engines for torpedo boats. In Singapore she picked up a further 120 tons of tin[5] in ingots, 59.8 tons of caoutchouc (raw rubber) in bales and 3.3 tons of quinine[6], then headed through the Indian Ocean to the Atlantic Ocean.

On June 6, 1944, the Japanese naval attaché in Berlin, Rear Admiral Kojima Hideo, signaled *I-52* that the Allies had landed in Normandy, thus threatening her eventual destination of Lorient. She was advised to prepare for Norway. She was also instructed to rendezvous with a German submarine on June 22, 1944. This message was intercepted and decoded by U.S. intelligence of the Tenth Fleet and a hunter-killer task force was targeted towards *I-52*.

On the night of June 22, 1944, about 850 nautical miles west of the Cape Verde Islands, *I-52* rendezvoused with *U-530*[7], which provided *I-52* with fuel, a Naxos[8] radar detector, an Enigma[9] coding machine, and two radar operators, and a German liaison officer for the trip through the Bay of Biscay.

Arriving in the area of the meeting on the evening of June 23d, a U.S. task force led by the escort carrier USS *Bogue*, launched flights of *Avengers* to search for the submarines. During the eventual encounter, *I-52* was sunk.

---

1. https://en.wikipedia.org/wiki/Kure,_Hiroshima

2. https://en.wikipedia.org/wiki/Tungsten

3. https://en.wikipedia.org/wiki/Opium

4. https://en.wikipedia.org/wiki/Caffeine

5. https://en.wikipedia.org/wiki/Tin

6. https://en.wikipedia.org/wiki/Quinine

7. *https://en.wikipedia.org/wiki/German_submarine_U-530*

8. https://en.wikipedia.org/wiki/Naxos_radar_detector

9. https://en.wikipedia.org/wiki/Enigma_machine

U-530 escaped undetected,[2] then proceeded with its orders to patrol the area around Trinidad.

On May 10, 1945, all U-boats were instructed to surrender. The *U-530* did not surrender[3] and disappeared until it appeared 60 days later in Mar del Plata. Captain Otto Wermuth did not explain why his submarine had jettisoned its deck gun, why the crew carried no identification, or why it had taken him more than two months to surrender.[4]

CHAPTER TWENTY-FIVE

Pinafore at Anchor – Donkey Island, Day Two

Back aboard *Pinafore*, we were in the cockpit engaged in our favorite pastime— eating. Charlie was with us. The shooter was still on the beach.

"Why did you leave it in the hole?" Liz asked.

"Liz, it's been sitting there for eighty years. Nobody will bother it for a few more days and I didn't want the shooter to see it." I said.

"Where's the rest of it?"

"Greedy, greedy. Liz, you always want more." I laughed.

"That's not true, but we seem to be in the mystery business, and it's the logical question."

"She's right. Where *is* the rest of it?" Ed said.

Tom opened another beer and had a drink. "What are we going to do with the stuff we found?"

"I guess you're going to put your kids through school with your share." I said.

"I can't take any of that gold!"

"Will you please stop teasing him? He's going to have a stroke." Liz said.

"Sorry Tom, but you need to lighten up." I said.

"So, what are we going to do with it?" Ed asked.

"That's up to Heraldo. He's running things. Who owns the gold?"

"I'm not sure. The Japanese will want it back, but I don't see that happening. The Germans will have their hands out. Since it was found in their territory, you can bet the Venezuelans will want a share. And yes, believe it or not, I can see the possibility of this intrepid crew receiving a share."

"Wow, that would be nice." Kelly said, giving Denise a high five.

"For now, I think we use it as bait. Maybe we take one bar and show it in all the wrong places. Tell everyone that we found the whole cargo. Use the island as a big trap." Heraldo said.

"You spread that around. You'll have a thousand people out here in 24 hours." Ed said.

"Ah, point well taken. Ideas?" Heraldo asked.

"The same tactic as last time. Let Charlie tell his friend that we found something, but not sure what." I said.

"How about we let our shooter do it? He must suspect we found something. Turn him over to the local police. If we don't press charges, they'll cut him loose and he'll run his mouth like all crooks do. Maybe he'll go right to Dieter." Ed suggested.

"And to make sure he says the right thing, we let him overhear our rehearsed conversations. Give him enough to know our next stop, wherever that is," Liz said.

Heraldo said, "a good idea, but we risk him being fearful of Dieter, in which case he tells his friends— "

"And we have the same thousand people here." Ed interjected.

"I think that leaves Charlie and his friend Mike. Should they be overheard, only Dieter and his associates will know what they are talking about," Heraldo said.

"Charlie, does your buddy have any hint of what we are doing out here?" Ed asked.

"No, I just told him you were anxious to come out here to dive on some coral. I don't think he believed it. This area is not known for that."

"Then I think that settles the matter. Now we have to come up with a radio message that will arouse Dieter's curiosity without his suspicion." Heraldo said.

I took another sandwich from the plater in front of us. "Well, we better come up with something before we drink any more beer."

The crew laughed.

"Keep it simple. Charlie just say we found traces of an old wreck, and we want to stay longer and explore." Liz suggested.

"I better say a wreck of an old fishing boat, so he doesn't want to come over himself."

"Good. Keep it plain vanilla." Liz said.

"Plain vanilla?" Heraldo asked.

"Uninteresting, boring."

"Ah *si*, very good."

"Assuming we're going to turn the shooter over to the authorities—"

"I thought we were going to drown him." Ed interjected.

"We have to convince him that all is normal, so he doesn't send the aforementioned hoards here. So, tonight, let's have a barbecue on the beach. That will deliver the message and give us all a break." I said.

"Great. Girls, if you help me get the food ready, I'm sure Mr. Colombo and Mr. Spade will take the grill and charcoal over to the beach and get the fire started." Liz said. "Tom, you're in charge of getting tables, chairs and coolers to the beach."

"I assume we want beer in the coolers?" Tom asked in jest.

"You assume correctly."

"What can I do?" Heraldo asked.

"Perhaps you would conjure up another one of your mother's recipes." Liz suggested.

"I'll make a salad," Kelly offered.

"I can make potato salad." Denise said.

"Wonderful, let's get to it," Liz said.

Ed and I dug out the grill and charcoal, which by now was at the bottom of the sail locker under tons of stuff. When I came up for air, I asked Charlie, "When is a good time to call Mike?"

Charlie looked at his watch. "Well, if he's out. Now is as good as any time."

"If we're going to be on the beach, maybe the call should wait until tomorrow, so we're not surprised," Tom suggested.

Ed stands holding the grill. "I think Tom has a good point."

"OK, Charlie, hold off on the call until tomorrow— when will Mike be coming out?"

"Usually around six in the morning."

"Then call him in the morning at what would be a normal time for you guys to talk."

By the time we had transported the grill, charcoal, paraphernalia, and crew to the beach, it reminded me of some troop movements I had been on, but less organized. Ed was a master chef when it came to hamburgers and barbequed chicken. Tired and happy, we all sat around the fire Tom had built in the sand, most drinking beer or soft drinks. Two were throwing a frisbee. A cooler sat beside a folding table topped with plates, cups, and food. The shooter sat about ten yards from the rest. I was sitting by the fire, I looked over to where Ed was lording over the grill. "Chef! How about those burgers?"

"One does not rush perfection." Ed replied.

"I'll take mine without perfection." Tom said.

The others laugh.

"For those unkind words, you may receive the one I dropped in the sand."

More laughing.

"OK, come and get it!" Ed said.

The sun was under the horizon, and it was almost dark. The crew sat around the fire, eating, drinking, telling lies and laughing. Charlie had been a little distant, but now walked over to me. "Mr. Spade, I can take that guy down the beach and make him disappear."

I looked at the prisoner sitting on the sand and eating. "Thanks Charlie, I think we will hold on to him for a while." Charlie nods and walks away.

"Did the prisoner get anything to eat?" Tom asked.

"I fed him." Liz said.

I turned to the prisoner and yelled. "Hey shooter! Do you want anything else to eat? *Máscomida?*"

"No, gracias."

"Guess he doesn't like your burgers, Ed."

"He had three. I fed him too."

Tom smiled. "For all your bluster, you guys are really softies."

"Tom, I think you will find Ed and I are the nicest guys in the world until somebody tries to hurt our family or friends. Excuse the overused expression— in the real world, rules and laws are often a long way off. As long as we can look in the mirror every morning and say we did the right thing, then life is good."

"Which does not include drowning the shooter, no matter how much we want to." Ed added.

Some laughing.

"But thank you for the sentiment." I said.

"I guess if we hadn't shot down that helicopter, they would have killed all of us and sunk the boat." He looked out over the water into the distance. "We would have just disappeared."

"Maybe he was trying to scare us. But when he came back for the second pass, I had to act or risk all of us. None of the stuff we do is worth the life of Elizabeth or any of you. As I told Liz long ago, these are not good people. They are paid soldiers in an army of thugs. They do what they do because they don't want to make an honest living, so they take their chances."

"Noted and accepted. And thank you."

"You're welcome, Tom."

"OK! Who wants another burger?" Ed asked.

Getting all the stuff off the beach at night with a buzz on had proved more than any of us could cope, so it remained on the beach. In the meantime, after a good night's sleep, we were enjoying a late breakfast in the cockpit. I looked at Heraldo, "Once we get your *Die Auserwählten* here, what are we going to do with them? The Gendarmes you're calling aren't responding. We can't get stuck on this island with twenty thugs without help and a place to put them."

"It may be over twenty, and you're right. My entreaties to the *Comando de Guardacostas* have met with little success."

Ed looked at me. "You and Elizabeth put Sabas in office. Call in your marker."

"While not entirely correct, your point is taken. The first thing he is going to ask is why isn't Argentina doing the heavy lifting?" I poured coffee in Heraldo's cup, then some in my own. "And he has a point."

"This is a joint effort between my country, France, and Israel. It will take months to work out the details, red tape, as you call it. We are so close to capturing these devils, I hate to lose our advantage."

"Forgive me, Heraldo, that's not an answer. Ed is right, we can call in a favor, but let's water it down a little so it's not a bitter pill." Liz said.

"How's that?" I asked.

"President Sabas is a good guy and I think he would help. But let's make it simple for him."

"Again, how?"

"We ask him to allow our special Ops to land choppers here. Corral the thugs and transport them. If we do our job right, our special Ops guys will be in and out in a few hours and no one will ever know they were here."

"This island is uninhabited so, no Venezuelans are in danger and there is no one around to watch."

"Except for the goats and donkeys. Heraldo what do you think?" I asked.

"Sounds marvelous to me. Are you really that close to the president?"

"We'll probably ask President Jackson to make the call. So, where do you want them?"

"In Argentina to stand trial."

You guys have some C-130s. Get one of them into Curaçao. Our guys will take the prisoners there and transfer them to your C-130." I said.

"Assuming we have any prisoners." Ed said.

"Assuming we have any prisoners." I said.

"Now, we have to bait the trap." Heraldo said.

Everyone looks at Charlie.

"You know these guys could come in by chopper instead of boat. If they do that, we won't see them until it's too late." I said.

"How are they going to transport two and a half tons of gold on a chopper? Ed asked.

"Good point. They will come by boat, probably two or three of them."

"Why is that important?" Denise asked.

Elizabeth and Kelly stand and start clearing the table.

"Our radar can see a boat out to 18 to 20 miles, maybe a little more. That will give us 20-30 minutes to prepare for their arrival." I said.

"OK, you have the logistics figured. What's the tactical plan?" Tom asked.

I passed some plates to Elizabeth below. "We can't make one until we have a day and time. Anyone have ideas?" I asked.

"Based on my days in narcotics, I figure we need to find Dieter and sit on him." Tom said.

"Yeah, he will lead the charge to get here." Ed said.

"Good in theory, but unless Charlie or Heraldo know where he stays, we're going to have to ask the Special Ops guys to sit at Curaçao for maybe days. I don't think that will sit well with them. So, Charlie, no talking with Mike until we get this all arranged."

"OK, mum's the word."

"I guess the first thing is to get the president in the loop. Then call General Barrett and get his help. I don't see anything happening until the day after tomorrow. Anything else?" I looked around the cockpit. "Then let's get the president on the phone. Hell, that could take a day." I sighed. "Next, we have to get all that stuff off the beach."

"We could just bury it." Ed said.

CHAPTER TWENTY-SIX

Pinafore at Anchor – Donkey Island, Day Three

We were all in the cockpit eating the breakfast Heraldo had prepared.

"Heraldo, if your law enforcement career doesn't work out, you may want to consider opening a restaurant." I said.

"Thank you. I would hate to turn a wonderful hobby into a quest for material gain."

My satphone rang. "Good morning, Madam President."

"Good morning. Rick tells me you want me to call President Sabas and request permission to invade his uninhabited island."

"Well, ma'am, I think invading is a bit strong. How about a temporary landing?"

"Have you talked to General Barrett about this?"

"No, ma'am, we wanted to get your approval first."

"OK, tell him I said OK, as long as we're not taking resources from something more important. At the moment, I can't think what that would be. I'll call you back as soon as I have talked to President Sabas."

CLICK.

OK, one down and one to go. I pushed a button on the satphone— "General Barrett, how are you . . ."

It was too hot for a Caribbean morning, Liz and the girls were sunbathing on the foredeck. Tom and Heraldo were on the beach looking after the shooter. He was getting par broiled, so we had to rig a tarp over him. Charlie, Ed, and I were in the cockpit drinking coffee. I was experimenting with the theory that if you drank warm liquid on a hot day, it would cool you off. So far, I didn't think much of the theory and was about to switch to cold beer, even if it was still breakfast time.

Ed put his coffee cup on the table. "Barrett is on board, so now what's the plan?"

"Charlie, do you have any more shovels or tools on your boat?" I asked'

"Just the shovel I gave you. I have some machine tools, nothing for digging."

"What I have in mind is as old as history, 5th century to be exact—

"Sun Tzu's, *The Art of War*," Ed said.

"Exactly—

"I've read your playbook," Ed said.

Elizabeth and the girls joined us in the cockpit. "Too hot for sunbathing." Liz helped herself to my beer.

"Anyway, we feign a retreat, more or less. Our prisoner will see us walk back and forth into the bush until one of us yells excitedly. Then soon he will see us carry the box we found and place it on the beach. Only it will be filled with sand."

"What do we do with the gold?" Liz asked.

"I'm getting to that— we will carry a duffle bag, chain, rope, cooler, and Charles' shovel, or anything that makes us look like we're working and digging. We carry one item per person across the beach and up the hill into the brush."

"Only the duffle and cooler will be filled with our weapons." Ed said.

"Right. Two of us will take the cooler back to the beach. It will contain two of the gold bars. We'll remove the bars and set them down in front of the shooter. Then take the cooler back to the dig site."

"His eyes will bug out." Charlie said.

"I hope so. Then later we'll bring the other bar to the beach."

"Eventually, the gold will be on the beach. Presumably, he'll think the cooler and metal box are full of gold too," Ed said.

"Right. And we will all be inland, well-armed."

"But why?" Kelly asked.

"When Dieter arrives with his thugs, he'll see the gold. His shooter will tell him all he's seen, and they will come looking for the rest of the gold and us."

"I get it. We won't be there." Kelly stands. "Is it OK to go swimming?"

"Sure, I'll go with you. Come on Denise." Liz said. The girls jump off the boat with what amounts to one large splash, getting the guys in the cockpit wet.

Tom and Heraldo came back aboard. We outlined the plan while they drank some beer. "Once we are up on the bluff where the shooter can't see us, we'll split into two-man teams and hike over to the left and right side of where Dieter will come ashore. Each team takes a flanking position on the beach." I said.

"I get it now. We cut off their escape until the special ops people get here." Tom said.

"I don't do rough stuff." Charlie says.

Everyone laughs.

"Charlie, I don't do rough stuff either. Unless somebody has another idea, this is the only way I can think of to keep the rough stuff to a minimum." I said.

"When do we start?" Heraldo asked.

"Charlie, make your call to Mike in the morning. I'll call Barrett to get things moving on his end. I figure— make that hope, Dieter will be here about noon, day after tomorrow.

I picked up a tissue and wiped off a smudge on what I referred to as our big radar screen. It was bigger than the repeater topside, so in that respect, it was the big screen. It was the morning of the day we were expecting our visitors. I was sitting at the nav desk with a handheld radio. Denise was on the other end of the radio. I studied the screen for a few moments. "Denise, it's them. They are about 18-19 miles out. Remember, you and Liz go to the right side of the beach. Now start hollering."

Denise was at the gravesite. "Yes, sir. Here we go."

I put down the radio and picked up the satphone and dialed a number. I waited while the phone went through all the macerations of up links, down links and scrambling.

Finally, a familiar voice answers, "General Barrett. Now would be a good time— Wait one." I looked at the radar screen. "Looks like two boats, 35 minutes max. — OK, Thanks." I slid out of the desk and ran up the companionway.

At the gravesite Denise is yelling, "Hey everyone! Up here! Up here! Hurry! Up here!"

The crew on the beach ran up the incline from the beach toward the shouting.

I was in *Gilbert & Sullivan* but could hear Denise shouting. I gave the throttle a boost, then cut off the engine as the dingy slid up on the beach. I jumped out, pulled it further up on the sand, then ran toward the shouting.

I met Tom and Elizabeth on the way down, carrying the gold box with the Japanese markings. Elizabeth winked at me, then shouted, "Look! We found the gold, we found the gold!" She and Tom continue to the beach, where they set it down and return to the hill.

The prisoner watches the activity intently.

I trotted up to the others standing around the gravesite. "Kelly, you and Denise use the cooler and carry the first two gold bars to the beach. Take them out of the cooler and put them on top of the metal box Liz just took down."

Kelly and Denise place two of the bars in the cooler. "Damn," said Denise, "this stuff is heavy."

"They're thirty pounds apiece. OK, off you go. Make sure the shooter sees them."

"He'll see them."

"Charlie, use the duffel and take the other bar down and do the same thing. Get back here fast."

"Right." He bends down and loads the gold in the duffel bag. Then walks to the beach.

I took a quick look at my watch. "Ed, when Kelly gets back, the two of you start your swing around to the left beach."

"OK, just remember not to let any of them get behind us."

"I'll do my best but keep your head on a swivel."

Kelly and Denise arrive. "Girls, you're our heavy artillery. Keep those guys on the beach. Don't let them get back to their boats. You'll be shooting toward each other. Do you know how setup a field of fire?" The girls looked puzzled. "Never mind, just don't shoot each other. I don't want any friendly fire accidents.

Liz walked up.

"Liz, you and Kelly take your places on the right beach."

Liz stepped over to me and gave me a kiss. "You be careful."

"I love you." I had a feeling of sadness as I watched Liz walk off, she was my everything. Not for the first time, I wondered what brought the two of us to such an enigmatic place in time and space.

Heraldo and Charlie walked up. Charlie was chuckling. "That guy's eyes almost popped out of his head. I couldn't resist telling him we found tons of the stuff."

I snapped out of my funk. "Good. OK, you and Heraldo get to the other side of this hill and hunker down."

"On our way." Heraldo said. They walked off, away from the beach, toward the other side of the island.

"Well, Tom, I guess you and I wait."

Looking at the M14 in my hands. "Is that the infamous automatic rifle?" Tom asked.

I looked down at the M14. "One and the same."

"I'm glad I'm on this side of it."

I looked around the immediate area. "Well, let's find a place that's protected and comfortable. We have a few minutes." Tom and I looked over the area until we found a shallow swale that commanded what might be called the path to the gravesite. In any event, nobody was coming up the hill without us seeing them. We waited a while. I looked at my watch for the 100th time. "I'm going to take a look over the rise. Watch Betsy for me."

"Great, you named it."

I grinned at him. "Not really— be back in a minute." I crawled to the crest of the hill and looked over. The sport fisherman and a trawler were anchored off the beach. Three men were climbing over *Pinafore* and two were on *Spankey*. Three dinghies were just landing on the beach. I backed away and scurried back to Tom. I whispered, "should be any minute they just hit the beach. You any good with that pistol."

He whispered back, "Now is a hell of a time to ask me that. Yes, I'm good with it. But I'm much better with a pencil and a calculator."

"Sorry about the accountant crack." I got lower to the ground. "Here they come." I whispered.

Ed and Kelly are concealed behind some brush and a small dune to the left of the landing area. All the boats were anchored to their right, or about 2 o'clock from their position. Ed and Kelly watched as several dinghies land on the beach. The occupants climbed out of the small boats and onto the beach.

Ed whispered into Kelly's ear, "That big SOB must be Dieter."

Kelly nods.

Dieter climbs out of an inflatable dingy and walked up the beach. He sees a man sitting on the sand. His hands are bound. Dieter walked over to the shooter. "So, you have survived."

"*Sí,*"

"Where are the others?"

Nodding with his head, "They are up on the hill. They have discovered gold."

"Ha, don't be foolish."

"It is true comandante. Look there on the beach. You will see for yourself."

Dieter walked to where the metal box and the gold bars were sitting in the sand. He picked up one of the bars. Then looked back at the shooter.

"There is more. They are up the hill digging for the rest." The shooter said.

Dieter looked up the hill and turned to his men. "You two stay here. The rest of you come with me. Untie him." Pointing to the shooter.

Dieter moved up the hill, followed by ten of his men.

From the right side of the beach landing area, Elizabeth and Denise watched from a rise halfway between the beach and the crest of the hill. The water and the anchored boats are to their left or at 11:00 o'clock. They watched as Dieter talked with the shooter. Dieter turned to look, then walked to the staged gold bars. As Liz and Denise watch, Dieter and ten of his men move up the hill towards the ambush.

Tom and I tried to get lower in the hole. As usual, the waiting was the hard part. "Here they come." I whispered. Dieter and four men, then six more men, walk over the crest of the hill toward where Tom and I are concealed.

I waited, then waited some more. "Stop!"

Dieter and his men stop.

"Throw your weapons on the ground."

"Who are you?" Dieter scowled.

"INTERPOL. You are under arrest."

"I think not. I think I kill you instead."

Bang!

Tom fired his pistol. One of Dieter's men falls face forward in the sand. Dieter looks at his fallen man.

"Throw down your weapons and raise your hands or we will kill you!" I yelled.

The man farthest to the rear turned and ran down the hill, yelling. In seconds, the others follow. I stood from our hidden position, followed by Tom.

"As you can see, we are well-armed. Now, do as I say."

We could hear automatic weapon fire coming from the beach.

Ed and Kelly watched as Dieter's men ran down the hill toward the dinghies. "Kelly! Stitch some rounds in front of those men."

Kelly stood, aimed, and fires her H&K.

RATATRATATRATATRATATRATATRATATRATATRATATRATAT!

Rounds from Kelly's gun impact and shoot geysers of water in front of the fleeing men. One of Dieters' men turned and fired a rifle in Ed and Kelly's direction.

BANG! BANG! BANG!

Kelly stood again and fired at the man, cutting him down.

RATATRATATRATATRATATRATATRATATRATATRATATRATAT!

Ed yelled at her, "Never stand up like that! You'll give away your position and get us both killed!"

Kelly ducked immediately and turned to Ed. Her eyes widen. "Ed, behind you!"

Ed turned, fell to his back, bringing up his shotgun.

BOOM! BOOM! BOOM!

A man standing feet away splayed backward. He and his M16 are flung to the sand.

Denise, fire into those dinghies and sink them!" Liz yelled.

Denise takes aim.

RATATRATATRATATRATATRATATRATATRATATRATATRATAT!
RATATRATATRATATRATATRATATRATATRATATRATATRATAT!
RATATRATATRATATRATATRATATRATATRATATRATATRATAT!

Geysers of sand and water stitch across the small inflatable boats. Rounds from Denise's gun shredded the boats until there were just pieces of rubber floating in the water.

Staying hidden behind the dune, Liz yells, "Everyone drop their weapons! Put your hands up! Do it now!"

"The men on the beach look at each other."

From his position on the left side of the beach, Ed yells, "Kelly! Fire a burst in the air."

RATATRATATRATATRATATRATATRATATRATATRATATRATAT!

Ed looked over his protected position at the men on the beach. *"Suelta tus armas. Ahora!"*

The men throw their weapons in the sand.

"De rodillas! Manos detrás de la cabeza!" Ed yelled.

The men got on their knees with hands behind their heads.

"Si te mueves, será sasesinado!"

On the right flank Denise looked at Liz. "What the hell does that mean?'

"He said don't move or you will be killed." Liz said.

"Works for me."

From our position on the hill, we could hear the automatic gunfire. Dieter turned abruptly.

"Yes, that's my men taking charge of the beach."

Dieter walked toward the beach.

"Stop! Put your hands behind your head."

Without turning, Dieter moved his right hand to his belt.

BAM BAM BAM BAM BAM BAM.

I fired a string of rounds across the back of his legs. Dieter went down screaming.

"Jesus, did you have to shoot him?" Tom asked.

I pointed the M14 at Dieters' remaining associate. "On the ground!" He jumped to the ground, hands over his head. "I just clipped his wings. Look in his belt."

Tom walked over and kneeled next to Dieter.

"Careful," I warned.

Tom stood. "You will not believe this. A Luger." He removed the magazine, ejected the round in the chamber, then threw the gun to me.

"Dieter, you watch too many movies," I said. "The Nazis quit using these things in '43. He probably has a Schmeisser in his underwear."

"What's a Schmeisser?" Tom asked.

"Nazi submachine gun. See if his friend has a Luger."

Tom searched the man on the ground.

Suddenly, there is a roar of engines. Two V22 Osprey's pass low overhead orbit into the wind and settle on the beach, throwing sand and dirt everywhere. In what seemed like one motion, the two aircraft land and disgorge Marines who line up Dieter's thugs and cuff them with zip ties.

"Come on, let's get Dieter and his friend down the hill."

"I'm not carrying that guy. You shot him, you carry him."

We left Dieter in the sand and walked down the hill to where all the excitement was. I looked up and down the beach. My heart tightened with dread.

"She's OK, helping a guy that got creased a little," Ed said, coming up from behind.

I let out the lung full of air I didn't realize I was holding. "Anybody hurt?"

"None of the good guys. The bad guys have one dead. I haven't seen Charlie or Heraldo."

"I told them to get lost, so I guess they did. There is another dead guy on top of the hill."

Staff Sergeant Williams walked up to the three men. "Hey Sarge. How are you doing?" I asked.

"I think we're good here. Before I forget, I'm supposed to tell you *Semper Fi* from Captain Schultz. Do you know him?"

"Sure do, great guy. Is he OK?"

"Far as I know. He was sitting behind a bunch of radios last I saw him. He said to tell you office pogues don't get out much."

I laughed, "That's OK, he's done his bit." I looked up to see Heraldo and Charlie trotting down the hill. Breathless, Heraldo ran up and said, "We heard the shooting stop and saw the airplanes come over, so we assumed the fight was over. By the way, we found the goats."

I chuckled, "Good to know. "Heraldo, this is Staff Sergeant Williams. I assume you will be going back with him to help transport the prisoners."

Heraldo shook hands with Williams, "If that's alright with you Staff Sergeant Williams?"

"You call, we haul."

Heraldo laughed, "*Si*, yes, very good."

"Speaking of prisoners," I said, "The object or objective of this whole exercise is up on the hill. You'll need a corpsman and a sky crane."

"Big, huh?"

"He has his own zip code. Are you going to have room for all these guys on those two birds?"

"I just asked for another one. Should be here in about 40 minutes."

Elizabeth, Kelly, and Denise walk up to the men. "Staff Sergeant Williams, it's nice to see you again," Liz said.

"You as well, Ma'am. I see you still have your window dressing with you."

Liz laughed and put her arms around Kelly and Denise. "We sure do. They just gave these jerks a lesson on fields of fire."

"Fields of fire. Sure, you weren't in the Corps?"

"Does sleeping with a Marine for 20 years count?"

SSgt Williams laughed, "Yes, ma'am, I'm sure it does."

CHAPTER TWENTY-SEVEN

Heraldo packed his gear and left with SSgt Williams so he could escort his prisoners back to Argentina. Charlie boarded *Spankey* and departed for parts unknown. The following day, we left the beautiful and serene Donkey Island, having never seen a donkey, and set sail for Tobago, retracing our route back to Pirates Bay. We were in the cockpit eating breakfast and doing our after-play review of the previous weeks. Elizabeth put her coffee cup down. "Well, it would have been nice if we had found the gold."

"We found it." I said.

"I mean the other 48 boxes."

"So do I."

"What do you mean?" Liz said.

I put my cup down next to hers and sat forward. "The first dive. Remember when Charlie said he found the deck gun and torpedoes?"

"Yes."

"The gold was down there too."

"It was! How do you know?" Liz asked.

"U-530 could have dumped the gun and torpedoes anywhere in the Atlantic, which means they had a specific reason to go to Little Tobago. And Charlie was way too eager for us to leave."

"That's right. He didn't want to stay in the bay, he wanted to come here." Ed said.

"Then on the way over to Donkey Island, using another channel besides 16 so we didn't hear him, he made a call to his buddy, Mike, or maybe even Dieter before he was supposed to. Then instead of sailing with us, he stayed way back—"

"I remember you thought he fell asleep. That doesn't mean he called Dieter." Liz said.

"In a million square miles of water, how did Dieter find the one island we were headed for? Charlie hung back, hoping Dieter would be waiting for us. Then, when we were out of the picture, he would go back and bring up the gold. But he didn't count on the helicopter. When we shot it down and Dieter ran, Charlie had to play along with us. And no one was more surprised than Charlie when we found that grave with the box of gold in it."

Tom finished a mouthful of eggs. "That's why he wanted to get rid of the shooter. He didn't want the entire Caribbean underworld to know about the gold."

"Well, now he'll go back and get it," Liz said.

"Let him. Everyone knows about it now. He'll spend weeks pulling it off the bottom only to have the Trinidad Navy waiting to scoop it up. Like Heraldo said, by the time Trinidad, Argentina, and the Germans and maybe the Japanese spend years fighting over it, he'll be lucky to get a finder's fee. If he's still alive."

"He'd been better off telling us about it." Liz said.

"Probably. Now every treasure hunter in the Caribbean will be looking for it. Charlie will get drunk some night and run off at the mouth. It's in shallow water. Somebody will find it, and soon."

"Well, I would have liked to have seen it. Maybe when it's found, it will be put on display." Liz said. Elizabeth's phone rings. "Good morning, Madam President."

"Good morning. Any civilians around?" The president said.

"No. Ma'am, we are down to the original six."

"Put me on speaker."

Elizabeth pushes a button on her phone. "You are on speaker."

"OK, I want you all to go to Havana and meet with some magazine photographers. Bruno and I think some exposure in some national magazines will help sell this new democratic movement and help tourism, which seems to be their only source of hard dollars, at least for now."

"Once we get there, what do you want us to do?" Liz asked.

"The magazine editor is a friend of mine and clued in on the *Pinafore's* mission. So, stick with the usual tourist routine. We want to use the boat as background for the photo shoot. She will have some models with her, so just go along with the program for a few days."

"Yes, ma'am."

I leaned to the phone, "Madam President. Using the *Pinafore* in photographs, as they say in the movies, could blow our cover."

"Can't be helped. It's the only place where we can control the process. This is propaganda in the truest sense, and I don't want some Cuban bureaucrat telling us what we can and can't do."

"When do you want us there?" I asked.

"Depends on how fast you can get there. I told her you were not close, so it might take you a week. That about, right?"

"We can probably be there next Thursday."

"OK, I'll tell her to meet you the following Monday morning. Let me know where you tie up."

"Yes, ma'am." I said.

"One other thing. I want you all to take in the sights, do the tourist thing, keeping your eyes and ears open. I want you to assess the public opinion of this transition government. Also, get their opinion of the new status with the U.S."

"Except for Ed and Liz, none of us speak Spanish, at least well." I said.

"See if you can get Heraldo to stick around for a few days. He owes us one."

"Ma'am, Heraldo left a couple of days ago. He took the prisoners to Argentina." Liz said.

"Then give Teddy and Adel Sabas a call. See if they want a vacation in Havana on me. I'd send Dr. Pérez down, but one never knows who he's working for."

"I'll call them." Liz said.

"Remember, for me, the important thing is ground intelligence. I hate to sound melodramatic, but that's the truth of it. I know it won't be a large sample, but do what you can, maybe take a trip to the country of some sort."

"I always wanted to see cigars made." I said.

"And rum" Ed said.

"OK, you get the idea. Talk to you later."

CLICK.

Pinafore slowly motored into Marina Hemingway, Havana, Cuba about a week later. The sail to Havana had been one of beautiful weather on a comfortable broad reach, port tack half the way. Then north of Dominican Republic, we turned more westward to an exhilarating close hauled, port tack to Havana. Winds were at 15 to 20 knots the whole time. We were able to get reservations at a Marina that dated to Hemmingway's fishing tournaments, and it now was named for the famous author. Ed and Kelly were on the bow, Tom and Denise were amidships, starboard side with boat hooks. Liz was on the stern with another boat hook. I was at the wheel. The chart showed the channel here was very narrow with coral on either side. It reminded me of a shorter version of the Nantucket channel.

"Coral on either side, so watch carefully, guys." I called out.

"What's the connection with Hemingway?" Tom asked.

"The guy is a God down here. I think he actually ran his fishing tournament out of this marina." I said.

Once tied up, as per usual, we sat around the cockpit drinking beer to celebrate docking without scratching the paint.

"We should drink mojitos in honor of Hemingway." Ed said.

"Or daiquiris." Liz added.

"I'll bet he drank beer, too." Tom offered. "What's the plan? Should we go into town?"

"Anything to get off this damn boat. How about some clubbing?" Liz said.

"OK, but we'll have to leave the girls here. They're not old enough." I said.

Denise and Kelly chimed in together, "We're old enough!

I laughed. "OK with me as long as we eat first."

In my day, we would go bar hopping, now I guess it's called clubbing. We caught a cab in front of the marina— an old Buick that had seen better days. It had room for ten, and that was just in the back seat. Downtown Havana, at least where the cab took us, was a scene of bars, nightclubs, and colored lights. Kelly and Denise gave instructions to the cabbie, and we ended up at the Habana Café. It was full of live music, dancing, laughter, and good food.

My favorite part of the club was the old cars and airplanes that decorated the place. Liz and I danced, then she took turns dancing with Ed and Tom. Other men in the club asked her to dance. So many men asked Kelly and Denise to dance. They never sat down.

"Damn, Tom, does your wife know you can dance like that? Ed asked.

"Of course, she does. Why do you think she married me?"

Liz returned from a trip around the dance floor. "My goodness, I'm exhausted. What a great time. Will you look at Denise and Kelly? Oh, to be 25 again."

I laughed, "You, my dear, are the perfect age, and I noticed you weren't being overlooked by what appears to be many admirers."

"Thank you, sweetie." Liz grabbed my hand, pulled me out of my seat, "Come on Sarge, dance with your wife."

"I thought you were exhausted."

"I've recovered." And we were off.

The next day we were all tired and hung over— except for Denise and Kelly— they found a shower, laundry and two handsome deck hands from a visiting yacht.

Liz was on her phone talking with Teddy Sabas. ". . . so, we thought you and Adel might join us. We always have room for a few more.

"Instead of staying on the boat, why don't we do this? You need to get to people that are inside the political machine. We have some influential friends, the Esperanza's. They have been after us to visit. Why don't we stay with them?

"Sounds perfect."

"No matter what they claim to be now, the Cuban *inteligencia* is still suspicious of everyone. But I'll work out a way to make introductions."

"I have an idea. Teddy, what does Mrs. Esperanza look like? I mean, is she attractive? Does she have a good figure?"

"The last time I saw her, she is what you Yankees call hot. Why?"

"Why don't we have her, and Adel be models in the shoot?"

"Really?"

"Sure, it's done all the time. What better way to break the ice? Tell them you met us when you were in D.C., which is true."

"So, you send Adel and Mrs. Esperanza an invitation to the photo shoot. That way, we can transition into a friendship."

"Exactly."

"Sounds fine to me. I know Adel will be pleased."

"OK, call when you get here, and we'll set it up."

On the prescribed day, the *Pinafore* and the adjacent dock were covered with photography paraphernalia. Models, producers, makeup artists, photographers, electricians, and assistants ran back and forth over the boat, to the dock, and back to the boat. The producer walked up to Liz.

"Liz, your two friends are quite beautiful. I also think you would make a wonderful addition to our shoot. One other thing . . . ."

With all the confusion, I was trying to negotiate the salon, to get to the galley, to get to the coffee. I wasn't having any luck, so I grabbed an uncovered spot on the settee and sat down. Ed and Liz were on the other side of the salon, in a tense discussion. Liz saw me and they made their way to where I was sitting. "Honey, they want Kelly and Denise to be in the shoot. Will that hurt their career?"

"I'm not sure. Where are they?"

"They're outside watching the setup."

"Ed, what do you think?"

"They won't be any good as field agents."

"Good, if the girls want to, let them. If nothing else, it might keep them out of harm's way."

"Great." Liz said. "Ed, one more thing, they want you too."

"Me!"

"They think you have the perfect physique for a mature man."

"I'm not mature!"

Liz stifles a laugh. "I'm sure it wasn't meant as an insult."

"I'm a seasoned, finely toned man."

I started laughing. "Wait until they see the scars. Your photo credit will read 'Zipper man.'"

Liz slugged me on the arm. "You should talk! Ed, I already told them you were a man of action. They said makeup and clothes will cover any deformity."

I laughed some more.

"I am not deformed!"

I laughed hysterically.

The next day, presumably the last day of the shoot, a half dozen models were using the *Pinafore* as a dressing room. The navigation station had been turned into a makeup cubicle complete with mirror and lights. I was doing a repeat performance trying to get some coffee, dodging woman, most of whom were all but naked. I turned to see Liz come out of the forward cabin. WOW! Her hair was up, and she was wearing camera-ready makeup, a lime sherbert colored sundress and heels. She walked over to me and gave me one of those a less than pleased eye arch thing she does.

"See anything you like?"

"Yes. I mean no. You look beautiful."

"Always the silver tongue devil. But thank you." She leaned over and kissed me on the cheek, then wiped off the lipstick off my cheek with her thumb.

"Liz, these women are all wearing high heels."

Two women came out of one of the aft cabins. Kelly and Denise chose that moment to come out of the other.

"Damn! Kelly and Denise are wearing them too."

Liz laughed. "All of us are wearing heels. It's a fashion shoot."

"They're going to tear up my decks!"

Liz steadied herself with the aid of my shoulder and removed her heels. "Dear, sometimes I worry about you. A half dozen beautiful, naked women running around, and you're concerned about your floor." She turned to the women. "Girls! Please wait until you're topside before you put on your shoes. Otherwise, my husband is going to have a stroke over his teak decks."

There is much giggling and laughter from the women.

Liz, Ed, Denise, Kelly, Adel and Mrs. Esperanza are featured with the professional models. Liz walked up to me as I was watching. "Don't Kelly and Denise look cute?"

"All of you look great! I think Adel and her friend Mrs. Esperanza have done this before."

"Adel said she and Sissy went to school in Paris together and worked summers as models."

"Where did the name Sissy come from?"

"Apparently, a nickname she picked up when she was a child. She invited us to a reception tonight, so be prepared."

"I didn't bring my tux."

She kissed me. "Coat and tie will be fine."

CHAPTER TWENTY-EIGHT

Esperanza Residence – Havana Cuba

The Esperanza Residence was a large pre-revolution affair, with beautiful furniture, paintings, sconces, and oriental rugs. I was dressed in a linin suit, Liz was in a white cocktail dress. We were greeted warmly by the Esperanza's who introduced us to several other couples. Teddy and Adel were already in attendance and soon joined us. When the Esperanza's excused themselves, the four of us walked onto a large patio to a formal buffet.

Elizabeth leaned into Adel. "I'm so happy you arrived. I was stretching my Spanish pretty much to the limit."

Adel was wearing a royal blue cocktail dress with matching jewelry. "I think perhaps you don't show you speak Spanish. I think it works better in our work."

"Thank you. I will take your advice."

The two women walk through the buffet line. Teddy and I followed closely behind.

"How's your father? I hear good things." I said.

"Very well, thank you. I don't see him as much as I would like."

"I thought he would put you in charge of oil production."

Both of us laugh loudly. The women turned.

"What is joke?" Adel asked.

"We will tell you later, dear."

The two couples sit and eat dinner in their laps.

"Will your children join you?"

"I think so. Initially, we were reluctant to bring them along, but if we're not home, I'll ask them to come down on Christmas break."

"We would love to have you for Christmas. It is quite the event." Teddy said.

"Yes. That would be wonderful." Adel seconded.

"Thank you." Liz looked at me. "Why don't we give that some thought?

"Consider me convinced."

Adel excused herself and walked away.

Turning to Teddy. "Do you suppose we could work in some dove hunting?"

"I'm certain that could be arranged. I have a new Beretta SO10 I want to try."

"Really. I have a Beretta EELL. It's not an SO10, but I love it."

"I don't blame you, the EELL is beautiful."

Adel returned and sat down. She looks worried. She glanced around to see if anyone was near, then quietly addressed the other three. "I was just in the *baño*. I overheard two women...."

Ed and I spent the next several days wandering the countryside visiting refineries, cigar manufactures, and eating at country roadside stands. If we were being followed, we didn't see them. Liz and the girls did the same, though I think they skipped the cigar manufactures in favor of shopping at the local *agros*.

A couple of days later, Liz was sitting at her vanity in the master stateroom, talking on the phone. ". . . the country people don't get what's going on. They are just trying to make a living. I think as the idea of collective farming subsides, they will see the benefit."

"How about the city folks?"

"Again, mostly ambivalent. They've heard it all before. Most would be happy to see their relatives in the states. They certainly like the idea of free travel."

"Any good news?" The president asked.

"They like the idea of more tourist dollars. There is a pretty sizable collection of tourists already here, but they think the U.S. could increase that substantially."

"So, this is all good, but prove it."

"Yes, ma'am, that pretty much sums it up. The good news was, I didn't hear any dissension. That brings us to the bad news."

"Now what?"

"We were at a party with Adel and Teddy, hoping to pick up some tidbits from the upper echelon. Adel overheard some conversation from the wife of someone who has a distinct dislike for Bruno and what he is trying to do.

"We're getting that from both sides."

"But this guy plans to arrest Bruno and take him before the Council of Ministers with enough incriminating information to have him put in prison, or worse."

"What information?"

"We don't know. The conversation ended."

"Great. Any ideas?" The president asked.

"First, keep Bruno in D.C. Second, Trust him or not, I think we need to get Pérez down here."

"I'll ask Bruno to stick around for a while, but I can't make him stay if he doesn't want to. I'll have Pérez call you. Explain the problem to him and see what he suggests."

"Yes, ma'am."

"And don't call me with any more bad news."

The days after Liz's call with the president were less than relaxing. The intelligence Adel picked up in the Esperanza Residence had put us on edge. There were no overt actions, not even a snide remark from any of the people we encountered. Nonetheless, we filled our fuel tanks and made sure the water was always topped off. Liz and the girls made a couple of trips to the *agros* for vegetables, eggs, and what meat they could find, which was mostly underfed chicken. I was sitting alone at the navdesk when my phone rang. It was the president. "Good morning, ma'am."

"Good morning. I need to talk with you in private for a moment."

"Yes, ma'am. Wait one." I slid out of the navdesk and walked to the forward stateroom and closed the door.

"Go ahead, ma'am."

"Sorry about the cloak and dagger stuff. When we're finished, you can tell who you like on a need-to-know basis."

"Yes, ma'am."

"I assume you know what Elizabeth told me the other day."

"About Bruno?" I said.

"Yes. Pérez is coming down there and hopefully will work things out. But I want all of you out of there pronto."

"Yes, ma'am."

"Do you know where that Nazi gold is?"

"Yes, ma'am, or I think I do."

"The Trinidad and Tobago government want it. Apparently, the mere knowledge of it is causing them headaches, which I won't go into. They say they're worried about crime, but politics is the overriding issue."

"Why don't they hire Charlie Whitt? He'd be tickled to death to show them, for a fee."

"Evidently, he's already been tickled to death. His boat was found 100 miles off Little Tobago, half-submerged. He wasn't on it." The president said.

"Oh, I didn't know."

"I would like you to meet with the British Submarine HMS *Hotspur* and show them where you think the gold is and give them what aid you can. Are you OK with that?"

"Yes, ma'am. Where do I meet them?"

"Have a pencil?"

"Just a minute, please." I hurried back to the nav station and slid behind the desk. "Go ahead."

"Meet the *Hotspur* at 19° 36' 58" N, 83° 57' 2" W at 9am on Friday."

I looked at the chart in front of me. "They must have thrown a dart at the map that's in the middle of nowhere." I said.

"I assume that's the idea."

"If it's OK with you, I'll put into the Caymans after our rendezvous. I can fuel and take on water. Maybe kick back for a day or so." I asked.

"Fine with me."

"What do I do with my CIA people?"

"Unless you think the British will try to 'burn, destroy or take you as a prize,' send them back."

"Me thinks you have read too much Hornblower." I chuckled.

"Patrick O'Brian, after *Master and Commander,* I was hooked. I can't put the dammed books down. Send the girls back so they can finish school. If you need them later, you can have them back."

"Yes, ma'am. Can Rick arrange a flight for them?"

"They can fly out with the magazine crew and the photographers. They're still down there but coming back tomorrow. It's our plane."

"I'll take care of it."

"One more thing, I told President Paula-Mae Medina that you will receive a 1% finder's fee for the gold. Talk soon."

CLICK.

I slid out of the nav desk and partially stepped up the companionway and stuck my head out. "Will you all come down here, please?"

The crew filed down into the salon and sat around the table.

"We just received new orders. Denise, Kelly, you two will fly home to finish your training. I'm sorry to see you go. I will give you my highest praise and any recommendations you need. Jerry McGuire will be told what superb agents you are. Get your stuff together. You fly out tomorrow with the photography crew." I laughed. "Maybe you can pick up a few more modeling gigs."

Denise and Kelly looked sad.

"You all have been very kind, and we learned so much. Perhaps you would let us work with you again," Denise said.

"And we got great tans." Kelly grinned.

"In places we normally wouldn't tan." Denise added.

We all laughed at their good-natured exit.

"Girls, there may be a stipend for finding that gold. If there is, the four of us will see that you two get your shares."

"That would be wonderful!" Denise said. The girls stood and walked to the rear cabins. Kelly could be heard telling Denise how she was going to buy a Corvette.

"As for the rest of us, we are to meet with a British submarine three days from now."

"What on earth for?" Liz asked.

"It seems the Nazi gold has ginned up a lot of interest, all bad."

"From the Brits?"

"No, its local politics. I guess their British roots run deep and Trinidad asked them to find help and recover it."

"Why don't they ask Charlie Whitt?" Liz asked.

"He has apparently met with an untimely death."

"Really?"

"One other thing. If there is gold, we are to receive a 1% finder's fee."

"Damn, bud, you can buy a bigger boat." ED said.

"The fee will be divided between the four of us and the girls."

"But I can't take—"

"Tom, I don't know the details, but the President of the United States just told me we would get a finder's fee, so just go with it. To save you all from doing the math, that's about two hundred grand each and I'm sure taxes will be involved, so you can't retire, but you can go on a nice vacation. For now, let's get ready to sail."

CHAPTER TWENTY-NINE

Pinafore - Two Hundred Miles West of The Cayman Islands

Re-provisioned, we got an early start the next morning. We sailed west then southwest to get around Cuba then headed almost due south or as us salts say, 171 degrees magnetic. Fortunately, we had a broad reach, port tack in about fifteen knots of wind: a couple of great days of sailing. On the morning of the third day, a large British submarine, supposedly *Hotspur*, surfaced about three hundred yards off our bow. The British Navy has been sailing in this area for some three hundred years, so I wasn't surprised that they nailed the navigation. They inflated and lowered a dingy with an engine, no less, and set a course for the *Pinafore*. The inflatable nudged against the starboard side of *Pinafore*. A distinguished-looking man in his mid-30s climbed the few steps of our ladder, stood on the deck, faced aft, saluted the flag, then turned and saluted me.

"Permission to come aboard, sir."

I returned his salute, "Permission granted and welcome."

We both stepped off the deck and into the cockpit.

"How do you do? I am Lieutenant Commander Ian Osborne."

I shook the offered hand. "A great pleasure, Lieutenant Commander. I'm Sam Spade. Turning to Liz, "This is my wife, Elizabeth."

Elizabeth shook hands with the Lt. Commander. "Hello Lieutenant Commander, may I get you some tea or coffee, or a soft drink?"

"I would love a cold Coca-Cola."

"Coming right up. Guys, anything?"

"Honey, bring up some sodas and we'll help ourselves." I turned to Ed and Tom. "These two are my closest friends, Ed Colombo and Tom Sawyer."

"Sam Spade and Tom Sawyer?"

I Laughed, "That's Tom's real name and I'm sure he has heard all the jokes, mostly from me."

Tom shook hands with Osborne. "How do you do? Very nice to meet you."

"Good afternoon, Commander, we don't get many visitors mid-ocean." Ed said.

"Full disclosure. Ed is with our State Department, and Tom is with our Federal Bureau of Investigation. Shall we all sit down?" I said.

We all sat around the cockpit table. Liz placed a bucket of cold drinks in the middle of the table, along with some chips. Liz sat next to me with a cup of coffee.

"So, how do you guys use a sextant when you're underwater?" I asked.

"Quite simple, we just step outside." Commander Osborne said.

Everyone laughed.

"What can we do for the Senior Service, commander?" I asked.

"As you know, we have been tasked with recovering some gold from a Nazi Submarine. Other than generalities, we don't know where to look. It was suggested that we ask you."

"We know where it is— maybe, but it's some 200 feet from the surface. How are you going to get it?"

"We'll put the boat on the bottom. Open a hatch and go out and get it."

"That simple?"

"Not quite, but we have done recovery work before."

Moving the bucket of drinks aside, I spread a chart on the table. "As you know, the submarine is long gone. As for the gold, I've never seen it, but I can tell you where I think it is, and by that, I mean, I'll bet the ranch on the location."

"Yes, well, despite the precarious tenure of your ranch. What makes you think you have found this submarine or its gold?"

"The submarine didn't surrender until some six months after the war. And before it did surrender to the Argentines, it was seen here." I pointed to a spot on the chart. "A witness saw the Germans dumping their deck gun and quote many boxes into the water. When we looked, we found the gun and torpedoes."

"But no gold."

"The bottom there is 230-280 feet. The diver we hired said there was no gold on the bottom."

"But you don't believe him."

"I don't. We found one box of the gold on an island some 200 miles to the west. Here." I pointed to the chart. "The box was found in a grave marked with a wooden marker etched in German with the words, *Good luck, my friend*. In the grave was a steel box containing three bars of gold."

"The box was marked with Japanese characters, and each of the bars was stamped with a Chrysanthemum." Liz said.

"The symbol of the Japanese emperor."

"Yes." Liz said.

"Plus, the wooden marker was etched with the numbers 530." I said.

"Why do you suppose it was left there?"

"Best we can figure, the captain left it there for a shipmate or relative. The important thing is we know the sub was in this bay," pointing at the chart. "And we know the gold was on the sub, and we know when it surrendered, it was not on board."

"So, you think it's in this bay?" Pointing to a place on the chart.

"I do. Did I mention after the dive, the diver tried to get us all killed? I think he went back to the bay and dived on the site again. He was probably pulling the gold off the bottom when he was killed. They found his boat with blood on the deck, but they never found him."

LCDR Osborne looked at Tom and Ed. "You gentlemen have unique qualities. One an expert in quantitative analysis and the other a representative of the U.S. Government. What do you think?"

"Deductive reasoning is probably more my line. In either case, one has to follow the facts. It's hard to ignore the ninety pounds of gold we found." Tom said.

"Once the diver surfaced, he spent most of his time trying to remove us from the picture. It wasn't because he coveted an antique deck gun," Ed said.

"I see. Well, we are under orders, so I guess we'll find out, won't we? How would you like to proceed?"

"On your sub."

"No, I'm afraid that would not be permitted. For one, you are civilians, and second, you are Yank civilians. Official secrets and all that. I'm sure you understand."

"I understand you can launch up to 30 Tomahawk missiles or Spearfish torpedoes, run 32 knots underwater, and this is your last cruise before you're decommissioned."

"Yes, well, your Department of State said we could expect full cooperation."

"Commander, I just came back from that island. It's a seven to eight-day sail, and I'm low on fuel and water. Fuel I'm not too worried about. We *are* a sailboat, but I absolutely cannot go without my bourbon and branch."

Smiling, Ed looks over at Osborne. "He means water."

"I am familiar with the term. Mr. Colombo, as I mentioned, your Department of State offered their full cooperation. As you are a member of that august organization, might I rely on your good efforts?"

"Wait one." I pulled out my phone and pushed a button. "Hello, hello. Rick. Hi, it's Sam Spade. I've run into a logistics problem. The Brits want us to go back down to Trinidad, but they don't want us near their sub. I have neither the fuel, water nor inclination to sail back down there— Because I like water in my bourbon, not in my diesel fuel— Yes, I mean it was contaminated. The water was crappy too, literally." I stood and climbed up on the stern holding onto the backstay with my spare hand. "How about this? The Caymans are about two days from here. Why don't I go in there and charter a plane? Ed can fly us down to Tobago, then we'll charter a boat to the island. Hell, we might beat the brits there."

I listened to Rick some more. "OK, sounds like a plan. See you then." I turned off the phone and looked at the assembled group. "He's coming down on one of our planes. Then we'll charter a boat and meet you at Tobago. Commander, you can ride down with us if you like."

"If I may ask, who is he?"

"The guy Ed and I work for."

"Commander, will you stay for lunch?" Liz asked.

True to his word, Rick was waiting for us when we put into the Caymans. He had chartered a new forty-foot sport fisherman and had it stocked with fuel and supplies. So, much to Liz's ire, we set off without so much as a shore-side shower. Commander Osborne went with the sub, but he was there to greet us when we arrived at Little Tobago Island. The following day, we began search operations as the Brits described it, which was mostly comprised of submerging *Hotspur* on top of the gold site and sending a diver out.

Commander Osborne was standing with the rest of on the stern of the chartered sportfisherman. The Commander finished talking on a handheld radio and turned to us. "They found one metal box that matches the description you gave us, but it's been opened and there is no sign of its contents. They're taking it aboard now. The divers said there are recent tool marks on the box where the lock should be."

"If the tool marks are recent, that must have been the work of our friend Charlie." I said.

"He's the diver, correct?"

"Yes."

"OK, they'll keep looking."

We all watched the empty spot in the water, where *Hotspur* sat 200 feet below. Occasionally bubbles would break the surface.

Forty-five minutes later, the sail of HMS *Hotspur* broke the surface, followed by the rest of the sub until its mammoth blue/black hull rose before them. Sheets of water cascaded off the steel skin, leaving a glistening leviathan before them. Hatches opened and men appeared on the sail and the hull below.

The radio squawks, "Lieutenant Commander Osborne."

"Yes, sir, go ahead."

"Ian, there is nothing down there but a 105mm gun and some old G7e torpedoes. The gun and the torpedoes are German WWII era. We found a steel box with Jap markings, but it was empty. Is that what we were looking for?"

Lt. Commander Osborne turns to me.

"Yes," I replied, "but there should have been 48 of those boxes."

"Sir, there should have been 48 unopened boxes." Osborne said.

"Sorry chap, nothing like that on the bottom."

"Right, sir. I'll chat with the U.S. Reps for a bit and get back to you."

"Very well. *Hotspur* out."

Everyone on the sportfisherman found a seat. Tom brought out some soft drinks from the galley.

"Well, we were beaten to the prize. Since we are here at the behest of the Trinidad government, I suspect we should let them decide on what's next." Osborne said.

"How long can you guys hang around?" I asked.

"I guess as long as Fleet says."

"Commander, we stand by our promise to assist President Paula-Mae Medina with the recovery of the gold. However, politically, I'm not sure this is the best use of anyone's time." Rick said. "I suspect voters will take a dim view of spending their money looking for what could be arguably called a myth."

"Right. I assume the captain will chat with the powers that be and tell them we are a bust. If they want to proceed, that will be up to them." Osborne said.

"I agree with Rick. But suppose we throw a caveat into the mix." I said.

"What do you propose?" Osborne asked.

"While Liz and I are supported by the State Department, we are private citizens sailing our own boat. Unless the boss calls us home, we'll be in the area, anyway. Should the Trinidad government pick up any clues as to the missing gold, we will investigate before they call you guys."

"Well, I should think that would please everyone, but it's not my decision. Let's pass it on and see what happens," Osborne said.

"Rick, what do you think? Do we need to get the boss involved?"

"It's a conservative use of resources. Let's go with it. I'll call and fill her in—"

"See if you can get the Doc down here too. I know she is a little hinky on him, but he knows all the players."

"Good Idea."

"Who is your boss?" Osborne asked.

"The president." Rick replied.

"You're joking."

"No, sir, we all work for her."

"Extraordinary."

"It certainly can be." I said.

The crew all laughed.

My phone rang. "Hi bud, how's the world of crime-fighting?— OK, thanks for letting me know. Call me when you can." I ended the call and looked at everyone and no one. "That was Heraldo, I guess we know where the gold went.— Dieter escaped several days ago."

CHAPTER THIRTY

Small Bay East of Little Tobago

We watched from our chartered sport fisherman as HMS *Hotspur* and Lieutenant Commander Osborne sailed away to the east. When they were almost out of site they slid beneath the surface.

"OK gang, let's get back to the Caymans and pick up *Pinafore* and Pérez."

"Then what?" Ed asked.

"I guess we find Dieter." I said.

'That should be easy. We just look for 48 boxes of gold." Ed said.

"I know you're joking, but I think you have an idea. I mean, where to you put 48 boxes of gold?"

"Where do we start?" Liz asked.

"Trinidad, I guess. Maybe the locals have picked up some information."

"Maybe Pérez will have some information." Rick added.

I laughed. "It's probably in his bank account. OK, troops, let's get this thing moving in the right direction. Tom, start the blowers please."

When the engines were running, Ed and I pulled up the anchor. Liz busied herself taking the awnings down.

"Tom, you have first watch."

Tom climbed the tower and slid behind the wheel. "Anchor up?"

"Anchor up and secure." Ed calls back.

Tom engaged the transmissions, eased the throttles forward, and our big sport fisherman headed east into the Caribbean Sea.

It was pure Caribbean weather on the way back to the Caymans. What would have been an exciting, relatively smooth ride in a sailboat was a bumpy, fast ride in the sport fisherman. I admit to enjoying the differences, at least in the moment, particularly since Rick was paying the outrageous fuel bill. We docked at the Cayman Islands Yacht Club and transferred what little gear we took back to *Pinafore*. The crew now included Dr. Pérez, who had agreed to the president's request. Per usual, we were all eating in the cockpit. This time, it was breakfast.

"Elizabeth, you are a wonderful cook. I have missed your excellent cuisine."

"Thank you Berto, but Ed did the heaving lifting this time."

"Eduardo, you have been holding out on me."

"You already know enough of my secrets, Doctor."

I chimed in, "OK, everyone, what's the plan? Doc, do you have anything you can share with us?"

"I have been in touch with Heraldo. He thinks Dieter and the gold are still in or near Trinidad. He believes Dieter will try to sell the gold in Europe and is waiting to reach a buyer."

"Why not the middle east or even China? Seems they would be less choosy." I asked.

"Perhaps, but his power base is presumably European, and I doubt he could trust either of your options."

"You dance with the one that brung you." Liz said.

"Quaint, but yes. I think you have, if I could also borrow one of your expressions, hit the nail on the head." Pérez said.

"Tom, do you think your Intel guys could sniff anything out?" I asked.

"Not without more to go on."

"How about surreptitious aircraft coming out of Europe?"

Tom chuckles, "Maybe, but I have to give them more than that and if I give them too much, they'll want to take over and I doubt if anyone wants that, at least for now."

"Chances are we will have to bring in the FBI eventually, but like you say, for now, we have nothing but a guess." I said.

"How about Schultz?" Liz asked. "He hears everything."

"Yeah, but we've been to that well a lot. I don't want to wear out our welcome."

"Bud, that's what he gets paid for, and we are working at the behest of the State Department." Ed said.

"OK, I guess you're right. Let's call him and see if he can snoop around. While we're at it, let's call it Teddy. Maybe he's heard something." I said.

"Maybe that *is* a well we don't want to dip into too much." Liz said.

"Before you call anyone, let me go ashore. I have some acquaintances nearby, perhaps lunch and a few adult beverages might not go amiss." Pérez said.

"Thanks Doc, good idea. In fact. Let's all take a break, clear out the cobwebs and we'll all meet here tomorrow for breakfast and trade information and ideas."

Everyone gets up from the table, most go below. Tom pulls out a book and puts his feet up, sipping from his coffee cup.

"Honey, do you want to go shopping or swimming?" I asked.

"To be honest, I just want to take a nap. I feel like I haven't slept in a month."

"You haven't. Sleep as long as you want, then if you like, tonight we'll get some dinner ashore." I said.

Liz climbs below out of sight.

"Ed, I'm going to try to get Schultz then, if you want, we can look around. Tom, you up for a shore trip?"

"No thanks. I'm going to stay here, finish my book and call my wife."

Ed and I left Tom reading and Liz napping. We walked along the main dock in the marina. I stopped from time to time to admire a boat or look at a rigging idea.

"Don't you ever tire of boats?" Ed asked.

"Do you ever tire of airplanes?"

"Probably, if I spent six weeks in one. Let's walk down to the Ritz Carlton and get some lunch."

"We just ate breakfast."

"I'm a growing boy."

OK, there are probably better local places."

"Probably, but I want to sit at a clean table with a white tablecloth, and sparkling silver and glass wear."

When we got to the Ritz, we opted for the dining room as opposed to the grill. We were seated at a table covered with a white tablecloth overlooking the water.

"This is the only Five Diamond restaurant in the Caribbean. Are you happy?"

"Let's see what the food tastes like. Did you get in touch with Schultz?

"Finally. He's a busy boy. He didn't have anything, but he said he'll call in some favors and let us know."

"Don't turn around, but Pérez is in the corner with a beautiful redhead."

"Good for him."

"Doesn't look like a date, more like a business meeting. Matter of fact, she looks pretty uncomfortable."

"Well, all we can do is eat our lunch. Are we doing wine?"

"Of course. You are not dining with a Philistine."

"I'll remember that the next time you cut off a guy's arm and kill him with it."

"Has no one told you it is boorish to bring up such distasteful matters at a pleasant repast. And I broke his jaw with it. You killed him."

The next morning, as agreed, we were all sitting around the cockpit eating breakfast. A catered breakfast, no-less. While Ed and I were at the Ritz Carlson, I arranged for them to deliver us breakfast.

"Thank you, honey, for the nice surprise." Liz said.

"I figured you and Ed could use a break. My way of telling you both how much we all appreciate your efforts with the meals.

Thanks bud. Nicely done." Ed said.

Tom helped himself to some eggs offered to him by a waiter. "There was a guy hanging around yesterday. He was white, maybe Spanish. I thought he was a guest or on a boat, but he kept looking over from different spots in the marina. Maybe nothing, but my cop instincts went on alert."

"Shit! They are on to us already. We haven't made a move yet."

"Maybe it was a guest." Pérez said.

"If Tom says it was a bad guy, that's what he was."

"As you say. On another matter, I was able to speak with Dieter's former girlfriend. Heraldo gave me the lead, but as it turns out, I had known her previously as, shall we say, a procurer of information. She remembers Dieter had a vacation home somewhere on the Orinoco River. She thinks it was what the old American westerns movies call a hidein."

"Hideout. That goon had a girlfriend?" Ed asked.

"It seems love triumphs all. She doesn't know where it is but once overheard a phone conversation when he referred to 'his place on the Orinoco.'"

"Can't she narrow it down? That's about the biggest river in South America." I asked.

"She said it was on a small uninhabited island. She doesn't know the name, but it had an oil platform next to it."

I jumped up, ran below, opened the chart table, and shuffled through the charts until I found the right one, pulled it out and went back up to the cockpit. "Let's see what we have." I studied the chart for several minutes while the others ate. "Here, I'll bet it's *Isla Cotorra*. It's on the *Caño Manamo*, which is a tributary of the Orinoco River. And look, there is the oil rig."

"How did you do that?" Tom asked.

"What?" I asked.

"Find that island."

"Well, we had the name of the river, not too many uninhabited islands and it couldn't be too far upriver, or it would take all day to get in and out. And the oil rig was a great piece of trivia."

"If his base of operations is or was Argentina. Why would his hide-out be so far from home?" Tom asked.

"Maybe because it is so far from home. We know he spent a lot of time in Trinidad. With that monster he was driving, he could be in Port of Spain in two and a half hours. Plus, he could slip into the Caribbean and disappear." I offered.

"Which is exactly what he did. His place probably has a chopper pad, too." Ed said.

"Good point. It's a good place to start, anyway." I said.

"Why don't we get Schultz to give it a couple of passes with a satellite before we go charging off? Maybe we can identify some other sites that look promising." Liz suggested.

"Once we do that, it gives me more leverage with my people, especially if there is an airstrip." Tom said.

"OK, let's make our way back to Port of Spain and work south from there. Tomorrow we'll head for Jamaica."

"It will take us about a week to get to Port of Spain, so that should give Schultz time to get some pictures. Berto, any ideas?" Liz said.

"No. But I should add it will be difficult to sell the gold and harder to arrange transportation, but once it's gone, I would doubt we will ever see it again."

"So, there is no rush, but hurry up." Ed said.

"Precisely."

We got into the Errol Flynn Marina at Port Antonio late the next day. Yes, that Errol Flynn. Apparently, he was a long-time resident of Port Antonio. For dinner, we walked down to the Ocean View Restaurant and Bar, where they sat us around a large table overlooking West Harbor, Navy Island, and the Windward Passage, beyond. I looked around to see if anyone was paying undo attention to us.

"Tom, do you see your bad guy from Jamaica here?"

"No, and I've been looking."

"OK, tomorrow we drop southeast. That should put us in Port of Spain by Thursday."

A waiter walked to the table and took our drink orders.

"By that time, hopefully Schultz will have something for us to look at."

"Then what?" Liz asked.

"If he has a target for us, we'll do our usual tourists thing and sail up the *Caño Manamo* river and check out *Isla Cotorra.*"

"What if he sees the boat? He'll know it's us?" Tom asked.

"Unless one is a sailor, or a boat broker— which he is not— to most people, one sailboat looks like another, especially from a distance. From what we know of this guy, he's always in a hurry, so I doubt sailboats are his thing." I said. "But your right, lets fly the smaller jib, and take *Gilbert & Sullivan* off the davits. It will change our appearance some."

"We know he's fond of Sport Fisherman. It will give us something to look for once in the river." Pérez said.

"So, we make like tourists." Ed said.

"Except for you and me. He had a close-up look at the two of us."

"And the two of you stand out like two bulls in a china shop." Liz said.

"Ed, I think we have just been insulted."

"It happens with us manly types,"

OK, so, Ed and I stay out of sight as much as we can."

"And definitely don't stand together." Liz said.

"Tom, he may have seen you, too." I said.

"I doubt it. He was too busy whining with his face in the sand."

"OK, anything else?" I asked.

"Yeah, let's eat. Insulted or not, I'm starved." Ed said.

CHAPTER THIRTY-ONE

CrewsInn Marina - Chaguaramas, Trinidad

Six days later we were back at the CrewsInn Marina, more specifically we were in the Lighthouse Restaurant overlooking the marina. The table was covered with a white tablecloth accented with red napkins. A glass of wine is in front of each of us. Tom put his menu down. "I have to tell you, this is the last place I would expect to see BBQ Baby Back Ribs."

"They are damn good, too." Ed said.

"You guys have been here before? Tom asked.

"Yeah, get Ed to tell you about Carnival." I said.

"You were here for Carnival?" Pérez said.

"Oh yeah. Go ahead Ed, tell them."

Elizabeth rummages through her purse and pulls out her phone. "Don't bother, I have pictures."

Ed leans back and puts his head down. "Oh, nooo."

"I warn the faint of heart. They are ex-rated."

Liz hands her phone to Tom. He thumbs through the pictures. "Wow. Liz, you look great!"

Using my best glare, "You're supposed to be looking at Ed."

Liz gave me her eye arch thing, "Thank you Tom, it's nice to be appreciated."

"I appreciate you— Just with your clothes on." That earned me an icy toned, "Thank you so much for that wonderful compliment."

"I mean in public. You know what I mean."

"Very smooth bud," Ed said.

"Ed, you look great too," Tom said.

Ed grunted. Tom handed the phone to Pérez. As he looks at the pictures, the waitress arrived to take our dinner orders.

An hour or so later, we were pretty much finished with dinner and the sun was pretty much finished with the day and my chances of marital bliss was pretty much finished for the foreseeable future. We sat quietly, looking out the window, mesmerized by the sun setting over the marina. I ventured to break the reverie. "I checked with the front desk. They have some rooms, so for a change, if any of you want to sleep in a private, clean room with a shower. Now is the time."

"You don't have to ask me twice. Not that I don't like the company of you, gentleman, but a girl likes her privacy once in a while." I got the official drop dead glare.

"I think I shall also take advantage." Pérez said.

"OK, everyone do as you like. Why don't we meet here for breakfast and plan the next leg of the trip?" I suggested.

Liz and I took one of the rooms. I was lying in bed reading. Liz walked out of the bathroom. Wrapped in a towel, she sat in front of a mirror and started combing her wet hair. "What are you reading?"

"A guy named Dewey Lambdin. He writes great swashbucklers."

Liz puts her comb down, stands and walks toward the bed, dropping her towel. "You may have noticed that for the first time in a month, we are alone."

"I noticed."

"Good. Now put the book down and show me how much you appreciate me with my clothes off." She climbed into the bed, reached over, and turned off the light.

Tom and Ed walked down Ana Street, in Woodbrook, an area in Port of Spain known for its nightlife. Taking in the sites, they stopped occasionally to look into a bar or club.

"You get the feeling we're being followed?" Tom asked Ed.

"About a block back, white pants, tie-dyed T-shirt and straw hat"

"Yep. Let's go into that bar up ahead. The one next to the alley. When we get in, you go right, I'll go left." Tom said.

"Lead the way."

Ed and Tom walked through the door of the Smokey & Bunty Bar then step to either side of the door. The man in the straw hat walked in a few minutes later. Before he got through the threshold, Tom, and Ed each took an arm and walked the man back out the door, backwards and around into the alley.

In one motion, Tom spins the man around, forces him against the wall and frisks him. "Gun." He hands the pistol to Ed and continues the search.

Ed pulls the magazine, ejects the round in the chamber, "Wow, a PPK. Don't see these every day. This must be James Bond."

Tom stands back from the man in the straw hat. "OK, James Bond, who the hell are you? And why are you following us?"

James Bond remained silent and looked at his feet.

Ed smacks James Bond in the solar plexus. The man gasps. When he was able to suck in a breath, he said, "I am following no one. You will return my property."

Ed pulls out a large spring knife. It snaps it open an inch in front of the man's face. "You will answer the nice man's questions, or I will carve you into pieces starting with your nose." Ed puts the tip of the knife in James Bond's nose and flicks outward, slicing the nostril.

"Ahhh!" The man grabs his nose. Blood trickles through his fingers. "You are crazy!"

Tom grabs the man's arm and twists it outward. "Well, well. Look at this. Young James has a tattoo, *Die Auserwählten*. Ed, I don't read German, do you?"

"So, James, what's that mean?" Ed asked.

"It girlfriend's name."

Ed placed the knife to the man's throat and pushed until blood started trickling. "Look, you little shit, you lie to us one more time and I'll start cutting."

"You know James, as a police officer I don't normally condone such brutality, but since I'm not a policeman in this country, I can only advise you to listen to my companion."

Ed pushes on the blade some more. The man screams.

"I can attest to the fact my companion cut a man's arm off and beat him to death with it."

"Why does everyone say that? I broke his jaw with it."

"OK, OK. I watch you under orders."

"The tattoo?" Tom demanded.

"In *Englisch* it is The Chosen."

Ed takes the knife from the man's throat, "Good boy, now who gives you your orders?"

"No. Even if you kill me. I can never tell."

"OK, Ed, kill him and we'll throw him in the dumpster."

Ed lifts his knife as if to cut James Bond's throat.

"*Warte*!"

Ed leaned in close to the man, "You have five seconds 5, 4, 3 ..."

"Dieter."

"Where is he?" Ed demanded.

"El Cidral Island."

"Where's that?" Tom asked.

"The Gulf of Paria. Across the river from a village called Pedernales."

"What else is around this island?" Ed asked.

"Nothing."

"Kill him." Tom said.

Ed pulls the man in the straw hat close by his shirt.

"Nein, *warte*! There is *erdöl* derrick 1-2 kilometers north of Island."

"What's on the Island?" Tom asked.

"I-I do not know. I have never been to the island. There is house, big house that's all I know."

Ed looks at Tom, who nods. "We know your buddy, Dieter. I suspect he will be upset when we tell him you told us how to find him. So, I suggest you go back to wherever you came from and get lost."

"No! No! I did not tell you this. He will kill me."

"Tough. We catch you again, you won't have to worry about Dieter. Now, get out of here."

The man in the straw hat runs off. Ed field strips the PPK and throws the pieces in a dumpster. "Still time for a drink?"'

"You bet."

We all sat around the same table as the previous evening. Pitchers of orange and tomato juice sit on the table. It was a beautiful morning, and the view out the windows was spectacular. Liz's and my morning started with a long lusty shower, so we were both in a particularly good mood, much noticed by the others, judging by the bawdy comments.

"If you all are finished with your lude remarks, I suggest we form a preliminary plan while we're waiting for breakfast." I said.

"Before we start. Tom and I were in Port of Spain last night and had a chat with one of Dieter's jackboots." Ed said.

"The same guy you saw in Jamaica?"

"Yeah, we snatched him up. He said he was ordered to follow us." Tom said.

"He had a tattoo on his arm, *Die Auserwählten*. When we mentioned Dieter's name, he turned as white as Dieter." Ed said.

"Damn, how in the hell are they following us?" I wondered.

"Port of Spain is a pretty logical stop for someone sailing east. Maybe it's good guesswork." Liz said.

"They are tracking us," Pérez said.

"Tracking? How?" I asked.

"The same way I do. Your AIS."

"Damn! How could I be so stupid? Well, the first thing we do is turn off the AIS."

Two waiters brought trays of breakfast and passed out plates of food. They either have great memories or have some kind of code because they got all the orders right.

"What the hell is AIS?" Tom asked.

"It's an automatic identification system primarily used for collision avoidance. But anyone with a smartphone can use it to track a ship, or in our case, a yacht." Pérez answered.

"It's sort of like a transponder in an airplane." Ed added.

"Doc, why are you tracking us?" I asked.

"So, I know where you are."

"Anyway, this guy said Dieter was on an island called El Cidral in the Gulf of Paria near a village called Pedernales."

"That lines up with what the docs girlfriend said." I said.

"He confirmed the oil rig, too." Tom said.

"I don't suppose you have heard from Schultz yet?" Ed asked.

"No, nothing. But I'll call and give him the update from Tom's friend," Liz answered.

"I suggest we press on. As I mentioned before, time is not our friend. If we don't hear from Capt. Schultz soon. We will have to improvise." Pérez said.

"OK, first, we have to find another boat." I said.

"Why?" Liz asked. "You said he wouldn't notice us."

"That was before I knew he was tracking us. We can't be surreptitious in a boat, Dieter's been tracking from the beginning."

"Yes, I see your point." Liz said. "Good word, by the way."

"What?"

"Surreptitious. Operating in secret or stealthy." She said.

"Right. Come on Doc, let's find a boat. We'll meet you all at the *Pinafore* in a few hours." Pérez and I excused ourselves from the table, left the restaurant, and walked down the dock to find a boat.

"I have a friend that may have the boat we need." Pérez said.

"Of course, you do."

With one phone call, a 'friend' picked us up in a white SUV. There was much hugging and palavering, most of which I didn't understand. About thirty minutes later, we were at a large private residence with a large private dock. Among the three boats at the dock was an *Alden 56 Downeast Flybridge Sedan* in perfect condition.

"Damn Doc, do you know what that is?"

"It is an *Alden 56*—

"I know what it is. I've just never seen one. It's beautiful."

"*Si*, we should take care not to scratch it."

After more hugging and shaking of hands, we were on our way to the marina to pick up our crew. In an hour, we were gliding into the slip next to *Pinafore*. The Doc shut down the engines. I threw the dock lines to Tom and Ed, who were waiting on the slip. Elizabeth looked on as the dock lines were tied off. "What in the world is that thing?"

"This, my dear this is an *Alden 56 Downeast Flybridge Sedan*. Very seaworthy, roomy, and pretty fast."

"A canoe is fast next to a sailboat." Ed said.

"Funny. You can pay the fuel bill." I responded.

"Well, no one will take that monster for a sailboat. Where did you get it?" Liz asked.

"You will be shocked to learn Doc here has a friend."

"He would prefer we bring it back without bullet holes."

"So, would I." Liz said.

"OK, let's get our gear transferred and get going." I said.

"We're leaving today? It's late." Liz said.

"Not for the *Foxy Lady*. She has twin CAT, 600 horsepower engines."

Liz walked to the end of the slip and looked at the transom. "My God, you're not kidding. I'm not getting in anything that's named *Foxy Lady*."

I winked at Pérez. "Good, we need someone to stay on the *Pinafore*."

"Dream on buster."

Pérez and I laughed.

We transferred and stored our gear, and by 3 o'clock we were underway. One thing I never get used to on a powerboat is the noise. There is nowhere on a powerboat that you can get away from it. By the time we were in the Gulf of Paria, I was over my fascination with the Alden. Then I remembered Alden makes some of the best sailboats in the world of which *Pinafore* was a distant cousin.

The Doc pulled the power back when we entered the Cano Manamo River. Once opposite the little town of Pedernales, we dropped the hook and broke out the beer.

Eating dinner in the oversized cockpit felt more like eating in a restaurant with a view than eating on a boat.

Elizabeth walked out of the salon with a bottle of wine. "More wine anybody?"

"Yes, please." Pérez said.

"Please." Tom said.

As Liz poured, I pushed my glass forward. "Thanks, honey."

"If I had known you guys were going to go for the wine, I would have brought more."

"Ed hands Liz his glass. "What are we doing tomorrow?"

"If we don't hear from Schultz, I guess we move slowly upriver until we see something fishy. No pun intended." I said.

"I don't think we should move until we hear from Schultz. No sense in being discovered for a gamble. Especially if we sail, I mean motor into an ambush." Liz said.

"It's still technically correct to say sail." I said.

"Good to know. Heaven forbid I be technically incorrect during an ambush." Liz said.

"I agree with Elizabeth. Dieter is no fool. If he suspects we are anywhere close, he'll move immediately. He may have already left." Pérez said.

"Criminals don't like to move out of their comfort zone. And of yesterday, we know he had someone following us, so he hasn't had time to move that gold." Tom said.

'OK, we stay put for now. You all may want to spend time splashing around in the water, cooking on the grill, that sort of thing making like vacationers until we have something from Schultz." I said.

The next afternoon, Elizabeth and Tom are floating on rafts next to the boat. Ed is on the forward deck asleep. Pérez and I were sitting in the cockpit drinking beer. Pérez is reading a book. I was staring across the water. I got up and peered over the side at Elizabeth. "When is he calling?"

"His text said about four our time and it won't be any sooner by asking me the same thing every 10 minutes."

I sat down and stared at the water again. The satphone rang. I grabbed it. "Hello— Oh hi, yes, ma'am. Nothing yet still waiting for Schultz to get back to us with the sat Intel— Yes, ma'am, as soon as we hear something." I hung up the phone and put it back on the table.

"Who was that?" Liz asked from her position in the river.

I leaned over the side of the boat. "The president. Seems the Brits are getting antsy. She says they can't keep their sub here for much longer."

"I thought we were doing this as a favor for them."

"It didn't seem prudent to mention that." I sat down again.

Elizabeth, wearing a white one-piece bathing suit, climbed up the boarding ladder and toweled off. "I'm going to try out the shower and change. You want anything?"

"Yeah, I want Schultz to call us." I said.

Liz walked into the salon and disappeared forward.

It was late afternoon, we were all sitting in the cockpit doing what we do best, eating sandwiches, drinking beer. The satphone rang. Liz picked it up.

"Hello. Hello. Speak up, please. Yes, hi, we thought you forgot about us. OK, OK, wait one—" Liz motions for a pencil and paper.

Tom jumps up and grabs a pencil and notebook from the nav desk and hands it to Ed, who places it in front of Liz.

"OK, go ahead—" Liz writes on the pad. "OK, OK— Right. Say that again— Got it. Yes, we will. Talk soon. Out. Liz puts the phone down and takes a drink from her beer. "Tom, while you're in there, grab the chart for this area."

"Tom, it's right on top of the desk." I said.

Tom pulled the chart off the nav desk, walked into the cockpit, and sat next to Liz.

"OK, we are here (pointing). See this little creek (pointing with the pencil) Schultz thinks the spot we are looking for is just south of where the creek intersects with the river. The property has a dock, but the main house is pretty far inland, maybe a quarter mile."

"So, we can't see anything."

"Not if there is any jungle or foliage."

"Good news. They can't see us," Tom said.

"Maybe. Schultz is sending us some pictures, but he thinks there is a tower."

"Of course." Pérez said.

The others look at Pérez.

"What?" Liz said.

"When the Fuhrer was defeated in 1945, nine thousand Third Reich cronies and collaborators escaped to South America via what they called the ratline."

"Why South America?" Liz asked.

"It is a long and controversial story, but one must remember, even before the War, there were already large German colonies in South America. In fact, Brazil had the biggest Nazi party in the world after Germany. Argentina was one of the most popular destinations because of Juan Perón laundered money for the Nazi war machine." Pérez said.

"You mean German business." I said.

"Exactly. The more senior of the Nazi refuges built large, protected estates in remote locations, some hoping to revive the Third Reich, others to avoid arrest for war crimes. These *grundbesitze's*, as they called them, had in common watch towers, sophisticated security, and escape tunnels.

"My father told me he worked with a Cuban to bring a Nazi into Brazil. Seems the Nazi had some special skills they wanted to help find Che Guevara. Was that you?" Ed asked.

Everyone stopped and looked at Pérez.

"The U.S. hated the Nazi's, but after the War they were seen as defeated, so all the OSS, later the CIA efforts were thrown into eradicating the new enemy, the communists."

"You didn't answer my question."

"Yes, I did."

Tom stands and disappears below.

Elizabeth turns to Pérez. "So, you think this place upriver is modeled on one of those Nazi estates?"

"Dieter molds himself after the Nazi escapees, so why wouldn't he follow suit with his hideaway?"

"Great. Just fucking great." I said.

"But. He doesn't have the resources his predecessors had, so maybe this *grundbesitze* will be less formidable." Pérez said.

Tom reappears with some papers. "Here, the photos just came over the Fax." He places a half dozen sheets on top of the chart.

Everyone picked up a photograph. They exchanged with each other.

"Looks like there is a chopper pad beside the house." I said.

"This looks like a vertical envelopment to me," Ed said.

"What the hell is that?" Tom asked.

"Basically, a frontal ground assault coinciding with an aerial assault by helicopter that seals off the back door. A pincer movement. You know, a vertical head'em off at the pass." Ed replied.

"Sounds like a lot of drug busts I've been on. Most of them went bad."

"Yeah, nobody on this boat is doing any assaulting for gold, especially somebody else's gold. We'll let the Brits do the heavy lifting on this one." I said.

"I say the Brits stand off and hit the site with a missile and save us all a lot of trouble. Can we go home now?" Ed said.

"We agreed to verify the location of the gold. If Dieter is here, that's verification enough for me, so let's at least do that much." I replied.

"You agreed to call the president as soon as we knew anything. Why don't I talk with her and see if there is any last-minute info?" Liz suggested.

"Liz, I will not do an armed assault on that house or estate or whatever it is; are we clear on that?"

Clear."

Liz sat on the bunk in the master stateroom and dialed a number. "Hello, please tell the president this is Elizabeth Hunter. Thank you." She waited for several minutes. "Good morning, Madam President. The satellites made three passes. They confirmed there is a large house where we suspected. There was a helicopter and a boat at the location. On the second pass, the helicopter was gone and on the third pass, the boat was gone. The photos don't show any people around the area. There is what we assume to be an observation tower."

"A tower?"

"Yes ma'am. Dr. Pérez thinks it's built to the same specs used by Nazis that escaped to Argentina after the war."

"Well, that alone is pretty good evidence of that creep, Dieter."

"Yes, we think so too."

"What's the plan?"

"We'll do our tourist thing and move the boat up the river to where the dock is and look around. We'll get back to you with what we find."

"OK, sounds good . . ."

"Madam President, we're pretty certain this is the place. If so, it's going to take a military type of assault to recover the gold. Captain Spade will not put our people in danger for gold."

"How big of a military operation?"

"You are former military, so I assume you know what a vertical envelopment is."

"I know what it is."

"Captain Spade and Ed think a dozen at the front, maybe from the British sub and at least a dozen more maybe from the Trinidad Defense Force at the rear using two helicopters."

"OK, I'll see what I can do. But remind your husband that Tom Sawyer and Ed Colombo work for the Federal Government, which means they work for me. And I set foreign policy, not him."

"Yes, ma'am."

"Talk later."

CLICK.

Liz walked out to the cockpit and sat down. "She didn't come out and say it, but there seems to be a political aspect to this adventure."

"Oil" Pérez said.

"I think that's the case."

"It's always about oil." I griped.

"I'm guessing it's LNG. We buy a ton from Trinidad." Liz said.

"OK, nothing we can do about it. Let's get underway and see what we can see." I said.

We weighed anchor and set a course upriver toward Dieter's place. As Liz had told the president, the plan was to anchor on the opposite side of the river from Dieter's dock and play in the water and make like tourists. I was driving from the pilothouse, Tom was on the flybridge as lookout. The rest were in the cockpit or salon. It was early afternoon when the *Foxy Lady* rounded a bend. To our left, on the far bank of the river, a sport fisherman was tied to a dock. Men were working on the boat.

"Ed, will you look at that boat and see if Dieter is on it? Stay back from the windows. Chances are he's watching us."

Ed entered the salon, takes the binoculars from the nav station, and looks through the port window at the sport fisherman.

"Yep, that's him and he *is* watching us through binoculars."

I eased *Foxy Lady* further to the right, away from Dieter's dock and his Sport Fisherman. "Listen, everyone, do not look at that boat! Just sit, read, or sunbathe, whatever tourists do. Repeat, do not look at the boat."

"OK, he's getting off— He's walking up the dock toward the house— Looks like his legs are in casts. He's off the dock and in the woods. He is out of sight now."

I called up to the flybridge. "Tom, take over the helm. Let's not hang around. Go further upriver around that point. Watch the depth. Once you're out of sight of that tower, keep station until we figure out what we're going to do."

About twenty minutes later, Tom called down, "I don't think they can see us."

"Thanks Tom! Liz, call the White House and tell them that as far as we are concerned, the gold is on this island, if not in the house." I turned to Pérez and Ed. "Anyone disagree? —No. OK, make the call. While Liz is talking to the higher ups. I'm making lunch. Any special requests?"

I banged around the galley and came up with a platter of sandwiches and a bucket of cold drinks. I stuffed a sandwich in my mouth, then climbed the ladder and relieved Tom at the wheel. "OK, bud I got it, go down and have some lunch. Ask Ed to go forward and ready the anchor."

"Will do."

Ed and I managed to get the boat anchored without too much drama. I shut off the engines and joined the others in the cockpit.

Later, Liz walked out of the salon to the cockpit where we were all sitting. She opened a beer and had a long drink.

"This can't be good." I said.

"Nobody is coming. The island is technically Venezuelan. Trinidad and the Brits don't want to risk an international incident."

"It's their damn gold!" I exclaimed.

"Don't shoot the messenger."

"Can we go home now?" Ed said.

Liz continued. "She would like us to hang around until she can get something worked out between Venezuela and Trinidad."

"OK, let's pull the hook, go back and anchor at Isla El Cidral. At least there we will be between Dieter and the Caribbean. Everyone get into tourist mode and don't look at Dieter's place when we go by. You can bet he has some powerful binoculars in that tower."

CHAPTER THIRTY-TWO

Foxy Lady at Anchor - Isla El Cidral, Caño Manamo River

"Good breakfast honey. Thanks."

"Ed and I will clean up." Tom said.

"Thank you, boys." Liz sits with a coffee and magazine.

"Would anyone like some more coffee?" Tom asked.

"Yes, please, that would be most welcome." Pérez hands his empty cup to Tom. "Any thoughts on what our instructions will be?"

"Sure. We do all the work and everyone else has plausible deniability." I said.

"I see. I take it you tire of the process. So, why do you continue to do this sort of thing?" Pérez asked.

I sighed and sat back. "I don't know. Seems I sign up for one thing and it snowballs into something else. Like this job, for example. Liz and I agreed to help you bring Cuba into the twenty-first century, and now we're chasing Nazi gold."

Elizabeth puts her magazine down. "We don't mind the chasing part, but our chases always seem to end in a gunfight. We have children and responsibilities like other couples."

"Our kids don't deserve to be orphaned for this kind of work. Especially not for gold." I said.

"I see what you mean. I have never had children, so I cannot share the depth of your concern, but I do grasp your point of view."

"It seems every fracas we get into has nothing to do with securing freedom and everything to do with controlling power for elites or politicians that wouldn't dare risk their own lives." I said.

'What you did for the people of Venezuela was certainly noteworthy."

"Yes. I am proud to have been part of that. I think we did a lot of good for many, many people." I said.

"Perhaps this venture will turn out the same."

"That's a nice thought." Liz said. The satphone rang. Liz picked it up. "Hello—Good morning, ma'am." Liz listened. "Very good. I'll get back to you shortly." Liz pressed a button on the phone, then placed it on the table.

Ed and Tom come out of the salon and sit around the table.

"The president brokered a deal with President Sabas of Venezuela. Apparently, there is an airstrip close to here in a town called Capure."

"It's the next town over from Pedernales. You can see it from here." I pointed.

They all look to the east across the water.

Is the airport on the chart?" Liz asked.

Tom looks at the chart. "Looks to me like Pedernales and Capure are actually one town divided by (pointing over the water to the shore) that little river. The airport is on the Capure side of the river."

"She will send some U.S. assets into that airport when we need them. They will be a short distance away, presumably at the old naval base in Port of Spain. By agreement, these assets will be unmarked and flown by civilians." Liz said.

"What kind of assets?" I asked.

"I have no idea. She was being purposely evasive, so I guess someone was listing."

"My bet is choppers. That's her default weapon of choice." Ed said.

"Any troops?"

"She didn't say."

"Shit, here we go again."

Suddenly, Tom sat up. "Dieter's sport fisherman is coming down the river! Man, that thing can move."

"Liz, how fast can we get the so-called assets?" I asked.

"She said we can have them now."

They all pretend not to watch as the huge sport fisherman speeds past them downriver toward the open Caribbean Sea.

"Tom, I don't suppose you saw who was on the sport fisherman?"

"No, sorry."

"That's OK. That thing set him back about a million, so where it goes, Dieter goes. And I doubt if he sold the gold yet," I said.

"He may have sold it by now, but I don't think he's moved it. And I'll wager it's going out through that airport," Pérez said.

"So, he has to move it by river at least a mile or two. Awkward, to say the least."

"Precisely." Pérez said.

"What if we take it in route?" Tom asked.

"We could be sitting here forever waiting for him to move it, then when we did try for it, there's a good chance it would end up at the bottom of the river." I said.

"Hard to control a moving operation, too." Ed added.

I stood and looked over water as the sport fisherman raced down the river. "OK guys, no time like the present. We're going to divide into three teams. Tom, you, and Liz take the dingy into Pedernales to buy groceries."

"We don't need groceries. We need wine." Liz said.

"You're not going to buy groceries, you're going to watch for the sport fisherman to come back. Take one of the hand-held's, but use— say, Channel 8. Dieter will have VHF too. He'll most likely be on 16," I said.

"Got it. Can I buy some wine and beer too?"

I glared at Liz. She wrinkled her nose at me. "Doctor, you're going to take Ed and I to Capure."

"Ed and *me*." Liz corrected.

"Ed and I will get off and make our way to the airport and meet our assets, whatever they are. When we get there, don't tie up, but make it appear you are. At least from the riverside."

"Why must I stay with the boat?" Pérez asked.

"Because you have more single-handed experience with a boat than the rest of us put together. If you see the sportfisherman, call us on Channel 8."

Unconvinced, "Very well."

"But just in case Dieter is listening, say, 'the water tanks need filling'. Be ready to retrieve the dingy or Ed and I at any time."

"Ed and *me*." Liz corrected again.

I turned to Liz, "Sorry, Ed and *me*. Liz, you use code too, say something like 'they're out of beer'." I looked around. "Questions?"

No one said anything. Tom pulled two VHF hand-held radios out of a duffle bag and handed one to Ed and shoved the other in his pocket.

"Liz, if possible, nose around carefully and see if you can find out how many people are in Dieter's house."

"There are probably 10,000 people in that town, and every one of them knows who Dieter is. Be careful what you say. You can never tell where allegiances lie," Pérez said.

"OK. Liz, call for our assets and tell them to meet us at the airport. Tell them to come in from the southeast— less chance that Dieter will see them."

Liz punches a phone number into the satphone, then disappears into the interior of the boat. The crew lowered the dingy into the water. Tom dons a life jacket and prepares to board the dingy. The other men clear away the charts and coffee cups. I started the engine.

Liz comes back to the cockpit. "OK, they are on the way, but they need a pilot."

"What the hell does that mean?" I asked.

"I don't know; it was all very cryptic. All they said was they are short a pilot."

"Who's they?" I asked.

"The president and Collins."

"If Collins has anything to do with this, no wonder it's fucked up. But I meant who is flying?" I asked.

"They didn't tell me that either."

"Can we go home now?" Ed droned.

"I tell you Ed, one more damn thing and we are gone!"

Liz kissed me, "By sweetie," then joined Tom in the dingy.

I watched as they motored off toward Pedernales. "OK Doc, get us over to the dock." I laughed at my stupid joke. Pérez gave me a withering look.

Once the engines were running, Ed pulled the anchor. Pérez turned us out into the river, and we were off toward Pedernales. I decided to tell the two men what had been running through my mind for some time. "Ed, sit for a moment, will you?"

"What's up?"

"Doc, I would like you listen too— I'm not going to fuck with this guy Dieter anymore. I'm *not* going to get anyone killed over oil or gold. When Dieter gets back, I'm going to kill him and go home."

"How are you going to do that?" Ed asked.

"Remember our little fight with the pirates off Block Island?"

"How can I forget?"

"As soon as we find out what's going on at the airport, we are hightailing it back to the place where we were anchored off Dieter's dock." I said.

"Then what?" Ed asked.

"I'm going to reach out and touch him. Then we send for the calvary, we go in and find the gold, call the Brits and be done with the SOB."

"Cut the head off the snake." Pérez said.

"Exactly."

"Sounds like a plan." Ed said.

I looked at Pérez. "Doc, do you have any objections or suggestions?"

"None. Good riddance— We're approaching the dock. I'll pull in front of that blue boat and you guys jump off. Be sure you have your radios.

The *Foxy Lady* slowly approached the dock. With the use of the bow thruster and engines, Pérez skillfully laid the boat alongside the dock. Ed and I jumped on the dock, then called back to Pérez. "We'll be back as soon as we find some beer!" Pérez smiles and waves.

Ed and I walked through the little town of Capure, looking into the small shops, smiling at the friendly people gradually working our way toward the airport on the east side of the town. "There it is." Ed said. We picked up the pace, walking down a small road through an unmanned gate. "Ed look." Sitting in front of the hanger are two Sikorsky UH-60 *Black Hawk* helicopters with 70mm rockets and .50 caliber forward firing guns. At the side are crew served MK25 Gatling guns.

"I see them, two *Blackhawks*. They look like the Army versions."

"With no markings. Well, let's find someone and introduce ourselves." Before we walked the remaining distance to the helicopters. Seven men walked out of the hangar and intercepted us.

"Bob, Jerry, how are you two? Admiral! What the hell are you doing here? —Sir."

The men shook hands and slapped each other on the back.

Chuckling, "I'm on leave. My wife and I are on vacation."

I've met your wife, sir, and that doesn't look like her." I said.

Briscoe turns, "Oh, this is Commander Rosenberg. Rosey isn't married, so he intrudes on our vacations. Heard you could use some artillery."

"Yes, sir." I turned to Ed. "You will remember Ed Columbo from our venture into Cuba."

Ed and Briscoe shook hands. "I do. Nice to see you again. I trust your wound has healed."

"Yes, sir, all healed. Thank you for asking."

Briscoe motions toward Jerry and Bob. "Barrett insisted I bring these two ruffians. I Thought maybe you could use some gunners too, so I brought some of my own. You may remember Ski, Lewis, and Ward." He pointed to the three men.

I waved at the men. "I remember your gunners very well. Ward, did you bring your grenade launcher?"

"Actually, sir, this time we brought some 2.5-inch rockets. Nice to see you again. I think."

I laughed. "My sentiments exactly."

"Before we go on, I'm a little sketchy on our mission," Briscoe said.

"You weren't briefed?"

"It was suggested by your General Barrett that I might like to vacation in Trinidad. Maybe do some flying."

"They asked a flag officer to fly a gunship for this cluster fuck?"

"Not really. He asked for suggestions—I volunteered. Cluster fuck, is it? Maybe I should go back to Port of Spain."

"Wish I could go with you. The short version is— our little unofficial crew were asked to help overthrow the regime in Cuba. Ed here was carrying bona fides for one of the principal architects of the coup. Ed was kidnapped— "

"That's what that ruckus in Cuba was about."

"Yes, sir. Then Richard Silvers and Dr. Pérez were kidnapped, this time for ransom-"

—"By the Cubans!"

"No, sir. By a Venezuelan drug cartel, we tangled with a while back. So, we were sent down here to meet with an intermediary who would facilitate their release. Only we found out the intermediary really wanted to use us to find some lost Nazi gold."

"You're kidding."

"No sir, I wish I was. Turns out the intermediary is really with INTERPOL, and he wanted the gold as bait for a neo-Nazi named Dieter."

"Stop. I need a scorecard."

"It gets worse. We found some of the gold."

"Really!"

"Yep, so we used it as bait to capture Dieter. It worked, and Dieter was arrested and sent back to Argentina. So, we started home. Then the boss called and said meet this Brit submarine."

"Submarine?"

"We only found one of the original 49 boxes of gold. Trinidad wanted the rest. They asked the Brits to help locate the gold, and they figured we knew where it was. So, they spoke to us. I told them where I thought it was. Unfortunately— "

"Dieter escaped, found the gold and made off with it." Ed said.

"Our friend, Dieter is about 5 miles that way," I pointed. "In a fortified house. We assume the gold is with him."

"Why do we care?" Briscoe asked.

"That's what I said. It seems Trinidad sells us lots of LNG and our administration wants to help with their problem, but covertly. Which means me and now you guys."

"What about the Brits or, for that matter, Trinidad?" Briscoe asked.

"We are in Venezuela— "

"No international incidents."

"Right."

"So, we are going to take this fortified position with what, 10 people?" Briscoe asked.

"Nine men, one woman."

"If Elizabeth is the woman, I pity this guy, Dieter."

I smiled. "I heard you could use some pilots."

"Ahh, yes, as you can see, I have two birds and two pilots. I need four pilots."

"Ed has his learner's permit."

"Well, not yet, but I play a lot of Flight Simulator." Ed said.

Briscoe sighs. "Guys, I have to take those things back in one piece."

I laughed. Ed has his ATP and was a chopper instructor for some outfit he won't tell me about. In fact, he taught our president to fly. Calls her Harriet when she's not around."

Ed glared at me. "All kidding aside, sir, I can fly your bird."

Briscoe motioned toward the three men in the background. "Ski, will you come over here for a minute?'

A man leaves his two companions and walked over to Briscoe. "Gentlemen, you may remember CPO Rutkowski."

"Sure, we remember. How are you Ski?"

"Fine, thank you, sir."

"Ski, you up to flying right seat on that bird over there?"

"Yes, sir."

"OK, you will fly with Ed here, go over and do a preflight— and don't bend anything."

Ed and Rutkowski shook hands.

"Aye, aye, sir. Don't bend anything, I'll write it down." CPO Rutkowski walked toward the nearest *Blackhawk*.

"He's a petty officer." I said.

"Do you care what rank he is?"

"No, sir, as long as he can fly."

"I taught him myself. He can fly rings around most of the nuggets out of flight school."

"Ed, you OK with it?" I asked'

"Sure, you don't have to be an officer to fly. They made me a warrant officer just to cover some stupid military regs. Let's go."

"OK, Rosy and I will fly Bird one. Ed and Ski will fly Bird two." Briscoe said.

"It will take me about an hour to get in place." I said. "We have to wait for Dieter and his sport fisherman to get back. Then this is what we will do."— I spread the chart over the ground then we all kneeled around as I told them the plan.

CHAPTER THIRTY-THREE

Foxy Lady - Caño Manamo, Orinoco River Delta

It was agreed that Ed would fly one of the *Blackhawks* and Admiral Briscoe the other. Ed would keep one of our hand-held's so we could communicate and, if needed, relay messages to Briscoe. Bob and Jerry came back to the *Foxy Lady* with me, where we joined Liz, Tom, and Pérez. We immediately shoved off and made for our anchorage across the river from Dieter's dock. Pérez was driving the boat. I was on the stern with binoculars looking down river. I turned to Liz. "Liz, take my place. If you see that sport fisherman coming our way, sing out."

Liz took the binoculars. "You going to take a nap? You can use the sleep."

"Great idea. Wake me when things get interesting." I walked forward into the salon.

"He's not really going to take a nap?" Tom asked.

Liz laughed. "I seriously doubt it."

Once in the forward stateroom, I removed a large duffle from the chain locker and placed it on the bunk. "Hey! Will you guys please come in here?"

Tom, Bob, and Jerry walked into the stateroom.

"Help yourselves." I said.

The duffle contained an S&W M19, a 1911A1 Colt .45, a TX4 shotgun, two H&K-MP7's, and a fully automatic M14. "Bob, open that locker please and pull out the ammo."

"You plan on evading Cuba again." Jerry asked.

"I'm going to cut the head off a snake. Neither my wife nor I will be getting killed over some dammed gold." I propped myself against the bulkhead to brace against the occasional lurch from the moving boat. "And I'm not getting anyone else shot either. Help me load these magazines."

We loaded the weapons, placing each on the bunk before continuing to the next.

"I am going to kill this bastard and go home. You guys need a weapon?"

"Na, we brought our own. You know, '*Have Gun Will Travel*' but without the horse."

"Cute."

Liz called back to me, "Hey honey, Berto says we are getting close. Do you want us to anchor?"

"I guess so. I'll be right there." Leaving the weapons in Bob and Jerry's care, I went back to the stern, climbed up the ladder to the flybridge and looked around. On the far-left bank of the river, Dieter's dock protruded into the river. "OK, Doc, this is fine."

Pérez stopped the engines. I called down to Liz, "Will you and Tom drop the anchor please."

A few minutes later, we were all sitting in the cockpit.

"Well, now we wait." I said.

"You guys want anything to eat?" Liz asked.

"No, thanks." Tom said.

"No, I prefer killing on an empty stomach." I said.

"Well, I'm getting some fruit." Liz said.

"Will you bring the chocolate chip cookies when you come back." I asked.

"I would enjoy some fruit also, please." Pérez said. He looked at me. "That's quite an arsenal you have assembled. Do you believe we will need it?"

"Yes."

Liz sets a bowel of fruit, cookies, and a couple of beers on the table and sat next to me.

"All is right with the world, beer and cookies." I said.

"So, what's the plan? I know you have one." Bob said.

I popped a cookie in my mouth and sat forward. "Simple. When that sport fisherman gets back. Dieter will have to get out on the dock. When he does, I shoot him."

"In cold blood?" Tom exclaimed.

"Hot blood, cold blood, as long as he's dead."

"How will you identify him?" Jerry asked.

"He'll be the only six-foot six albino in leg casts on the dock."

"Leg casts?" Jerry asked.

"Tom and I shot him up the last time we met. Should have killed him then. It would have saved us all this trouble."

"And Charlie would still be alive." Liz said.

"Then what?" Bob asked.

"The five of us launch an amphibious assault and surround them." I said.

Bob laughs. "Sounds a trifle optimistic."

"First, we call the calvary. One chopper seals off the back, the other takes the front. They hose down the house and tell the survivors to surrender.

"We don't even know how many people are in that house. It could be a hundred or ten," Tom said.

"Strike your enemy with such ferocity and lethality that he is dead before he even knows you're on the field of battle." Bob said.

"Who said that?" Tom asked.

"The United States Marine Corps." I said.

"Sun Tzu said, 'The supreme art of war is to subdue the enemy without fighting.'" Pérez said.

"Well, whoever said it first, the idea is to scare the crap out of them, so they surrender." Ed said.

"Elegantly put. Two *Blackhawk* helicopters should do the trick." Jerry said.

Tom stands and shields his eyes. "Looks like we have company."

"OK guys, spread out and look touristy." I said.

We all spread ourselves around to look like we were lounging in the sun. Tom pretends to read a book. "I went forward and came back with the M14."

A large sport fisherman slid effortlessly into Dieter's dock. Two men jumped off the boat and fastened the bow and stern lines to the dock. Another man rigged a spring line while the other two prepared the gangway. I could see a crewman on the boat handing crutches to a large man standing on the stern. The large man limped from the boat down the gangway to the dock. He is both large and extremely white, as if he were an albino. His movements are hindered by a brace on one leg and a full length cast on the other.

Once on the dock, he glanced toward the *Foxy Lady*. Then, helped by both companions, he turned and trudged down the dock toward a waiting jeep.

I placed a seat cushion on the teak combing of the transom, laid the M14 on the cushion and kneeled behind the rifle. I took a deep breath, let out part of it, then gently squeezed the trigger.

BANG!

The large and extremely white man fell forward to the dock. His companions stooped down, looked in our direction, then ran down the dock, passing the Jeep running into the woods.

I stood and turned to the others. "Liz, get on the radio and get Ed and Briscoe on the way."

Liz turned and quickly went into the pilothouse.

"Very good shot." Pérez said.

"You shot him in the back." Tom said.

"What did you want me to do, Tom? Yell four! I'm trying to save lives, including yours."

Liz returned. "The choppers will be here in three minutes. You can see them over Pedernales already."

"The dingy is ready to go," Jerry said.

"Thanks. Liz, I may ask you to bring the boat over when things cool down. I'll have a radio, so stay up on channel eight."

Liz walked up and kissed me. "Please be careful. All of you, be careful."

We climbed down in the dingy. I carried my shotgun and .45. The others carried H&Ks. I called back to Liz, "Honey, keep that M14 handy. Watch the near bank. Maybe Dieter has friends on this side of the river."

"Will do."

Tom put the dingy in gear and motored off toward the dock. "Here come the choppers."

Two *Blackhawk* helicopters swooped out of the northeast. One pulled up almost to a stall, then low hovered over the ground. The other one swept past and made a steep bank to the left. An MK25 Gatling gun fired out of the left side toward the ground.
BZZZZZZZZZZZZZZZZZZZZZZZZZZZZZZZZZZZZZZZZZZZZZZZZZZZZZZ BZZZZZZZZZZZ

The first helicopter orbited left and fired two missiles at the tower.
SWISSSSSSSSSSHHHHHHHHHHHH
SWISSSSSSSSSSHHHHHHHHHHHH
BOOMM!

The tower disappeared into a ball of fire.

The same helicopter orbited right, nosed down and fired two more missiles at the ground.
SWISSSSSSSSSSHHHHHHHHHHHH
SWISSSSSSSSSSHHHHHHHHHHHH
BOOMM! BOOMM!

Two enormous explosions followed.

"Jeez, I guess they're blowing up the entire house." Tom said.

"Hopefully, they are just beating up the front and rear yards of the house." I said.

Pérez said, "Scaring the crap out of them, I believe you called it."

"Yeah, me and Sun Tzu."

The dingy rapidly approached the dock.

"We are almost there. What do you want me to do?" Tom asked.

"Pull in behind Dieter's boat. We'll use it for cover. Guys, be very careful. We don't know how many of these guys are around."

"There may still be people on Dieter's boat." Tom warned as he steered the dingy in behind the sport fisherman.

Pérez and I tied up the dingy. Jerry and Bob moved low and slow down the dock, stopped and kneeled. Tom remained in the dingy, pointing his H&K at Dieter's sport fisherman.

Bob nods to Jerry. In a whisper, "I think we need to clear that boat before we do anything." Doc and I joined them.

Jerry, in a low voice, said to the three of us, "Doc, watch our backs. We'll go on the boat and take a look." All three of us approached the sport fisherman carefully.

Tom yelled, "Get down!"

Bang! Bang! Bang! Bang!

Chips of fiberglass fly off the sport fisherman.

Rat-a-tat Ratatat Ratatat Ratatat!

Pérez fell flat on the dock, and I jumped beside him. Tom, now on the dock, is on one knee. Bob and Jerry are prone, all firing at the tree line. I pulled out my radio and keyed the mic. "Ed you there!"

"What do you need?"

"I need one of you guys to hose down the tree line just in front of the dock. They're shooting the crap out of us!"

Ed and Ski sit in front of their instrument panel. Ed handles the cyclic and collective like a musician. Inputs were smooth and coordinated.

"On the way."

"Ed! Remember the chopper pad to the east?"

The helicopter banked hard to the right, circling out over the river, then levels.

"Nothing on it. OK bud! Keep your head down!"

Ed put the nose down and fired two missiles, then the .50 Cal.

SWISSSSSSSSSSHHHHHHHHHHHH
SWISSSSSSSSSSHHHHHHHHHHHH

BangBangBangBangBangBangBangBang   BangBangBangBang BangBangBangBang

"Lewis, I'm going to orbit the tree line in front of the dock. I want you to mow that brush down."

"Give me some time on station and I'll turn it into a putting green." Lewis said.

The *Blackhawk* swung out over the water again, passed over the sport fisherman and banked left orbiting the tree line. Lewis fired his MK25 Gatling gun at the brush and tree line, turning a basketball court sized area into chopped vacuity.

BZZZZZZZZZZZZZZZZZZZZZZZ
BZZZZZZZZZZZZZZZZZZZZZZZZZZZZZZZZZZZZZZZZ
BZZZZZZZZZZZZZZZZZZZZZZZZZZZZZZZZZZZZZZZZZZZZZZZZZZZZ
BZZZZZZZZZZZZZZZZ
BZZZZZZZZZZZZZZZZZZZZZZZZZZZZZZZZZZZZZ

Satisfied, Ed swings out of harm's way and hovers over the water. With Bird Two out of the way, Bird One fires more missiles at the rear of the house. Then Briscoe orbits around the house. Briscoe sits in the right seat, handling the controls. Rosy is in the left seat, acting as a weapons officer and monitoring the radar and radio. "Ward, hose down the areas around the house. Walk a few rounds in the front door."

"Aye, aye skipper. You get this thing doesn't do just a few," Ward said.

Briscoe laughs, "Just don't cut the house in half."

The helicopter circles the house. Ward fires his MK25.

BZZZZZZZZZZZZZZZZZZZZZZZZ
BZZZZZZZZZZZZZZZZZZZZZZZZZZZZZZZZZZZZZZ
BZZZZZZZZZZZZZZZZZZZZZZZ
BZZZZZZZZZZZZZZZZZZZZZZZZZZZZZZZZZZZZZZ

The grounds around the house look like they were plowed by a farm tractor. The wide wooden veranda at the front was turned to splinters. Briscoe banks away, then takes a position over the water about a half mile south of Ed and Bird Two.

Pérez, Tom, and I were still laying prone on the dock. I keyed the mic on the radio. "Good lord did you guys leave anything standing?"

"We didn't touch the house— sorta." Ed replied.

"Ed, do you have a hailer on that thing?"

"Wait one—" Ed turns to Ski, "we have a hailer on this bird?"

"Sure." Ski throws a switch on the radio panel, "OK, just key the mike when ready."

Ed keyed the hand-held, "Yeah, we have one."

"Get as close as you dare and tell them to come out of the house with their hands in the air. In single file, walk down to the sport fisherman, get on the boat, and leave or they will be killed."

"Roger that."

Bird two flies slowly and stops to hover in front of Dieter's house.

"Lewis, I'm going to orbit right and hold. If you so much as see a face in a window, take that fucking house down. For all we know, they have Stingers in there. I've suffered that misfortune once."

"Got you sir, once is enough."

"Either of you guys know German?"

"My grandmother was German. I know a little." Ski said.

"Did you hear what the ground boss said?"

"Some of it."

"Tell them to get out of the house, get on der Fuhrer's boat, and leave. Otherwise, we kill all of them. They have three minutes."

Ski moves the switch on the radio panel and starts speaking. "*Aufmerksamkeit. Wenn Sie das Haus nicht verlassen und Dieters Boot nehmen und gehen. Du wirst getötet werden. Du haben drei Minuten Zeit.*"

"Tell them again in German and English" Ed instructed.

"*Geh oder du wirst getötet. Sie haben zwei Minuten Zeit.*"

"Hope they don't speak Spanish." PO Lewis said.

"You in the house. We will destroy the house and everyone in it if you don't leave and get on Dieter's boat. You have one minute to comply."

"Switch that hailer to me." Ed said.

"*Sal de la casa, sube al bote y vete o te matarán. Tienes un minuto.*"

The helicopter continues to hover.

"Skipper! Look at the front door. They're coming out. Guess Spanish was the magic touch." Lewis said.

"Who would have thought? A bunch of Nazis speak Spanish. I'm pulling back. You guys watch every move they make. Ski, ask Bird One to come in and help herd these guys to the boat." Ed said.

"Ed, anything happening?" I asked into the hand-held.

"Yeah, they are coming toward you."

"OK, come on guys, let's get out of sight. I don't want them to know there are only five of us." I said.

The helicopters hovered overhead as the men file down the path, onto the sport fisherman. Once aboard, they just sit.

From my concealed position, I keyed the mic of my radio, "Ed, tell them to start the engines and go home. Use Spanish."

"Roger that."*Encienda los motores y tome el barco. Vete a casa. Ahora!*

The engines on the sport fisherman start. A man jumped off the boat and untied the dock lines, threw them on board, then jumped back on the boat. The boat turned away from the dock and started downriver.

The five of us came out of our hiding places and watched until the boat disappeared.

"Hope the gold wasn't on that boat," Tom said.

"Pleasant thought. The least they could have done was take Dieter. OK, let's go clear that house." I said.

The men walked up the path toward the house. I pulled out the radio. "Ed, how you guys doing for fuel? I would like you to stick around until we can go through that house."

"Stand by."

"Guys, please watch yourselves. There could be a dozen more in that house." I said.

"As you said, a most pleasant thought." Pérez said.

Ed came up on the radio. "We're OK for another 30 minutes. You watch your ass."

"Thanks."

CHAPTER THIRTY-FOUR

Dieter's House on the Caño Manamo - Orinoco River Delta

The approach to the house reminded me of a five-man fire team sweep I conducted a lifetime ago.

"I hope this turns out better than the last time we did this," Bob said.

"At least this time we have air support." I said. I prayed this time it would turn out better. We spread out and approached the front door and what was left of the veranda from different directions. "I'll go right, Jerry follow me. Tom, you, and Bob follow next, then go left. Doc, watch our backs, particularly that tree line behind us."

The four of us went single file through the door. Pérez knelt half in, half out the door, watching the tree line and the stairs to the second floor.

Jerry and I crept into a large room. In the middle of the room are stacks of metal boxes. Each is identical to the one we recovered from Donkey Island but corroded from being underwater. "Jerry, watch my ass while I try to count these things." I slowly approached the boxes and started to count—

"Behind you!" Pérez yelled.

Jerry and I swung around. A man was standing on the stairs from the second floor. We all fired at the same time.

Ratatat Ratatat Ratatat Ratatat! Ratatat Ratatat RatatatRatatat Ratatat RatatatRatatatRatatat!

The man toppled down the stairs. Pérez ran forward pointing his gun up the stairs. He watched for several moments. "I don't see anyone else. Anybody hurt?"

"I'm OK." I said.

"I'm OK. Scared the crap out of me," Jerry said.

Bob and Tom ran into the room, weapons at the ready.

"What the hell happened?" Tom asked.

Looking at the man on the floor. "Guess this guy wanted to keep the gold. Did you kill him?" Jerry asked.

Bob kneeled next to the body. "At least twice."

"Thanks Doc, you saved our collective asses." I bent over and picked up the gun the man was carrying. "Tom, look at this. Remember when we had Dieter back on Donkey Island and you asked me what a Schmeisser was?"

"Yea, sort of."

I handed Tom the sub-machine gun. "This is a Schmeisser. Take it home and add it to your collection. The thing is worth a fortune." I said.

"Thanks, I'll stick to collecting baseball cards." He pulled out the magazine, cleared the chamber and threw both on a stuffed chair.

"Sorry, I shouldn't have let him get that far down the stairs." Pérez said.

"As I said, you saved our lives. Thank you. Let's clear the house and make sure there aren't any more little Führer's around."

Once we were convinced the house didn't contain anymore of Dieter's men, we came back to the foyer.

"Did you find the gold?" Tom asked.

"Yeah," I pointed to the other room. "It's in there."

We all stepped into the living room and looked at the metal crates.

"I wouldn't mind collecting some of that stuff. For historic reasons, of course." Tom said.

"Before we do any collecting, let me take a look." Jerry said. He walked carefully around the stack. When he got to the far side, he stopped. "Guys don't move! Wires are coming from the center of the stack and leading out to the kitchen. Let's all back out of here."

"OK, everyone out, let the Brits open it. Plus, this guy may have buddies." I took pictures of the crates, then followed the others to the front door. Once out of the house, I keyed the radio. "Ed, we're going back to *Foxy Lady*. Will you watch our backs until we get to the boat? Dieter left a friend."

"Anybody hurt?"

"No one that counts."

"Did you find the gold?"

"Yep. Still in the Japanese crates. Jerry thinks it's sitting on a charge."

"Ouch. OK, we're covering your exit."

In a scene reminiscent of videos and pictures of soldiers threading their way through jungle trails in Vietnam, we made our way down the path toward the dock. When we got to Dieter, Tom asked, "What do we do with him?" I turned him over. His arm flopped on the dock. A swastika is tattooed on the arm. A large hole in his chest seeped blood.

"Take his picture and leave him for the Brits."

Tom aims his cell phone at the corpse and takes several pictures. "The sea gulls will have most of him by the time they get here."

"Tough." I said. "Everyone in the dingy."

Once back across the river, we climbed aboard *Foxy Lady*. Liz greeted us with hugs and kisses, saving a special kiss for me. Jerry and Tom pulled the dingy aboard. Doc and Bob made drinks.

Liz put her arms around me. "How are you?"

"Fine, not a scratch. But I don't like this place, so let's go."

Liz turned. "OK, if a couple of you will get the anchor up, we'll be on our way." Liz started the engines. When Ed gave her the signal, Liz put the boat in gear and headed toward the Caribbean.

The two *Blackhawks* were still orbiting over the *Foxy Lady*. Ed called on the radio,

"Hey Bud, our fuel is getting dicey. I see nothing in front or behind you, so we're heading for the barn. I'll see you in Port of Spain tomorrow."

"Roger that. Thanks for watching over us. Out."

The two *Blackhawk* helicopters bank and fly off to the north.

Foxy Lady left the Orinoco River in the late afternoon, motoring toward the mouth of the Delta and the Caribbean Sea beyond. We were all in the pilothouse. Liz was at the wheel. The guys were sitting around a table with cold beverages and sandwiches.

"Guess I need to call the boss." I said.

"No time like the present." Ed said.

"OK. Let me finish my beer. I need my strength." I procrastinated some more, then grabbed the satphone and went forward, sat on a bunk, and dialed the number. "Hi, will you please tell the president that Sam Spade is on the phone— Afternoon ma'am."

"Did anyone get hurt?"

"No ma'am, not a scratch."

"OK, what do you have for me?"

"The short story is we pretty much dismantled Dieter's organization and found the gold."

"Where's the gold?"

"In Dieter's house or estate or whatever they call it. It's in the middle of the living room floor. Tell the Brits or whoever is going after it, we think it's booby trapped."

"What happened to Dieter?"

"He didn't survive the encounter."

"OK, you can give me the long version the next time I see you. Where are you headed?"

"Port of Spain to pick up Ed. He had to take the choppers there. What do you want me to do with my three draftees?"

"Keep Jerry. Send Pérez and Bob home. Bob is supposed to be retired. If something happened to him, his wife would have my head.

"Good job., I have another project for you, but I'll have to call you back."
CLICK.

CHAPTER THIRTY-FIVE

CrewsInn Marina, Trinidad

We got into Port of Prince early in the evening and tied up the *Foxy Lady* next to *Pinafore*. Ed was on the dock when we arrived. He said Briscoe and his wife left for some real vacationing. Rosie and the other guys were going to try their hand at deep sea fishing before heading home. By the time we had transferred all the gear, it was too late to return *Foxy Lady* to her owner, so we all went out and had a late dinner.

Early the next morning, Ed and Doc took the Alden back to her owner. No one mentioned the fuel bill, so I didn't bring it up.

We sat around the boat for several days waiting for the powers at be to decide what they— meaning us, were going to do next. After three days I made an executive decision and set sail for home or at least for the keys, our temporary home.

About 10 days into the sail, I was sitting at the nav desk busying myself by organizing the charts. My phone rang. It was the boss. "Good morning, ma'am."

"Good morning. I need to talk with you in private for a moment."

That was always a bad beginning. "Yes, ma'am. Wait one." I walked forward to the master stateroom and closed the door. "Go ahead, ma'am."

"Sorry about the cloak and dagger stuff. When we're finished, you can tell who you like on a need-to-know basis."

"Yes, ma'am."

"I assume you know what Elizabeth told me several weeks ago?"

"About Bruno?"

"Yes. After talking to Liz, Pérez decided to go down there and hopefully work things out. But I want all of you back here pronto."

"You think it's that bad?"

"It's not good, and the truth is, I don't know. When can you be in the Keys?"

"In two maybe three days. We left Port of Spain about 10 days ago."

"Good. That way if we need you back in Cuba you can get there fast if Pérez needs help."

"Do you think he's in trouble?"

"Again, I don't know, but he has the knack for it. OK, talk soon."

CLICK.

CHAPTER THIRTY-SIX

Pinafore – Marathon, Florida Keys

It was evening, the sun was low, about ready to depart for the day. We were all sitting in the cockpit drinking whisky, gin and tonics and the occasional beer contemplating dinner.

"I think a month at sea is enough for a while," Liz said.

I laughed. "We were never out of sight of land, more or less."

Pushing the skin on her face, "Do you think my face is getting too much sun?"

"I don't see how any sun gets through all that sunscreen you slather on. I think you have a nice glow."

"Do I have a nice glow, too?" Ed asked.

"Oh, shut up, you two."

Ed and I laughed.

"Now, if you all will excuse me, I'm going to get off this damn boat and take a real shower."

"I'm with Liz. I'm ready for an actual shower and a restaurant." Ed said.

Liz and Ed gathered their shower gear, climbed off the boat, and walked down the dock to the showers.

"Tom, another drink," I said.

"Don't mind if I do." Tom said. "Does opting for a drink instead of a shower make us heathen's?"

"I should think so. But wiser for it." I said.

Once the true believers returned from their showers, we all walked down the dock to the Lazy Days Restaurant & Bar, which is located under a large, covered patio, as one would guess, overlooking the water. We all sat at a round table drinking cocktails.

"The last time we were here, we had steaks." Liz said.

"I'm having the steak again." Ed said.

The waitress walked up to the table, took our dinner orders, then left.

"What's on tap for tomorrow?"

"I guess we are going to be here for a few days so you all can do your own thing."

"I've never been to Key West. Wouldn't mind seeing Hemingway's house, especially after staying at his marina in Cuba. Anybody else want to want to tag along?"

"Sure, I'll go." Liz said.

The next day while Tom and Liz were gone, I thought I'd use the downtime to check fluid levels, belts and the electrical connections that take a beating when cruising. I was in what is euphemistically called the engine room.

"Hey, Ed hand me that can of engine oil, will you?"

"Just a minute." Ed gets up from the couch, takes the oil can from the counter and bends down in front of the engine compartment. "Here you go."

"Thanks."

The satphone rang.

"You want me to get that?"

"Please."

Ed picked up the phone and pressed a button. "Hello. No, this Ed— He's in the engine room— Wait one." Ed turns, sits at the nav desk, pulled out a pen and notepad. "OK, go ahead— OK, got it." He pushed the button on the phone again and placed the phone on the desk. "That was Collins. Apparently, the good doctor has incurred the wrath of some unpleasant people, and we are to pluck him from the grasp of villainous person or persons unknown."

"When and where?"

"We are to meet a boat off Cayo Fragoso in three days."

I backed out of the engine room, stood, stretched my back and faced Ed. "Where in the hell is Cayo Fragoso?"

"I have no idea. You're the intrepid mariner. I'm merely a supernumerary. I have the coordinates, though. Us aviators do know about such things as latitude and longitude."

"I think the intrepid aviator has been at the sauce. Let me see what you have."

Ed hands me a piece of paper. "True, but the sun *is* over the yardarm— What is a yardarm anyway?"

Ignoring Ed's dearth of all things nautical, I looked at the slip of paper. "Bud, grab that chart on top."

Ed opens the desk, removes a chart, and lays it on the desk. I replaced the cover on the engine compartment, then walked to the navdesk. "OK, let's see what we have." Pointing, "Here. This must be it."

"Looks like it's about 100 feet in diameter." Ed said.

"If that."

"Man, that's close to the mainland."

"You're right. What do you think?" I asked.

"The same thing you do. The Indians could be planning to ambush the calvary. I'd call Collins back and say not only no, but fuck no."

"OK. Let's wait for the gang to get back from their road trip and we'll toss it around."

The satphone rang. I picked it up and pushed a button. "Hello— Hi John. Yeah, we have been discussing it. Can't you send the Coast Guard in there? — Because it looks like a trap. — Because they don't like us, or they want to embarrass the president." I walked over to the settee and sat down. "Get in touch with him and tell him to find another place. Tell him it's too shallow for us. — OK, call us back." I disconnected the phone and tossed it on the settee. "Damn that guy." I stood, "Come on lets go get something to eat."

As we walked down the dock to the restaurant, I harangued Ed with my opinions of Collins. "I don't trust that guy. I don't trust his motives and I don't trust his competence."

"So, you're saying you don't trust him."

"And I don't like him."

Ed and I walked into the Lazy Days Restaurant, opted for a table on the patio, and ordered drinks and dinner at the same time.

We were well into dinner when Liz and Tom arrived.

"Look who we found." Liz announced.

Denise and Kelly were standing next to Tom with baggage in hand. I stood, kissed Liz and hugged the two girls.

"Long time no see. To what do we owe the pleasure, though I suspect I already know the answer."

"We were told to get on a plane, and you would fill us in." Denise said.

Steele finds Liz a chair. Everyone start talking all at once. They pull chairs up to the table and sit.

"You all want something to eat?" I asked.

"No thanks, we ate on the way back."

"Best Key lime pie I've had." Tom said.

"We ate on the plane. Best ham sandwich I've had." Denise said. Everyone laughs.

Liz looks around the table. "How about something to drink?"

"Sure." Kelly said.

"I can use a beer.' Tom said.

Elizabeth motioned to the waitress, who came to the table and took drink orders.

Ed and I continue eating our dinner.

"So, did you all have fun?" I asked.

Again, everyone started talking at once. Eventually, Tom and the girls excused themselves and went back to the boat for some sleep. After coffee, Liz, Ed, and I walked back to the boat enjoying the coolness of the evening.

"Boy, the girls were really tuckered." I said.

"So am I. It was a long day." Liz said.

"We heard from Collins this afternoon. He wants us to pull Pérez out of Cuba. Seems he got himself in trouble."

"So, that's why the girls are here. What kind of trouble? Liz said.

"We don't know." Ed said.

"And the place they are sending us is right up against the mainland. Ed thinks it's a perfect spot for an ambush. So, do I."

"An ambush! Why on earth would they do that?" Liz asked.

"I don't know, but Ed and I have to rely on our instincts."

"It's kept us alive this long." Ed added.

"Which reminds me you two and I are going to have a talk someday." Liz said.

"Anyway, we asked Collins to come up with another plan. We're still waiting. So how was Key West?"

"I think Tom got more out of it than I did. I did enjoy seeing the Hemingway house. There were pictures from his fishing tournaments, but I didn't recognize the marina in any of them."

The next morning started like most, somebody volunteered to cook breakfast, usually Liz, somebody volunteered for clean-up, usually Ed. The girls and Tom went down the dock to take showers. Ed, Liz, and I were having coffee in the cockpit when the Satphone rang. I picked it up and pushed a button. "Hello— Hey Rick, how are you? You're on speaker. No civilians."

"Doing well, thanks. The good doctor really screwed the pooch this time."

"What happened?"

"He killed someone."

"Why?"

"The guy was about to throw a wrench into our whole deal. So, Pérez invited him to dinner and then stuffed him into an oil drum."

"That must have been the man Adel heard about at the party." Liz said.

"So, he got caught." I said.

"More likely betrayed. As they say, he's on the lam and we have to get him out of there. He understands you not liking his first choice. He said he can probably make it to a place called Cay Sal Bank, a small group of islands at the southern end of Bimini, about thirty miles from Cuba. Says he can be there the day after tomorrow."

"Wait one" I went below, pulled out several charts and scrambled back into the cockpit. Looking at the chart, "That's about 70 miles, or 8 hours. So, that will work."

Ed looks at the chart. "I know that place. Rick, tell him to go to the main island, Cay Sal. He'll know it too. It's uninhabited, but it has an old airstrip."

"Will do."

"If it has an airstrip, why not just pick him up?" I asked.

"He's wanted for murder. The U.S. Government can't be involved. You remember what we did to our friend Victor?" Rick said.

"OK, we'll go get him." I said.

"One thing may be useful. Under agreement with The Bahamas, the U.S. Coast Guard monitors Cay Sal, and the nearby islands frequently."

"That's something. Might come in handy. Thanks." I said.

"Talk soon. Out."

CLICK.

"Ed, how did you know about that airstrip?" Liz asked.

"I used to fly in there during my misspent youth."

"Gotcha."

Though it was a short trip, voyaging on a sailboat, or any boat for that matter, isn't like getting in the family chevy and tripping to grandmas. Eisenhower's wonderful interstate system does not equate to the peculiarities of weather, winds, and currents of traveling by sea. So, the astute navigator tries to build a contingency into each trip. In this instance, contingency wise, we were out on a limb. Meaning we had no plan B. By late morning of the next day, we were in the Straits of Florida, sailing about 146° on a broad reach, starboard tack in about 18 knots of wind. Tom was behind the wheel, the rest of us were sitting around the cockpit table having lunch.

"Tom, turn on the autopilot and sit down so you can enjoy lunch." I said.

"And our company." Liz added.

"I'm having a great time, but I am hungry."

"We'll make a sailor out of you yet." I said.

"Too late, I'm hooked. Wasn't too crazy about the squall the other day." Tom leaned down and pushed a button on the autopilot, then sat next to Liz.

The table is festooned with a basket of fruit, a plate of different cheeses, ham and tomatoes and various drinks.

Tom takes a plate and starts making a sandwich. "Anyone want this last beer?"

"Help yourself. There's more below." Liz said.

"Squalls are nothing to fool with, they're almost like miniature hurricanes. Nowadays you can usually see them coming on the radar, which helps." I said. "OK, as we get deeper into the Florida Straight, we run a good chance of meeting Cuban coast guard or gunboats, which is the same thing— "

"Girls, he's telling us to break out the bikinis." Liz said.

The girls giggle.

"How about the H&Ks?" Kelly asked.

"I think we should put all the guns in the locker. That way, if under some pretext we get boarded, they won't have an excuse to seize the boat."

"Not that they need one." Ed added.

"I'm hoping this new 'peace in our time' political atmosphere might— shall we say, temper their belligerence towards us innocent, fun loving, recreational sailors." I said.

"Neville Chamberlain." Liz said.

"What?"

"British Prime Minister, Neville Chamberlain, 1938. He's the one that said, 'peace in our time.'" Liz said.

"That's an ominous thought." Tom said.

"Why?" Kelly asked.

"Many think his clumsy, naïve attitude started the war between Germany and England. I'm one of them." Tom replied.

"Harriet is not naïve."

Everyone looked at Ed.

"Harriet, huh?" I said.

"Leave him alone." Liz said.

"I didn't mean to imply President Jackson was naïve." Tom said.

Ed gets up, stands behind the wheel and turns off the autopilot.

"Great lunch, honey." I said.

I stopped during the night, keeping station and a watch throughout so we could come up on Cay Sal early in the morning. The sun had been up for about an hour. We were under full sail until we were about five miles northwest of Cay Sal, then we took some sail in reducing speed until we could locate Pérez. Kelly was behind the wheel, the others were sitting around the cockpit table.

"Capt. Spade, there is a boat off the starboard beam coming our way. About six miles away. I think it's a patrol boat," Kelly reported.

I jumped up and grabbed the binoculars and looked to starboard. "Damn, you have good eyes. Probably coming out of Havana. Everyone do the low crawl, get below, and put on bathing suits."

"With or without tops?" Liz said caustically.

"What? Oh, with, of course."

"Just checking."

Kelly and Denise giggle. The crew scrambled below. I leaned down the companionway. "Make sure all the firearms are in the repel borders locker." I watched as the small patrol boat got larger. One by one, the crew came back on deck and placed themselves around the boat, ostensibly looking like tourists.

When it was obvious the patrol boat was preparing to intercept us, I furled the main and jib. Tom and Ed put fenders over the side, so our inquisitor didn't take chunks out of the hull. The patrol boat pulled alongside. Captain Gonzalez, walked out of the bridge and looked down at *Pinafore.*

"Good morning, Captain Gonzalez. We meet again. How nice." I said.

"Gonzales looks the length of *Pinafore.* "No tits today. Too bad, I like tits."

"You may have heard too much sun can cause cancer, so we try to stay vigilant. And we are still in international waters."

"Perhaps I arrest you anyway and take beautiful woman with me."

"Captain, please. The U.S. and Cuba are now allies. You would not wish to harm our friendship over some mere woman."

"*Capitán*, do not take me for fool. I think you are looking for a fugitive, as I do."

"Fugitive? No, we are not policemen. Captain, as I said a month ago, we are on vacation."

"Perhaps. I can be clever too. Now go." He turns from the rail and enters his bridge.

The gunboat motors off to the south.

"That guy is going to follow us right to Pérez." I said.

"Now what?" Ed asked.

"I don't know— Kelly start the engine, steer 146 same as before."

Still in the Straits of Florida, still sailing southwest, Kelly is still behind the wheel, and I was still in a pickle. We had probably covered three miles since we left *Capitán* Gonzalez and his miniature battleship. We all lounged in the cockpit, finishing lunch and discussing events.

You mean our good *Capitán*, Gonzalez, will merely follow us to Pérez and then arrest him?" Kelly asked.

"They'll arrest him, but he'll never make it back to the mainland." Ed said.

I stood and looked toward the Cuban gunboat, still sitting just under the horizon.

Ed stood beside me, looking through binoculars. "You're right, he's going to follow us right to the rendezvous."

I said nothing and continued to look off into the distance. After a moment, I strolled forward to the bow. Holding on to the forestay, I leaned over watched the mesmerizing bow wake.

Liz came up behind me and put her arm over my shoulder. "Penny for your thoughts?"

"Remember the last time you asked me that?"

"The airport in Caracas . . . you figured it out then and you will figure it out now."

"Yeah, this time let's hope I can figure it out without getting someone hurt— Hey, maybe that's the answer!" I grabbed Liz by the face and kissed her, then hurried to the cockpit and went below.

Liz stared after me. "What did I say?"

It had been several hours since *Capitán* Gonzalez had graced us with his presence. We were now a mile off Cayo de Sal making just enough headway to keep the bow pointed in the right direction. I was sitting in the cockpit. "Kelly, where's the gunboat?"

Kelly looked at the Radar. He's moved in to about seven miles."

"Not closer?" I asked.

"No, seven miles, give or take a few yards." Kelly replied.

"Staying out of Bimini waters." I said.

"Won't that keep him off our back? Bimini territorial waters, I mean," Denise said.

"No. Even if it did, he would just intercept us on the way back to the Keys." I picked up the satphone and pounded in some numbers— "Rick, it's me. Our satphone's are scrambled, right?"

"They're supposed to be. Why?"

"OK, I'll be cryptic. Have you heard from our friend?"

"About two hours ago? He says he is in a flatiron fishing skiff, whatever that is."

"It's a small flat-bottom boat rigged like a catboat, and it's the last thing you want to take to sea. How is he talking to you?"

"Satphone ."

"Does he have a cell?"

"Yes, I'm sure he does."

"Call him and tell him to turn on the AIS on his cell and find us."

"You can do that on a cell phone?"

"I didn't know it either, he's the one that told me."

"OK. Then what?" Rick asked.

"Tell him to talk us in. Back to you soon."

CLICK.

"Kelly, do you see anything on the radar?" I asked.

Kelly shielded the screen from the sun. "No. Nothing other than the gunboat."

"Use that x-ray vision of yours and see if you can pick Pérez's boat out of this haze. You're looking for a small boat with one mast." I said.

Kelly picked up some binoculars and slowly scanned 360 degrees— "He could be behind that spit of land, but I would probably see the mast."

"Unless he took the mast down. OK, everyone keep a sharp eye. Denise, how about going below and let me know if you can see anything on the big radar screen? And keep an eye on that gunboat."

Denise ran below. We spent the next 20 minutes scanning the low island just ahead of us and the horizon for sight of anything besides the damn gunboat.

"Capt. Spade look! About (looking at the compass) 125 degrees. I saw a flash."

The satphone rang. Liz snatches it from the table. "Hello!" She turned toward the spot where Kelly was pointing. "Yes, we see you! Stay down! There is a Cuban patrol boat not far away— OK, see you then." Liz disconnects and puts the phone down. "He is right over there where Kelly saw the flash. He's going to leave his boat on the beach and walk north. He wants us to come around the point and he will swim out to us."

"Kelly, move the boat slowly to the point at the north end of the Cay. Denise, if that patrol boat moves an inch, I want to know about it." I said.

"Right!"

"Ed, you and Liz put the ladder down and get ready to get Doc on board." I picked up the mic to the VHF radio and keyed the transmitter. "MAYDAY, MAYDAY, MAYDAY. This is the sailing vessel *Pinafore*. We have a heart attack victim and need immediate medical assistance.

"MAYDAY, MAYDAY, MAYDAY this is the sailing vessel *Pinafore* we are at 23° 41'35 North — 80° 22' 56 West. We have a heart attack victim and need immediate medical assistance. Over."

All the crew members stopped what they were doing and stared at me.

"Sailing vessel *Pinafore*, sailing vessel *Pinafore*, this is Coast Guard Station Miami. Identify your boat. Over."

"Coast Guard Station Miami, sailing vessel *Pinafore*, we are a 50-foot sloop with dark blue hull, white superstructure. There are seven people on board. We are located at 23° 41'35 North — 80° 22' 56 West. Over."

"Sailing vessel *Pinafore*. Coast Guard Station Miami. ETA five, zero minutes. Continue first aid. Over."

"Roger, Coast Guard Station Miami. ETA five, zero minutes. Continuing first aid. Sailing vessel *Pinafore* out."

"What the hell is that all about? Nobody is sick." Liz said.

"We want Pérez out of here, right? So, he rides out courtesy of the Coast Guard. Maybe the good captain heard our transmission and will hightail it out of here."

Ed looks through the binoculars at the gunboat- "Silvers and Collins are going to roast your chestnuts for this stunt. Denise! Is he moving?"

From below, "He's still paralleling our course."

"Another thing, he could come bounding over here to render aid. No one will fault him because he would be complying with international law." Ed said.

"Yeah, I know, but nothing says we have to submit to his aid." I said.

Kelly steps up on the stern pulpit, holding onto the backstay. "I can see the Doctor on the beach! He's in the water."

"Kelly, get as close to him as you can. Watch the depth! Denise. Keep an eye on the depth down there too!"

Kelly turns the wheel and applies some power to the engine.

Denise called up. "It's twenty-five feet right here!"

Moments later, Pérez was alongside.

"Liz! He's alongside!" Kelly called out. She stopped the engine.

Ed and Liz lean over the stern and help Pérez into the boat.

Denise called out. "The patrol boat has altered course. He's heading right for us!"

Everyone looked up and across the water. The patrol boat was coming straight for us, the bow wave forming a huge white mustache. Everyone hugged Pérez. Then Liz pushed him below. "Towel off and get into some dry clothes."

I called Rick Silvers. "Rick, it's me. As soon as we disconnect, I need you to call Coast Guard and tell them there is a 50-foot sailing yacht at Cay Sal suspected of smuggling drugs. Tell them to intercept and seize the yacht. Tell them the name of the boat is *Pinafore* and we are heavily armed.

"What! Are you crazy?"

"Rick, as soon as we get back in international waters, this gunboat is going to sink us."

"How do you know that?"

"Just please believe me. I'll try to hide behind the Cay, but those Coast Guard boats are our only chance."

"Can't you hold him off?"

"Rick, the guy is driving an old Stenka class patrol boat with twin 30mm rotary cannons! Inside of two and half miles, he can blow us out of the water in seconds. He knows who we are, and he knows who we're trying to recover."

"Do you have Pérez yet?"

"Yes, we have him, at least for now."

"OK. Give me the coordinates. You're going to get me fired."

"23° 41'35 North by 80° 22' 56 West."

"Talk soon. Out."

"I noticed you didn't mention Pérez suffered a massive heart attack." Ed said.

"I didn't want to give Rick one, plus I'm not so sure those guys would be all that enthusiastic about saving our asses if Pérez wasn't on board."

"Is the gunboat really going to sink us?" Kelly asked.

"He's going to try." I said.

"I thought this was going to be a vacation."

"We aren't dead yet." I said.

"If Doctor Pérez gets away, why would Captain Gonzalez sink us?" Denise asked.

"He was ordered to do a job. If our plan works, he will be in trouble. And because he can. There's no downside for him. And there is no law that says he can't, at least not out here." Ed answered.

"How fast can Gonzalez get here?" Tom asked.

"Kelly, you said he's about seven miles out. He can do 40 miles an hour, you do the math."

"Ten or twelve minutes. How long will it take the Coast Guard to get here?" Tom said.

"The chopper can get here in about 40 minutes. The boats will take three hours from now." I said.

Everyone looks at their watches.

"OK, *mi capitán*, what's the plan?" Tom asked.

"I have one. Get the hell out of that guy's way." Ed volunteered.

"Good idea. Tom take the helm. Kelly, get my M14 out of the locker."

Kelly ran below.

"Oh good, you're going to kill the big bad boat with a rifle. You know those Stenka's are sub chasers; they have torpedo tubes on them." Ed said.

"They use the tubes to store rum. They couldn't launch one anyway, it's too shallow."

"That's what they said about Pearl Harbor." Ed countered.

"Anyway, if they get shitty, I thought I might break some glass." I said.

"The good news is this class boat traded missile launchers for the tubes. Bad news, the guns are radar controlled. They don't need to look out the window. All you'll do is piss them off." Ed said.

"Piss them off are the operative words. How do you know so much about those boats?"

"I was supposed to steal one once."

"No kidding? For who?"

"Whom. Remember when I was—

"Guys! Can we focus, please? For Christ sake, you're giving a grammar lesson while trotting down memory lane!" Tom yelled.

"Sorry Tom. What's the depth?" I said.

"Twelve feet. Bottom coming up." Tom said.

"Tom, I would like you to ease around the point and keep this little island or Cay between us and the patrol boat."

"What's keeping Gonzalez from following? As you told me once, *Pinafore* can't go faster than nine knots, even with a jet engine strapped to it."

"I'm still hoping he will respect Bimini's territorial waters." I looked over at Ed. "What's it draw, about 12 feet?"

Ed nods. "Twelve, six."

"So, the patrol boat draws 12 - 13 feet, we draw four. He has to stay out in the Nicholas Channel, which keeps him at least a mile away."

"You may remember a 30mm has a range of two miles probably more. He can stand off and shred us." Ed said.

"If he gets inside 600-700 yards, I'll shoot up the bridge and that arrogant prick will get so pissed he'll fuck up and run aground."

"You know this how?" Tom asked.

"I have an advanced degree in psychology from Sears."

"Probably why they went out of business. The first thing you better do is shoot up that radar dome." Ed said.

"Good point. Tom! Watch the depth or we'll be the ones stuck." I said.

"Sorry. I get distracted every time I have thoughts of being ground to pieces by a 30mm gun." Tom said.

The patrol boat was a mile or more to the south. Liz walked to the companionway and called up to me. "Honey, you're wanted on the phone."

"What?"

"The radio— It's Captain Gonzalez, he would like to speak with you."

"Shit. Kelly, you drive, Tom. Come with me."

I climbed down the companionway and slid behind the navdesk, turned up the volume and picked up the mic. "This is SV *Pinafore*, over."

"Go to channel nine." I voice said.

I dialed the frequency to channel nine. "Anybody have a recorder on your phone?"

"I do." Tom said.

"Record this conversation."

Tom takes his cell phone out and turns on the recorder. I keyed the radio mic.

"This SV *Pinafore*, go ahead."

"You have my prisoner. Deliver him immediately."

"Captain Gonzalez, how nice to hear from you, but I have nothing that belongs to you."

"You have Alberto Pérez on your boat. He is wanted by the *Policía Nacional Revolucionaria* for murder."

"Even if we had such a person, we are in the Commonwealth of the Bahamas. The PNR has no authority here."

"You will turn him over, or I will come and get him."

"This is Bahamian territorial waters and frequently patrolled by armed U.S. Coast Guard aircraft."

"You have 10 minutes."

I tossed the mic on the table. I yelled, "Denise, trade places with Kelly, keep station here. Everyone else below."

Everyone but Denise climbed below and sat around the salon.

"You all heard the radio. Anyone have an idea?" I looked at my watch. "We still have 30 minutes before the medivac gets here. Gonzalez can't get much closer, but like Ed said, he can stand off and pound us into splinters. Which reminds me." I stood at the bottom of the companionway. "Denise, pull down our radar deflector, will you? No sense giving him a better target." I turned back to the crew.

"Maybe I should just go with him. I'll be OK at least until we get to Havana." Pérez said.

"The president said bring you in, we're going to bring you in."

"No. That's a good idea." Liz said.

Everyone stared at her.

"Call Gonzalez and tell him if he promises to return Berto to the authorities, we will send him over—"

"The Doc will never make it to the beach, let alone Havana." Ed said.

"Let me finish. By the time we negotiate the surrender, inflate the dingy, get it in the water and get three people outfitted with life jackets, and in the dingy, it could be at least 30 minutes."

"By that time, the Coast Guard will be here." Tom said.

"We hope." I said.

"Anybody have a better idea?" Liz asked.

We all looked at each other.

"OK, somebody besides me needs to start the conversation, make like we had a minor mutiny." I said.

"From what I have seen of the good *capitán*, his name is in the dictionary under misogynist. So, I am probably not the best choice." Liz said.

"Tom, have you ever taken one of those hostage negotiator courses?" I asked.

"Yeah, a long time ago."

"You're elected."

The radio crackles. "*Cinco minutos.*"

Tom sits behind the navdesk and picks up the radio mic. "My name is Sawyer. I have taken, shall we say, temporary charge of the *Pinafore*. We will comply with your wishes provided you give us some guarantees. Over."

"Ha, I guarantee not to sink your boat."

"You will do more than that. You want to complete your mission. We want to go home. So, you will agree to our terms."

"What terms?"

"The man you call a prisoner will be turned over to the American Envoy in Havana."

"*Si*, I can do this."

"The prisoner will be unharmed."

"*Si.*"

"Good, I will call our State Department in Washington and tell them of our agreement. Once we get approval, he will be sent to you."

"I want him now!"

"Captain, you have two choices. An international incident, and you fail in your mission, or agree to our terms, and complete your mission. Which I suspect will keep you out of jail."

"I can sink and kill all of you and complete my mission."

"True. But captain, if we are who you think we are, don't you suppose our government knows precisely where we are? If you harm us, it would be a major incident. Ask yourself who would get the blame for killing six U.S. government officials?

There is a long period of silence.

"Captain Gonzalez, do you copy? Over."

Another long pause.

"Captain Gonzalez, do you copy? Over."

"*Si*, I agree to terms. My government says OK."

"Standby." Tom looks around the salon. "Now what?"

I slapped Tom on the shoulder. "Damn good job. Now we wait." I looked at my watch. "You already used up eight minutes."

"He must not have heard that radio call for the medivac." Liz said.

"Those guys are very compartmentalized. Even if the radio operator heard the call, he may not have told the captain." I said.

"Especially this captain. One wrong word and you're fish food. Better to say nothing at all." Ed said.

"OK, we sit tight until Gonzalez squawks. Tom, while you're sitting at the navdesk, crank up the range on the radar. We may see the chopper coming."

Tom adjusts dials on the radar.

"You don't suppose he would shoot that chopper down, do you?" Tom asked.

"If he does, I'll be spending my retirement in Leavenworth."

The Satphone rings. Liz answers it. "Hello— Hi, Rick, wait one." Liz pressed a button on the phone. "OK, you're on speaker."

"Two Sentinel-class cutters out of Key West are on the way. They aren't battle ships but please do not screw with them. They can punch large holes in your boat."

"I want them to punch large holes in this fucking gunboat." I said. "Rick, in about 45 minutes, I want you to call the cutters and tell them we are the good guys, and the gunboat sitting next to us is the bad guy. It is heavily armed, so warn them to be careful."

"Why didn't you just say that in the first place?"

"Because there was/is no time for an outbreak of international cover our asses. We have minutes, not days. I'm hoping the medevac chopper will get here before the gunboat starts shooting."

"What medevac chopper?" Rick asked.

"Pérez had a heart attack, so I had to call the Coast Guard to get him out of here."

"The hell he did! You are going to get us fired and sent to prison!"

"Relax. The only one that's going to get in trouble is me."

"Jesus H Christ! You are really something. I'll get back to you— Keep your head down."

The radio belches with the voice of Captain Gonzalez. "*Pinafore*! I do not see any boats in the water. I lose patience. You will not like what I do if you make me angry."

Tom picks up the mic. "Relax, our dingy wouldn't inflate, so we are fixing it. The patch is done—" Tom waves at the crew, motioning them to go on deck. Everyone but Pérez and I ran up the companionway. "And we're inflating it."

"You lie!"

"Look for yourself. We have the whole crew working on it."

"You have 15 minutes!" Captain Gonzalez yelled. "Then I come get him!

Denise called down from the helm. "Capt. Spade! There are two targets at 10 miles to the northwest. I think it's the choppers."

I ran to the navdesk and looked at the radar. I looked at Pérez. "Doc looks like you're going for a ride. Stuff anything you need into your pockets." I took a few steps up the companionway and stuck my head out. "Liz! Get to the bow and get the jib and its gear out of the way. Choppers are in bound."

"Will do."

Stepping down and turning to Pérez, "Doc, when the choppers are close, I want you to crawl through the forward hatch, lay on the deck and play dead.

If they see you lying on the deck, I think they will send down a basket. Get in quickly. This type of rescue is hard to manage from a sailboat."

"I understand. Just tell me when to go up on deck."

"OK, go forward and wait for the signal."

Denises yelled, "Capt. Spade! Choppers almost overhead."

I ran forward and lifted the forward hatch. "Liz! Are you ready?"

"Send him up!"

Pérez squeezes past me, climbs on the bunk and shimmies out of the hatch. The hatch closes. Now on the foredeck, Pérez lies on his back. A Coast Guard *Sikorsky* MH-60T Jayhawk hovers over *Pinafore*, already sending down a basket. The noise and hurricane strength wind are intense. The basket bounces on the deck as the boat pitches and the helicopter's hover varies. Ed and Liz unceremoniously shove Pérez into the basket, then give the helicopter a thumbs up. Slowly, then with a jerk, the basket swings away from *Pinafore* out over the ocean. They all watch as the basket is winched up to the door and pulled into the helicopter. Both helicopters fly off to the west. The penetrating noise and wind die away.

The radio is screaming profanities.

"OK, Tom you're up."

"What the hell am I going to tell him?"

Ed climbs down the companionway followed by Liz. "Your new best friend is working closer. Guess he didn't read his manual about minimum depths."

Denise calls down, "Hey guys, I think the gunboat just trained his guns on us."

"Shit! Ed, take a look. Tom, get on the radio and say something."

Ed climbs back up the companionway. Tom sits at the navdesk and keys the mic.

"This is *Pinafore*. Go ahead."

"You tricked me! I am going to turn that scow into scrap."

"We are in waters protected by U.S. Bahamian treaty. If you fire into our boat—

Ed slides down the companionway. "That SOB is getting ready to fire. If you think the M14 will reach his radar, now is the time."

I ran to the forward cabin, returning with the M14 and ran up the companionway.

"—Captain you will create an international incident which I'm sure will be grounds for your arrest." Tom continued.

I rested the M14 on the top of the cabin and aimed at the Stenka. "Kelly, grab some glasses and watch that boat."

Kelly grabs some binoculars and focuses on the gunboat.

"He's got to be at least 700 yards, which is a crap shoot with iron sights, but if he shoots, I'll aim at the radar dome. Can you see it?"

"I have it." Kelly said.

"OK, if I shoot, try to see where my shots hit."

BOOM! BOOM!

Two large splashes erupt in the water next to the *Pinafore*.

"Guess that qualifies as a first shot— Everyone down! Girls, you're going to earn your pay today. Denise, try to maneuver as much as you can, changing the profile and location of *Pinafore*. Don't give him a stationary target. Kelly! Here we go."

BANG! BANG! BANG!

Denise turns the wheel, and the big boat swings 180 degrees.

"Up two feet and right about a foot," Kelly yelled.

"Denise, steady!" I yelled.

BANG! BANG! BANG!

Denise turned the wheel, changing the profile of the boat.

"You're on it! Come right another foot and fire for effect!"

"Steady Denis!" I yelled again.

BANG! BANG! BANG! BANG! BANG! BANG! BANG! BANG! BANG!

You got it! You tore it all to hell!" She jumped up and kissed me on the cheek.

Grinning, "Denise, start maneuvering again. He can still shoot. He just doesn't have eyes." To prove my point.

BOOM! BOOM! BOOM!

The gunboat fires three more times, but the shots are wide.

"Kelly, I'm going to fire at the pilothouse, keep an eye on what's happening. Denise steady up."

BANG! BANG! BANG! BANG! BANG! BANG!

"You're breaking a lot of glass."

Denise yelled, "Look! He's turning the boat toward the shore. He's trying to get closer."

Down below the satphone rings. Ed stands, grabs the phone, then jumps back on the deck. "Hello!"

"I have some news." Rick Silvers said.

"The cutters aren't coming."

BOOM! BOOM! BOOM! BOOM! BOOM! BOOM!

"No, they are on the way— What's that noise?" Rick asked.

"What do you think it is! The guy is shooting the crap out of us!"

"Shit! OK, the Navy is sending two F-5s out of Key West. Hopefully, they will be there in minutes."

"Rick! We have no way to talk to the pilots. Please give them the situation and ask them to kill this guy before he kills us," Ed yells.

"Done!"

BOOM! BOOM! BOOM! BOOM! BOOM! BOOM!

CRASH!

The mast shattered and fell over the side with a screeching sound, just missing me and Kelly. The deck was fouled with wire, rope and what's left of our radar dome.

"Denise! Stop the prop now! — I need some help up here!" I yelled.

Tom and Ed appeared from below.

"Get that rigging out of the water before it fouls the prop! Liz, do your thing with the Coast Guard!" I yelled.

I fired at the gunboat again. Ed and Tom strain to get the damaged rigging out of the water.

"Rick says Navy fighters are on the way! Should be here in minutes." Ed yelled over the noise.

"We won't live that long." I said, mostly to myself.

Liz came up from below. "The radio is out!"

"Shit! Yeah, the antenna went over the side with the mast. Use the handheld!"

"OK, I pulled out the life jackets."

"Honey, get below, make your calls, and lay flat on the cabin deck. Drowning is not the problem."

"OK, we got all the stuff in." Tom yelled.

"Thanks, everyone but Dense below." They hesitated. "Do it! Denise! Keep bobbing and weaving."

The crew dived below.

BANG! BANG! BANG! BANG! BANG! BANG!

CLANG!

The boat shook and there was a loud sound, like a bell being struck by a huge hammer.

"What was that!" Denise yelled.

"They hit the anchor. We won't need it, anyway."

BOOM! BOOM! BOOM! BOOM! BOOM! BOOM!

Waterspouts exploded next to the boat as the heavy 30mm projectiles hit, throwing mud and bottom debris on the deck.

I took aim again just as two jets screamed over so low that it looked like water was sucked up in their vortex. The jets pull up to the vertical— almost out of sight, they pull back until they are inverted— they snap rolled level— then nosed down into a steep dive.

ZZZZZZZZZZZZZZZZZZZZZZZZZZZZZZZZZZZZZZ! ZZZZZZZZZZZZZZ! ZZZZZZZZZ!

SWOOSH! SWOOSH! SWOOSH! SWOOSH!

BOOM-KABOOM!

The gunboat disintegrates into a ball of fire. The jets make another low pass, then fly off to the west. I watched what was left of the gunboat sink into Nicholas Strait.

Ed walked up beside me.

"Jesus Ed, what were those things?"

"Navy F-5s with 20mm guns and Zuni rockets. They're used mostly for training."

"They sure schooled Captain Gonzalez."

CHAPTER THIRTY-SEVEN

I looked over *Pinafore*. My once beautiful boat was strewn with broken aluminum, shards of fiberglass, steel cable and Dacron rope. My ears rang incessantly from the gunfire. I looked at where the gunboat had been. Not even an oil stain marked its loss.

"Anybody hurt?" I asked.

There followed a chorus of various negative replies.

"Anybody hungry?" I asked. Incongruous as it sounded, I was hungry, and for the others it would keep shock at bay.

"I could eat." Ed said.

"I'll fix some sandwiches." Liz offered.

"I'll help." Kelly said.

Both women moved slowly through the rubble and went below.

I turned to Denise. "Denise, is the engine, OK?"

"I've been watching the oil and water temps. Both are normal."

"Good, because the engine is now our only way home. See if there are any holes in the hull, look below the waterline first.

"On it." Denise runs below.

"Tom, will you move us away from the island until I can rig the spare anchor."

Tom shifted the transmission into gear and eased the throttle forward. As he turned the wheel, the big sailboat turned powerboat, swung away from the island and pointed north.

The satphone rang. I picked it up. "Hello. Hi Rick."

"You guys, OK?"

"No injuries. The boat took a beating. Lost the mast, a hunk of the bow was shot away. The engine seems OK."

"Very happy to hear you all are OK. What happened to the Cuban gunboat?"

"It's sitting on the bottom in about 30 feet of water."

"Any survivors?"

"We didn't look, but I doubt it. The Navy hit a fuel bunker, or a magazine, and it went poof."

"As you so distinctly put it, everyone here is now in 'cover my ass' mode. Do you think the Cubans saw the jets?"

"As for the patrol boat, no. We were all pretty busy. We didn't see them until they were literally on top of us."

"How about mainland radar?" Ricked asked.

"Rick, those guys were so low they were sucking fish through the intakes. When they popped up for the strike, it was just seconds. The pilots were in the O-Club having cocktails before the gunboat hit the bottom. It's likely the Cubans on the mainland never saw them. Rick standby for a second." I put my hand over the phone. "Tom, stop here. Ed, will you pull the spare anchor out of the chain locker then hook it up? If you have questions, ask Liz or Denise."

Ed goes forward.

"OK, Rick I'm back."

"We think you should cross the Santaren Channel, then move northeast to Nassau."

"Nassau! Rick, that's 200 miles from here maybe more. The boat is all torn to hell. I'm not sure we would make it. Why can't we just go back to the Keys or Miami? That's only 70 miles?"

"Because once you're in the Florida Straits, you'll be sitting ducks."

"What do you mean sitting ducks? Who's hunting us?"

"The Cubans. Once they figure out what happened to their gunboat, and they will, they'll be looking for an opportunity to save face or restore their *machismo*, however you want to put it."

"I thought these guys were going to be our allies?"

"Most of them are, just not the Coast Guard, or the Airforce, or maybe the Army."

"Jesus, Rick, are you sure this is all worth the damn hassle? If these people don't want to be friends, then fuck them. What do we need them for?"

"All we want you to do is go to Nassau or go to Andros if you have to. That way, you stay in Bahamian territory. Leave the boat and come back here."

"I can't get to Andros or Nassau without crossing the Bahama Banks!"

"So?"

"You ever heard the saying, it's too thin to plow and too thick to drink?"

"What the hell does that have to do with anything?"

"The Bahama Banks are too deep to walk across and too shallow to float across. Most of it is about six feet deep!"

"Look, figure it out. Then get back to me."

"This sounds like some stupid crap Collins made up."

CLICK!

I threw the phone down. "OK, let's eat before I have a stroke!"

Sandwiches and beer were the focus of the next hour. Being shot at makes you hungry, it made me hungry anyway. We sat around the cabin eating quietly, nobody saying anything until Tom spoke up.

"What's the plan?"

"We'll spend the night here. The lunch hook Ed put out should hold fine. It's not too deep here. Let's toss all the broken stuff overboard so we're not tripping over it. Plus, it will lighten the boat some, the mast alone is about 200 lbs. Don't throw the wire over, it will end up around the prop. In the meantime, I'll be huddled up with the chart trying to find a way across the Banks."

I slept surprisingly well. No nightmares, no flashbacks until Denise nudged me early in the morning.

"Capt. Spade. Capt. Spade, wake up."

Thinking it was a nightmare, I turned over and ignored the noise. It didn't go away.

"Capt. Spade, wake up."

"Good morning, Denise. What's up?"

"There is another gunboat on the other side of the Cay."

"Crap!" I carefully crawled out of the bunk so as not to wake Liz, pulled on some shorts, then hurried to the companionway and climbed up to the cockpit. Ed and Tom are already on deck.

"Morning skipper, nice day." Ed said.

"How long and what's he doing?" I said.

"My we are in a mood. He was here when Tom and I came topside about 20 minutes ago, and he is just sitting there."

"Looking for his buddy, no doubt." Tom added.

"No doubt." I said.

"I'm all atwitter as to what your plan is?" Ed asked.

"Coffee first." I said.

"Ahh. Logical and concise. I feel better already." Ed said.

"I don't. Those nervous nellies in D.C. are never going to send us fighters again." Tom said.

"You can bet they already threw our phone number in the trash." I turned to Ed. "Mr. Expert. What is that thing?"

"That is a Zhuk-class patrol boat. Good news, no heavy artillery, just twin .50s. Bad news, it draws four feet and can do 30 miles per hour."

"So, all bad news."

"I am a 'cup half full' kind of guy," Ed said.

"How is it you know so little about boats, but you know about these things?" I asked.

"I steal them, I don't drive them. I actually stole one of those Zhuks."

"Will you guys please tell me what the hell you're talking about?" Tom implored.

"Our comrade here has a dark and shadowy past as a boat thief."

"I got that part."

"Sorry. The problem or our problem is they only draw four feet, so they can go anywhere we can go. The twin .50s you can figure out for yourself."

I waved a pleasant good morning at the gunboat. Nobody waved back. "Let's look normal. Get the anchor up and start the engine. We'll work our way out to the channel. Maybe they don't know what happened to their friends."

"They can figure it out just by looking at us. We're all shot to hell." Tom said.

"The mast or the lack of one is probably a big clue." Ed said.

"Maybe they won't notice." I said.

"You think they won't notice 50 feet of our mast is missing?" Ed asked.

"They're power boaters. What do they know? I thought you were a glass half full kind of guy. And I'm open to ideas."

Tom moved over to the wheel and started the engine. Ed and I went forward and pulled up the anchor. Even pulling up the lighter 'lunch hook' was a major feat without the windless, which was now sitting on the bottom.

Once back in the cockpit, I called down to Elizabeth. "Liz! You girls get into swimsuits. Kelly break out the H&Ks and the rest of the heavy artillery."

Liz comes to the bottom of the companionway. "What's up?"

"Another gunboat. I'm not sure they know what happened, so we make like tourists. But keep your tops on." I said.

"You're never any fun. Can I have some coffee first?" Liz said.

I chuckled. "Sure."

The radio crackles. "Unidentified vessel, this is patrol boat '*Libertad*' identify yourself."

I picked up the mic. "*Libertad*, this is *Pinafore*. Switch to channel nine. Over.

I dialed in channel nine on the radio."

"This is Captain Eduardo Mendoza of the Cuban Revolutionary Border Guard. Over."

"Good morning, Captain Mendoza. How can we be of service?"

"You may tell me your business in these waters."

"These waters are Bahamian territory, but we are tourists on vacation."

"Your boat has been in big storm, yes?"

"You are most astute, captain. We encountered a squall yesterday which caused a good bit of damage."

Elizabeth and the two girls came up from below, walked forward, put towels on the deck and laid down.

"I think you should come to my ship. We have fine *almuerzo*. You bring ladies, yes."

"That is very gracious of you, captain, but we must decline. Unfortunately, there are repairs that require our attention. Have a good day. *Pinafore* out." I tossed the mic on a seat cushion.

"That ought to hold him for about five minutes." Ed said.

"Liz! You and the girls stay put. I don't want the good captain to see us in a parlay."

"Eye, eye skipper. This is hard work, but we are up to the task."

Kelly and Denise laugh.

I sat down and laid a chart on the cockpit table. "Last night, I plotted a course over the Bank. I suppose the patrol boat could follow. If I were him, I wouldn't try it, but mostly I guess we rely on him not wanting to enter Bahamian waters."

"Especially if his plan is to sink us," Ed said.

"Cheery thought." Tom said.

"If we sink, at least it will only be in about six feet of water." I said.

"Oh good, we can walk home." Ed said.

"Tom, ease away from the Cay and move out toward the east. Let's see what this guy will do."

Tom swings the boat to the northeast and adds some power. "Depth is steady at 28 feet."

"So far, so good." Just as I looked back at the gunboat—

BANG! BANG! BANG! BANG! BANG! BANG!

Plumes of water explode alongside of the boat.

The girls dove for cover behind the cabin roof. I grabbed the mic and keyed the radio. "What the hell do you think you're doing, you prick!"

"Courtesy and gentle persuasion has always been our credo," Ed needled.

"Turn your boat 180 degrees or we fire into you!" Captain Mendoza yelled.

"Tom! Do as he says!" I keyed the mic again. "You fired on an unarmed civilian craft in Bahamian Territorial Waters!" I yelled.

"Cuba considers this international waters. My men were performing maintenance and the gun misfires. We are sorry." Captain Mendoza said.

I threw the mic at the radio. "Misfire my ass. Liz, where is the satphone?"

"You keep throwing that mic around were going to have to child proof it." Ed said.

"The phone is right here. I already called Rick." Liz handed it to me.

"Rick! You remember the duck hunters you were talking about? They found us and already fired the proverbial shot across the bow."

"Are you guys, OK?" Rick asked.

"Yeah, we are OK. But what about getting us out of here?" I said.

"I'll take it to the committee right away."

"Committee, what fucking committee!"

"After yesterday, you earned yourself an oversight committee to determine policy."

"Collins is behind this— he going to earn himself a broken jaw!"

"He's the committee chairman." Rick confirmed.

"Can you get me to the President?" I asked.

"Not yet. She's under a lot of pressure to get this Cuba thing done, and there are those that see you as a hinderance. Let me work some back channels."

I sat down and put my head in my hands. I was exhausted, and for the first time I was scared. "OK. I get it. We are expendable."

"I didn't say that." Rick said.

"You didn't have to."

CLICK.

Tom, will you and Ed anchor the boat? Liz, how about feeding everyone?" I said.

"Sure. Are you OK?" Liz asked.

"No. For the first time, I'm scared. I'm sacred for you, for me and for the people on this boat."

"Now you're scaring me. What can we do?" Liz said.

"I don't know, but whatever it is, we are on our own."

Liz fixed a big pot of spaghetti, not the usual fare for breakfast in the tropics, but we wolfed down every bit. Kelly and Tom helped with the clean-up and afterwards we all sat around the salon with coffee. Tom had beer.

"I can see some men watching us through binoculars from time to time, but other than that, they don't seem to pay us much attention." Tom said.

"Liz, what do you think?" I asked.

"I think we take Rick at face value. As for the Cubans, they are waiting to see how much starch President Jackson has in her back. I bet they won't provoke anything for a day or two. In the meantime, we're running out of food."

"Denise, how's the fuel situation?" I asked.

"Depends on where we're going. We can get home, but not to Nassau."

I scratched my head, trying to get the weeds out of my brain. "Ed, how many crew on that boat?"

"Supposedly, two officers and nine enlisted. And I don't like where this is going."

"I'm going to like it less." Tom added.

"You haven't heard the plan." I said.

"You've been reading too much Horatio Hornblower." Liz added.

"Who's Horatio Hornblower?" Kelly asked.

"Sounds like fun," Denise said.

"Tonight, we are going on what the famous Captain Hornblower would call a cutting out expedition. First, we control the deck, then . . . .

CHAPTER THIRTY-EIGHT

Pinafore – Cayo De Sal, Bimini - Night

Ed, Tom, Kelly, Denise, and I were all in dark clothing. Each carried a weapon. Quietly, we slipped into the dingy, which was tied on the far side of *Pinafore* so to be out of view of the gunboat. Once we were all aboard, Tom and Ed rowed slowly around the stern of *Pinafore* toward the gunboat, making a wide arc to come up on its far side. The moon was out but it was cloudy— for how long was the question. As the guys rowed, the girls and I watched the gunboat paying particular attention to the deck house. One of the guys missed a stroke making a noisy splash. We all froze, afraid to breathe, waiting for a machinegun to stitch through the night. The dingy drifted for a few minutes. No one on the gunboat came to look. We continued, in what seemed an eternity, we finally came along the dark side of the gunboat, which was now between us and the moon, keeping us in dark shadow.

Slowly, the five of us climbed on board. Tom went forward. Kelly moved aft. Denise went to find the engine room. Ed and I entered the pilothouse. Sleeping in a chair was an enlisted crewman, presumably the anchor watch. Ed clamped his gloved hand over the man's mouth. The man's eyes bugged out with surprise. I shoved my 1911A1 Colt in his face and made a sign with my finger and lips to be quiet. The man nodded. Ed wrapped duct tape around his mouth and head. Then bound his hands and feet with the same tape. We laid the man on the deck and proceed below.

Once in the passageway, we located Captain Mendoza's cabin and slipped inside. The captain was in his bunk, asleep. Ed stuck a shotgun in Mendoza's face and shoved the barrel into his nose. He awoke instantly, only to be shoved back in his bunk by Ed. I put my pistol under the man's chin.

Almost whispering. "Do you know what kind of pistol this is?"

Captain Mendoza nodded.

"Do you know what kind of hole it will make in your head?"

Captain Mendoza nodded again.

"If you make the slightest noise, I will kill you and everyone on this boat. Do you understand?"

Captain Mendoza nodded.

"Good. Ed watch the companionway. Now, Captain, where is the PA system?"

Captain Mendoza shakes his head and shrugs his shoulders.

"*Direcion publica.*" I said.

There is a flicker of recognition in his face, but Mendoza shrugs again.

I ground the Colt into Mendoza's neck. "Listen, you putz, you fucked with the wrong guy when you shot at my wife! The last guy that did that is fish food. Now you get me to the *Direcion publica* or whatever the fuck you call it and do it now."

From the cabin door. "Shussssh. Not so loud," Ed cautioned.

"Fuck it. Let's kill all of them and get out of here."

"You're the boss. It's easier anyway."

I pulled Mendoza out of his bunk, shoved him on the floor, and pointed the pistol at Mendoza's forehead.

"Nooo. Please. . . by the desk."

I pulled him off the floor and dragged him to the desk. "How many crew are there?"

"Nine crew, two officers."

"Wrong!"

"No! Please! That's all I have."

"You tell the crew to assemble on the aft deck, fantail or whatever you call it, and do it immediately. All of them. That man at the door with the shotgun speaks Spanish, *perfecto*. You say the wrong thing and I'll kill you right here. *Entendar.* "

"*Si*, yes." Mendoza leans over to a box on the bulkhead and turns on a switch. "*Atención, atención. Este es el Capitán. Todas las manos se encuentran en la cubierta de popa. Todas las manos se encuentran en la cubierta de popa.*"

I sat Mendoza in a desk chair and then taped his mouth and hands. I then bound his torso and legs to the chair. When finished, I tipped the chair backwards until it fell to the floor. I pointed my pistol between Mendoza's eyes. Mendoza looked terrified.

"You shot at my wife. If I ever see you again, I'll kill you."

"OK, it's getting busy out there. Let's go." Ed warned.

Ed and I let a couple of crewmen pass, then stepped out into the passageway and walked up to the flying bridge. We peeked out onto the aft deck. The crew are milling around. One of the petty officers calls them to attention. I unslung my M14 and walked out starboard of the radar mast and moved to a position overlooking the deck. Ed did the same thing on the port side. I fired the rifle in the air.

BAM! BAM! BAM! BAM!

Instinctively, the Cuban crew ducked.

Silencio! I yelled.

Kelly and Tom work around the port and starboard sides of the main deck. Both point H&K submachine guns at the gunboat crewmen.

"Kelly fire a burst over their heads. "

RATATATRATATATRATATATRATATATRATATATRATATAT!

I said silence! You men that speak English translate for the rest. The crewmen look shocked, but they are quiet.

"You do one thing I don't tell you to do. You will be killed and thrown overboard. You give any of my people the least provocation, and you will be killed and thrown overboard. If you strike, touch, or talk back to any of my people, you will be killed and thrown overboard. Am I clear!"

The crew talked among themselves. I petty officer stepped forward.

"I am chief petty officer. May I speak?"

"Go ahead." I said.

"What is your intention?"

"That should be plain. My intention is to take over your boat. Which I have done. Are there any crew below?"

"No. You will not harm us?"

"Not if you follow my instructions."

"Why are you doing this?"

"Because you fired on my boat! The attack was unprovoked. And my wife was aboard that boat! And that pissed me off."

"We were following orders."

"That's the usual excuse isn't it. Well, now you're going to follow my orders. Ed throw him the tape. Tom you too."

Tom and Ed threw the petty officer my year's supply of duct tape. I hoped it was enough. I wondered if Cubans used duct tape. "Now, you will one-at-a-time bind the hands and feet of your men. Then they will lie on the deck and be quiet. Do it!"

The petty officer picked up one roll of tape, called one man forward, bound his hands and feet, helped him to lie down and repeated the process until all the crewmen were lying on the deck. Then Tom did the same to the petty officer.

Denise came on deck.

"Well?"

"Done."

"Tom?"

"Done."

"OK, let's go."

As soon as we got back to *Pinafore*, Liz had us underway. We motored through the rest of the night. By midday, we were about twenty miles off Marathon, Florida, our temporary base. Denise was driving. The rest of the crew were sitting in the cockpit.

"Denise, don't let anybody come up behind us."

"I'm watching. Fuel is getting low."

"Nothing we can do about it. Let's just get inshore, if we need to stop, we will."

"You going to call Rick?" Liz asked.

"Guess now is as good as any time." Liz handed me the satphone . I punched the buttons. "Hey Rick."

"I'm sorry I haven't got back to you yet. I just don't have a decision from this damned committee yet." Rick explained.

"That's OK, we are just outside Marathon, FL. Should be at the dock in an hour."

"What? So, they let you go. Great!"

"Sorta."

"What do you mean, sorta?" Rick asked suspiciously.

"We took over the boat. Disabled the crew, engines and radios and threw the .50 cals over the side."

"You're kidding!"

"No. And if the Cubans tell you any differently, it's a lie. We didn't hurt anyone. But I understand the engines will probably never run again. They sucked up some sand or something like that."

Denise giggled.

"The radios needed updating too, so no loss there," Ed said.

"You guys are going to start a war!" Rick exclaimed.

"Listen, slick! I thought we were friends. But you left our asses hanging way out, and from what I could tell, with absolutely no plan to get us back. Now you tell Collins, his fucking committee, and anyone else that was involved in this fiasco, and I mean anyone, to go fuck themselves! And never call me again!"

CLICK!

"Well, there goes my pension." Tom said.

"Remember our credo— courtesy, and gentle persuasion." Ed said.

CHAPTER THIRTY-NINE

Pinafore – Marathon Marina, Florida

Ed and I were drinking beer in the cockpit. I was reading an old copy of *Sail* magazine. Liz and the girls were sunning on the deck. Tom was drinking beer and reading a book.

"So, have you guys been contemplating your retirement?" I asked.

"I'm thinking Walmart greeter." Ed said.

"You were a private detective. Why don't we go into business as partners?" Tom said.

"I'd love to. As soon as I get out of Leavenworth, I'll call you."

Liz raised her head. "Will you three stop. If you're bored, go into town, and do the grocery shopping."

"I'm not that bored." I said.

Ed was looking over my shoulder at the dock. "Boy, someone is going to get their ass handed to them."

Tom and I look up at Ed.

"Why?"

"Some idiot is driving on the dock."

I turned to look at what Ed was describing. "I wanted to do that myself more than once. I hate humping gear back and forth to the boat."

"Try it with groceries sometime." Liz said.

I turned back to my magazine.

"Hey guys! Heads up." Ed said.

"Now what?" I turned to look down at the dock.

"It's Harriet." Ed said.

Liz sits up. "No, no, no, she can't see me like this."

Kelly and Denise sit up and look around.

Two men dressed in suits walk on board *Pinafore*. One of them says, "You gentlemen have any firearms on your persons."

"No, but you might want to check the girls. They've been known to conceal H&Ks in their bikinis." I said.

"You would be the smart ass."

"That's Captain smart ass to you and nobody invited you on board." I stood and pushed my way past the suits and stepped to the gangway. Ed and Tom followed. The girls all stood in place.

I could see two more Secret Service Agents on the dock.

The President of the United States, Harriet Jackson, walked up the gangway, giving me her hand. I helped her aboard.

"Good afternoon, ma'am." I said.

"I got your message." The president said.

"The redacted version, I hope."

"I suppose so, nonetheless, I felt I owed you a face to face."

"High honors from the president." I said.

"Yes, it is. May I sit, probably in the cabin or as you nautical types say, down below? The Secret Service loathes open-air meetings."

"Probably those unfortunate incidents with Kennedy and Reagan." I said.

"Probably."

"Right this way, ma'am." I proceeded her down the companionway.

President Jackson looked up to see Liz and the girls standing forward. "You all look comfortable. Elizabeth, you'll notice I'm not wearing a pencil skirt. Why don't you join us? Ed, you, and Tom too."

Liz went down the forward hatch. Kelly and Denise followed everyone else down the companionway, then hurriedly shunted off to their cabin. After the president was seated, I opened the reefer.

"Ma'am, would you care for something to drink?"

"Do you have a cold beer?

"I don't think Tom drank it all." I pulled a half dozen beers out of the reefer and placed them on the table. I then gathered a like number of classes from the cupboard and put those on the table. I went back into the reefer and pulled out four soft drinks and handed them up to the Secret Service.

Liz walked out of the forward stateroom dressed in a pink polo shirt and white shorts. "Madam president, please excuse my informality."

"I hardly expected you to be dressed in a business suit. Though if you recall the last time we were on a boat, you were in a blue suit with heels and pearls."

Both started laughing.

"With a pencil skirt, no less. I can't imagine what I was thinking." Liz said.

"Well, the sailors liked it."

Liz blushed, then laughed.

Ed, Tom, and I found seats. Kelly sat at the nav desk, Denise stood beside her. They were both dressed in shorts and T-shirts.

"Madam president my I present Special Agents Denise and Kelly, both work for Jerry McGuire."

"Ladies, it's very nice to meet you. I've heard many wonderful things."

"Thank you, ma'am." Kelly replied.

"Thank you so much. It's a pleasure to meet you, ma'am." Denise said.

"OK. Let's hear what happened. Please remember, no one is in the loop except those present." The president said.

"You know what happened with the first gunboat. After that, we were ordered to cross the Santaren Channel and into the Bahama Bank and make for Nassau. I told Rick that I thought it was too shallow. Plus, we didn't have the fuel, but I'm not sure I told him that part."

"What's the depth of the Bank?" The president asked.

"Six to eighteen feet on the chart. I plotted a course that may have worked, but the next morning, another gunboat showed up. We tried to make like tourists. We waved, and the girls paraded around in their swimsuits—"

"Topless?"

"Ahh no. You heard about that?" I said.

"I did, quite ingenious."

Liz blushed, Denise and Kelly looked at their hands.

"Anyway, we pulled the anchor and motored east away from the gunboat. The Cuban opened fire with their twin fifty's."

"Did they hit the boat?"

"No ma'am. All the damage you see was done by the first boat, the one the Navy sank."

"Then what?"

"They said it was an accident, but they also said if we tried to leave, they would fire into us. So, we anchored and called Rick Silvers, but he was less than helpful."

"How so?"

"He said everyone was trying to cover their ass and Collins was in charge of some committee, which would determine policy regarding our situation. I asked to speak with you but was told you were under a lot of pressure, and it wouldn't be a good idea."

"Policy?"

"Yes, ma'am."

"Then what?"

"Liz has a lot of experience with this stuff, so I asked for her thoughts."

"I told him to take what Rick said at face value. I said I thought the Cubans were waiting to see what you would do. My exact words were, they wanted to see how much starch President Jackson has in her back. I then prophesied they would do nothing for a day or two." Liz said.

"In the meantime, we were running out of food. We can make water, but other than the occasional fish we bring our food and fuel—"

"And you weren't planning for a long stay."

"No, ma'am." I said.

"Then what?"

"Dwindling food, seemingly no chance of help and hinky Cubans we— I decided to take over the gunboat. "

"Tell me about it."

Tom and the girls shuffled in their seats.

"No one will hear this except me. There are no career enders here." The president said.

Everyone looked relieved.

"About three in the morning, we rowed over to the gunboat and boarded. The watch was asleep, so we got on with no problem. Tom took over the bow and Kelly took aft. Denise went below to disable the engine.

"Ed and I went to the captain's quarters and persuaded him to muster all his crew aft. We then wrapped them in duct tape. Tom threw the 50s over the side, Ed disabled the radios, and we left. Liz was standing close by with the engine running and we high-tailed it home."

"You didn't shoot anyone?"

"No, ma'am, we fired a few rounds over their heads to get their attention. But no one was hurt. But I don't think the engines will run again."

Denise giggled a little.

"Denise, are you a mechanic?"

"No, ma'am, but I grew up in my father's marina. I know boats and engines. I'm sorta Captain Spain's chief bosun."

"Madam President, I'd like to call attention to Denise's conduct. During the fight with the first gunboat, I ordered the crew to get below the waterline. Denise, the most qualified, was ordered to handle the boat while I attempted to disable the gunboat's radar. At no time did she falter under the Cuban's 30mm gunfire."

The president looked at Denise. "I see. High praise from a decorated Marine."

Denise looked quickly at me, then looked at her hands, then at the president. "I just drove the boat, ma'am."

"Humm, any regrets about your chosen career?"

"No, ma'am, none."

"I have a jaundice view when it comes to woman in combat. Having been one, I'm entitled, but that's another conversation. Anyone have anything to add? Tom, how about the FBI?"

"That's how it happened, ma'am."

"Ed. Anything to say. Any throat cutting to report?"

"No, ma'am. They may have lost some skin taking off the duct tape, but no throat cutting."

"Damn. A slow week for you."

Ed chuckles.

"Is that restaurant down the dock any good?"

"Yes, ma'am." Ed replied.

"OK, let's all go down and give them something to talk about. Not to mention the collective stroke my protection team will have."

"Can we all go." Kelly asked.

"Yes, ma'am. I'd like you to sit next to me. Denise, you'll sit on the other side of me." The president said.

It was reminiscent of several troop movements I've been on, but we all finally made it to the restaurant. The manger wasn't sure he was happy about cordoning off one of his rooms, but he seemed ecstatic to host the President for dinner. The crew of the *Pinafore* and President Jackson sat around a family sized table, seemingly all talking at once.

I clinked my water glass with a spoon, then stood holding up a wine glass. "Ladies and gentlemen. The President of the United States."

Everyone but the president stood and repeated the toast. After we were all seated, the president spoke.

"Thank you so much. What a great country, a woman president. Not even a hope 50 years ago. Now I'm just one of the boys."

Everyone laughed.

"While we wait for our food, let's get some business out of the way. First, Elizabeth was right. The Cubans were waiting for me to grow a set."

There were some snickers.

"Like I said, just one of the guys."

Laughter.

"The Cuban government is sending a delegation to D.C. next week to finalize what we're calling the Celebration Agreement."

"No complaints about the gunboats?' Liz asked.

"None. Second, Ed, I want you to go up to Tampa and hold Dr. Pérez's hand, take him to a movie. Whatever it takes, just be sure to have him in D.C. by next Wednesday."

"I thought he was wanted for murder."

"Well, now he's everyone's best friend. So have him there. I'll send a plane. Third, Kelly, Denise, you are to report to Langley as soon as you can get to D.C."

"No more school?" Kelly said.

"No. For all I know, you'll be teaching whatever it is they teach."

President Jackson looked at me. "The people at Hinckley in Stuart, Florida, will pick up your boat in a few days. They have instructions to repair or replace anything that needs fixing or replacing— Do you know the Hinckley organization?"

"Yes, they're the best."

"Good. Once you're satisfied the boat is in good hands, I want you to get back to D.C. Elizabeth, I want you to come back with me, so pack a toothbrush."

"Yes, ma'am."

"Tom, you hang out with Capt. Spain until the boat is picked up. You're now his official protection team, a team of one. When you guys get back, Capt. Spain will go home. Tom, after you spend some time with your wife, report to the Hoover Building."

"Yes, ma'am. Are we expecting trouble? For ah, Capt. Spain."

"Let's eat first."

Elizabeth darted a concerned look at me. Two waiters walked up to the table with trays of food.

"OK. everyone please enjoy this fabulous meal. Lunch is on Ed."

Ed groaned. "My pleasure, I think."

The crew laughed. Tom and I looked at each other.

Our late lunch, early dinner, turned into a two-hour affair. Everyone, including me, was on their best behavior. The conversation was lively and unusual for it was generally devoid of politics and the latest Cuban affair. I noticed the president and Ed were unusually chatty at times, then one or both would draw a curtain and they would all but avoid each other. At the end, the table was strewn with empty glasses and dessert plates and the faces of my crew, as I had come to think of them, were full of smiles and comradery.

"This has truly been a wonderful interlude, but I must ask all of you to excuse me for a few minutes. I need to talk with Captain Spain and Agent Sawyer." The president said.

The crew, minus Tom and I got up and walked back to the boat. Everyone was talking at once. Liz and Ed gave me a look.

Once the room was empty, the president turned her attention to Tom me. "Do you know a Captain Gonzalez?"

"Yes ma'am, he was CO of the gunboat the Navy took out." Tom said.

"He also stopped us back when we were looking for Rick, Bruno and Pérez." I said.

"He's the one you ran the topless tourist scam on." The president said.

"Yes, ma'am. Why?"

"His brother is a big deal in the National Assembly, and he thinks you murdered Captain Gonzalez."

"We didn't murder anybody. He was shooting at us, and the Navy fighters blew up his boat with him on it." I said.

"Well, apparently, he didn't die in the explosion. There were two survivors, and they said Gonzalez was killed by long-range gunfire."

"That boat was 700-800 yards off." I said.

"So, you don't know anyone that could make that shot— You were just praising Denise for helping you knock out the radar."

"I shot up the deck house and I know I broke some glass. Kelly was watching with binoculars and saw the glass break. I suppose Gonzalez could have been hit with one of those rounds."

Tom interjected, "Ma'am, he was firing at a 30mm rotary gun. Perhaps you don't realize—

Mr. Sawyer, I flew combat missions with a M230 chain gun strapped to my ass, which for your information is a 30mm weapon. I know what they are capable of. Now, your credibility is not in question, but I have to know what transpired, so I know how to deal with the problem."

"Yes, ma'am." I said.

"Yes, ma'am." Tom said.

"So, you may have hit him?"

"Yes, ma'am, if the survivor is telling the truth, and Kelly is correct, then, I'd say it was likely I killed Gonzalez."

"Tom, go get Kelly and bring her back here."

"Yes ma'am." Tom got up and jogged down the dock.

"Gonzalez's brother has put, what they call in the movies, a contract on you."

"Just great. That means I can't go home, not with Liz and the kids around."

"Call Captain Schultz and see if anything has come up on his radar, so to speak."

"Yes, ma'am. Good idea, there's not much that gets past him."

"I have my moments." The president said.

Tom and Kelly returned to the restaurant and walked to the table and sat down.

"Agent Kelly, Capt. Spain says you were acting as spotter when he was shooting at the gunboat. Did you see any of his rounds penetrate the bridge?" The president asked.

Kelly looked at me. I nodded. "Yes, ma'am. He probably broke every window on the boat. I think he may have hit the driver because the boat sort of jerked to the right after one series of shots. It was hard to watch for long because they were shooting at us with a Gatling gun. Capt. Spain is one of the best shots I've seen. I know because I'm pretty good myself."

"I'm glad you approve. Thank you, Agent Kelly. You may leave."

Kelly stood and walked out the door.

"She's a good shot?" The president asked.

"She's an artist with an H&K."

"Such a wonderful skill for a young woman. OK, this is what we are going to do. I don't give a fig if Pérez is at the celebration in D.C. And I sure don't want Ed there, it would be like the proverbial bull in the china shop. The four of you are going to find this hit man and remove him from the scene and if you can find the brother, do the same with him. I will not have this back-ally thug stuff screw up all my good work."

"Any instructions?" I asked.

"Don't start a war— One other thing, somebody inside my administration is feeding Gonzalez information."

"Why?" I asked.

"I don't think it's political, I think it's personal."

"Collins."

"Collins."

"You two should take that routine on the road."

President Jackson left for the airport, leaving a car for Elizabeth. When I walked into our stateroom. Liz had an assortment of clothing spread over the bunk. She was busily folding things into a suitcase.

"Hi honey. Off the races again." She said.

I moved behind her, turned her around, and gave her a long kiss. "I'm going to miss you. I think we've spent more time together in the last few months than we have in the last few years." I said.

"I know, even with all the escapades, it's been wonderful, but you'll be home in a few days."

"Probably not. Some Cubans are annoyed with me, and I have to smooth some ruffled feathers before I can come home." I said.

Liz sat down hard on the bunk. "Now what? Can't we ever get a break?"

"I want you to have the kids stay away from the house and I don't want you there either. Change your routine, don't use our cars. And most important, divulge nothing to Johnathin Collins, or any of his associates, including Rick Silvers."

"What about Harriet?"

"Work with her as before, but don't talk to her in front of Collins, or any of his minions, including that new girl Suzi Van what's-her-name. Harriet will know why."

"Are you going to have any help?"

"Ed, Tom, and Pérez. And I think I'm going to make a quiet call to Jerry. Don't mention that call to anyone, even the president."

"OK, I thought the guys were going to D.C."

"No, they'll be with me."

"Good, I feel better."

"I think our phones are OK but be careful what you say to me and about me. Preferably use a satphone. And listen to what I say about not using the cars and changing your routine."

"OK. I won't go near the cars."

"If you use a rental, change it every day. I you rent a hotel room change it every day."

Liz put her arms around me and kissed me. "I love you. Please be careful."

I walked Liz to the waiting car and kissed her goodbye one more time, then watched as she was driven away. Because of the small airport, on this occasion Air Force One was a Learjet 35. The Lear was a physical and I suspect psychological departure from the norm of what most know as Air Force One. I also suspected President Jackson's experience as a combat pilot gave her a different perspective from other chief executives. The Lear was, in many ways, like a fighter, fast and nimble. I could imagine the president asking to sit in the right seat for the all but supersonic flight back to Andrews.

CHAPTER FORTY

Pinafore – Marathon Marina, Florida

When the President of the United States tells you that your life is in danger, the wise man takes her word for it. My first plan was to enlist one of the few men I knew that excelled in the murky world deceit and mayhem. I picked up the satphone and dialed his number.

"Do you know who this is?" I asked.

"I know who it is."

"Did you hear that some of Hemingway's friends are upset with me? It comes from the top."

"No."

"The misses will be in D.C. tomorrow. Will you have one of your golf pros give her some lessons?"

"Yep. What else?"

"Maybe you could nose around and pick up the latest gossip, then come down and play a few rounds. Some of our old golfing buddies will be here too."

"I'll pack the clubs and be down tomorrow. Same place?"

"Same place. By the way— "

"Yeah?"

"Nobody, and I mean nobody, knows about our golf game— one more thing, one of the club pros is playing for the other team."

"See you soon."

It was late the next morning, Tom and I were standing on *Pinafore* talking to two men from Hinkley. They were there to make a preliminary inspection and take the boat to their yard in Stuart, Florida.

"Why don't you guys come aboard and take a look around." I said.

The two men walked up the gangway and then went forward, looking at the damaged hull and rigging. They then came aft.

"Please, sit down. Can I offer you some coffee?"

"No, thanks. You mind me asking, what the world hit this boat?"

"A 30mm Gatling gun. And that's all I'm going to say and all the questions you're going to ask." I said.

"Guess that's why the State Department is paying."

I just looked at both men. Finally, the other guy said. "Well, what's left is beautiful. What is it?"

"It's a one-off built by the King Dragon yard in Taiwan."

"Same people that built Passports."

"Right, the original owner was enamored with Passport's and Alden's, so he tried to build his favorite parts of each into this boat. It worked pretty well. It's a great sailor, stiff in a heavy wind, and reasonably fast."

The first guy laughed. "Just not bulletproof."

The second man said. "Wonder what the designer had against Hinkley's?"

"He thought they were a bit narrow in the beam, but you guys are the last of the best, which is why you have the job. When do you want to get underway?"

"That's up to you. We can get started anytime. It's about 22–23-hour trip. Is the engine, OK?"

"Seems to work fine. I just checked all the fluids. You'll need to top off the fuel. The water tanks too. I installed a water maker a couple of months ago, but I had a crew of six on board."

"Got it. Fill the tanks. How tall was the mast?"

"Fifty-one feet. Look, it's already about noon. Why don't you be here first thing in the morning? My buddy and I will have all our stuff off by then, and you can take it from there."

"OK, we'll see you in the morning."

Later that afternoon, I was trying to talk on the phone, eat a sandwich and drink a beer all at the same time.

"Why don't you put the thing on speaker? Tom asked.

"I didn't know you could— shhhhhss, yes, Capt. Schultz, is he there? OK, I'll wait — Gunner! It's Sgt. Spain— I'm fine. Your CO in chief suggested I call you. She says the Cubans have a contract on me— Yeah, just like in the movies. Can you look into it for me? The main thug is a guy named Gonzalez. He believes I killed his brother— Probably, he was the captain of the gunboat the Navy clobbered last week— Yeah, that's the one. Anyway, Gonzalez is a member of the Cuba's National Assembly, so it may be more about gumming up the works for the chief, but I'm worried about my family— OK, thanks.

Jerry got in at about five and Ed and the Doc got in about 8:30. We were sitting around the cockpit table, drinking beer, and eating from an assortment of chips and crackers.

"Drink up guys. What we don't finish the yard guys will get." I said.

"When are they coming?" Ed said.

"First thing in the morning."

"Hey, one of my girls has been nominated for a valor award. I was asked to do an informal assessment. Since she hasn't worked for anyone else, I guess you're the one I need to talk to."

"Denise? She's the real deal, Jerry." I said.

"What happened?

"I had to have her stand in the open while the Cubans were hosing down the boat with a rotary gun."

"What were you doing?"

"Shooting back."

"Where was everybody else?"

"We were digging a hole in the cabin floor." Ed said.

Laughing. "I sent everyone below the waterline. I didn't see the point of getting everyone killed, particularly my wife."

"My wife appreciated it too." Tom added.

"Why Denise?" Jerry asked.

"She knows boats better than I do. She's my go-to gal for anything to do with the boat."

"She has brass too. She went into a Cuban engine room by herself, in the middle of the night." Ed said.

"I remember her resume said something about boats." Jerry said.

"Her dad owns a marina. She worked there until she went to college. If there was any justice in the world, she would be skipper of one of those Navy LCACs."

"You really think she's that good?" Jerry asked.

"I do."

"What's an LCAC?" Tom asked.

"Huge hovercraft used for amphibious assaults."

"Jarheads never saw a beach they didn't want to assault." Ed said.

"While we're on the subject, how's Kelly doing?" Jerry asked.

"She's a shooter." I said. "And by the way, she was my spotter when I was trying to fuck up the gunboat's radar."

"No kidding? So, she's no shrinking violet either."

"As I told the president, an artist."

"We figured you're the one that taught her." Ed said.

"I teach a couple of courses. Guess she was paying attention."

Ed looked at me. "OK, what's up? The Doc and I thought we were on our way to D.C. for the big celebration."

"The president told Tom and I the Cubans have a contract on me issued a guy named Gonzalez."

"Captain Gonzalez?" Ed asked.

"No, his brother." Tom said.

"I know him. His name is Enrique Gonzalez, former DGI. He's a member of the Cuba's National Assembly. He is a pig, but ruthless. Also, a coward, he will hire someone to do this," Pérez said.

"He believes we killed his brother, the Captain Gonzalez we know or knew. A survivor told the authorities that Captain Gonzalez was shot before the Navy jets attacked." Tom said.

"He does not give shit about his brother. Enrique opposes the new regime because it will affect his pocketbook and will use this to ruin the proceedings." Pérez said.

"The president agrees with the Doc. She thinks this may be more about gumming up the works." Tom agreed.

"We have been ordered to find this guy and get rid of him. Of course, those orders do not extend to Berto, but we sure could use your help." I said.

"You shall have it." Pérez said.

"I called Schultz to see if he could confirm the hit and dig up info on the shooters, if any. Doc, would this guy go after my kids?"

"I doubt it, but since Elizabeth was on *Pinafore* during the incident, it would be prudent to presume he would go after her. Provided he was paid to do so," Pérez said.

"Shit— OK, subject to information coming from Schultz, we need a plan. Ideas?"

"You have to bite the head off a snake." Pérez said.

"How do we get to the snake?"

"Ed and I have contacts that may be of use in that area. But I may already have the vestige of a plan." Pérez said.

"I'm all ears." I said.

"This pig has a weakness— "

"—Woman." I said.

"No. Motorcars."

"Cars!" I said.

"Not just cars, Duesenberg cars."

"Hard to think of anything I know less about."

"Then it's a good thing it wasn't women." Ed said.

All the men laughed.

"I know very little about woman either, but It may surprise you. I know a good deal about cars," Pérez said. "A former associate was an avid collector, and I took a fancy myself. You may remember Estéban Morales."

"First, nothing would surprise me about you. Yes, I remember Morales. Who could forget? Guess he had to do something with all that money."

"The one thing he could not do, was buy a 1935 Duesenberg SSJ. Only two were built. Your movie actors Gary Cooper and Clark Gable each owned one."

"You have everyone's attention." I said.

"The Amelia Island Concours d'Elegance is in a few days. We make it known to Gonzalez that one of the SSJs is for sale. When he arrives, we will have a chat with him."

"That will get him up here to Florida?" Tom asked.

"Yes. He could not resist."

"How do we know one of those cars will be at the show?" Tom asked.

Warming to the idea, Jerry jumped in. "We don't. But I'll have some of my guys fix up a catalog with the car and we'll make sure he sees it."

"Can he get into the country?" I asked.

"Between Jerry and I, we can fix that. Besides, this is the new era. All he has to say is he's stopping off on the way to D.C. for the celebration." Tom said.

"Guess we have a plan. I'll call Schultz and make sure he can't shoot holes in it, then we proceed. In the meantime, we have to find some place to stay. *Pinafore* is being picked up tomorrow."

"The Concours d'Elegance takes place at the Amelia Island Ritz-Carlton. I suggest we stay there." Pérez said.

I looked around the cockpit. "Any objections?"

"I'm not sure how I can live without a two-foot square shower that ceaselessly moves, but if you guys insist." Ed said.

"I'm appalled at such spurious abuse from one who portends to be of the 'glass half full' society of seers." I said.

Patrons of El Del Frente in Havana, Cuba, are seated in the sumptuous restaurant, temporarily shielded from the simmering tropical heat of the midafternoon. Two patrons are eating and talking animatedly. One of the men stops, holds up his hand, then dives into his briefcase. He pulls out a pamphlet, opens it to a page and shows it to his lunch companion. At the top of the pamphlet, the heading reads, *Amelia Island Concours d'Elegance Auction Catalog.* In the middle of the page is a large picture of an antique car described and labeled as a *1935 Duesenberg SSJ.*

We divided up and charted planes into Cecil Airport. Jerry and I arrived first so we were cooling our heels in the Tidewater Grill, which was in the Amelia Island Ritz-Carlton.

"Did the other guys get in OK?" I asked.

"Yeah, I told them Gonzalez won't be here until tomorrow, but not to be seen together. We are all going to meet in your room at 8:30 tonight."

"Did you find out what room he'll be in?"

"Yep. He'll have a bodyguard with him in the adjoining room and one in the room across the hall."

We finished our drinks, then left separately for room 372.

One by one the others showed up, soon we were all sitting my room.

"What did you hear from Schultz?" Ed asked.

"He confirmed what the Doc and your guys said. Gonzalez took the bait and will be here tomorrow. Nothing on the hit yet." I said.

"We should probably take Gonzalez tomorrow night. He and his bodyguards will be tired and less observant. Once he's gone, all of us will use our contacts to get the word out that the paymaster for the hit changed his mind. Permanently." Pérez said.

"What the hell are we going to do with him after he has retired?" Tom asked.

"I have arranged for some friends to take him and his bodyguards on a fishing trip. They will pick him up in what will look suspiciously like a laundry truck." Pérez said.

Some laughing.

"When the laundry truck gets here, everyone collect their stuff and get back to Cecil Airport. A G-IV will be waiting. Then on to D.C." I said.

"In a few days, his family and associates will start receiving e-mails and postcards from Portugal, saying he is having a wonderful time. Over time, he will disappear." Jerry said.

"Tom, you will be our emergency reserve. Stay in your room and monitor the radio. The Doc brought in a couple of friends. They will be in the lobby to watch for bad guys, if any—

"I don't mind—"

"Tom, nobody doubts your skill or courage. We need you to watch our backs. If the Doc's guys in the lobby see something or someone they don't like, you need to delay those people. If everything goes to shit, get back to D.C. pronto. Tell the president what happened, then keep your mouth shut— Any questions? — OK, sleep well. See you tomorrow night."

The next day we all stayed in our rooms. I mostly slept and spent a lot of money on room service. I don't know what the others did. Late that night, everyone but Tom was on the fifth floor. Ed and Jerry are poised at a guest room door. The Doc and I were across the hall at another door. A look up and down the hall, then Pérez nods. All four enter their respective rooms.

Once inside our assigned room, Pérez walked to the door of the adjoining room. He opened it and stepped inside. In the dim light, a man was sitting on the side of the bed, looking at his cell phone.

PHITT! PHITT!

The man fell back on the bed. Pérez closed the door carefully. We walked over to the other bed. Another man is on his stomach and snoring noisily. Pérez slaps the man on his rump.

"Uh, what?" He tried to rub the sleep out of his eyes and turned over. "Who are you?"

"Mr. Gonzalez?" Pérez said.

"Yes."

"Do you know Dr. Alberto Pérez?"

Gonzalez sits up quickly. "Have you captured him?"

"No, he has captured you."

Enrique Gonzalez sputters. "What? I demand to know who you are."

"I am Alberto Pérez. You have one chance to save your life. Who did you send after Elizabeth Hunter?"

"Who?"

"The woman that was on the sailboat, your brother tried to sink." Pérez said.

"He wasn't trying to sink it, he was told to just scare them."

"He succeeded. Now, who is looking for my wife?"

Enrique Gonzalez sputters more, "You're him! You killed my little brother."

"And I'm going to kill you too if you don't tell me who you sent after my wife."

"Guard! Guard!"

"He is already dead. Who is it?"

"You wouldn't dare hurt me."

PHITT! PHITT!

Enrique Gonzalez is thrown back onto the bed.

"You are wrong, my friend," Pérez said.

We waited for the laundry truck, then caught a couple of cabs to the airport. The G-IV was waiting, so in no time we were high above the depravity in which we found ourselves. That said, orders or not, I would not allow my wife and family to be destroyed for another man's lust for wealth.

I was sitting next to Pérez. I leaned over, "My wife would have said, '1865, John Singleton Mosby.'"

"Pardon?"

"You asked Gonzalez if he knew Dr. Alberto Pérez? He asked if you had captured him and you said no, he has you. Liz would have followed with, 1865, John Singleton Mosby."

"Yes, I remember Elizabeth's penchant for quotes. Who is Mosby?"

"Famous Confederate guerilla. He captured a Union Brigadier under almost identical circumstances, except they weren't in a Ritz Carlton."

"How do you know this?"

"Big fan, I grew up in his area of operations. There was even a TV series about him called *The Gray Ghost.* "

Pérez laughed. "Ahh yes, in that context, it may surprise you that I now remember my father mentioning him."

"OK, you surprised me this time."

"As a young officer, my father attended lectures at the Virginia Military Institute where Mosby's tactics were taught. However, I had not heard your strangely coincidental anecdote."

Pérez looks out the window for a while. "What have you heard from Captain Schultz?"

"All he knows about the hit is that there are two guys, probably ex-DGI. One was sent to Marathon and one to D.C. — He said something strange. The man sent to D.C. is not Cuban. He is South African."

"Fouché. He is white, so he will be all but invisible in Washington." Pérez said.

"I was surprised Jerry hadn't heard of him, but he put some men on Liz and the kids."

"Fouché is not an intelligence operative, and he was not DGI. He is a hired assassin, very good and he enjoys killing."

"Will he have a Cuban passport?"

"Yes, he will have a Cuban diplomatic passport. You must kill this man on sight. He will not give you a moment's chance. And as I said, he travels with diplomatic immunity. Speak with Edward. He knows this man."

CHAPTER FORTY-ONE

White House - Presidents Working Office

The president, Elizabeth, Tom, Pérez, Ed, Jerry, and I sat around a small conference table in the president's office.

"I'm sorry, this will have to be short. As you can imagine, there is a lot to do and little time. First, Jonathan Collins no longer works for the administration, he has decided to retire in favor of spending more time with his family. I will announce a new chief of staff shortly. In the meantime, Rick Silvers will fill in. OK, give me the short version. Dr. Pérez, I understand you were the lead on this, so you have the floor."

"We tricked Enrique Gonzalez into coming to Amelia Island. We had a conversation with him and then put him on a fishing boat to Portugal."

"My, that was a short story. I trust he will be happy in his new life, and we won't be hearing from him in the future."

"Yes, ma'am."

"Next on the agenda. Jerry, what's the latest on the assassination attempt?"

"Ma'am, I have every man I can find on it without going official. The guy in Florida took off when he heard his paycheck left for Portugal."

"Not before scaring the crap out of the yardmen at Hinckley— excuse me, ma'am. The guys at Hinckley had a bit of a fright." Ed said.

"There is still the one here in town. Ed and the Doc know this guy, so they have taken the lead." Jerry said.

The president looked at Ed. "Another of your kindred spirits?"

"He is a South African named Fouché. I met him when you and I were—
"

The president taps her pencil on the table. "Continue."

Liz and I glanced at each other.

"I met him in North Africa. We were on different sides but got caught up in a political reshuffle and spent several months in the same cell. He's a sociopath, lives for the life, kills anyone, anywhere for anyone as long as the money is good. His only allegiance is to money."

"Well, if Mr. Gonzalez has left for Portugal, perhaps this Fouché will follow his associate's lead and go home." The president said.

"Maybe, my bet he got paid first." Ed said.

"That would be a certainty." Pérez followed.

The president leans back in her chair. "Damn. I'm open to suggestions."

"Doc, Ed, does this guy have any weaknesses?" I said.

Ed and Pérez look at each other.

"Maybe arrogance. He thinks he's the brightest bulb on the tree. In fact, he's sure of it." Ed said.

"Is there any reason to think he knows we are aware of him?" I said.

Ed looks at Jerry and Pérez. "No. And it probably wouldn't make any difference. That may be another chink in his armor. He's not very sophisticated, more like a big bear. He just keeps coming."

"Then I guess we make the arrogant bear come to us." I said.

Liz and I spent the next twenty-four hours in several local hotels trying to keep a low profile. We were able to get in touch with Brad but had been unable to get Emily by phone or text. Under normal circumstances, this would not have been a concern, but now we were on the verge of panic, but there was nothing we could do but proceed with the plan. We received word from Schultz that Fouché was on his way to Reagan National. Jerry pulled out all the stops to confirm his arrival. Armed with the date and time we met everyone at our home in the Mount Vernon area of Virginia. Elizabeth and I sat with Jerry, Tom, Pérez, and Ed around our dining room table. Normally, the dining room was one of my favorite places in the house. Floor to ceiling windows offered an unmarred view of the lawn and the woods beyond, a source of birds and deer. This time when I looked out the window, I could only summon the feeling of dread.

"Honey, did you hear me?" Liz said.

"What? Yes, OK. Cars in the driveway, some lights on, doors locked—are we sure about the locked door?"

"He'll suspect something if they are unlocked." Jerry said.

"OK, what else?"

"Where do you want me?" Liz asked.

"You'll be at Bob Osborn's place." I said.

"No!"

"Liz—"

"You had me mowing down a bunch of thugs in some jungle 2,000 miles from here, but I can't protect my home. I don't think so."

I looked around the table for allies. All I got were a few shrugs. "OK, but don't use the M14. I don't want to chop the house down."

There are a few sinkers.

"I told you it didn't know it was on automatic."

I looked at my watch. "I guess we go hunker down and wait. Help yourselves to what's in the fridge.

The wait was interminable, we still hadn't been able to get in touch with Emily. Ed confirmed what Doc had said assuring me that Fouché wouldn't go after Emily, but I was less sure, and for all I knew they were just trying to reassure me.

It was getting close to mid-night, I was in the dining room. Except for a light in the den, and what light made it in from the street, it was pitch dark. Then I heard it. A noise, a faint sound— It was the laundry room door opening. Lying on the floor, I carefully looked through the kitchen into the laundry room. A tall figure warily inched out of the laundry room into the kitchen. He peeked into the lit den, then stepped through the door into the den. I gently got to my feet and walked through the kitchen toward the den—Suddenly, the front door opened.

"Mom! Dad! Where are you! How was your trip! Hope you have something to eat food. I'm starved. Wait to I tell you where I've— Who are you? — Let me go! Put me down. Put me down!"

I looked into the den. Fouché had Emily around the neck, dragging her from the foyer into the den.

I stepped into the doorway between the kitchen and den. "Put her down!"

Fouché turned to face me and smiled. "I have no wish to hurt the girl. But you must do as I say. You will please put the gun down. Hurry! I suspect we have little time."

"OK, OK. Just don't hurt her." I leaned over—

BANG!

Within the confines of the house, the noise was like an explosion. A piece of Fouché's shoulder was blown off. He dropped Emily and turned toward the shot—

BANG!

I fired my Colt and hit Fouché below and just forward of his right ear. The lower part of his head disintegrated. The room immediately filled with the others, all with guns drawn. I walked through the den to where the first shot came from. Liz is standing in the foyer holding Emily. The M14 hanging from her other hand. I carefully took the rifle and walked into the living room and sat down. Shaking, I put my head in my hands and gave a silent prayer.

From the foyer, "Please get that piece of garbage out of my house. He's ruining my oriental carpet!"

I stood and walked over to Liz and put my arms around her and Emily. "Guys, please drag him into the garage until the police get here."

It was the better part of the week before we got the house cleaned, delt with the local and federal authorities. Even though she had been immersed in the final days of the big celebration, I had the feeling that President Jackson had taken time to ease our way through all the investigations.

Liz and I were finally in our own bedroom watching the television from our very own bed with a real mattress and box spring. I confess, *Pinafore's* bunk got old.

Probably for the third time, we were watching a rebroadcast of President Jackson's speech from the Rose Garden. "*. . . my administration has ordered the restoration of full diplomatic relations with Cuba and the reopening of our embassy in Havana. Please join me and our most honored guests at this celebration. Today, for the first time in more than a half-century, we celebrate the end of perhaps one of the last vestiges of the Cold War. . . .*"

"Stop that." Liz giggled.

"Stop what?"

"That."

"You mean that?"

She snuggled closer to me.

Yes, that. Don't stop.

She turned her face up and kissed me, and I reached out for the remote and turned off the TV. The room went dark.

"You're doing it again."

"You said don't stop."

"Humm. So, I did."

A phone rings.

"That's my new phone, it's the president."

"She can wait."

"Did I tell you I was her new chief of staff?"

"I'll read about it in the paper."

"Hmmm. Good idea. Do that some more."

Pinafore and Her Crew will Return

AUTHOR'S NOTE

Be it at the beach or by a fire, I hope you enjoyed this novel. Except for bits of history, most of the restaurants, geography, and some trivia, the novel is researched make-believe. U530 was real, as was its rendezvous with I-52. All the ship handling, rigging, sailing, equipment, and navigation is autobiographical. The firearms used in the book are real and the descriptions of their use are more than possible by a competent marksman. The aircraft and the military equipment are real, as are some of the military units.

The chief character and I share some traits and values. Unlike the hero, I rarely drink, Blanton's or otherwise, preferring iced tea and chocolate milk. I have an aptitude with firearms and think sailing is a gift from the Almighty.

The character Elizabeth is a tribute to my former wife. The two women are quite similar in their beauty, uncommon skills with firearms, languages, and music. They also share a penchant for clothes and shoes and an oblivious disregard for hot water on a boat.

The character Ed is a composite of two of my oldest friends and their exploits. They are both from the Palm Beach area, they are about the same age, and they are pilots. Both are of Italian descent, and graduates from universities in D.C., yet they have never met.

Pinafore is a composite of two of my favorite sailboat designs.

Emily, Brad, and Sable are based on their namesakes.

ACKNOWLEDGEMENTS

Those times when I thought this project was ill-advised or an unending chore, there were always family and friends who pushed me back in the right direction.

To Katherine Shemeld, for the endless hours of proofreading, your spelling and grammatical prowess, and your unceasing support in all things. Thanks, mom, you are the best!

To Ed Galasso and Sam Aurilio, for your forty-year friendships. You guys lived a life of fiction; the backstory for Ed Colombo is a composite of your adventures. Ed, thanks for teaching me to fly.

To Mayne Berke, for his encouragement, support, ideas, and editing skills. Mayne, you, sir, are a true gentleman.

To Dana Briscoe, for taking his time to edit my copy.

To many family and friends, for their support and encouragement.

ABOUT THE AUTHOR

Robert Shemeld is the author of the award-winning political thriller, *The Narraganset Files.* He has been published in a national magazine and has written numerous scripts for television dramas.

A former Marine and decorated combat veteran, he was a private investigator for fifteen years and a real estate broker, developer, and financial consultant for twenty years. An avid sailor, he favors New England, Chesapeake, and Caribbean waters. Robert is also an accomplished skeet and sporting clays shooter.

Mr. Shemeld used experiences from these and other vocations to give his writings its labyrinth of realistic narratives, persuasive conflict, and vivid images.

He makes no pretension to being a pilot, however; he has flown solo many times, and it is with some pride he alleges his landings equaled his takeoffs.

Mr. Shemeld is a native and resident of Northern Virginia. He attended American University in Washington, D.C. He the proud father of three. His last nautical venture was a four-week navigation of the Intracoastal Waterway.

www.robertshemeld.com

---

[1] Sensuikan

[2] History of WW2DB

[3] War History Online

[4] Wikipedia